Shadow Blind
Shadow Warriors Book One
Trish McCallan

Also by Trish McCallan

Acknowledgments

With endless gratitude to the following people for their help with this book!

David Steele and Michele Gwynn for their most excellent copy-editing skills.

Author Nicole Flockton for her insight into Australian lingo and critiquing my scenes with an Australian character.

Author Nadia Lee for allowing me to mention her books and in Shadow Blind's Book Brigade discussion.

About This Book

Navy SEAL Aiden Winchester is not okay.

Shattered by loss and betrayal, he's been thrust into a world where love, loyalty, and the fate of humanity collide.

When a devastating new weapon claims the lives of Aiden's teammates, yet spares his own, he's left grappling with the aftermath—broken bonds, a lost love, and a shattered career. Fate takes an unexpected turn when Aiden is rescued by his mysterious half-brother, Wolf, leader of a covert Native American special ops team operating from the enigmatic Shadow Mountain.

As Aiden unravels the secrets within the shadows, he discovers that the weapon's threat is far more ominous than imagined, with the power to decimate humanity. Now Aiden faces an urgent mission to thwart the weapon's deployment, expose the shadowy culprits behind its creation—potentially his own superiors at WARCOM—and reclaim the love of Demi Barnes, the woman he has always loved.

Thus begins a race against time as the mastermind behind the weapon targets Aiden, determined to uncover the anomaly that spared him. In a desperate bid to save Demi's life and reclaim her love, Aiden must navigate a perilous path, confronting enemies within and beyond the shadows.

Shadow Blind weaves a gripping tale of second chances, the bonds of brotherhood, found family, and a hero's quest for redemption against the backdrop of a super-secret Native American special ops base. This electrifying blend of romance, suspense, and action will leave you breathless until the last page.

Are you ready to step into the shadows?

Chapter One

Author's Note

This note is for those readers who read the Red-Hot SEAL series and noticed discrepancies between those books and Shadow Blind.

Originally, Aiden, Kait, Wolf and the rest of the Native American special ops warriors based out of Shadow Mountain were Arapaho. The Red-Hot SEALs series, was written over ten years ago, before I knew about the own voices movement. Once I realized how offensive it was to the Arapaho people to mix my imagined supernatural elements with their history, culture, and tribal customs, I decided not to continue with the Arapaho story element.

However, for my Shadow Warriors series to work, I needed a Native American tribe. So, I created my own mythical tribe, with its own history, culture, language, and tribal customs. Thus, Aiden, Kait, Wolf, and the rest of the Shadow Mountain warriors are now from the Kalikoia tribe. My imaginary Native American tribe is not based on any living or dead indigenous culture and came straight from my imagination. Unfortunately, I cannot change the Arapaho element in my Red-Hot SEALS series as my publisher owns the copyright to those books, but I have changed these tribal elements in Hearts Under Fire and my new Shadow Warriors series.

For those interested, a glossary of Kalikoia words can be found at the back of this book.

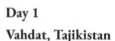

Day 1
Vahdat, Tajikistan

"Fuck." Aiden Winchester glared at the secure laptop's screen with its spinning wheel of doom.

The SAT link was always iffy this far into shitkicker territory, particularly with the cloud cover. Sometimes the radio heads got the link reestablished, sometimes they didn't. But dammit, did it have to go down during his scheduled FaceTime? Sure, he could reach for his secure squad SAT phone, but then he wouldn't be able to see Demi.

Sometimes snarky, sometimes sweet, always sexy as hell, Demi's pixie face broadcast her every thought and emotion. Listening to her voice wasn't enough. He needed to see her too.

"Yo, Squirrel." His shout turned his team brother's scalped head his way. Squirrel was the only one of his squad mates who still went in for those buzz cuts of old. "Get hold of the brainiacs and find out what's going on with the SAT link."

"Bro, you're so apron whipped. Can't even last a day without kissy-facing your gal?" Squirrel asked with his patented squinty eyed smirk. But he turned and headed for the weighted door of the tent. That was his best friend in a nutshell—smartass quip, followed by immediate action.

The ruddy tattoo of a coiled rattler glinted across Squirrel's neck as he shoved open the door and hunched his way out into the snow-crusted tundra that surrounded them. A blast of icy wind swept through the door, prickling against Aiden's shoulders and the back of his head, before the door banged shut again. It was ass-crack cold and too windy for comfort during February, in the wilds of Vahdat, Tajikistan. Particularly at twenty-three-hundred hours.

Aiden turned back to the spinning circle of doom, and for a moment, a bone white face seemed to unfurl across the laptop screen. A twisted, elongated face with a gaping mouth and slits for eyes. A face surrounded by mist and fog.

He tensed and closed his eyes. When he opened them again, the image was gone.

Fuuuuck.

He leaned back in the desk chair and scraped his palms down his face. What the fuck had that been about? This was the first time the damn dream had followed him into wakefulness. He'd like to pin that weird moment on stress—after all, they were about to spin up for another assault—except he didn't do stress.

The rotating circle froze. The monitor flickered, and Demi's face filled the screen.

Aiden cleared his throat. "Hey babe, like the hair."

The pixie cut was the same, but the color was new. Blueish green this time. Not a surprise. This was her third color swap in the three years they'd been together. Demi liked to experiment.

Someone toward the back of the tent—Grub, if he wasn't mistaken—made exaggerated kissing sounds. Most of the crew was sacked out on cots around the tent, trying to catch some shuteye before the chopper went skids up. But without a doubt, Grub wasn't the only asshole listening to the conversation. The rest would start up with the razzing as soon as he hit the 'End Call' button.

Such were the annoyances of team life.

"This isn't a good time, Aiden. I'm headed out the door," Demi said in a flat voice. "Is there something you need?

Something I need?

The cool response caught him off guard. This was not how their sporadic FaceTimes went. Had she heard Grub's bullshit? Was that why she'd shut the conversational door in his face? It was too bad he hadn't found a warm, private space to place this call. But there had been plenty of less than private chats in the three years they'd been together. She'd never complained, nor had she cut the call short before.

He frowned, leaning closer to the screen. Her gaze was dull with crinkles of tension around her eyes. And her face was...guarded. *Flat and guarded?* His gut tightened. This was not the Demi he knew.

"What's wrong?" he asked quietly.

She gave him a look, one he couldn't quite decipher. Maybe accusatory? Maybe sad? Maybe both?

"I'm just tired. Today's been a bad day." She ran a hand over the top of her blue-green hair and looked down, avoiding his eyes. Her shoulders slumped. When she looked up again, her smile looked forced. "I'm sorry, Aiden. I've got to go. Keep yourself safe out there..." her voice trailed off and her lips twisted with something that looked almost cynical. "Wherever *there* is."

Cynical? Demi? That couldn't be right.

The screen went blank.

Aiden sat there, ice shredding his gut. Something was very wrong in sunny Coronado. It was ten-hundred hours in California. He always timed his calls so they wouldn't be too late or too early for her. This was the first time she'd cut one short. Hell—they hadn't even had a call. Not much of one, anyway.

He reached for his secure cell phone. It was nine hundred hours in Alaska. His sister Kait should be up, with all synapses firing thanks to a bucket full of coffee. His twin did like her coffee, something Kait and Demi had bonded over.

It took her so long to pick up the call, he was about to hang up and try again later.

"Aiden." Her voice was breathless. "Sorry, I couldn't find the phone. What's up?"

He grimaced, certain that her breathless voice and raspy breathing had more to do with Simcosky's sexual shenanigans than frantically searching for a ringing phone. And Christ help him—that was not an image he wanted in his head.

"It's nine hundred hours, for fuck's sake. You two should be out of bed by now. You've been married for two years. You left newlywed status behind months ago."

"I told you not to answer it," Cosky grumbled in the background. And then much louder, "Thanks for the cockblock, bro." Cosky's voice was so clear, he'd obviously snatched the phone from Kait.

Jesus. Aiden jerked the cell from his ear and pinched his nose, desperately trying to purge that knowledge from his brain. There were some things he simply didn't want to know when it came to his sister. Her sex life was at the top of that list.

There were scuffling sounds over the line and Kait's voice was back, sounding more breathless than ever.

"To what do I owe the pleasure of this highly irregular call? I mean, this is what, the first call from you in a month?"

"Personal calls are off-limits in sensitive areas." He reeled off the excuse with practiced deftness, hitting the perfect balance of apologetic and regretful. Still, a twinge of guilt accompanied the half-truth. He really should call Kait more often.

"Suuure." She drew the word out sarcastically and added a scoff in case he hadn't picked up on her disbelief. "Let me guess, you've got yourself in trouble again and need a healing. It's been what—" she paused as if she was doing the math. "Thirty days since Cosky and I healed your ass after that idiotic stunt up at Snow Valley?"

He almost objected to the idiotic stunt comment. Everything had been under control until an out-of-control snowboarder barreled into him. Thank Christ Kait and Cosky had joined him and Demi for that weekend ski trip before he'd shipped out. They'd been right there beside him on the slope and healed his floppy knee without his team brothers or CO being any the wiser. He'd gone wheels up with the rest of his team, right on schedule.

"I'm not in need of your miraculous gift." He wasn't even being facetious. What his sister could do, particularly when Cosky was with her, truly *was* miraculous. Unlike his damn talent, which was nothing but a farce. His chest tightened beneath a surge of frustration. He shoved it back. This wasn't about him. It was about Demi. He nudged the conversation in that direction. "I just wanted to check in, see how you're doing, that's all."

"Right." Kait's skepticism sharpened.

A scowl followed his grimace. Hooking up with Simcosky had made Kait immune to his excuses. As a former SEAL, Cosky knew when an explanation rang hollow. And no doubt the nosy bastard was listening to the conversation, his head on the pillow next to hers.

"You want to get on with why you called, bro? Your sister and I would like to continue the...activities...that you interrupted with your lying bullshit."

Aiden grimaced, pinched the bridge of his nose and purged his brain some more.

"Have you talked to Demi today?" He knew they called each other several times a week since Kait had settled in Alaska. But it was early in both their locations. He wasn't sure what time their convos took place.

"Not yet. I thought I'd give her the day to wallow. I'll call her tonight. We'll have a nice long chat where I'll encourage her to cry and then distract her with plans for a girls' trip somewhere. With luck, all the emotions and crying will exhaust her, and she'll be able to sleep tonight."

Woah. Wallow? Encourage her to cry. He was right, something was wrong.

"Is there something I should know?" His question was operator code for '*What the hell's wrong?*'

Silence hit the line. A long silence. He counted the seconds off in his head. 1...2...3... Yeah, that pause was lingering in dangerous territory.

"Seriously, Aiden?" Kait's voice turned sharp. "You've been dating her for three years and you don't know the significance of today? Donnie died six years ago today."

Ah, shit. Aiden closed his eyes. Well, that explained Demi's doldrums.

"Maybe if you had an honest to God conversation with her when you hit stateside instead of hauling her into bed and screwing her the entire time you're on leave, you'd know how hard this day is on her." The acidic quality in Kait's voice spiked. "It gets a little easier for her each year. But this date will always bring back the sorrow of losing him. Donnie was her heart."

Aiden's chest went hot and then cold at the reminder. He was aware of how much Demi had loved her husband. It had taken her three years to come out of that grieving fog she'd drifted around in after his death. Three damn years before she even noticed he existed, and he'd been able to claim her.

A distant, rumbling voice came over the line, breaking into his reverie.

Kait sighed. "Marcus says I'm being unfair. With the lengths of your deployments over the past three years, you've barely spent any actual time with her, anyway." Her voice lost its sharpness. "Honestly, I'm surprised she's put up with your absences for so long."

Aiden froze. "For so long? What the hell does that mean?"

The silence that fell between them was almost as long and even more dangerous than it had been before. Every muscle in his body tightened. This was bad. He could sense it.

"I'm sorry, I shouldn't have said that. But Aiden, you must know how difficult these deployments are for her. Demi isn't part of the SEAL community. When you leave, she's completely alone for months at a time. It's not fair to ask her to put her life on hold for you."

Aiden couldn't have been more surprised if a shitkicker had sprung up from beneath his feet and popped him one between the eyes.

"What exactly are you saying, Kait?" he asked, surprised to find his voice even, rather than breathless. "Is she thinking about breaking it off with me?"

There was another pause, shorter this time but fraught with tension. At least on his end.

"I don't think your current friends with benefits arrangement is working for her. I think she's ready for something like she had with Donnie. A partner, marriage...someone to have kids with."

If Aiden got any tighter, his muscles were going to snap. His temper, too. Kait didn't know what the fuck she was talking about. Demi had never mentioned being dissatisfied with their relationship.

"I wasn't the one who wanted a friends with benefits package," he said tightly. "She was." And he'd agreed to it, because...hell, he would have agreed to anything to get her into his bed, which would give him a chance to worm his way into her heart. Granted, the past three years hadn't worked out like he'd planned—she still hadn't admitted she loved him. He knew she did, though. She wouldn't be so open with him in bed if she wasn't in love with him. That kind of openness required trust and love. "If she's changed her mind and wants the white picket fence and diamond ring, I can do that."

"Aiden," Kait replied, surprised, then her tone grew weary. "Getting married won't make the problems disappear, not when you're gone so much. She'd still be alone while you're deployed or off on those endless training missions. And when the kids came—she'd be a single mother. She's not looking for a part-time marriage. And unless you opt out of your next reenlistment contract, that's all you can offer her."

A knife twisted in Aiden's chest. "Mom didn't consider her marriage to dad a part-time one."

"Didn't she?" Kait retorted. "How would you know? She died when we were ten. We never discussed personal stuff—like whether she was happy with dad being gone so much." She broke off and took an audible breath. When she spoke again, her voice was quiet. "Look, I shouldn't even be telling you this. It's between you and Demi."

Aiden wandered to the tent door and nudged it open, staring out over the shadowy tundra. A thin skiff of snow flocked the sturdy grass, brightening the night. It was gray outside, and miserably cold. An artic wind flayed him through the open flap. Yet it didn't come close to matching the icy chasm spreading within him.

"Aiden?"

"Yeah," He turned back, letting the door fall back into place. "She's talking about breaking things off then? No matter what?"

Kait sighed. "Yeah. She's planning on telling you face to face once you hit stateside. And unless you're willing to leave the teams and settle into a 9 to 5, I don't think you'll be able to change her mind."

"That isn't happening." His resistance to the idea was instant. Violent even. The SEAL teams were his fucking home. His teammates were his brothers. They were all he'd ever known, all he'd ever wanted. He wasn't giving them up.

Even if it meant losing Demi?

No, goddammit. No. He wasn't losing her either. There had to be another way.

"You could join Shadow Mountain. Wolf said there will always be a spot for you among his warriors."

"Not gonna happen." The refusal was curt. Final. Shadow Mountain was not home. Wolf's men were not his brothers.

There had to be another way, a way that would satisfy Demi and allow him to stay on the teams. He was a smart guy, he just needed to think of something. Something that would change her mind and open her eyes to what they had. There had to be a compromise they could both live with.

He just needed to find it.

Chapter Two

Day 1
Coronado, California

Demi sat in front of the blank computer screen, back straight and chest tight, as the knowledge that she meant nothing to the man she loved spread throughout her body creating a hollow ache.

Aiden hadn't remembered the significance of today's date. More evidence he didn't know her, didn't care about her. At least, not like she cared about him. If the situation were reversed, she'd know exactly what this day meant to him. She would do everything possible to see him through it. But then, she loved him, while to him, she was nothing but a convenience. A warm, willing body, on those few occasions he was on leave and horny as hell after months of abstinence.

A sour burn climbed her throat.

You have no right to be upset about this. This is what you asked for. Sex without emotions. Sex without love. You want more now, but he's fulfilling the terms of the agreement.

Her gaze focused on the 'Call Ended' button. The rectangular box was the color of blood. It reminded her of Donnie, of how that foul baseball had struck the side of his head. His blood was so red and there had been so much of it. It had soaked into her hands and then into her mind.

Even now, six years later, the memory sliced through her heart. Her breathing hitched. She could taste the bitterness of shock, smell the metallic tinge of terror, feel the gritty fragments of bone as she tried to hold his skull together.

Demi flinched from the memory, struggling to release her caged breath as her thoughts returned to Aiden.

She should have known better, split from him sooner, before she fell for him, before their arrangement started to hurt. His obliviousness to the memories attached to today's date confirmed what she'd suspected for the past year and a half. He didn't care about her, and she wasn't cut out for a fuck buddy bargain. For her, the physicality of sex required the emotional support of love.

But that love had to be reciprocated, and hers wasn't.

At first, the arrangement was wonderful. He was the perfect counterpart to her libido. Not only was he the sexiest man she'd ever known, but she was wildly attracted to him. Their sexual chemistry had been off the charts—still was. They didn't just heat the sheets; they burned them to cinders.

But then she'd developed *feelings* for him, feelings that were tearing her apart. And it wasn't just the pain of loving someone who didn't love her back. Nope, there were other emotions all tangled up inside her, too.

Like the fear and anxiety during those endless deployments when she didn't know where he was or what he was doing or if he was okay. SEALs led dangerous lives, with the threat of death constantly hanging over their heads. One misstep, one piece of wrong intelligence, one bad guy where he wasn't supposed to be, could send Aiden's superior to her door with the news of his death. Just the thought of that possibility knotted her stomach.

And then there was the loneliness and sexual frustration while he was gone. He'd kickstarted her libido, only to leave her hanging for months on end. Her handy dandy vibrator and agile fingers didn't quell her sexual cravings anymore. She needed more than the physical stimulations of toys. She needed his weight on top of her, his thickness inside of her, the distinctive male scent of him enveloping her.

The craving and fear were bad enough, but her evolving feelings were the third strike. The fact he hadn't remembered the significance of today was just one sign he didn't reciprocate her feelings. His endless secrets were another sign, the ones he refused to share with her, the ones he hid from her.

Oh, not his SEAL secrets. She understood the necessity there, as well as the intention behind them. But his personal reticence, his unwillingness to share anything with her, was much harder to swallow. There was no love without trust, without the sharing of oneself.

And Aiden shared nothing; at least, with her. Not the nightmares that plagued him while he slept beside her. Not the injuries he accrued while in service to his country. Not even the injuries he received during his downtime, while in pursuit of his own enjoyment.

He'd never told her about the accident up on the slopes of Snow Valley, or the injury he'd received to his knee that had been so severe it had required both Kait and Cosky's combined efforts to heal the damage. And she'd been there. Oh, not on the slopes. She'd been in the resort spa. But she'd been there, sharing a room and a bed with him, dining across from him. They'd even had dinner together hours after he'd taken that hit on the slopes. Yet he'd never said a word about the accident. Not one damn word.

Kait had been the one to tell her after Aiden had shipped out.

That's when she knew she had to get out, that their *friends with fucking privileges* wasn't working. It wasn't what she wanted anymore. She wanted a partner. Marriage. Someone to have kids with, to build a family with. To live her life with. Someone who shared the important details of his life with her.

And while she loved him, Aiden didn't fit those parameters. Nor would she find the man who did, when she was emotionally and physically tied to Aiden. She needed to break things off with him before her feelings grew even stronger. And she needed to do it as soon as she saw him again—but face to face, not over video.

When he returned home, she was going to tell him goodbye.

A sudden musical tone erupted from her cell phone. She grabbed it from where it vibrated next to her laptop. *Ocean View Vet* lit up the screen. Instantly, anxiety tensed the muscles of her shoulders and spine, which was ridiculous. It shouldn't matter whether the cat had survived its surgery. She had no emotional investment in it. She'd simply been the one to see it get hit by the car and, like any good Samaritan, had rushed it to the closest vet.

"Yes." She steadied her voice.

It doesn't matter if it lived or died. I did what I could for it. My conscience is clear.

Too bad her tense muscles and churning stomach didn't agree with that statement.

"Could I speak to Demi Barnes?" a woman asked.

"Speaking." Demi's voice climbed. She forced it back down.

Why was she so anxious over the fate of this stupid cat? Maybe it was because of the day. Death stalked this day in her mind. It would be nice to cheat the Grim Reaper out of another soul for a change.

"This is Doctor Morrison with Ocean View Veterinary Clinic. You asked me to let you know whether the cat you brought in survived surgery." The woman continued in a calm voice.

"Yes. Did it?" She braced herself. The animal had been in terrible shape. So mangled and bloody, she hadn't been sure it was still alive when she'd reached the animal clinic.

"It did. We removed the back right leg and left eye, as we had discussed. But we also had to remove the tail. The nerves, vertebra and ligaments were too badly damaged to save it."

Demi winced. The poor thing. "Will it survive, do you think?"

The veterinarian paused before saying in a quiet voice, "At this point, we've done everything we can. Its survival will depend on its will to live." Her voice turned brisk. "You mentioned when you brought the cat in that you'd pay for any lifesaving procedures and left us a credit card number as a security deposit. Is this still the card you want us to put the charges on?"

"Yes. Do you have a total on the charges yet?" She was obviously crazy. She wasn't responsible for this creature. Why in the world had she offered to pay for the medical charges?

"As of right now, we're looking at $2,987. This includes several projected days in intensive care. If the animal dies before those days are used, or if he recovers more quickly, you may get a slight refund."

Demi winced, then shrugged. She had the money, might as well use it on something worthwhile. "Fine. Run the charges. Where will you send him after he recovers?"

The vet made a sound that showed surprise. "We were under the assumption that you'd be taking him home."

"Oh, no," she said automatically. "Aiden hates cats."

"I see." There was a long pause.

Demi felt compelled to fill the silence. "Maybe the local shelter would take him?"

"I'm sure they would." The woman's voice was neutral. "But with his injuries, he'd likely be euthanized to make room for more adoptable cats."

"Oh…" Demi's voice was small.

"We can look into some of the local rescues, see if any of them have room for a special needs cat."

Special needs? She grimaced. Of course it was. With the extent of its injuries, it could hardly go back to living on the streets.

"We have a couple of days before we need to decide," the woman continued. "He may not even make it through the night. He's lost a lot of blood and the damage to his body was catastrophic."

Demi scowled. The vet's tone suggested that death might be the best option.

"I've changed my mind. I'll take him." The decision burst from her with no input from her brain. No, Aiden didn't like cats, but his preferences didn't matter anymore. He might not know it yet, but they were officially broken up.

"Okay…" the vet sounded hesitant. "Are you certain?"

"Absolutely." To Demi's surprise, she was sure. The cat needed a home, and she had plenty of space. "Can I visit him?" At least a visit to the animal clinic would get her out of the house. And if she was going to bring him home, they needed to bond. There would be bandages to change and medicines to give. He needed to learn to trust her and let her take care of him.

"Of course," the doctor assured her.

After making an appointment to visit the cat, Demi hung up. Looks like she had a pet. A roommate, to keep her company as she moved on with her life.

Chapter Three

Day 1
Denali, Alaska

"You appear indifferent about this trip to the *Brenahiilo,*" Samuel observed as the cafeteria doors slid apart and they stepped into the corridor beyond. "Are you not meeting with your *anistaa* and *le'ven'a?*"

"I am."

It did not surprise Wolf that Samuel had sensed his dissatisfaction with the upcoming visit to the Twin Peaks Reservation. His *Caetanee* had been kin to him since their early rotations of running wild through the forests and fields of the *Brenahiilo.* They had been accepted into the warrior clans and bound to the *Neealaho*—the neural web that tied all warriors as one—during the same ceremony. No one, within or without the Shadow Realm, knew him as well as Samuel did.

"If you do not wish to go, why do so?" Small lines knit Samuel's forehead.

Wolf grunted but offered no explanation. Spending time with Jillian, his shadow *le'ven'a,* at least of late, brought nothing but frustration and longing.

He could not prevent her from wallowing in her shadow life, existing in her memories. No matter how many spirit walkers he sent to perform the recalling ceremony, no matter how many times they attempted to rejoin the pieces of her shattered soul, they could not reunite her spirit. Sometimes, when the spirit broke too brutally, it could not be made whole.

"Ah." Samuel stared straight ahead. But his words proved he knew the situation well. "She does not retreat from the Shadow Realm, then?"

Samuel's face showed nothing, neither did his matter-of-fact tone. But Wolf felt his second's sympathy. It shimmered through the mental link that tied their minds.

He bled all emotion from his face, voice, and the neural connection that bound them. "She does not."

After three cycles of drifting with one foot in, one foot out of the Shadow Realm, it surprised him she had not succumbed to her spirit children and joined them at the web of her ancestors. Once, her resistance to death had offered hope that her spirit might return to her, and thus to him.

That had not happened. And such hope was long gone.

"Do you train with Daniel today?" Wolf shot his second a quick glance.

"I do. He becomes more skilled with each rotation." Pride shined in his *Caetanee's* eyes. As it should. Samuel had been more father than uncle to the young one and coached him well.

As Jude had done for Wolf.

Perhaps he should join them. He could use the exercise of his mind and body. Samuel's nephew had become a fine tactician, and a fine warrior, although he'd yet to set foot on his first *aggress*. It would be soon, though. The young one was ready.

"*Betanee. Caetanee.*"

A raspy, parchment-thin voice drew Wolf's attention to the right. Milky eyes caught his gaze. He stopped and turned, instinctively bowing his head and shoulders. All elders were accorded respect for the cycles they had walked the Earth. But Benioko—the *Taounaha* or earthside voice of the Shadow Warrior—was due instant obedience as well.

The *Taounaha's* visions led the Kalikoia. Not just the warriors who called Shadow Mountain home, but the entire tribe. He was the voice, ears, and eyes of the Shadow Warrior, and thus, the most influential of the *Hee'woo'nee.*

"Come," the Old One said. Turning, he shuffled toward the utility vehicles parked at the charging station beside the cafeteria.

The shuffling was a fresh worry. So were the faded and filmed eyes. Once Benioko had stood tall, walked with pride—even arrogance. He had faced all challenges with fierce strength. But his years of walking the Shadow Realm and battling the younger gods hung heavy on him. The shaman had long since left the energy and health of youth behind. He had been old before Wolf had joined the warrior clans. He had one foot across the veil now.

As did Jillian.

With Samuel beside him, Wolf followed the *Taounaha* to an electric cart with seats for four. They climbed in, Benioko settling behind the wheel.

The fact that the Old One had addressed him and Samuel by their warrior designations, rather than their given names, meant this meeting was about warrior matters. Benioko silently confirmed that expectation when he drove the vehicle straight to Shadow Mountain Command.

Wolf listened to the whisper of the *Taounaha's* shuffling steps, as they entered the decades old stone building and traversed the cold, echoing halls.

They entered the briefing room and took seats around the massive table. Wolf scanned the archaic wood, his eyes skimming over the names carved into the surface. Hundreds of names, each representing the spirit of a warrior—one who currently walked or had once walked these halls. His gaze easily found Jude's name. His mentor. His mother's brother. The loss of his *anisbecco* still stung his heart, even though the wound was three cycles old.

In the corner of the ancient wood were his and Samuel's names. It was customary for young warriors to carve their name into the table of memory, but only after they survived the binding ceremony and joined the warriors' neural web.

All warriors, in and out of the Shadow Realm, except for O'Neill and the four white warriors, were represented on the table. But then the four SEALs were not bound to the *Neealaho*. And while O'Neill had survived the binding ceremony and joined the warrior clans, he was an outsider, an unwelcome addition to the *Neealaho*. O'Neill knew this; thus, his absent name from the table of memory.

Wolf still did not understand why Benioko had forced the *jie'van* upon them.

Custom dictated that the *Taounaha* speak first, so Wolf and Samuel waited for the Old One to gather his thoughts. As he waited, Wolf studied the crevices digging into Benioko's forehead. His gaze dropped to the lines bracketing the ancient one's nose and cheeks. He recognized the vacant look in the elder's eyes, and the exhaustion folding his face. The slow, shuffling gait he noted earlier came to mind. All were signs of a splintered soul.

Benioko had spirit walked again. And recently. It often took several rotations for the *Taounaha* to reclaim the pieces of his spirit from the Shadow Realm.

Wolf straightened in concern. It was never wise to walk among the shadow gods without an attendant—someone versed in drawing the spirit back into the physical realm. Sometimes the ancestors were capricious, or the tricksters paid a visit, or the younger shadow gods refused to allow return.

Since Jude's death, he had attended the elder during the crossing ceremonies. He bore witness as the shaman pierced the veil to the Shadow Realm and consulted with the Shadow Warrior.

Yet, the last request to attend the Old One was long ago.

"Last night, the Shadow Warrior walked my dreams. He showed me a rising darkness, one that will blot out all peoples, across every web of life," the Old One said, his voice tattered and thin.

Wolf jolted upright in his chair. He must have misunderstood. The Shadow Warrior did not seek out his earthside mouthpiece. His *Taounaha* went to him through dreams, or if the mind and spirit were fatigued, through the crossing ceremony and the ritual smoke.

Benioko read Wolf's shock and offered a single solemn nod. "He came to me. In my sleep. I did not seek him out."

Wolf tensed. If the Shadow Warrior had invaded Benioko's dreams, something was very wrong in the waking world. So wrong, the elder gods had interfered.

"What did the Shadow Warrior show you?" Wolf asked, dread drilling down to his bones.

"He showed me *Hokalita* swallowed by a new—" the Old One paused, and frowned, as though contemplating his words. "People," he finally said. "A people unlike any before. Dead, yet not dead. Connected by thought as one mind, like our sisters the ants and bees. They rise as few but multiply to many and lay waste to all peoples, from all places and customs. They become the one, the only. A swarm of locusts across sister earth."

A swarm of new people, connected by thought... A hive mind? Dead but not dead. Zombies? The warning would have been amusing—zombies, for shadow's sake—except...the Shadow Warrior had invaded his *Taounaha's* dreams to give warning.

This had never happened before.

"Where do these new people come from?" The dread lay heavy in Wolf's gut and chest.

Creation was the providence of the Shadow Warrior and the Blue Moon Mother. Not even the most jealous of their shadow children carried this kind of power.

"From the *woohanta*, prodded on by the lower realm's trickster children." Benioko shook his head tiredly.

So, this new threat had evolved through the Anglo tribe and the elder gods' envious, capricious shadow children. This was never a good combination. Wolf grimaced. Of course, the Shadow Warrior's lower realm children, those banished from the upper realm because of maliciousness and spite, were behind this new global menace. While they did not hold the power of creation like their parents, they often maliciously meddled in the affairs of the elder gods' favorite children. Erasing their parents' creations from the face of *Hokalita* would please them greatly.

"Did the Shadow Warrior show you how to defeat this new enemy?" Wolf asked. It was impossible to discuss battle strategies when they did not know what they fought.

"He showed me your *javaanee*, the one who follows the white warriors' ways."

Wolf shook his head. He had only one javaanee and Aiden was staunchly against his Kalikoia heritage.

"The Shadow Warrior should have chosen more wisely." Wolf's voice turned dry, and outright sacrilegious. It was never wise to question the elder gods. But Benioko knew Aiden refused to learn the ways of the *Hee'woo'nee*. "Aiden will not join us to neutralize this threat."

The Old One released a long, tired sigh. "You must convince him. He is in great danger. Your *javaanee* is the arrow in this new war. Without him, the *Hee'woo'nee* and all the peoples who walk *Hokalita* will be no more."

Then they were in trouble.

Wolf had spent many cycles trying to convince Aiden to join Shadow Mountain Command and adopt his tribal heritage. Time after time, Aiden had brushed aside the requests. Wolf had long since stopped asking. You could not force knowledge on those unwilling to hear.

"Your *javaanee* is in great danger. If those who created this new enemy find him, he will cross the veil and the *Hee'woo'nee* will perish." The Old One looked up; his hooded eyes sunken with concern. "You must find him and quickly. Others seek him. If they reach him first, this war is lost." He gestured weakly at the huge computer monitor that stretched across the far wall. A map of Tajikistan and the Karategin Mountains filled the screen. "You will find him there. Choose your men and go. Quickly. Take your *javaacee* and the new Thunderbird. Aiden will have need of your sister's *Hee-Hee-Thae* magic and your new toy's speed and veiling."

Aiden would need healing? And not just any healing, but from Kait, who was the strongest healer among the *Hee'woo'nee*? This was unwelcome news.

Yet, his gift of future sight had not warned him of a threat to Aiden. Not this time.

Wolf frowned, unease stirring. Three cycles ago, the future sight gift had failed him, and Jude had died. Aiden's fate could not echo his *anisbecco*'s.

According to Benioko, Aiden's death would end the world.

Day 2
Vahdat, Tajikistan

In the past, when Aiden spun up for an op, he did so with a focused mind. A good operator—and he was a damn good one—knew that distractions led to death. But this time…fuck…strategies aimed at convincing Demi not to dump him plagued his thoughts.

He was too damn distracted, which didn't bode well for his survival.

"The chopper will drop you eight klicks from your target."

It was zero-one-hundred, half an hour from go, and he found it impossible to concentrate on the final mission brief. The news he was in line for a *Dear Aiden* speech kept swirling through his mind. But it didn't help that Dipshit Dwight Dawson was giving the briefing. The CIA analyst charged with monitoring this region of Tajikistan had the worst voice *ever*. Didn't the Farm teach their agents not to bore their audience into a stupor? This particular spook spoke in a low, droning monotone. No pitches or valleys. Just an endless, dull buzz.

"Our target is Grigory Kuznetsov, an arms dealer brokering stolen military tech." The most boring spook alive continued.

Dipshit Dawson didn't look like your average spook. And yeah, spooks had a look. Nondescript, flat-faced, cold-eyed. Not Dawson, though. Nope, he was tall and lanky, with warm blue eyes.

"…Karaveht is the smallest of the villages on…"

To his right, Squirrel's shorn head bobbed, the bronze and red scales of his rattler tattoo shimmering. Aiden leaned over and drove an elbow into his buddy's muscled ribs. If he had to listen, so did the rest of his crew. Squirrel grunted and jolted upright.

The spook kept droning on and on, periodically tapping his pointer against the huge monitor that stretched across the front of the command tent. The monitor displayed satellite images of a small settlement tucked between steep, rocky hills. Mud-brick houses lined both sides of a dirt road. Metal roofs, along with the jagged hills surrounding them, were splashed with white from the recent snow.

Their target was Karaveht, a remote village amid the Karategin Mountains. While a narrow road ran through the village, connecting it to the rest of the towns along the Rasht Valley, they wouldn't be using it. The road would expose them to unwelcome eyes. Instead, they'd insert into town by climbing and descending the hills surrounding it.

According to Dipshit Dawson, Karaveht was small. Only two hundred and fifty souls called it home. It seemed odd that Kuznetsov had set up shop there. For fuck's sake, the place didn't even have internet, or electricity. Gasoline generators powered what electrical resources they had. But perhaps that was the point. Who'd expect high-tech military arms for sale in such a low-tech place?

"You're looking for the schematics and prototypes of the A7V02 Drone. Be advised that Grigory Kuznetsov and his men have access to the deadliest weapons available," Dwight Dawson droned on.

Aiden scoffed beneath his breath. What the fuck? Did the bastard really think they'd underestimate one of the most prolific arms dealers in the world? News flash, he and his brothers *never* underestimated their targets.

"Once you've neutralized Kuznetsov and his men, search the target's dwelling. Remove any prototypes, schematics, and hard drives."

Aiden rolled his eyes. They'd been doing retrieval ops for years. Nobody had to tell them how to do their damn jobs.

"Who has the AN-M14 grenades?"

Grub, the squad's explosives technician, raised his hand and offered a two-finger wave. "Checked out five of 'em."

"Five? One is overkill in this case," the spook said.

Grub shrugged. "Could be all sorts of shit that needs incinerating once we're on site."

Truer words had never been spoken. It was best not to assume the intel gathered for this op painted the entire picture.

"Questions?" The spook glanced at his watch.

"Yeah, what's with the continuous video feed?" Aiden split his questioning look between the spook and Trevor Montana, his Lieutenant Commander.

Hannah Montana, as they called him behind his back, was a tier one prick, more concerned with toeing the company line than sticking up for the men beneath his command. Zane Winters, his previous CO, was by far the better man. But then, his loyalty and morality led to his downfall.

"The camera feed is a direct order from WARCOM." Montana shrugged. "It's a thinner, lighter camera with a longer battery life. They're testing its durability and battery charge in the field."

Aiden shook his head in disgust. The standard cameras worked perfectly fine. What a waste of time and money. Should have known the order came directly from NAVSPECWARCOM or WARCOM for short. At least he wouldn't be the one slogging through hours of snow crusted desert and wintery skies.

Chapter Four

Day 2
Karaveht, Tajikistan

They were still two klicks from Karaveht when Aiden's get-the-fuck-out-now alarm started screaming. It wasn't a premonition, at least not like the ones Wolf got. It was more like a feeling that something was wrong...or about to go wrong.

His breath steaming from the mesh mouthpiece of his balaclava, Aiden stopped to scan the jagged peaks surrounding them. Their target was just over the next rise. The scrubby, snow-crusted terrain surrounding them was a luminous green beneath his NVDs and cold weather goggles. No furtive movements up ahead. No shimmer of metal as snipers lined up their shots. The steep, rocky hill above them looked barren. No sign of a welcome party. No sign anyone was out and about.

What the hell was he picking up on?

The night huddled around them—hushed and still. Even the tread of their boots against the snow crusted path sounded muted, instead of crunchy. That was when it clicked. The night was too quiet. Unnaturally so.

"Alpha One, problem?" Grub's question was a flat growl through Aiden's comm. They all knew voices carried in the cold, crisp air.

"Possibly," Aiden said in a toneless whisper. "Anyone getting the willies?"

A pause traveled the line, followed by Montana's cool response. "Alpha One? What's the problem?"

Aiden scanned the hills again. Still no signs of life. No indication of an ambush.

"Alpha One." Montana's voice again, this time with a hint of impatience. "Is there a problem?"

Aiden frowned. The prickle down his spine sure thought so. But his eyes saw nothing concerning. "Unclear."

"Target is over the rise. Two klicks away," said Dawson.

"Copy that." Aiden scanned the hills again. His internal danger alarm was getting louder and more insistent. "Any new SAT intel?"

Another pause crawled over the comm. Then, "Pulling."

Minutes ticked by while his team shifted uneasily behind him. As they waited, the cold dug in, chilling skin previously warmed by adrenaline and exercise. They needed to get moving again. Movement was their best defense against the sub-zero weather—at least until they returned to their exfil site and dug into their cold weather kits.

"The newest images are consistent with the earlier ones," the spook said. "Nothing concerning. We are a go. Repeat, we are a go."

Aiden stepped forward, forcing his resistant muscles to move. Something sure had his bowels in a twist.

When they reached the summit, they went belly down on the rocky, snow-smudged ground. Karaveht lay dark and silent below. A chill skated down his spine as he examined the messy rows of houses. Not a damn light on in any of them. Sure, it was late, barely zero-three-hundred, but you'd think someone would have left a light on.

His chest, abdomen, and legs tried to root themselves into the ground. Christ, he didn't want to go down there.

Just do your job.

He forced himself up and over the ridge. The ground was rocky and slick. They took their time, testing each step, descending as stealthily as possible. By the time they reached the outskirts of Karaveht, his danger alarm was shrieking nonstop.

They moved forward, rifles up. A dozen paces in, his scope fell on a huddled lump in the middle of the street. They slowed, cautiously approaching. The smell of blood was faint at first but grew stronger with each step. It was minus ten degrees. There had to be a lot of blood involved for him to smell anything at all. In subzero temperatures, the olfactory system had trouble detecting and categorizing scents.

The lump separated into two forms as he got closer. Humans. Both dead. A lake of red surrounded them. No one could survive losing that much blood. One body lay face down, the other, face up. He tapped the heel of his boot against the pool of blood. It crunched and splintered. Frozen. Which meant these two had been dead so long their blood had cooled and froze.

The body facing up was a male in his sixties, with a gaping split across his throat. A bloody serrated knife still touched his fingers. Squirrel squatted beside Aiden, watching him turn the second body over. It was female. Younger than the male. She wore the traditional straight dress, trousers, and colorful embroidered shawl of a mountain woman.

Squirrel used his rifle barrel to nudge the tatters of her dress aside. "She was stabbed. Repeatedly."

Grubb scanned the scene. "If someone killed them and left, they'd leave bloody footprints behind. There are none, and the knife is next to him. Looks like he used the knife on her first and then slit his own throat."

Had this asshole killed his wife and then himself? Suicide by slitting your own throat was unusual. Plus, they'd been dead for hours. Why hadn't anyone moved the bodies out of the road?

"Let's find Kuznetsov, collect the drone shit and get out." Aiden rose to his feet.

According to their intel, their target's residence was a narrow, one-story mud-brick building in the middle of town. They moved toward it, clinging to the shadows, their boots crunching against the crusty snow. The door to the second house stood wide open. And the blood smell was even stronger than up the road. Aiden's chest tightened. An open door in the middle of February? In minus-ten-degree weather? Along with the scent of blood? This could not be good.

He skirted the door and froze at the sight of the bodies behind it.

A whole damn family. All dead. All bloody as hell.

"Fuck. She's just a kid." Aiden squatted next to the closest child and turned her over. Eight or nine years of age, with a bloody hole in her forehead. Her tattered, tiny dress and pants were iced with blood, indicating she'd suffered more than just the gunshot wound. His gut churned. It was always hard to see a dead kid. So senseless, so much lost potential. But this...

He rose to his feet, turning to the other bodies. Squirrel and Grub had flipped them over until they faced up. Their bodies were covered with frozen blood, half their faces and heads gone. A rifle and two handguns lay on the ground among them. The carnage was senseless. This hit hadn't come from a terrorist sect. Shitkickers didn't waste ammo.

"What the fuck happened?" Benny asked, his wiry body rigid.

"Again, no footprints walking away." Grub's voice was thin. "And these wounds are close range." He glanced at the guns on the ground. "Looks like the adults killed each other and the kids."

A single lover's quarrel was one thing. But a mother and father killing each other, *and* their kids? Plus, the sheer violence of the scene. It looked like the couple down the road and this family here had gone fucking crazy and slaughtered each other.

Something was very wrong in Karaveht. Was Kuznetsov behind the bloodshed? That's when he remembered the live camera feed.

"Base," he said. "You see this?"

"Affirmative." Montana sounded nonplussed.

"You know anything about this?" Aiden's voice went hard, accusatory.

What were the odds they'd walk into something so messed up while testing this new continuous video feed? Had someone up the ladder known his team would stumble into this shit show?

"How the hell would I know about this?" Montana sounded pissed, like he'd picked up on Aiden's unspoken accusation. "Get the drone intel and get out."

Aiden glanced down as Grub rose from where he'd turned one of the kids over.

Turned the kid over...

Ah, hell.

"No more touching them," he ordered sharply. God only knew what had caused these people to snap, but if it was contagious...

He shuddered, staring down at his gloved hands. He was wearing his winter wear gloves, which were thicker, with more insulation, but still, he'd touched two bodies.

You're wearing gloves. You're fine.

Unless his gloves were contaminated and he'd touched his face, spreading the taint to his unprotected skin. But, hell—the contaminant could be airborne. They could be infecting themselves with every breath they took. He shook himself and regrouped. While there was still the chance these two instances of violence were aberrations, they needed to take precautions.

"Everyone mask up." They all carried Avon M50 respirators in their packs. They'd be a tight fit with the balaclavas, but they'd make it work.

"Don't touch your face. Before attaching your respirator, take your gloves off without using your hands. Once the M50 is hooked up, switch to a pair of fresh gloves. From here on out—*don't touch anything*."

He moved away from the second kill site. Far from the bodies and blood, he eased out of his assault pack. He used the toe of his boot to anchor his gloves and pulled them off. After plugging the M50 into the Electronic Communications Port, he pulled on a fresh pair of gloves.

Were their precautions too late? Had they already been infected by whatever caused these people to snap? The question sat like a cold, hard lump in his chest.

More bodies appeared as they advanced into town. They didn't stop to investigate, but the bloodshed was incredible. Men...women... children. One guy had a shovel buried in his abdomen; another was hacked to pieces with a machete. The violence was unreal.

No fucking way was an outside force responsible for this insanity. The entire town had gone bonkers and slaughtered each other. Most of their weapons were household items. Several of them had used skillets to pulverize their victim's skulls.

Had Kuznetsov tested a psychotropic drug here? Had it turned everyone insane?

"Jesus." Squirrel's breathing was choppy and sporadic. "That asshole used a goddamn chainsaw. He cut their fucking heads off."

Aiden didn't look. He didn't need more horrifying images clogging his memory. "Keep your distance from the bodies."

Not that anyone needed the warning. Nobody wanted to catch whatever had infected these poor bastards.

"We touched the first two sets of bodies." Grub's voice was hoarse, horrified. "We had our gloves on, but still."

"Yeah." Aiden shook aside his own dread. "Can't do anything about that now. Focus. Get this job done and let's get out."

"Golden Eagle," Aiden said, addressing his CO by the moniker the prick had chosen for himself. He could almost feel the bastard preening on the other end of the comm. But it was best to keep the ass pliable. "It's too dangerous to bring anything back from here, nor can we evac. Whatever caused these people to snap could be contagious. We can't risk infecting base." He paused, his voice tightening. "We need a CDC risk assessment team."

A small town in the middle of bumfuck nowhere would make a perfect test site for a viral, bacterial, or psychotropic weapon. Was that what Kuznetsov was up to in Karaveht, testing something new and horrific? Had their camera feed been ordered to record the aftermath of the test? Was that the real reason they'd been ordered to run a continuous feed? Were they part of the goddamn test?

If that was the case, then he had a big problem, because someone within WARCOM had to be calling the shots.

Rage coiled in his gut, vibrating like an angry rattler.

This whole situation felt like a damn set up.

Kuznetsov's house was exactly where Dawson said it would be. Its door stood open. The interior was dark. Complete silence from inside. They assaulted into the building low and quick, rifles up and sweeping. Pure muscle memory at work.

"Clear."

"Clear."

"Clear," echoed through the silent rooms.

Their search of the house revealed nothing.

No Kuznetsov. No signs of habitation. No computers. No cell phones. No drone specs or drone prototypes. Nothing but empty rooms and layers of dust.

"Golden Eagle." Aiden's voice echoed through the silent house. "Our target is cold."

This house hadn't been occupied in months, maybe even years.

They'd been set up.

Fuck. Fuck. Fuck. Fuck.

The litany went on and on in his head.

"Copy, Alpha One." Montana's voice was muffled as though he were consulting with someone to the side. "Light it up and search the town."

They left the house with Grub releasing the M14 grenade and rushing out to join them. The explosion rocked the eerie silence behind them. A ball of flames and debris leaped into the sky. Nobody came to investigate. They searched the entire town, their bodies tense, their breathing choppy, their silence ripe with fear. They didn't find Kuznetsov, or the drone specs, or any survivors. Whatever hit this town had a 100% fatality rate.

If he and his brothers were infected...

Don't think about it. Focus on the job and get out.

"Golden Eagle, target is cold," Aiden announced into his comm once they'd searched the last house.

"Copy," Montana said. "Hold for orders."

"If these new orders involve collecting samples from this hellhole, they can go fuck themselves," Lurch muttered.

Aiden grunted in agreement and hoped his buddy had turned his comm off.

"Alpha One." Montana's voice sounded tense. "Head to exfil. Be aware, evac is delayed. We have a CDC team en route. Keep us apprised of any changes to your team's health and mental acuity."

Montana's terse order shortened Aiden's stride. Translation. Let us know if you, or any of your teammates, go nuts.

Aiden flinched.

Fuuuck.

Did base think this insanity bug came on so fast it would infect his team within hours of leaving town? How soon had it affected the villagers?

When had they died? The subzero temperatures made it difficult to assess time of death.

He keyed his mic. "Agent Dawson. You said the latest SAT images were consistent with earlier ones. Did any of the images pick up the dead bodies? Any evidence of when they died?"

"No. There were no bodies on the SAT scans." Dawson's voice sounded defensive. But then, he knew how fucked that was. The bodies should have been visible...unless someone had scrubbed the images before sending them on. "I've sent them in for analysis."

Aiden grimaced. Great. It would take days for the Farm to issue a report.

As they scaled the hill toward their exfil site, the ice-shrouded grass crackled beneath each footfall. Aiden listened to the harsh breathing of his teammates as they climbed beside him. Never had their breathing been so loud, or their tension so sharp, after completing a mission. He could taste the fear in the air—both his and his brothers'. The sharp, metallic taste of it filled his mouth. They all knew their lives were at risk the second they hopped off a chopper—hell, even before their boots hit the ground sometimes—and that each mission courted the ultimate sacrifice—the giving of their lives.

But not like this. Not through insanity and violence. Not through the ultimate betrayal and the slaughter of his brothers, the men he'd sworn to protect. He wanted to believe that wouldn't happen, that his team had escaped whatever had driven the inhabitants of Karaveht crazy, driven them to kill each other.

But he couldn't push the fear aside, because that damn internal alarm was still screaming in his head, warning him that the danger was far from over.

Chapter Five

Day 2
Washington, D.C.

Clark Nantz braced his right ankle on his left thigh, repositioned his laptop closer to his torso, and leaned forward in the elephant chair. His heart pounded harder than normal as he clicked the first small window on the screen. Finally, after months of preparation, his new weapon had come out to play. The aftermath of its testing, which was about to play across his laptop screen, would change the landscape of human conflict and propel him to the top of the world's billionaires list.

The video—which came from Aiden Winchester's camera, according to the name below the feed—was jerky, alternating between a wintery dark night, snow crusted road, and shadowy hills. Suddenly, it steadied and zeroed in on a lump in the middle of the road. The lump got closer.

The breathing on the video was calm...even...barely discernable.

Clark scoffed. Winchester didn't have a clue what he was walking into. His breathing would turn choppy soon enough.

He glanced across his penthouse office toward his desk, his African Blackwood desk—created from the most expensive wood in the world. A Pininfarina Xten Chair accompanied it. The desk and chair were more comfortable than his thirty-million-dollar elephant chair, but not nearly as satisfying. He scooted backwards a bit, trying to ease the ache in his back. Watching Winchester's and his SEAL team's reaction from the Art Deco chair, surrounded by what the antique represented, was worth any amount of discomfort.

Nothing was more thrilling than watching the aftermath of the testing of his new cash cow from a priceless antique made possible by his previous successes.

"She was stabbed. Repeatedly," one of the SEALs said, as he used the tip of his rifle to lift a torn section of the woman's dress.

"If someone killed them and left, they'd leave bloody footprints behind. There are none, and the knife is next to him. Looks like he used the knife on her first and then slit his own throat."

Ding, ding, ding. Give the SEAL a reward. He'd read the situation correctly. How long would it take them to realize what had happened in Karaveht, and fear it happening to them?

The SEALs moved away from his weapon's first set of victims. While Clark waited for them to stumble upon more fatalities, he idly skimmed his fingers down the antique chair's elephant tusk armrest. The ivory slipped beneath his fingertips, dipping and rising with each intricate carving. The tusk felt like satin beneath his hands, luxurious and timeless.

The elephant chair was one of his touchstones, physical proof of how far he'd climbed since those long-ago days in the homeless camps. From nothing to billions, thanks to the brilliance of his mind. Although his willingness to venture into territory most people—those too pious, or lazy, or mired in morals—refused to dwell had a lot to do with his success too.

Territory like the one scrolling across his laptop's screen.

Winchester squatted next to a child and turned her over. "Fuck. She's just a kid."

Clark leaned forward again, studying the scene through Winchester's video feed. So, the weapon bypassed the parental impulse to protect their children. Excellent. The earlier testing had showed as much. But it was nice to have that potential borne out in the field.

"Base," Winchester said. "You see this?"

"Affirmative." The responding voice sounded baffled.

"You know anything about this?" Winchester's voice was tense, even critical.

"Tsk-tsk." Clark smiled. So much drama, with so much more to come.

He gazed out his fifteen-floor office window as the SEAL team proceeded through town. The huge, floor-to-ceiling windows offered an unparalleled snapshot of the city. A billion-dollar view. The obelisk known as the Washington Monument speared the sky to his right, along with the towering white dome of the Capital Building and the pillars of the Jefferson and Lincoln memorials.

The view from his office was another touchstone. Visual this time. Proof that he'd escaped the poverty and shame of his childhood. Escaped a life of dumpster clothing and homeless camps, where he'd sweltered in the summer and froze in the winter and fell asleep listening to his rumbling belly.

"No more touching them," Winchester snapped.

And why, yes—the team leader's breathing was noticeably louder. Clark smiled.

This new weapon was quite a departure from his earlier patents. The first of which had come some thirty years ago—a revolutionary anti-sand, anti-heat, laser guided firing system for anti-armor missiles. Over the past thirty years, many other patents followed, all of which were innocuous compared to the weapon he'd just tested in Karaveht. His new baby would make the old-fashioned war machine of infantry, missiles, tanks and fighter jets obsolete, while simultaneously making him the richest man in the world, by billions upon billions of dollars.

"Golden Eagle." Winchester's voice echoed through the video feed. "Our target is cold."

Clark frowned over that statement. It had to be code for something. Maybe the drone? Maybe the arms dealer they'd been sent to find? If so, then yes. Their targets were cold. But then, they'd been sent to find targets that didn't exist.

At least, not in Karaveht.

So far, every inhabitant of Karaveht on the video was dead, which gave his new weapon a perfect score. One hundred percent fatality. Excellent.

He was so focused on the images streaming across his laptop, he didn't hear the door to his office open.

"Sir? Dr. Nantz?"

He jolted at Bernice's, his administrative assistant, tentative voice and quickly hit the button to shut the screen off. The footage was being recorded. He could go over it at his leisure, as many times as he wanted.

"I know you said no interruptions," she continued, her voice diffident, "but Admiral Hurley is on line one. He's demanding to speak with you."

Of course, he was. Right on time, too. It might be 3:30 a.m. in Karaveht Tajikistan, but it was 6:30 p.m. at the pentagon. Hurley probably hadn't left his office yet.

"Of course. Put him through."

He breathed in the gardenia scent of her perfume and preened. She was wearing the perfume he'd given her for Christmas. Proof that they both had excellent taste. He rose and stretched as the door closed behind her. With the laptop beneath his arm, he headed for the desk, set the laptop down, and dropped into the Pininfarina Xten Chair. It gave beneath his weight with a hushed *whoosh*. He picked up the phone receiver and hit the button for line one.

"Nantz, are you—"

"Admiral," Clark broke in, doing his best to impersonate someone in the throes of frustrated annoyance. "What the hell's going on over there? I've seen no evidence from the camera feed that Kuznetsov is in Karaveht, like your people predicted. Nor have I seen the A7 Drone's prototype or any of its schematics anywhere on the video. This op of yours has been a complete disaster. We *must* get that drone back" He inserted confused horror into his voice. "And what the hell killed all those poor people?"

A hoarse huff came down the line, followed by a gravelly voice.

"From what we can tell, the whole damn town slaughtered each other." Hurley sounded winded, like a pin had just pricked and deflated his righteous fury. "You wouldn't know anything about that, would you? The timing of this test on your new cameras is suspicious as hell."

But Hurley didn't sound accusatory, more frustrated and confused than anything.

"How the hell was I supposed to know that your men would run into problems on this mission? We weren't even supposed to be testing the cameras today. They were scheduled for testing last month. Remember? Only your supply chain lost the damn battery packs, which—I'll remind you—was your crew's fault, not mine."

The missing batteries had been easy enough to set up. A bribe here, another there, and the batteries had become separated from the cameras. Hell, he'd even gotten paid for the second shipment.

"Look, I have no idea what happened in that village." Clark leaned back and swiveled his chair until he could look out over the lights of Washington, D.C. below. "You're the one who tracked Kuznetsov to that place and assured me he'd set up shop there." All of which was true. "How the hell would I know what went down there?"

Except, of course, he knew exactly what had happened in that doomed town. Hell, he'd instigated it. Not that anyone would ever know that.

He had no intention of being brought up on charges of crimes against humanity.

"Our CIA team is still insisting their intel was solid, and that Kuznetsov and the A7V02 Drone prototype were there."

"Obviously, your analyst was mistaken," Clark snapped. "There's no evidence the drone was *ever* in this town."

Because it hadn't been in Karaveht.

Hell, it hadn't been stolen. Kuznetsov had done an excellent job of planting the fake intel throughout the dark web, to catch the CIA's attention and lure the DOD into sending a retrieval team.

"Our analyst thinks Kuznetsov chose Karaveht to run a test using a biological or psychotropic agent. We're mobilizing a full biological and chemical team to investigate."

Clark smirked. By the time Hurley's teams arrived, there wouldn't be anything to investigate.

He had proof, on video no less, that his weapon had activated the civilian population. Too bad he didn't have footage of the violence taking place. Kuznetsov had installed cameras throughout Karaveht for just that purpose. Unfortunately, the satellite upload link had failed. Footage of the inhabitants going crazy and attacking each other had never made it out of town. No matter. When his cleanup crew arrived, they'd retrieve the cameras, along with the dead villagers. If his luck held, the video on the cameras would still be accessible. But then, the footage of the villagers going crazy wasn't nearly as critical as phase two of his test.

SEALs were a breed apart. Hell, a breed above. They were practically superheroes—physically stronger, mentally resilient. If his weapon affected them—which Clark fully expected it to do—and they turned on each other, as the townspeople of Karaveht had done...then he'd have proof that his baby could take down any military organization in the world.

It was only a matter of time before the infected SEALs tore each other apart. Only this time, the carnage would be caught on film. And the footage of Hurley's mighty SEALs slaughtering each other would sell his new weapon for him.

Chapter Six

Day 2
Karaveht, Tajikistan

They took the M50 respirators off as soon as they cleared Karaveht, which made it easier to breathe. Aiden focused fiercely on the *shushushu* of the wind as it swept over his winter BDUs. The icy burn of the breeze slipped past his balaclava, numbing the bridge of his nose and his forehead. Thank Christ for the goggles, otherwise his eyes would be sealed shut. He'd unzipped the armpits of his tactical jacket to vent the body heat buildup from the hard climb up the hill, but sweat still trickled down his back and under his arms, which was never a good thing in cold weather ops. Still, the itchy sensation was a welcome distraction. Anything to avoid the what-ifs pushing against his mind.

What if he was infected? What if Karaveht's insanity bug was spreading through his brain? Was he about to go crazy and slaughter his teammates—his best friends?

The squeak of boot treads against ice and snow drifted up from behind him. So did heavy breathing. Steam plumed through the mesh mouthpieces of their balaclavas. The path to exfil was steep and winding, slick with ice and snow. Still, the physicality of the climb shouldn't tax them. They'd scaled more difficult paths dozens of times before. The only difference this time was the knowledge they might not have left the danger behind once they left town. They might carry the danger with them…inside them.

As that danger alarm in his brain insisted.

Squirrel was the best friend he'd ever had. But the rest of the men on his six were his brothers in every way that mattered. He'd covered their backs for years, just as they'd covered his. He'd attended their birthdays, weddings, and anniversaries. He'd hiked and fished with them, shared beers and barbeques.

The thought of snapping and putting a bullet into their brains was far worse than dying himself. He'd kill himself before he'd harm any of them.

Working up a sweat in sub-zero temperatures was a recipe for hypothermia. But the quest to put that doomed town and the horrifying possibility it represented behind them pushed them forward. They had extra warmies, thermal blankets and even puff jackets in their ditch kits. They could dry off and keep warm back at the exfil site.

Managing the threat of insanity was more difficult.

If they'd been exposed to a drug that caused psychotic behavior, wouldn't they be symptomatic by now? The symptoms would have presented as soon as the body absorbed the dose. Karaveht was an hour behind them. Plenty of time for a drug's side effects to show.

Infections, on the other hand, whether viral or bacterial, had incubation periods. Some were long, some short, but they all had them. How long was the incubation period for the sickness that attacked the inhabitants of Karaveht?

Hell, what were the early symptoms? It would help if they knew how long it took from exposure to the first incident in Karaveht.

He stopped walking and triggered his mic. Instantly, the cold pressed in. "Agent Dawson, have you received any new intel on what happened in Karaveht?"

"Negative, Alpha One." The response came from Montana. "Any up-dates on you and your team's condition?"

"Status quo," he said after a beat of silence. "It would help if we had a timeline on Karaveht—an understanding of how long it took for the insanity to progress."

"Understood, Alpha One." Montana sounded sympathetic, which il-lustrated how serious the situation was. "I'll reach out to our contagion crew, see if they have anything to offer." The sympathy gave way to a harsh demand. "Keep us apprised of your team's health."

"Copy." Aiden let go of the mic.

An hour later, hot and sweaty, they climbed the final hill to their evac site.

He knew his teammates as well as he knew himself. He'd recognize irreg-ularities in their behavior. If any of them started acting...off...he'd restrain them. If he started acting weird, they'd have to restrain him. It was the only thing available to them until the chopper arrived.

"We need to take precautions." Aiden stopped next to the cold weather rucksack he'd ditched behind a boulder as soon as they'd hopped off the chopper. He shrugged out of his assault pack and squatted to unzip the ditch kit.

The assault pack contained the essentials of an active op—extra ammo, distractors, frag grenades, flares, extra gloves, the M50 respirators, breach-ing equipment, and an extra radio. It was small, light, and easy to maneuver in. The ditch kit, on the other hand, was his home away from home. It was also heavy, bulky and unwieldy in the field. It was ditched at drop-off and returned to once the op was completed. It carried all the extras that made life bearable but weren't necessary for an insertion: extra cold weather layers, thermal blankets, three days of water and MREs, a puff sleeping bag and jacket, a camp stove, and a rudimentary med kit, along with the ever-present ammo and secondary hand weapon. The ditch kit carried everything necessary for cold weather survival if exfil didn't go as planned and they had to hunker down for a day or two.

"What're you thinking?" Squirrel asked. He'd removed his goggles, and his brown eyes were grim as he shrugged out of his assault kit and lowered it to the ground.

Good question. Aiden's fingers paused as they rummaged through the compression bag at the bottom of his rucksack with the thermal layers of clothing. Now that he'd stopped moving, the cold was getting grabby. Everything was separated by compression bags in the ditch kit. The lightest and fluffiest bags at the bottom, the heavier and bulkier bags towards the top.

"First step is monitoring ourselves." Aiden grabbed a T-shirt and a dry thermal top to layer over it. "Anyone feeling..." He frowned before shrugging, "...different?"

"Different? Like how? Like I suddenly have a hankering to use the lot of you for target practice?" Benny asked, pulling his balaclava down to free his mouth. "I got ketamine in my kit. If anyone melts down, we can knock them out."

Benny was their combat medic. In their years together, he'd patched them all up. He knew what drug would serve them best if someone went schizoid. But all drugs had their disadvantages. And ketamine took a while to work—not a long while, somewhere between two and five minutes, but those minutes would feel like forever if they were trying to hold someone down.

"We'd have to restrain until the drug takes effect," Aiden said, pulling his balaclava down as well.

Which presented a problem. Restraining a dude in peak physical condition, a dude who'd been taught a dozen ways to kill someone without the use of a weapon, a dude caught in an "excited delirium" state...

He grimaced. Hell, that sounded like a surefire ticket to death.

"We'd be better off removing our weapons and hiding them, then restraining each other now, while we're stable, while we can cooperate," Aiden said, his voice reasonable, knowing with absolute certainty that his brothers would hate that suggestion.

He wasn't fond of it himself. Taking such extreme action would leave them vulnerable. Not just to each other, but to any shitkicker regime patrolling the area.

But which outcome was more likely, death by an enemy that might be in the area, or death by each other, if any of them carried the contagion that had decimated Karaveht?

"No fucking way," Grub snarled as he yanked his balaclava over his head and tossed it toward his ruck. The dude's thin beard appeared to shimmy in agitation. "We don't even know if we're infected. If we are, we don't know when the insanity will hit." He threw his assault kit to the ground hard enough to pop the bolt cutters out. "For all we know, those poor bastards were infected days, even weeks ago."

Aiden shrugged. "Once the chopper reaches us and returns to base, medical can screen us. But if the insanity hits before the chopper arrives, we need to take preventative measures, for the exfil crew, as well as for each other."

"By restraining each other?" Grub snapped. His fists slammed down on his hips, and his wiry body seemed to radiate frustration and fury. "By leaving ourselves vulnerable to any motherfucking local who passes by? Hell no. We keep our eyes peeled and act when necessary."

Act when necessary?

The hairs on the nape of Aiden's neck shot up. He stood and angled closer to get a better look at his teammate. What did Grub mean by that? Only two possibilities came to mind. Restrain the affected or kill them. God help them if Grub meant the latter.

They better tie him up now.

Aiden ran a hand over his head and studied his buddy. The dude's face was jumpy as hell. Grub was one of the cooler guys on his crew. When shit went south, he reacted with caution. He assessed the situation. He was a stone steady kind of guy. Aiden had never seen him so worked up before.

His gaze settled on the twitch at the corner of Grub's left eye.

That was new.

But then Grub had never faced the possibility of insanity before. That shit could stir up stress. How were they supposed to differentiate an abnormal response from a fear-based one?

You don't. You tie him up and let the docs sort it out.

He wasn't the only one focused on Grub. Squirrel and Benny were too. Both men had discarded their goggles and were watching Grub closely. Lurch was crouched over his rucksack, ignoring the lot of them. And Hutch...where the hell was Hutch? The dude had disappeared.

What the hell?

Aiden returned his focus to Grub. The corner of the guy's eye was twitching even worse. Like a grotesque wink. With careful, slow steps, Aiden edged toward his pack and the 550 cords. Flex cuffs wouldn't hold Grub. He'd snap them within seconds. It was much harder to escape from 550 cord and tight knots.

"Where the hell are you going?" Grub asked, an edge sharpening his voice.

Aiden stopped and twisted to face him. "Just getting my thermal blanket. He held the thermal underwear up as evidence. "It's getting cold."

"Liar." There was no humor in Grub's tense laugh. "You don't get cold." His rifle lifted. "Don't fucking move."

Aiden froze, his gaze locked on Grub's hands. The cold weather gloves wrapped around the rifle grip were twitching, too, like his fingers were flexing inside the leather.

"Calm down, bro," Squirrel said in a soothing voice. He took a cautious step forward, moving between Grub and Aiden. "We're just talking. No need to get riled up."

As Grub's gaze shifted toward Squirrel, Aiden eased toward his pack again. He needed the damn cord, and he needed it now. Although...how the fuck was he going to restrain Grub when the dude was armed up the ass and twitchy as hell?

He caught movement out of the corner of his eye and glanced over. Benny was closing on his pack, no doubt going for the ketamine.

"Stay the hell away from me." Grub's voice rose until it was close to a shout.

Fuck. Grub didn't raise his voice. Never. Until now.

He should have restrained everyone as soon as they escaped Karaveht. Exfil could have come to them. But with evac delayed, they'd needed their cold weather kits. Besides, how was he to know the insanity bug would hit so soon?

"How about this, you prick? How about you give me that rifle before you kill someone?" Squirrel snarled.

Aiden jerked. Where the fuck had that tone come from? Nothing soothing or placating about it at all. He shifted to face his two deadlocked squad mates. The step Squirrel took toward Grub was predatory. His rifle rose.

Squirrel glanced back at him. It was just for a second, but long enough for Aiden to get a look at his eyes, his muddy, bloodshot eyes, the corners of which were twitching.

No! Fuck no!

His gaze dropped to his best friend's fingers. Twitching.

Motherfucker.

"Fuck you," Grub snarled, his rifle rising higher. "Nobody is *restraining* me. Nobody is stealing my ability to defend myself. I'll see you all dead first."

Squirrel lifted his rifle, his feet squaring up. "Of course you'd see us all dead, you selfish prick. You've always been more *me* than *us*."

Shit. Shit. Shit.

As his two teammates squared off, Aiden scanned his remaining three teammates for help. Twitching fingers and bloodshot eyes. All of them.

Son of a bitch.

How had this happened so fast?

He keyed his mic. "Base. We're infected. Early signs are twitching faces and fingers, and bloodshot eyes." He dropped the call as voices exploded over his comm. How to stop this brewing blood bath? They were about to shoot. He could feel the animosity crackling in the air all around him.

He gathered himself, about to tackle Squirrel. "Benny," he yelled. "Take—"

Lurch, the squad's sniper, suddenly charged his bickering teammates. Dimly, it registered that Lurch, his teammate most proficient with rifles, had left his M4A1 carbine hanging.

"Lurch!" Aiden roared, putting every ounce of command he could muster into his shout. "Stand down!"

In unison, Grub's and Squirrel's rifles turned toward their attacking teammate. They bypassed his chest, which was protected by ballistic plates, and aimed at his face. Between one breath and another, rifle fire lit the exfil site.

Crack. Crack. Crack. Crack. Crack.

Lurch flew back, a cloud of brains and blood where his head used to be.

No! Aiden's scream was silent and useless.

Grub and Squirrel turned their weapons on each other.

Crack. Crack. Crack.

They knew where to target for maximum damage. Above the armor. Below the helmet. Both men's heads reared back, and vanished in a mist of blood and bone. Their bodies dropped to the ground.

Thump. Thump.

What the hell...what the hell...what the motherfucking hell...

Aiden sucked in a choking, wheezing breath. He rocked back on his heels as the ground seemed to buckle beneath his boots.

This can't be happening.

"What did you do to them?" Hutch screamed.

Aiden pivoted. The movement felt slow...clumsy. Like his body was two steps ahead of his mind. Everything was happening so fast. Too fast.

"Alpha One, Sitrep! Sitrep!" Montana's voice thundered through his headset. "Someone give me a damn Sitrep!" Like the bastard wasn't watching this shitshow through those damn cameras.

Hutch had pulled off his balaclava, exposing his red, sweating face, his lips, eyes and fingers twitching. There was a blind sheen to his bloodshot gaze, the same sheen Grub and Squirrel had worn before they'd killed each other.

"You killed them! Why did you kill them?" Hutch screamed, spittle spraying from his mouth. He lifted his rifle, targeting Aiden's face.

Aiden dropped to the ground. The muzzle of Hutch's rifle followed the movement. He rolled.

Crack.

A stinging pinch hit Aiden's left thigh. He rolled again. Hutch shook his head, slow to respond, slow to re-sight.

"Drop it! Drop it!" Aiden spun onto his knees, ignoring the screaming agony in his left leg the movement unlocked.

He lodged the rifle stock against his shoulder, steadied the M41A with his right hand on the rear grip and his left on the fore stock, only to hesitate.

No. No. Don't make me do this.

Images of barbeques and birthdays flashed through his mind. Glass bottles clinking at The Bottoms Up Tavern. The slow stretch of Hutch's lips as he said, "One more rotation behind us."

Hutch's chin lowered. His blind gaze locked on Aiden's face. The muzzle of his rifle dropped.

No.

Crack. Crack.

Hutch's face disintegrated. He wavered on his feet for a moment, then fell backwards.

His breath lodged in his throat. Still on his knees, Aiden trembled. His rifle wobbled. Had he pulled the trigger? He didn't remember pulling the trigger.

Jesus, what have I done?

Movement to his right snapped him back to the present. He twisted, his rifle scope following his eyesight. A distant, sharp pinch dug back into his thigh. Benny stood slightly behind him; his rifle muzzle locked on Hutch's splayed frame. Had Benny fired on Hutch, or had Aiden? Did it even matter?

Aiden's gaze lifted to Benny's bare face. It was twitching. So were his hands. But the bloodshot eyes that held Aiden's own were aware. The blind, blank sheen was missing.

"Tell the docs it started with a tingle, an electrical buzz in my brain."

Aiden found his voice. "You tell them. You're still you. Fight it while I get the rope." He tried to spring to his feet, but his left leg buckled. He hit the ground again. Grunting, he rolled back to his knees. That dull pinch was getting sharper by the second. "Fight it, brother. You can beat this."

"No time." Benny's face twisted. "I can feel it taking over. The rage. The paranoia. The certainty I need to fire on you before you can fire on me. I don't own my mind anymore." His hand dropped to his holster and drew his sidearm. "Find out who did this to us. Make them pay."

When Benny's hand rose, Aiden was too numb, too stunned to evade the shot. Only Benny didn't aim at him. He stuffed the barrel in his mouth and pulled the trigger.

And then there was one.

Aiden ripped off his helmet, tipped his head back, and howled his grief and rage into the dark sky. When he fell silent and looked down, his hands were twitching.

Chapter Seven

Day 2
Washington, D.C.

Clark took a sip of coffee, picked up his Montblanc diamond-studded ballpoint pen, and paused to admire it. Not only was the pen subtly elegant and fabulously expensive, but it was a pleasure to use. The ink flowed with fluid ease and dried quickly. No smudges. No fuss. Just expensive excellence. The best the world had to offer.

Life was good.

But then he'd promised himself such a life back on those street corners of LA where he'd hooked for food and shelter. And again during his education at MIT, which he'd attended thanks to a very exclusive escort service that had booked him out to their wealthy female and male patrons as both arm and bed candy. The clients he'd met through the service had given him an appreciation for the finer things in life and a distaste for sex. A fair trade.

He glanced at the time stamp on the video feeds scrolling across his laptop screen and jotted down a note.

Subjects infected 6:30 pm 2/08. He listed the D.C. time rather than Tajikistan. Tracking was easier that way.

The new cameras combined video and audio, which helped track the progression of his new weapon. When the bots hit the inflection point, the subjects devolved into violence, which got loud. Shouting, screaming, and slamming things around was common. He'd know through the audio feed the instant his little soldiers had seized their hosts' brains.

It was two hours since the SEALs had been infected by his NNB26 bot prototype. In earlier test subjects, the mental deterioration showed about now. But these six were SEALs—with all the stamina and mental fortitude the title implied. Perhaps they could withstand his weapon's grip a little longer.

No matter—two hours, or three hours—the six men were living on borrowed time.

His laptop display was split into six mini screens. Each small window was tagged with a name. Thomas Acker, Nathan James, Peter Hutcheson, Aiden Winchester, Sean Backman, and Chris Jennings. It was nice to have actual names attached to his subjects, rather than those adolescent nicknames.

Squirrel? Grub? Lurch?

Ridiculous.

As he settled back in his Pininfarina Xten Chair and waited for his new weapon to seize the SEALs' amygdalae and hypothalami, he gazed out his penthouse window toward the Pentagon. The Potomac River looked like a ribbon of black velvet from the fifteenth floor, while the Pentagon was glowing. No doubt Admiral Hurley was huddled somewhere in that radiant building, with the rest of the brass watching and waiting. Possibly praying—to whatever entity he prayed too—that his men would escape the insanity of Karaveht.

But there would be no reprieve. His nanoweapon would make sure of that.

The test had gone remarkably well. Sure, his planning had been meticulous. He'd identified every conceivable obstacle and removed them, but some things were beyond his control. Such as the delivery system in Karaveht. The distribution and subsequent infection of the locals had been time sensitive. It was essential the weapon deploy, infect, and kill the residents prior to the SEALs' arrival. If the SEAL team arrived too early, the locals, in their infected state, would kill them before the bots could take hold, and he needed to prove his bots worked on special forces types.

Injecting the citizens would have given him more control over the timing. But injection would lead to scrutiny, and possible detection. Nor could they send infected individuals into the village. For exposure to occur through an infected individual, there had to be direct physical contact. A touch. A kiss. A hug. Sex. And it was difficult to control when such events took place.

Eventually, he'd chosen the well to disperse the bots. On his orders, Kuznetsov had dropped five vials of his little soldiers into the water. They'd tested this delivery system in the lab, so they knew the approximate time between the vial dump and the first infections. They'd adjusted the parameters for the size of the well and the distribution through the water pipes. The first people to drink the water would have infected their families and friends. From there, the infection rate would just keep escalating.

His new technology really was the perfect weapon.

From the condition of the bodies on Winchester's camera, the villagers had died late last night, long before the SEALs arrived. Perfect timing.

The six SEALs had been infected the moment they turned the dead locals over. The bots would have entered through their hands and fingers. Possibly even through the soles of their boots. Gloves and boots didn't prevent bot penetration. His little soldiers could pierce anything but the densest of metals. A weapon that could be circumvented by protective clothing wasn't much of a weapon, was it?

Once a person was infected, the bots immediately began scraping biological materials from within the host's body—calcium from the bones, iron from the blood, proteins from the various cells, as well as a multitude of other elements. Then they began replicating, creating hundreds and then thousands more bots. Most of the bots would migrate to the brain to attack the amygdala and hypothalamus, as well as disrupting the neural connectivity of the brain. The remaining nanobots shed into the skin and surrounding areas, waiting to infect additional hosts.

He settled back, and took a sip of coffee.

"Where the hell are you going?"

The question came from the laptop, but it was the edge to the voice that caught Clark's attention. He focused on the window that was greenlit, showing—he glanced at the name—Sean Buckman was speaking.

Winchester responded in an unnaturally calm tone. "Just getting my thermal blanket."

"Liar." Buckman laughed. An ugly, taunting bark of a sound. "You don't get cold." His rifle lifted. "Don't fucking move."

Five of the six cameras were locked on Sean Buckman. He leaned closer to the screen. There was a distinct twitch in the corner of Buckman's eye—his bloodshot eye.

"Fuck you," Buckman snarled, his rifle rising higher. "Nobody is restraining me. Nobody is stealing my ability to defend myself. I'll see you all dead first."

The twitching had doubled. Yep, NNB26 had infected them. Clark smiled in expectation, almost vibrating with anticipation.

The confirmation came seconds later.

"Base, we're infected. Early signs are twitching faces and fingers and bloodshot eyes," the squad's leader said.

Wow. Winchester had certainly identified those symptoms quickly. He glanced at Buckman's camera feed, which was focused on the squad leader. Interesting... Still no yelling or screaming—at least from the SEALs. There was plenty of yelling coming over the comm, but all from the base.

Clark dialed the base audio down so he could hear what was happening between his subjects.

"Lurch!" the squad's leader shouted. His video feed jittered, before centering on a huge Viking of a man, charging toward Buckman. "Stand down!"

Lurch? Oh, yeah, Nathan James. Damn, these nicknames were annoying.

The meltdown came fast after that.

Chuff. Chuff. Chuff.

The rifle fire didn't sound like he'd expected. No sharp staccato reports. More like a couple of subtle coughs.

Nathan James's head disappeared, and he dropped to the ground. More *chuffing* and two more men went down.

"You killed them! Why did you kill them?" Peter Hutcheson screamed. The man's face was red, sweating. The skin next to his red eyes twitched. His stare was a thousand miles blind.

Hutcheson lifted his rifle, aimed it at Winchester. The squad leader dropped to the ground; his camera feed chaotic. Another burst of *chuffs* hit the audio feed. Hutcheson fell. Clark checked the remaining camera feeds. How many men were left?

Just Winchester and Chris Benton.

The two men's cameras were focused on each other. Clark's eyebrows rose. Benton didn't have his rifle up. He leaned in to get a better look at Benton through Winchester's camera feed. The face on the feed was twitching, and the eyes were bloodshot, but the gaze staring back at him was self-aware. The guy hadn't gone crazy yet.

"It started with a tingle," Benton said. "An almost electrical tingle in my mind."

Interesting. Clark made a note on his tablet. Nobody had mentioned that symptom before.

"Find out who did this to us."

The command startled a laugh from Clark. Good luck with that.

Through Winchester's camera, Clark watched Benton shove the barrel of his handgun into his mouth and pull the trigger. He dropped to the ground.

A guttural sound, like a horrified rasp, broke from Winchester before his camera jerked away. The camera feed bounced and swayed, before lifting and filming the dark sky. A raw, primitive howl filled the silence.

All six cameras were still filming, three of them pointed at the dirt and snow and three of them at the dark sky. Was Winchester alive, or had he killed himself, too?

Clark frowned, settling back in his chair. The squad leader's camera wasn't moving. He was likely dead as well. While he hadn't heard a gunshot, Winchester could have used a knife. He'd have to rewind the camera feeds to see how the man had died.

But for now, it was time to shut the test down.

Leaning forward, he hunched over the laptop, exited the camera feeds and laid down a string of passwords. A new window popped up. He entered another string of letters and numbers. Same with a third screen and then a fourth. He'd encrypted this program to hell and back. It would be difficult for someone to hack into that first login screen. Nobody could hack all four.

Seconds later, a fifth screen appeared. *Kill switch activation. Yes. No.*

He clicked *yes.*

Please verify. Another login screen popped up. The cursor sat there at the first box, blinking patiently. It was a good thing he had an eidetic memory. A lesser mind would have to keep all the passwords in a notebook—which was never secure. After he typed in the last password, the screen turned red and then blue.

NNB26 prototype has been deactivated.

He went through another series of passwords and screens until he was looking through the atomic force microscope mounted on the top of the NNB26 testing tank. The AFM sent the images through Wi-Fi to the main computer terminal, where the images were recorded and stored and could be accessed remotely.

He assessed the NNB26 robotic structures, which were viewed under a magnification of 1,000,000x. The microscopic bots were matte black and round. Normally, they scurried around like a colony of energetic ants, but currently, none of them were moving. As expected, they'd shut down on implementing the kill trigger—exactly as he'd programmed them to do.

Excellent.

He rubbed his hands together, his smile wider than ever. It was critical to prove that his weapon could be turned off. The video would prove what his new weapon was capable of, but nobody would bid on the technology if it couldn't be controlled.

He'd have to program each batch of bots he sold with their own kill switch code, but now he had proof the prototype could be deactivated as easily as activated.

Let the bidding begin.

Chapter Eight

Day 2
Karaveht, Tajikistan

Hunched over on his knees, with his palms braced on the cold, hard ground, Aiden struggled to breathe. A thick, aching lump sealed his throat, cutting off access to fresh air. Lightheaded, he yanked the balaclava off, wheezed a couple of times and concentrated on the sensation of cold seeping through his gloves. He stared at his fingers as they dug into the ground. They trembled.

He was infected. Like his brothers. His dead brothers.

"Huh." The raspy sound was part groan, part cough to clear his throat.

Burning, acidic pain washed over his left leg. He looked down. The white and gray camo of his winter BDUs were soaked with blood. Or at least his left thigh was. He grunted as the pain swelled. He must have taken a hit. He should bind and treat the wound.

But apathy stilled his hands. Why bother? He'd be dead soon, anyway.

A faint, urgent voice came from his headset. Instinctively, he reached out and pulled his helmet closer. The voice grew stronger. It was Montana demanding a sitrep.

Heat flashed through his chest, exploding in his gut. His lips tightened. Montana knew *exactly* what the situation was. He'd had a front row seat for it. Unlike every other op since he'd taken the trident, these new moth-erfucking cameras were still rolling. A continuous feed from drop-off to exfil. Those had been his orders. What a damn coincidence.

The brass, along with whoever had set them up, had watched five of the bravest, most loyal men on the teams sink into insanity and slaughter each other. The rage churned hotter, thicker.

It was inconceivable. A Special Operator's creed was bound by loyalty. Your life for your brothers. To create a weapon that bypassed that loyalty and forced an operator to turn on his teammates, to massacre them—his gut twisted, caught between horror and grief.

He should have 86'd those damn cameras as soon as they went skids up, left the bastard behind this setup to stew in the dark.

Another voice from his comm, another demand for a sitrep.

Fuck that. No way was he updating the motherfuckers behind this situation. Nor was he killing himself on camera for their goddamn data collection. He turned his helmet over. The new camera was a thin cylinder mounted to the right side of his helmet. He flipped the tiny power switch from on to off and forced himself to his feet. The pain shifted with his movement, radiating up and down his leg, before sinking back into his thigh in an agonizing rush. He gritted his teeth and shuffled toward the splayed body of Hutch. All his teammates' cameras needed to go dark. Damned if he'd give the bastards any new insights through those live camera feeds. He hobbled from helmet to helmet, half of which were still attached to his crew's bloody, fragmented heads, and flipped the cameras off.

By the time he finished, his whole body was trembling. Exhausted, he sank down, landing on his ass, and stared at his hands. They were still shaking. Not a surprise. He was infected. He already knew that. He'd touched the same bodies his brothers had. No, he hadn't gone insane yet, but it was coming. Maybe the delayed insanity was because his metabolism was different. Or maybe his infectious load had been lighter and slower to spread.

Tilting his head back, he stared dully up at the gray, fluffy sky. The wind had died. A lazy, faltering snow was falling. It would be a peaceful morning, if not for the bodies of his dead teammates surrounding him.

He needed to take himself out now, while he still had control of his mind, before the exfil crew arrived. Before he attacked anyone.

He unsnapped and unholstered his sidearm. Too bad it wasn't dawn with a clear sky. The sunrises in the Karategin Mountains were gorgeous—all pinks and purples. They reminded him of Demi's hair, of the way she'd looked three years ago, when he'd finally claimed her. The way she'd glowed, all pink hair and flushed skin as she'd writhed beneath him in bed. His chest went hollow and hot. He closed his eyes and burned the image of her into his mind. The sexy smirk on her red lips, the hungry glitter in her eyes, the way she welcomed him into her body with urgent hands and breathy moans.

He wanted to ask Montana to patch her through to his comm so he could tell her he loved her, tell her how sorry he was for the past three years, how he regretted not spending those years with her. How he wished he'd filled his memory with her, instead of endless ops and training missions.

Fuck, he'd been an idiot. He'd cheated them of the only thing that mattered. Time. Now that he had none left, he realized how badly he'd squandered it.

With a drained sigh, he lowered his head and stared at his helmet. But he didn't reach for it. Demi had one man haunting her already, a better man than him. Donnie had understood what mattered in life. He'd given Demi everything he had to offer, while he'd had the chance to give it.

Aiden, on the other hand, had hoarded his time with the teams. Sure, he loved her, but she'd always come second—behind the missions, behind the training, behind the teams. It wasn't fair to load his biggest regret onto her shoulders, where she'd carry it, along with his memory, for the rest of her life. He'd do her a favor and let her grieve his death, without the agony of unborn possibilities.

After one last look at the snow floating down from the fuzzy sky, he lifted his weapon, shoving the muzzle into his mouth. His gaze locked on his hands, and the finger resting on the trigger guard. It took him a second to realize what he was seeing—or rather, not seeing.

His fingers were steady. Still as a rock. Not a tremble in sight.

What the hell?

He lowered the gun, his gaze transfixed on his hands.

Still no shaking.

With Squirrel and the rest, the twitching had gotten worse, not better, as time went on. And come to think of it, their faces had twitched as well. After holstering his weapon, he carefully shucked his gloves and cupped his face with his hands. His skin felt icy beneath his touch, but he felt no twitching. Hell, his face was as still as his hands.

Was he infected?

Sure, his hands had been shaking earlier—but fuck, he'd barely escaped a bullet to the face and watched his team slaughter each other. Plus, he'd lost a lot of blood. Adrenaline, shock, and grief could have caused the shaking.

Was he infected? Maybe. But maybe not.

It had been fifteen minutes since his team went insane. And they'd all gone down that rabbit hole at the same time. He hadn't joined them, not then...not now. Plus, Benny had mentioned a tingle in his brain, which he still hadn't experienced.

He sat there, frowning. He didn't want to die. Sure as hell not by his own hand. But he couldn't allow himself free rein either. This sickness came on fast. If he was infected, just slower to succumb, he needed to protect the exfil team while he still had the chance.

First things first, though. He scowled down at his blood-soaked leg. He needed to take care of that. Blood loss could kill him as easily as a round to the mouth. No sense in trading one ticket out for another. He'd treat the wound, change into some fresh warmies, wrap himself in the heat sheet, and tie himself up.

And hope he was still alive and sane by the time the evac crew came to pick him up.

Day 2
Washington, D.C.

Clark exited the NNB26 programming and navigated back to the camera screens. There was no new imagery, but according to the seconds accumulating on the individual camera clocks, the six units were still filming. He pushed back the desk chair and rose to his feet, about to exit the feeds and call it a night, when a sandy colored object encroached on one of the camera feeds. It paused in the frame.

It was a boot laced to above the ankle. A bare, blood-stained hand skimmed through the camera feed and the camera went dead.

Clark sank back down, staring at the remaining camera feeds. Two were dark now. Winchester's and Hutcheson's. The boot—or more accurately, a pair of them—appeared again, this time in Acker's feed. The hand reached down again, and the video feed went dark. Feed after feed, the tan boots appeared, followed by the bloody hand, followed by the camera feed going black.

Someone was moving from body to body and turning off the cameras. Why? Who? A local? But why would a stranger turn the cameras off? Besides, wouldn't there be audio if a local showed up? Shocked exclamations when they came across the bodies? It couldn't be anyone from the evacuation team. Hurley hadn't sent his evac crew out yet.

There was only one possibility.

One of the SEALs was alive.

The only man who hadn't died on the feeds—was Aiden Winchester. Was the squad leader still alive? Of course, even if he *was* alive, he wouldn't—or shouldn't—be mentally stable.

He glanced at the clock on his laptop screen. It was fifteen minutes since the other SEALs had succumbed to the bots. He shifted in unease, his desk chair squeaking beneath him. Moving from body to body and turning off the cameras was not a sign of someone suffering a mental lapse. It was too methodical. Too focused. Winchester was eerily silent, too. No shouting. No ranting. And then there was his hand. His fingers hadn't trembled while turning the cameras off.

Was Winchester infected? He remembered the SEAL touching at least two of the bodies. That alone should have been enough to infect him.

He rewound Winchester's camera footage until just before the SEALs entered Karaveht and pressed play. He stopped the feed when they reached the first set of bodies. Only two of the men were wearing tan boots: Winchester and Acker. And he'd watched Thomas Acker take a bullet to the face. The SEAL turning off the cameras had to be Winchester.

Slowly, he pressed play, and the video inched forward. He paused it again as Winchester turned the first woman over. Clearly, he'd touched her, at least long enough to roll her over. Sure, he'd been wearing gloves, but his gloves weren't made from a metal alloy that prevented bot penetration. He allowed the feed to advance forward again until the SEALs reached the second set of bodies. This time an entire family—kids and all. He paused the video again as Winchester reached for one of the children. His hands made contact again. It was right there on film.

Frowning, Clark's gaze dropped to the volume of blood surrounding the bodies. Winchester's boots were standing in the middle of all that red. Of course, everything was frozen, but that wouldn't make a difference. The NNB26 bots would have been in the blood when the family bled out. When Winchester made contact with that lake of red, the bots should have penetrated his boots, and then his skin and muscles, before entering his circulatory system.

Winchester *should* have received an infectious load through his gloves and boots—like his teammates had. Clark slowly leaned back, staring at the computer screen, then jerked forward again and fast forwarded the video.

He didn't remember seeing any signs of infection from the team leader. But he hadn't focused much on the man, not when there was so much drama through the other camera feeds. Maybe he'd missed the symptoms. He slowed the video again, watching as the SEALs went crazy, and methodically searched the various camera feeds for footage of Winchester. He found plenty of instances of Winchester on the various video footage—different angles, different cameras. Like the others, the squad leader was wearing one of those damn face covers. But the cloth left his eyes free, which were not bloodshot. In none of the video feeds were the corners of his eyes twitching, nor were his hands. And there was no sign of erratic behavior.

Winchester didn't look compromised at all.

Had he been infected? It seemed unlikely. He would have been infected at the same time as his teammates, so he'd have gone crazy at the same time they had. At the very least, he'd be showing symptoms by now. This new weapon was incredibly predictable. There was little variation in how it affected its victims. If Winchester had been infected, he would have had symptoms. He would have succumbed to the insanity by now.

Clark's stomach tightened. A sudden, vicious throb pounded behind his eyes. A tension headache. He recognized the pinch and pull, although he hadn't suffered one in years.

It was inconceivable, but Winchester was apparently immune to his NNB26 prototype. But how? There was only one way to find out.

He needed to get Winchester in his lab.

Immediately.

Chapter Nine

Day 2
Karaveht, Tajikistan

Aiden buried his weapons at the eastern edge of the exfil site and the ammo at the western edge. If he went crazy and attacked the evac crew, the distance between the weapons and ammo, along with his bound wrists and ankles, would neuter his lethality. He'd just have to hope no shitkickers stumbled across him while he waited.

He collected the medical supplies from Benny's assault kit and rummaged through his slain brothers' ditch kits, gathering all the water, propane canisters, MREs, thermal blankets, puff jackets and puff sleeping bags. God only knew how long before the exfil crew arrived. He'd need to hydrate, eat, and stay warm until they collected him.

He thought about scrounging for firewood, but the mountain tundra provided little fuel, and his leg was bleeding enough to cause concern. Just burying his weapons and collecting the extra supplies had increased the bleeding twofold. Besides, every step hurt like hell.

After unfolding and stacking two of the thermal blankets on top of each other, he sat down and unlaced and pulled off his boots. His tactical pants were designed with easy access zippers that ran from calf to pelvis. If he unzipped both sides and took a knife to the thermal underwear below, he'd be able to treat the wound without removing his boots. But he'd also be stuck wearing his blood-soaked thermals and pants until the evac crew arrived, which would make it difficult to tell if the bleeding started up again after he treated the wound. Besides, the zippers might not even work considering they were slick with blood.

Moving quickly, he stripped out of his blood-soaked tactical pants and bottom thermals. The cold hit instantly. Shivering, he packed the entry and exit wounds with hemostatic granules, working the granules into the bloody holes until the wounds stopped bleeding. He bandaged the injury and eased a fresh pair of thermals and tactical pants over the bulky bandages. The bullet had gone through the meaty part of his thigh, missing both bone and arteries. It wasn't a life-threatening injury. If he controlled the blood loss and shock, he wouldn't even need a saline IV or tourniquet.

Most of the water bottles were frozen. He pulled a small camp stove, propane canister and pan from his cold-weather kit, thawed the bottles and tucked the warm water against his side, beneath the layers of warmies. His body heat would keep the water from freezing again. If he ran out of thawed water, he had plenty of frozen bottles piled next to him, along with extra propane canisters for the stove.

Before draping his legs over his cold weather kit to combat possible shock, he sliced off several lengths of 550 cord, wove them together, and bound his ankles. Binding his wrists was more difficult, but a slip knot and a couple of hard tugs on the cord with his teeth did the job.

Three hours after burrowing into the mound of warmies, he awoke to the sensation of warm liquid sliding down his thigh.

"Son of a bitch." Scowling, Aiden sat up. He nudged aside the thermal blankets and pile of warmies covering his left thigh. Fresh blood gleamed wetly against the white and gray camo of his pants.

Hell. He grimaced. He'd have to unzip his pants and cut through the thermals to treat his leg again. Only this time, because of his bound ankles, he wouldn't be able to change into dry clothes afterwards. Plus, it was going to be a bitch treating the wound with his hands tied together.

He'd buried his FFK, along with his other weapons hours ago, so he couldn't use the knife to cut through the thermals. But there was a pair of scissors in Benny's med kit, as well as an assortment of scalpels. He'd find something to cut through the fabric. Before getting started, he clasped a bottle of water between his bound hands, worked the cap loose and carefully lifted the plastic to his lips—staring at his fingers the entire time. Still no twitching.

Thank Christ.

His rationality seemed intact, too. No paranoia or murderous rage. Not yet, anyway.

The snow had stopped an hour earlier, and the sky had cleared from fluffy clouds to slate gray, not a cloud in sight. When he tipped his head back to take a gulp of water, he noticed a slightly darker pinprick against the wintry sky. He lowered the bottle and took a harder, longer look. The speck, which was barely visible, only stood out because it seemed to move. Hell, it could be a trick of the eye. Except...

He frowned and leaned forward. Was it bigger than it had been even seconds ago?

He tensed. Fuck, yeah, the damn thing was getting bigger as he watched it.

The object was coming from the west. The exfil chopper would come from the north, which made it unlikely this aircraft was his pickup service. But it *was* some kind of aircraft. It had to be. Its steady, quick progression across the sky spoke of its mechanical origins. But what the hell was it? It was close enough now he should be able to hear it. The roar of its engines or the beat of its rotors. Instead, the damn thing moved like a shadow. Dark and silent.

As it drew closer, it took shape. A giant, sleek, bird-like craft almost the same color as the sky. WARCOM had nothing like this in its hangers. It became clear, as the craft slowed and circled overhead like a giant, predatory eagle, that it was here for him. Who the hell was piloting it? The bastards behind the brutal attack on Karaveht and his team? Were they here to pick up their test subjects?

Hell with that.

Without taking his eyes off the object above, he lurched toward the med kit sitting beside him. He needed something sharp to cut the cords binding his wrists and ankles. The craft's wings angled up, like a bird on the verge of diving. Its tail rotors lowered and slowed, then reversed, leisurely spinning backwards. It inched slowly and steadily toward the ground. Its exterior color pulsed, shifting between gray and cream, before turning white.

"What the hell!" he whispered. His fingers froze inside the med kit as he watched it descend.

For the first time, he could hear it. Or at least he assumed the low whirring sound mixed with a soft trilling was coming from the craft. How bizarre. It even sounded a bit like a bird. Within the whirring and trilling came the occasional chirp. Also like a bird, the damn thing's wings and tail rotors were flexible rather than immobile. How the hell could it fly like that? Or lift off? Or land? What aerodynamics would allow this thing to even exist in the air? The hull pulsed between gray and white a couple more times before bleaching out completely. When it finally settled onto the ground, its exterior was a perfect match for the white, wintry tundra surrounding it. Like a chameleon, it had blended into its surroundings.

He closed his eyes, then lifted his bound hands and pressed them against his eye sockets. Obviously, he'd gone crazy. There was no way this mechanical bird could exist...or fly...or land. His insanity had simply manifested in a different direction—weird-ass hallucinations rather than rage, paranoia, and violence. But when he dropped his hands and opened his eyes, the craft was still there. He glanced at his fingers. No twitching.

The faint whirring and chirping fell silent. The tail rotors stopped moving.

He went back to rummaging through the med kit, opting for a scalpel rather than scissors. If he hadn't gone crazy, if that damn thing was real, he didn't want to be stuck here on the ground, helpless, while whoever manned that craft disembarked.

Assuming the thing was real and wasn't a figment of his infected brain.

The wings of the craft folded down and back, tucking neatly against its side. His fingers closed over a narrow scalpel. He fumbled with the instrument, until he got it positioned beneath the cord, but his transfixed gaze never left the strange object now sitting still and silent in front of him.

Damned if the thing didn't give new meaning to the military slang of *bird*. It looked eerily like some metallic, prehistoric avian. Even the front of it—which had to be the cockpit—was slightly bulbous and elongated, with one dark slant of an eye curving across the exterior of the cockpit.

It was probably a good thing his hands were tied, and his weapons were out of reach. For all he knew, regardless of his brain's imaginings, the craft in front of him was the evac Black Hawk with the hazmat team. At least with his hands secured and his weapons out of reach, he wouldn't be able to attack them.

There was a scraping, grinding sound like a helicopter's cargo door sliding back, followed by the heavy thumps of multiple boots hitting the ground. A squad of huge men decked out in tactical gear and armed to the gills rounded the corner of the craft. Their rifles were up, gloved fingers light on the trigger guards. Most of the men stopped at the sight of Aiden's dead teammates. Rifles swept the surrounding area, only to lower again.

"Sweet Jesus," a voice said, the southern drawl thick with shock. The dude's helmeted head turned toward Squirrel's sprawled, faceless form.

It had been close to three years since he'd bunked with the dude, but he recognized the slow, lazy drawl of Seth Rawlings. The knowledge he recognized one of the men who'd arrived in the possibly imaginary aircraft struck him dumb. Was Rawls a figment of his infected brain too?

"What the hell happened?" A harsh, gritty voice asked from his right.

It was Mackenzie's voice, his old commander. Aiden's gaze swung in that direction. He would have recognized that stance anywhere. Knees locked, shoulders back, hands on his hips. Arrogance and dominance in every muscle of his body.

Well, fuck, his former crew had swooped in to rescue him. Aiden's throat tightened, and he avoided looking at the corpses surrounding him, the visual reminders of his current crew, the ones he couldn't save.

"Is this what Benioko saw in that dream you told us about?" One of the other men asked, his helmeted head slowly turning as he considered the carnage.

Aiden recognized that voice, too. Cosky. His brother-in-law. Fuck, he'd just talked to the bastard the day before. Or, at least, he'd heard him speaking over Kait's phone.

What. The. Hell?

The guy Cosky had questioned shook his helmeted head. "No..." Another slow, methodical shake of the helmet. "This is not what the *Taounaha* spoke of." He paused before adding, "Yet he advised we hurry. Perhaps this is why."

Aiden recognized this voice as well, the rich, yet controlled tone of it. He recognized the way the speaker moved, too, as he headed across the clearing. Fluid and powerful. He was staring at Wolf—his half-brother.

It made sense that both these men would bleed into a hallucination since they were family, or close to it. Perhaps he was dreaming.

But fuck, this felt too real to be a dream.

Chapter Ten

Day 2
Karaveht, Tajikistan

Was he hallucinating?

Aiden's gaze slid to the batshit crazy aircraft. Hell, the mechanical bird fit right in as an insane hallucination. But it could be real too. As the commander of Shadow Mountain, a high tech, quasi-military base, Wolf had access to all kinds of nifty toys, including experimental aircraft. This weird chopper-plane hybrid could be something the Shadow Mountain aeronautical engineers had whipped up. Plus, there was the craft's crew. Mac, Rawls, and Cosky—former SEAL teammates of his—had joined the Shadow Mountain base three years ago. It was possible the three had joined Wolf in a rescue mission.

He still hadn't decided whether he was hallucinating when Kait flew around the corner of the mechanical bird and headed straight toward him.

"Aiden!" she dropped to her knees beside him and pressed her palms against his bloody thigh. "You're hurt!"

She was dressed in the same tactical garb and ballistic plates as the men disgorged by the aircraft, but without the helmet. Her hair swung against her back in a long, golden braid.

"Don't touch me!" He knocked her hands off his thigh with his bound wrists. Dream or not, damned if he was going to expose her to insanity and death.

That's when he caught sight of her bloody fingers and palms. His chest went hollow, his muscles tight. Hell, his blood painted her hands. If he was contagious, she might be infected now, too. Although...she'd only touched him for a second. Maybe that wasn't long enough to transfer the pathogen. Thank Christ, Kait's gift required skin-to-skin contact. She couldn't heal him through the layers of fabric.

Kait, being the resolute sort, refused to let that stop her. She glanced at Benny's open med kit and grabbed the small pair of scissors in the top compartment.

When her hands closed on his bloody thigh with the scissors, he slammed his bound fists into them again, forcing them away. "Dammit, Kait, don't touch me. There's a good chance I'm contagious."

"Contagious?" Cosky spun, saw Kait kneeling beside Aiden, and leaped toward them. "Goddammit, we told you to stay in the Thunderbird until we called for you."

Cosky's comment convinced Aiden he wasn't dreaming. His stubborn sister never obeyed an order she didn't agree with.

Her focus completely on Aiden's blood-soaked upper thigh, Kait dodged Aiden's hands and lowered the scissors until the tip pressed against the sodden fabric. "Grab his hands, Marcus. I need to get to the wound, but his pants are in the way, and he won't let me cut them."

Aiden didn't care about his pants, but Kait wasn't listening. He lifted his head and caught Cosky's gaze.

"Get her away from me. I'm probably infected by whatever killed my team." He tilted his chin toward the closest body, which was Squirrel.

A wave of grief hit at the sight of his best friend's corpse, with its blood-iced face—or what had once been his face. A fist plunged into his chest and squeezed the breath from his lungs. *Jesus*—he struggled for air. Jerking his gaze away, he counted to ten and fought for control.

"Benioko wouldn't have sent me if danger was present." She braced herself when Aiden swung his fists at her hands again. "He sent me with Wolf and the others for a reason. To heal you."

Who the hell was Benioko? One of the Kalikoia elder gods? Wolf, their Kalikoia half-brother, had exposed Kait to their father's Native American heritage. But joining the Shadow Mountain team as one of their healers had sucked her deep into the Kalikoia culture.

"Besides," Kait's voice turned dry. Her hand with the scissors dodged his fists again. "It's too late. You've already bled all over me."

True, but beside the point. The more she touched him, the stronger the chance of infection. Maybe by some miracle she'd escaped contamination the first time she'd smeared his blood all over her hands.

Thank Christ Cosky had more common sense than his sister. Aiden relaxed as his brother-in-law leaned down, wrapped his arms around Kait's waist, and lifted her completely off the ground.

Kait lost her grip on the scissors as she squirmed violently in her husband's arms. "Dammit! Let me go! He's bleeding."

"He's bled worse." Cosky tightened his hold on her squirming body and cautiously backed up. "Let's find out what happened and why he's tied up before rushing in."

"I already touched him." She stopped struggling long enough to present her bloody hands. "If he's infectious, it's too late. Might as well let me heal him."

Cosky's jaw hardened. He angled his head toward Aiden. "What the fuck happened? Who tied you up?"

"I tied myself up to avoid attacking the exfil crew when they arrive." He blew out a tight breath. Adopting an even monotone, he recounted what they'd found in Karaveht and what had happened to his team brothers.

"Whatever infected the locals infected my crew, too. It stands to reason that I'm infected as well."

"Sweet Jesus."

Rawls's tight voice caught Aiden's attention. He glanced over in time to see Rawls straighten and back away from the closest frozen, faceless corpse.

"That's Squirrel. I recognize the tat."

Aiden's chest went tight and hot. He coughed to clear the ache from his throat. "Yeah. Squirrel and Grub took out Lurch and then each other. It happened so damn fast—" His voice gave out beneath the pressure in his chest.

"I crewed with all three men," Cosky said, his voice grim. He lowered Kait until her boots touched the snow crusted ground but didn't let her go. "They were experienced operators, not men who break under stress." His head turned toward Wolf. "Was this what Benioko saw in his dream?"

Benioko again. Who the hell was this dude?

Wolf shook his helmeted head. Slowly he turned, as though surveying the carnage. "No. The Old One described something much different. Although, perhaps, what happened here is related. He says Aiden is the key to defeating this new enemy."

"Enemy?" Aiden sat up straighter. "Did he see who was behind this attack? Who infected the locals and my men?"

"You keep saying infected," an unfamiliar voice interrupted. A dry voice with sharp undertones. "Not a word I'm fond of. What kind of infection? How does it spread?"

Aiden cocked his head, taking an immediate dislike to the lip flapper. The dude was decked out in the same tactical gear as the others, but his skin tone was more ruddy than terra cotta, like Wolf and his Kalikoia warriors. Plus, the dude had the strangest eyes—metallic green, not brown or black, like the rest of his brother's crew. This dude didn't look Native American at all, which was odd. Kait said that most of Shadow Mountain's personnel and all of Wolf's warriors were of Kalikoia descent. Well... except for Mac, Cos, Rawls, and Zane—ST7's former leadership—who'd joined the base a couple years back.

"Unclear," Aiden drawled, not bothering to hide his instinctive dislike of the dude. The bastard hadn't said or done a damn thing to elicit this immediate animosity. So, why was he having so much trouble leashing his hostility?

Probably just fallout from this shithole day.

"Which answer is unclear to you?" the asshole asked, his voice sharpening. The metallic green eyes narrowed and...glittered?

"Both," Aiden drawled.

"Great," the asshole said. This time, his tone was downright condemning. "Let's revisit. Something lethal affected the people of Karaveht and your team, turning them into psychotic, violent monsters. But you don't know what caused their reaction or how it spread."

"That sums it up." To piss the bastard off, Aiden offered an exaggerated shrug.

"Which means we could be infected now, too. Isn't that just peachy?"

Wolf turned toward the sharp-tongued bastard. "*Taounaha* would not have sent us if danger still lingered here."

Even from where he sat, at least fifteen feet away, Aiden could see the hardness stamped across his brother's cheeks and chin. And there was more steel than calm in Wolf's normally neutral voice.

"Yeah? Well, I wouldn't know about that, as the Shadow Warrior doesn't favor me with his visions." The sharp tone swerved into sarcasm.

Wolf stiffened. A stare-down began. The disagreeable dude set his shoulders and boots. What he didn't do was back down. The balls on that guy. Not to mention an obvious chip on his shoulder.

"Pay O'Neill no mind," Rawls said, dropping to his knees beside Aiden's bloody thigh. "He's an ass. Dude could start a fight in an empty house," he added, his voice wry.

So, the guy's name was O'Neill. Aiden studied the dude. Wolf obviously had issues with him, so why was he on the payroll?

"Let's see where that blood's comin' from." Rawls shrugged out of his attack pack, untied it, and pulled out a bulging red and white canvas bag.

Aiden glanced at Benny's open med kit, which was sitting within touching distance. Field medics were all alike, whether with USSOCOM or Shadow Mountain. No med kit was as good as the ones they packed themselves.

"Just cut my wrists free without touching me." Aiden lifted and extended his hands. "I'll treat the wound myself."

Rawls hesitated, his fingers resting on the zipper to his med kit. "I ain't gettin' loco vibes from you."

"Thing is, we can't chance that I'm not infected. I touched some locals down there. Just like my crew. Everyone...absolutely everyone else went insane. Why haven't I? No, I don't have any of my crew's symptoms, but that doesn't mean I escaped it. Hell, I could be infected, just asymptomatic. Or the agent—whatever the hell it is—could be taking its time with me."

"Squirrel and the boys had symptoms?" Rawls brow furrowed as he unholstered his blade and sliced through Aiden's wrist and ankle bindings. "What kind?"

"Twitching mostly—around the face and fingers. Bloodshot eyes." Aiden leaned over and picked up the scissors Kait had dropped when Cosky grabbed her. "Benny said his symptoms started with a tingle in his mind."

"You havin' any of those?" Rawls asked as he sheathed his knife and returned it to his tool belt.

"Not yet." Aiden leaned over his thigh, carefully cutting through his tactical pants and thermals. "But that doesn't mean I won't."

"How long since your squad succumbed to this insanity?" Rawls settled back on his haunches. His gaze narrowed on Aiden's thigh as the bloody bandage came into view.

Aiden glanced at his watch, then peeled the soggy dressing from his leg. "Three-and-a-half hours, give or take."

Rawls digested that in silence before nodding toward the blood streaming down Aiden's leg. "How bad?".

"In and out. Missed all the important shit. Just needs to stop bleeding." Aiden pressed a clean wad of gauze against the bloody hole and pushed down hard.

Once the red stream slowed to a trickle, he tossed the soggy gauze aside and dumped a small mound of hemostatic granules onto the wound. Gritting his teeth against the burning pain, he massaged the granules into the wound. Only this time, the bleeding didn't slow. Hell, it sped up. Fresh blood washed the granules away as soon as he dumped a new batch into the hole.

A red pool spread beneath his leg. Fucking shit, he was bleeding a lot worse than he'd bled before. The round must have nicked a vein, which had opened beneath his recent activity. An admitted concern, since he hadn't been all that active.

"Better let Kait have at it," Rawls said, his gaze locked on the blood streaming down Aiden's thigh. Worry touched his blue eyes. "She's got your blood all over her hands anyway. If you're incubating that loco sickness, she is, too, now. Just sayin'... No sense in you bleedin' out when she can stop it."

Aiden scowled. "I might not have infected her the first time she touched me. A second attempt may be all it takes. I'm not chancing that."

"Benioko would not have sent her to heal you if he saw danger to her," Wolf said, his voice reasonable. "The danger here has passed." He turned and looked up, scanning the sky. "But others come. We must be gone before they arrive."

Aiden followed Wolf's gaze and scanned the horizon. Was he talking about the exfil crew? "My evac crew won't arrive for hours yet."

Wolf's gaze dropped to Aiden's face. For the first time, Aiden saw the grimness in his brother's black eyes. "I do not speak of your people." He turned to address the equally tall, grim-faced dude standing next to him. "Bag and load the dead. We have little time left."

Aiden frowned. "Montana's sending a hazmat team. They'll know how to handle the bodies."

Wolf simply looked at him. "There will be no bodies when your people arrive."

"If we leave them here—"

Wolf shook his head. "They will not be here, nor will you, when your people come for you."

Aiden thought about that. Dammit. "Whoever's behind this field test is on their way in?"

"So I am told," Wolf said.

It made sense. The motherfuckers would want to collect their test subjects. They wouldn't want evidence of their fuckery to get out. He was damn lucky the bastards hadn't already showed up and grabbed him.

"In consideration of this news, your Benioko mobilized you boys pretty damn late, don't you think?" Aiden drawled. "We're lucky the bastards behind this FUBAR test didn't snatch me already. I've been waiting for hours."

Wolf shrugged. "It is unwise to question the elder gods. We are here. Our enemy is not. When they come, we will be gone."

And thank Christ for that. If the bastards coming for him had arrived before Wolf and his crew, his teammates' bodies would have vanished forever. And Aiden would be dead.

Or worse.

Chapter Eleven

Day 2
Karaveht, Tajikistan

Aiden pressed down harder on the blood-sodden gauze, hoping the extra pressure would slow the bleeding. Footsteps crunching across the frozen ground brought his head up. He watched Wolf stop in front of Cosky. Their shared brother-in-law still held Kait in a tight embrace, one more restrictive than loving.

"Kait speaks the truth," Wolf told Cosky, his voice mild. "The Old One specifically requested her presence on this mission to heal Aiden. He would not have sent her if Aiden was a threat to her. The danger comes in lingering here. She must heal him. Now."

Cosky responded with a thunderous scowl and tighter arms.

How the hell would Wolf's Old One know if Aiden was contagious or not? Not that it mattered. This decision was not Wolf's, or the aforementioned Old One.

"I'm not risking Kait. We don't know whether I'm contagious. This isn't your decision, Wolf. It's mine. And I'm a no. End of discussion."

"There is no time for this." Wolf's voice was calm, although he set his shoulders and boots as though preparing for battle.

Abruptly, Wolf's warriors swarmed Cosky. An explosion of swearing—all from his brother-in-law—painted the air black as the Shadow Mountain team seized Cosky's arms. The cussing doubled when they wrenched his elbows behind his back, forcing him to release Kait. Freed, Kait sprinted for Aiden. Her golden braid fell over her shoulder, bouncing against her torso with each stride. More warriors converged on Aiden, pinning him to the ground.

Cold bit into Aiden's shoulders and back, even as heat swallowed the burn and throb in his thigh. He twisted and lurched, struggling against the implacable hands forcing him down. It was his choice, not Wolf's—dammit. The heat consuming his leg swelled, a clear sign Kait's healing was well underway. He craned his neck, catching sight of his sister's intent face and furrowed brow.

Too late to save her now.

He shot a furious glance toward Wolf's expressionless face. From the savage curses erupting from Cosky, Aiden wasn't the only one enraged by this breach of trust.

"Son of a motherfucking bitch. You goddamn bastard. You have no right—" Cosky roared. He broke off to take an audible breath and stopped struggling. His voice was lower, but tighter when he spoke again. "She'll heal him faster with my help."

Wolf didn't make a sound. Hell, he didn't even move, yet the men imprisoning Cosky let him go.

"This isn't over," Cosky snarled as he stalked past Wolf. A nerve twitched in his stone-cut jaw. The gray eyes that sliced through Wolf were livid.

Aiden had never seen his brother by marriage so furious.

When the fire swallowing his thigh doubled in intensity, he grunted and settled back. The increased heat meant Cosky had joined Kait. Somehow, when his brother-in-law laid his palms on top of Kait's hands, his sister's healing ability increased tenfold. Together, the pair could repair catastrophic injuries—wounds Kait couldn't handle on her own. Aiden wasn't sure how their combined abilities worked. He just knew that they did.

But there was a downside to the pair working together. The heat they generated could be brutal. It often blistered their own palms and the flesh of their patient. While the damage invariably healed on its own, and quickly, too, it was exceptionally painful while it lasted.

Like now. Hell, his leg felt like he'd shoved it in a pit of lava, as if his flesh was melting and bubbling away. Sweat rolled down his chest and shoulders. He clenched his teeth to keep the groans inside.

The burning, sweltering agony went on and on. Far longer than it should have for a simple repair to punctured flesh, and a nicked vein. That's when it hit him. She wasn't just healing his wound. She was trying to neutralize whatever agent he'd been exposed to. Fuck, she was trying to prevent the insanity from manifesting.

Suddenly, as if a switch had been thrown, the fire vanished. Or, if not vanished, at least diminished. The agony fell from two thousand back to a ten, then eight…five…

Aiden lay there gasping for breath, his BDUs and hair soaked with sweat. His thigh still burned with the flames of hell, but the intensity was lessening by the second. The men pinning him to the ground released their grips and backed off. On the plus side, he wasn't cold anymore. He forced himself up to check on Kait. A healing that intense must have wiped her out.

He found Kait and Cosky flat on the ice-crusted ground, with Rawls dribbling water over their faces and hands. Aiden grabbed a bottle for himself and took a long swig before pouring the rest of it over his lobster red thigh. The water appeared to bubble for a second after hitting his skin. When it slid off, it took a good bit of the redness with it. He flopped back with a long, beaten sigh.

"They good?" he asked. Rawls would know who he was referring to.

"Good as can be for now, I reckon." Rawls's voice grew stronger. Aiden opened his eyes as his former teammate crouched over him. "At least you ain't bleedin' out no more."

Aiden frowned. "I wasn't bleeding out."

Rawls offered an unconvinced scoff and poured more water over Aiden's pinkish-red thigh. A guttural groan came from behind them, followed by a scuffing sound. Aiden propped himself up on his elbows and watched Cosky gently take Kait's curled hands and turn them toward him. The hiss that escaped his brother-in-law's tight mouth told Aiden the extent of the damage. A sliver of guilt pierced the exhaustion. She'd been hurt because of him. But dammit...

"I told her to leave it alone." The frustrated admonishment burst from him as fear set in again. What if he'd infected her?

"You're welcome," Cosky said sarcastically, but his voice lacked heat.

He reached out and grabbed Rawls' open med kit, dragging it closer. After a bit of rummaging, his hand emerged with a tube of cream, which he squirted generously on both of Kait's hands. After spreading the white cream across both of her palms, he returned to the med kit for gauze pads and wraps. Other than a couple of hisses, Kait lay there placidly, letting Cosky tend to her.

That alone told Rawls how much energy the recent healing had taken. Kait hated being babied. Guilt prickled again. He pushed it aside. Dammit, her exhaustion wasn't his fault. He'd tried to stop her.

After a few long minutes of silence, Kait stirred. "I'm okay." She pushed Cosky's hand away.

Cosky pulled back. After a moment, he shifted and scooted over to Aiden. His jaw was still hard, although the nerve tick had stopped. But the eyes staring at Aiden were chips of silvery ice. He'd locked his rage at Wolf down, but it was still there, simmering below the surface.

"Did you find the stolen drone specs you were sent in to recover?" he asked, his voice grim.

Aiden shook his head, his mouth tightening. "No drone specs. No sign of Kuznetsov, the arms dealer, either." Bile burned his throat as an over-whelming sense of betrayal crested. "And get this—we were fitted with a continuous feed video camera for this mission. Ordered to keep the cameras running from skids down to evac. Montana said they were testing a new prototype. What a coincidence, don't ya think? The bastard behind this got a bird's-eye view of everything, including Squirrel and the others—" his throat closed.

Cosky's muscular body went rigid. "You were set up?"

"I'm not counting it out," Aiden said tightly. "Feels like some asshole was testing an infectious weapon and we were their guinea pigs."

"Yeah. Feels like that." Cosky shifted, scanning the bodies strewn around the clearing. "Scuttlebutt during the flight was that what happened here is connected to what Benioko dreamed about the other night. And you're so crucial to the Shadow Warrior's plans, the old man sent us to collect you in the new Thunderbird. First time it's been released for duty."

Thunderbird, huh? Aiden stared at the craft. The name was certainly apropos. But then Cosky's comment sank in. This Benioko had sent them to rescue him?

He drained a bottle of water and stuffed it back into his pack. "So big bro didn't foresee my imminent demise and haul ass out here to save me?" It had happened before.

"Not this time." Cosky glanced toward Wolf, his face hardening. "Be-nioko, Wolf's CO, who's the base shaman, had a dream...a bad one. An end of times dream. The kind where humanity goes bye-bye." Cosky's helmeted head swung back in Aiden's direction. "He says you're instrumental in stopping the apocalypse. That's why he sent us to rescue you. Any idea what the old guy is talking about?"

A chill swept Aiden's spine. It quickly spread to every inch of his flesh. *Fuck.*

He slowly turned his head, scanning the clearing. Dead friend after dead friend met his eyes. *Double fuck.*

"Maybe." He grimaced. A horrific feeling was rising inside him. An ugly premonition. "If this damn insanity bug gets out, it could get bad fast, Cos. Really fast." His voice tightened. "Yeah, it could turn apocalyptical. There wasn't one survivor in Karaveht. Not one. The insanity infected the entire town. The residents slaughtered everyone—their neighbors, their families. Hell—even their kids."

Which was terrifying. Parents were programmed to protect their children. Sure, sometimes that wiring misfired. Occasionally, a parent killed their kid. But filicide wasn't common, and it sure didn't happen en masse.

Not like it had in Karaveht.

His audience had swelled to all of Wolf's warriors, along with Kait, Cosky, and Rawls. A dozen pairs of grim eyes were trained on him, waiting for more information. Gathering his thoughts, Aiden dug his fingers into the crystalized shards of field grass beside his bed of warmies and thermal blankets. The cold speared into his fingers, numbing them. But they remained steady. No trembling. Still no signs of infection.

Thank Christ.

"It spreads fast," he continued tightly, still staring at his hand. "So fast there'd be no way to contain it. We were two hours out of Karaveht when the insanity hit my team."

An uneasy stirring swept through the group.

"How come you weren't infected?" Mac asked bluntly. But the question was obviously on everyone's mind. Including Aiden's.

"I don't know. Hell, I can't be sure I'm not contagious." He lifted his chin toward Squirrel. "Or that they aren't." He paused, adding emphatically. "Don't. Touch. Anything."

"Not touching them won't keep us safe if every time you exhale, you're infecting us," O'Neill ground out.

Aiden stiffened, his fingers curling into a fist. O'Neill wasn't wrong, but hell—he could have eased back on his tone and delivery. "What the hell do you suggest? That I stop breathing?"

O'Neill didn't respond, but then he didn't need to. From the uneasy reaction sweeping through the men surrounding them, others were wondering the same thing. Could the infection be in the air they were breathing, the ground they were walking on? Shoulders grew tense, jaws hardened, boots shifted—crackling against the icy grass.

Wolf stepped forward, his dark gaze skipping from warrior to warrior, holding each gaze a heartbeat, before moving on. "The *Taounaha* saw no danger here. Not to us. This infection—the one Aiden speaks of—has passed." He paused before adding grimly. "For now."

The men he'd addressed relaxed, the tension vanishing. Muscles softened, faces smoothed, fingers flexed. They trusted Wolf. His declaration assured them. They trusted this Benioko, too. It must be nice to have such instant, implicit faith in one's leaders.

Aiden doubted he'd ever trust a superior again.

Chapter Twelve

Day 2
Karaveht, Tajikistan

His right hand deep in the side pocket of his tactical pants, O'Neill studied Wolf's heralded half-brother. This was Wolf's squid brother? The SEAL proclaimed by Benioko, Shadow Warrior's *Taounaha,* as the chosen one, the protector of the Kalikoia people—hell, the entire world? He didn't look like a savior.

He did resemble Wolf to a startling extent—minus the long hair. Their father had certainly put his stamp on the pair. Winchester was broad-shouldered and fit, with short dark hair. His eyes were almost identical to Wolf's. Same color. Same hooded lids. What set them apart was the expression within. Wolf's gaze was aloof, while Winchester's was shimmering with rage and betrayal.

Still, the bastard didn't look special. No halo of light illuminated him. No aura of power surrounded him. Judging by the blood that had flowed from the bullet wound in his thigh, the asshole was made of flesh and bone like the rest of them. He bled like the rest of them. So, what set him apart? What made him so special to Benioko and the Shadow Warrior?

Was it because he shared genes with Wolf? Or because he'd been chosen by the eagle clan? Word of mouth indicated the asshole was so fucking clueless about his heritage, he didn't even realize the spirit eagle had claimed him.

O'Neill's gaze shifted to Winchester's neck. There was no leather thong. No clan totem. While the bastard might have been claimed by the *thae-hra-ta*, he'd left his induction gift at the claiming site. What a complete moron.

Hell, Aiden Winchester wasn't even part of the *Hee'woo'nee*. He was *jie'van*, an outsider. He knew nothing of his own people, not their heritage, their culture, their origin. He was other. An interloper...or he should be.

Instead, Benioko and Wolf and every warrior had dragged him into their hearts because he was their prophesied messiah.

Nope, Winchester wasn't the outsider. O'Neill had that honor, even though he'd been raised on the *Brenahiilo* among the *Hee'woo'nee*. Even though he'd been chosen by the *heschrmal* and had the totem to prove it.

Not that anyone outside of the *Taounaha* believed him.

His fingers closed around the satin-soft pouch in his pocket. He'd created the misshapen thing himself, stealing needle and thread from his grandmother's sewing box and a rabbit pelt from his grandfather's shed. He'd been beaten for that—for the thefts. He'd been seventeen then and much bigger than the old woman and old man who'd never accepted him as kin. He could have stopped their fists and belts. Instead, he'd taken the beating as a memory, something to remind him of things best forgotten.

Among the Kalikoia—or at least normal families among the *Hee'woo'nee*—the claiming pouch was gifted to each child chosen by a spirit clan on puberty. For young males, the gift was delivered by the eldest male in their father's family line. For females, the eldest female among the mother's family line. The totem pouches represented the Shadow Warrior and Blue Moon Mother, and the spirit animals they sent forth. This remained true for all the *Hee'woo'nee*...except O'Neill.

But then, his family had never been *normal*.

With a disgusted shake of his head, he turned, watching as Samuel, Wolf's second in command, wrapped one of the dead SEALs in a plastic sheet. Good ol' Samuel, one of Shadow Mountain's most venerated warriors, didn't look worried about handling what could be a highly infectious body.

Another face, a feminine version of Samuel's, tried to transpose itself over the warrior's face. O'Neill shoved it away. He had plenty of practice shoving it away. Particularly since her son, who looked so much like her and Samuel, had joined Shadow Mountain for training.

No, Samuel didn't appear concerned about handling the dead bodies, but then why would he? Benioko, the Shadow Warrior's earthside mouthpiece, had assured everyone they were safe, assured everyone no harm would come to them while rolling the corpses of Aiden's infected teammates in plastic, stuffing them in the body bags and sharing the cramped space of the Thunderbird with them for the five hours it would take to fly back to base.

O'Neill would have rolled his eyes at that insanity if he didn't believe the Old One too.

He might be an outsider, but he'd grown up on the *Brenahiilo* alongside mysticism and clan magic. He'd seen things that couldn't be explained by science or logic. But what carried the most weight was that he'd never known Benioko to be wrong about anything.

Infallibility walked hand in hand with access to an elder god who foresaw all futures and all likely paths. Benioko's infallibility was why O'Neill had joined Shadow Mountain and currently put up with the warrior assholes who ran it.

After that God-awful moment two years ago, when the Old One appeared on his doorstep in Hebron Palestine and *showed* him the horrific events about to unfold, he'd needed to do *something*. He needed to do everything in his power to stop Benioko's vision from coming true. To stop humanity from turning on each other and disposing of everything that made humans...human. No more cruelty, or greed, or violence. But no more love, creativity, or compassion either. Only programmed precision and endless emptiness.

To prevent that future, he'd broken every promise he'd made to himself and returned to the *Hee'woo'nee*, to the very ones who'd shunned him, who labeled him a thief and liar. Who called him *jie'van*. Outcast. Outsider.

In all his years, only two of the Kalikoia had seen him with unfiltered eyes. And one of those two...well, hell, she'd proven to be a mirage, nothing but an illusion, spawned by his own mind.

Even now, a year after the *Taounaha* had appeared on his doorstep in Palestine and showed him the fate of humanity, he questioned whether joining Wolf and Samuel and the rest of the assholes at Shadow Mountain had been necessary. Why couldn't he do his part to prevent Benioko's nightmarish future from coming true while tucked into his own little niche in the shadows? Why upend his life and resume his position as *jie'van* among those who had no clue who he was, or why he'd returned?

A muted thud caught his attention as Mackenzie dropped Aiden's rucksack next to the Thunderbird's open cargo door.

"Hey, asshole," Mackenzie growled. Angry black eyes locked on O'Neill's face. "You want to help us here, instead of standing around with your thumbs up your ass?"

Ah, Mackenzie and his poetic insults. The rest of Wolf's warriors might feel the same disdain, but they never acted upon it. They were too busy pretending the *jie'van* didn't exist.

That old familiar resentment rose. Fuck them. Fuck them all. He should have never fallen for the Old One's machinations and joined him at Shadow Mountain.

"Wouldn't want to deprive you of workhorse duty. You do it so well," O'Neill drawled, loading his voice with mockery. Maybe he could annoy the former commander into throwing a punch.

Mackenzie was the easiest to rile, although the other SEALs weren't far behind. Simcosky and Winters were easy to needle, too, although they never lost control and launched a physical strike, just spewed biting verbal assaults. But their response was enough to provide some entertainment while the skirmish lasted. The southern one, though...he just shrugged the needling off and shot him a knowing look—like he knew there was more to the taunts than sheer arrogance.

His eyes volcanic, his fists clenched, Mackenzie let loose with a string of mother fucking this and mother fucking that. Before he could stomp over to where O'Neill waited, Rawlings blocked his way. Good old Rawlings, forever the peacekeeper. At least among his SEAL brethren.

There wasn't much need for peacemaking among Wolf's warriors. It was impossible to push their buttons, although O'Neill prodded them as often as he could. The urge to antagonize was instinctive after a lifetime of using sarcasm and derision to deflect and shield. Not that such tactics worked on Wolf and his men. They responded to his taunts with placid faces and flat, distant eyes—like he was an annoying fly buzzing around their heads. Or worse, like he didn't exist.

Except for Benioko. The Old One just shook his head and watched him with chiding eyes.

"Why even come if you ain't gonna make yourself useful?" Rawlings asked, although he sounded more curious than annoyed.

"Good question." O'Neill grimaced.

Joining the go team hadn't been his idea. Or Wolf's. Wolf was never thrilled to have O'Neill shoved down his throat. Nope, the *Taounaha* had insisted on his inclusion in this mission.

But why? He wasn't needed here. What was he supposed to see? Benioko knew better than to expect O'Neill to use his cursed talent with so many eyes as witnesses. Besides, there wasn't anyone to use it on. Was he supposed to learn something up here? Something about this new enemy, this new war? He scanned the few corpses that hadn't been shoved into body bags yet. This wasn't the vision that Benioko had shared with him all those months ago in Palestine. But it was related. He sensed that.

His gaze drifted to Winchester, who was just now climbing to his feet. Maybe Benioko's insistence that he join this op was because of Wolf's little bro. Did the Old One want him to meet and bond with the chosen one? That seemed unlikely. The shaman knew better than that. There would be no bonding with anyone from the eagle clan, even those unaware they'd been claimed by the *thae-hrata*.

Winchester's instant animosity toward him illustrated that point.

Cats and birds didn't mix.

Day 3
Washington, D.C.

Clark raked tense fingers through his hair and scowled down at his iPhone. What the hell was going on? His crew captain should have checked in by now. He was over an hour late. Unacceptable.

It was utterly unbelievable how *everything* had suddenly gone to hell.

He had contingency after contingency in place to make sure his specimen retrieval went smoothly. For Christ's sake, he'd booked three Chinook helicopters with three complete crews. All three choppers had been inspected and tested yesterday. All three had been mechanically sound and took to the sky without delay.

But today? Not one of them had left their pad on time. And now the captain in charge of retrieving the SEALs, both dead and alive, was MIA. If Clark was the type to believe in superstitious nonsense, he'd think lady luck had turned against him.

A couple of deep, slow breaths slowed the urgent thump of his heart.

Calm down. There's still time to get this done. Hurley's evac crew and the CDC scientists haven't even left their base yet. Yes, it's annoying, even frustrating as hell, but this doesn't impact your plans.

Another slow, deep breath and he relaxed into the elephant chair. This wasn't the end...it was barely the beginning. Worst-case scenario—he'd send his deep cleaning team, which was currently at work in Karaveht, to the SEALs evacuation site. They'd get there in minutes, well before Hurley's Blackhawk set down. He glanced at his Patek Philippe watch, barely noticing the rose gold dial and blue diamond hands. He still had some time. Best not pull the cleaning crew off their Karaveht duty just yet.

Ten minutes later, the call finally hit his burner phone.

"We have a problem," a laconic voice informed him.

No shit. The bastard would have contacted him before now if the body extractions had gone smoothly. Still, it couldn't be that much of a problem. According to his spy among Hurley's men, the WARCOM chopper hadn't even left base yet.

"What's the problem?" Clark asked, surprised to find his voice was even when he felt like a pressure valve about to erupt.

"There were no bodies at the coordinates you gave us," the voice said flatly.

Clark's mouth fell open. "What the hell are you talking about?"

The SEALs had to be there. Hurley's team hadn't arrived yet.

"There was nobody at those coordinates. Living or dead."

"Then you went to the wrong site," Clark snapped. "Dead men don't walk away."

Although the living, which apparently included Aiden Winchester, could certainly walk away. Had Winchester hidden the bodies? Why the hell would he do that?

"We dropped at the correct location." The guy's voice sharpened. "We found lots of frozen blood, but no bodies."

Clark shook his head numbly. This news made no sense.

"We searched the area. No tracks leading out of the clearing. Although there were multiple boot prints on-site, more than would account for six soldiers." The speaker's voice turned terse once again. "My guess is some-one grabbed them before we got there."

Clark pinched the bridge of his nose. Had his spy lied to him? Had Hurley's team already swept in and grabbed Winchester and the dead SEALs? "Where are you now?"

"Back in our hidey hole, awaiting your orders."

"Hold tight for now." Clark disconnected the call and leaned back in the elephant chair. For the first time, the prestigious armchair felt painful beneath him, a claustrophobic prison.

Five hours later, he had more questions than answers. According to his contact in the admiral's office, Winchester and the dead SEALs had been missing from the evac site when Hurley's crew had arrived. USSOCOM was as much in the dark about their whereabouts as Clark.

Previous testing indicated NNB26 prototype had a one hundred per-cent infection rate, which had led to a one hundred percent fatality rate. Until now. According to his eyes and ears on Hurley's team, Winchester was still alive. Fuck, Hurley had spoken with the SEAL multiple times after his teammates' deaths, until six hours ago when he'd abruptly gone radio silent.

Clark would have assumed he'd stop talking to his superiors because he'd finally succumbed to the bots, except...his body had not been at the evacuation site. That didn't mean he wasn't dead. His body could have been taken along with the other SEALs.

Or he could be responsible for the missing bodies.

This uncertainty left Clark in a hell of a conundrum. If Winchester hadn't been infected by NNB26, Clark needed to know why. An immune host carried incalculable risks. Someone could use Winchester to create a cure. A cure to his prototype would render his new weapon worthless.

He needed to find that damnable SEAL and get him into his lab, ASAP. It was the only way to figure out why he hadn't been infected. It was the only way to patch this unexpected failure to infect. As a bonus, if the bastard was strapped down in one of his labs, nobody else could get their hands on him and use him to create a cure.

Chapter Thirteen

Day 2-6
Denali, Alaska

This call wasn't going as smoothly as he'd hoped.

"Demi—" Aiden barely got her name out before she broke in again.

"No. It doesn't matter how many times you ask; the answer is no." Frustrated exasperation framed each word. "I'm not putting my life on hold and flying to God knows where, just because you want to see me." An annoyed breath blasted the line. "I told you I have responsibilities now."

"The cat." Aiden scowled as he paced the linoleum floor of his isolation chamber in his borrowed surgical scrubs. The scrubs were surprisingly comfortable—soft as silk as they brushed against his arms and legs. "You can bring the damn cat with you."

"No, I can't," she retorted. "I just picked him up from the vet. He's in no condition to travel."

Her life was more important than a damn cat.

Not that he could tell her that. She didn't know he'd brought danger to her doorstep, or why it was imperative that she join him. Hell, he couldn't even tell her where she'd be flying, not over the phone, not when anyone could be listening in on her line.

"It's just a cat," he growled, his frustration getting the better of him. "It's not even your cat. There's got to be a dozen animal rescues in the San Diego area. Farm it off to one of them."

He regretted the suggestion immediately. Demi wouldn't appreciate his cavalier attitude. But damn it, he couldn't tell her *why* he needed her to fly out and meet him. Wolf had arranged a phone for him, assuring him the cell was secure. But that security didn't extend to Demi's phone. Anyone could be listening in on her line.

Whoever was behind that test in Tajikistan had access to WARCOM. Those fucking cameras proved that. They knew who he was. Since he'd been in contact with Hurley until Wolf whisked him away, they knew he'd survived. They'd come after him to find out why. And when they couldn't locate him, they'd go after those he loved to smoke him out. Kait was inaccessible, but Demi was vulnerable.

He completed another circuit of his chamber and paused next to the right wall, which was constructed of smoke colored glass or plastic or something similar. He had to convince her to fly up to meet him. The safest place for her was tucked away in this secret base, surrounded by lethal warriors.

"He's my cat now. I accepted responsibility for him." The flat, calm tone screamed 'pissed off.' The angrier Demi got, the calmer and more rational she became. "I'm not abandoning him."

Great. She'd dug her heels in.

It would help his case if he could explain why he needed her to join him. Demi wasn't stupid. If she knew the reasons behind his request, she wouldn't be so intractable.

"I've got to go."

"Hold on a second." This approach wasn't working. He needed to pivot.

He reassessed his strategy. The assholes behind Karaveht's death toll probably hadn't tracked Demi down or tapped her line yet. It hadn't even been ten hours since Wolf had dropped in to rescue him. But if they were listening in on this conversation...so what? If he was careful about what he told her, if he stuck to information the assholes behind the test already knew, then he wouldn't be giving anything critical away.

Releasing a slow breath, he rearranged his talking points. "Look—"

"Give it a rest, okay?" she interrupted. "I know what this request is about."

His eyebrows rose. He doubted that.

"You want to meet with me, so you can convince me to continue our relationship." A soft sigh followed before she added, "Kait told me she spilled the beans. I know you know I want to break off our friends with benefits arrangement."

Fuck. "That isn't what this is about."

Her voice firmed. "I haven't changed my mind. Nor am I abandoning my responsibilities and flying off to meet with you. A face-to-face chat will just lead to sex, which will just fuck with my mind all over again."

Before he'd found out she wanted to dump him, he'd have teased her about fucking with more than her mind. A sliver of sorrow pierced him. Was that easy, teasing repertoire a thing of the past now?

"I'm sorry, Aiden, but I really have to go."

"Demi—" His protest came too late. She'd already hung up.

His hand clenched the cell phone. He fought the impulse to hurl the damn thing as hard as he could against the glass door of his isolation unit.

Instead, he dialed her number again, his teeth grinding with every ring that rode the line. By the time he gave up and ended the call, his jaw ached. He paced from one smokey wall of his chamber to the other, while strategies marched through his mind.

If he couldn't convince her to fly up to him, and he couldn't fly down to her, the next best option was saddling her with a security team, men he trusted to protect her until he was free to do the job himself.

An old roommate of his, Lucas Trammel, had joined Forged, a San Diego security company, after he'd left his leadership role on ST7. Aiden knew several other dudes from the firm, too, excellent operators that he'd crewed with in the past. An hour later, he had a surveillance team on Demi. Men he could trust to monitor her and step in if anyone tried to grab her. He suspected she'd be furious if she found out he had her under surveillance, so the protection crew was under orders not to engage with her unless it was absolutely necessary.

He'd fly down and haul her up to Alaska in person as soon as the Shadow Mountain docs released him from isolation.

It was ironic, really. While Benioko, the base shaman, had convinced Wolf's warriors that Aiden was not a health threat, he hadn't been as persuasive with the base scientists and doctors. No surprise, really. Scientists and doctors dealt with the physical, not the mystical. When the Thunderbird set down in the Shadow Mountain air hanger, a small hoard of men and women in lab coats and PPE had swarmed the craft and hustled everyone off to the isolation complex.

Aiden was relieved the scientists were taking precautions. Although he wasn't nearly as concerned about infecting people now as he'd been earlier. So far, neither he, Kait, or any of the warriors aboard the Thunderbird were showing signs of insanity. Besides, it shouldn't take long for the tests to clear him. A day, maybe two, and he'd be on one of Shadow Mountain's jets—Wolf claimed they had three—heading down to Coronado to collect Demi.

Three days later, he wasn't nearly as optimistic.

The insides of his arms were an ugly black and blue and looked like a pair of pincushions. He'd been x-rayed, ultrasounded, and stuffed into so many mechanical hollow tubes that he'd developed an itchy sense of claustrophobia.

Yet he was still here, in this damn isolation chamber, with no end in sight.

He knew there were others in the isolation unit—Wolf, Kait, and Cosky, along with the rest of the warriors who'd arrived on the Thunderbird. But he couldn't see anyone on either side of his chamber.

The walls of his prison were an impenetrable smoky gray with a glass-like texture that flowed smoothly beneath his fingertips. There was an adjustable hospital bed against the back wall, with a small table beside it. An enormous television was mounted above the door, and a bathroom, complete with a pulsing shower, tucked into the left corner of the chamber. The head was enclosed by the same smokey gray glass as the walls. He could adjust the temperature of the room to his comfort level. He even had privacy when he wanted it. By some marvel of engineering, the punch of a button on the control strip embedded into the table beside the bed would shift the front of the enclosure from clear to smokey.

The space would be comfortable enough if he wasn't locked in, and if he was getting some damn sleep. But no, those freaky, white-faced demons with the elongated mouths and eyes from his nightmares seemed to have an impenetrable hold on him in here. His nights were whacked.

He paced from wall to wall, absently listening to the faint hiss of air circulating through the chamber by the vents along the back wall. Periodically, he'd glare at the clock merrily ticking down the wasted hours above the bed. That damn clock had become an obsession, a constant reminder of passing time, of what he *should* be doing, rather than pacing the linoleum floor, or pumping out dozens of pushups and sit-ups, or wasting time watching TV.

He *should* be tracking down the bastards behind that ugliness in Karaveht. He should be down in Coronado with Demi protecting her from whatever nightmare he'd brought to her door.

At least she was safe...for the moment. Tag said there was no sign she was in danger. Nobody was showing interest in her. Nobody was staking out her condo complex—except for the men he'd hired to do so. But his instincts insisted she was in danger. Or that she soon would be.

And goddammit, she still wasn't answering his phone calls. The frustration of that left a metallic taste on his tongue.

When the pneumatic door hissed open, he expected a nurse in a protective suit, intent on drawing more blood. Instead, Wolf and a small herd of doctors entered his chamber. Wolf had been released from isolation? That was news. Even more newsworthy was that none of his visitors were wearing protective equipment.

"I'm not contagious?" he asked as his lead doctor, Soloman Brickenhouse, crossed the linoleum toward him.

"No, you are not," Brickenhouse said. "Every test came back clear. We waited an extra twenty-four hours out of an abundance of caution. But after the latest test results, there's no need to keep you in isolation any longer."

Huh...

Aiden frowned, absently rubbing his chin. "It's not a virus then?"

From what little he knew of viruses, they had unpredictable incubation periods. It seemed unlikely the docs could be certain he wasn't contagious after four days.

"Not a virus." Doctor Brickenhouse advanced on the bed and unhooked a clipboard from the metal bar stretching across the foot of the frame. He plucked a pen from the breast pocket of his lab coat. A scratching sound filled the room as he scrawled something unreadable on the paper clipped to the plastic board. "Nor is it an environmental pathogen." A long, silver braid swung against the back of the white coat as he turned and beckoned a short, round dude forward. "Doctor Cole can explain this better than I."

Aiden turned toward the dude Brickenhouse had gestured at. This new doc was built like a buoy, if a buoy grew arms and legs and sprouted a bowling ball for a head. He was short enough that the white smock hit him mid-calf. Fuck, the dude looked like a kid playing dress up.

The bowling ball of a guy stepped forward, one finger pressed against the old-fashioned square glasses swallowing his round face. His brown eyes looked enormous beneath the lenses. "We've identified the..." he paused as though searching for the closest word, before shrugging, "culprit, that caused your friends to attack each other."

Culprit? Aiden's forehead furrowed. That seemed a weird choice of words. Still, at least they'd identified what had caused the insanity. You couldn't solve a problem without identifying it.

"What was it?" He paused, his muscles bunching. "Do I have what they had?"

"No." The human bowling ball bounced slightly on his toes. His face was earnest yet concerned. "We found none of the nanobots in your blood, muscle tissue, or skin samples."

"Nanobots?" He froze. "That's what killed my team?"

What. The. Hell?

"Well, nanobots are the closest representative to what we found in your teammates' samples. But it isn't a clear identification of the...objects...either. We've seen nothing like them. While these structures are of an organic nature, they aren't composed of virus and bacterium DNA cells, or polynucleotides, like typical organic nanobots, nor of metals or diamonds as the typical inorganic bot. Instead, they appear to be composed of organic proteins and elements found within the human body itself. Elements such as iron, calcium, salt..." The doctor shook his bald head. "It's ingenious really."

Baffled, Aiden frowned. He'd heard of nanobots, knew they existed. But that was where his knowledge ended.

"Aren't nanobots a medical thing?" he asked.

Had a medical experiment gone wrong? Two seconds later, he cast that possibility aside. Every instinct he possessed insisted he and his team had been sent into a test zone—the test of a new weapon. Apparently, a nanobot weapon.

"They can be." Doctor Cole pushed his glasses back up. "They're microscopic, so they move through the human body and blood with ease. The ones we found in your friends are inactive, so we can't be certain how they progressed through their hosts. But they must have moved from the original point of contact, as we found heavy concentrations of them in your teammates' brain tissue. Particularly in the amygdala and hypothalamus, which explains the scenario you described." When Aiden stared at him blankly, Cole frowned and rocked back on his heels. The movement sent his glasses sliding back down his nose again. He pushed them up. "The amygdala and hypothalamus are two of the structures in the brain that control extreme emotion, as well as violence. There were also heavy concentrations of the bots in the hippocampus, thalamus, and nucleus accumbens, structures within the brain. These structures have been associated with psychotic and schizophrenic behavior and audio and visual hallucinations." He dropped his hand and lifted his gaze to Aiden's face. "In short, these nanobots appear to be drawn to the areas in the brain that control violent emotions, along with violent and psychotic behavior."

Aiden's entire body tightened. That sure as hell sounded like a fucking weapon to him. A weapon that turned ordinary people into psychotic killers. "You find any of those damn things in me?"

Cole shook his head. "All the samples we pulled from you were clean. Of course, under the circumstances, we couldn't pull brain tissue, but the bots were not present in your blood, muscle, or skin samples under the

AFM—atomic force microscope. We found large concentrations of them in all your teammates' samples. Plus, while there were high concentrations of the bots in your teammates' brains—there was no evidence of them in the multiple MRI, SPECT, EEG and FMRI scans we did of your brain."

Aiden's chest tightened. Unease crawled through him. "You said they were microscopic. Would they even show up on brain scans?"

"They do if there are enough of them," Doctor Brickenhouse interrupted. "They form concentrated clusters that can be identified at high magnification. These clusters were visible in your teammates' brain scans. There were no concentrated masses in yours. With the lack of the bots in your tissue samples and no indication of a large collection in your brain scans, we're fairly confident that you're not infected."

Fairly confident.

Aiden flinched, his stomach cramping at the thought of microscopic bugs crawling through his brain. They might not be insects, but Jesus... The idea of tiny bugs eating away at his brain until there was nothing left but violence and psychosis gave him the willies.

"We're releasing you from isolation." Dr. Brickenhouse handed Aiden's chart to a serious-looking woman in light blue scrubs standing to his right.

That was the best news he'd heard in days. Aiden turned to Wolf. "I'll take that jet now."

Thank Christ. He could finally take care of Demi.

Wolf shook his head. "Not yet—"

"I'm afraid you misunderstood," Brickenhouse interrupted, a polite expression on his high cheek boned face. "While we are releasing you from the isolation chamber, we aren't releasing you from the medical facility. You're being transferred to the clinic. We need to do more testing."

"Why?" Aiden tensed beneath a surge of frustration. "You just said I wasn't infected. Why keep me here? Why run more tests?"

"Well," Brickenhouse took a step back, as though he were startled by Aiden's reaction. Maybe even apprehensive, like his patient was exhibiting overly aggressive behavior.

Aiden forced his rigid shoulders and arms to relax and loosened his clenched hands, trying to project a less lethal attitude.

Brickenhouse relaxed. "The question isn't whether you carry the bots any longer—"

"—it's why the bots didn't infect you," Dr. Cole nodded in agreement. "If we can zero in on why the bot's avoided you, we may be able to manufacture a cure. If this is a weapon, as you and others believe, an antidote is essential."

"The tests we'll be running next rule out conditions that could have caused the nanobots to reject you as a host. By running a full battery of tests on you and comparing them against your teammates' results, we might be able to pinpoint why you're immune."

Well...hell. He could hardly skip out on that approach, since it might save lives. "How long are we talking about?"

"At least seventy-two hours," Brickenhouse said, his dark eyes narrowing. "We don't know what we're looking for yet. This could take time."

"You have twenty-four hours," Aiden interjected. "Get your testing done by then. I'm out of here tomorrow morning." Both doctors looked like they'd swallowed a lemon. Aiden turned, catching Wolf's guarded gaze. "I mean it, bro. Demi needs me." Although she didn't realize it. "You get me a chopper or a plane and I'll give you twenty-four hours of testing. No plane, then I'm out of here now. I'll book my own trip to Coronado."

Wolf stared at him in silent contemplation, then turned and left the room.

Was that a yes or a no?

"Mr. Winchester," Dr. Cole's face folded into lines of disapproval. "Such testing cannot be put on a timetable."

Aiden shrugged. "Testing can resume when I get back, right? I'll only be gone a day."

"Oh," Dr. Cole's face turned hopeful again. "You plan on returning?"

"Don't have much choice." Aiden left it at that. It wasn't like he had any other place to go.

Chapter Fourteen

Day 7
Denali, Alaska

With a muffled grunt, Aiden settled back against the plush pillow of his hospital bed. The constant *beep-beep-beep* coming from the medical monitors next door was irritating, but that annoyance was mitigated by the spring-fresh scent of his recently laundered pillowcase. The nurses must have changed his sheets while he was in that last CT scan.

Now that he was free from testing, it was time to rustle up that jet. He picked up the borrowed cell phone from the bedside table and dialed Wolf's number. When the call went to voicemail, he left a message.

Since there wasn't anything to do until Wolf hooked him up with a plane, he relaxed into the freshly laundered sheets and closed his eyes. Might as well nap until Wolf showed up. Fuck, he was tired. Ironic, since he hadn't done a damn thing all day except get wheeled from test to test. He was pulled from dreams of twisted, nightmarish trees and a misty, alien terrain thirty minutes later by the whisper of footsteps outside his door.

"Lunch is served. Chicken fried steak and mashed potatoes with a vegetable medley." The perkiest nurse in the history of perky nurses slipped through the privacy curtain. She set the plastic covered platter on the swivel tray parked along the side of his hospital bed and rotated it until the food was in front of his chest. "Applesauce for dessert." She stepped back and beamed at him, the smile brightening her hazel eyes. "Never let it be said we don't treat our patients right. Don't forget to leave us a positive review." She winked at him before brushing past the curtain on her way out.

Aiden grunted in response. All that cheerfulness was downright exhausting. The thick, meaty smell of chicken fried steak and gravy soured his stomach, so he pushed the swivel tray aside. Before he reached for the phone to call Wolf again, the squeak of rubber soles against the rubber flooring brought his head up. His visitor wasn't wearing tactical boots, not with all that squeaking, so it wasn't Wolf outside his door.

Sure enough, Kait squeezed through the gap in the curtain. Cosky didn't bother with squeezing in, he just shoved the drape aside. The shriek of the plastic curtain rings against the metal rod followed him into the room.

"Either of you see Wolf? I need that plane." Aiden watched the pair advance on his bed.

Although he'd talked to them on the phone over the past four days, he hadn't actually seen his sister or Cos since they'd been hustled to the isolation units. But the two looked good, bright eyed and bushy tailed. He suspected he didn't look nearly as bright eyed. But then, unlike them, he'd had gallons of blood drawn, and dozens of tests run.

"I try to avoid the bastard as much as possible." Cosky dropped into the second chair and grabbed the swivel tray, maneuvering it toward him. He popped the plastic lid off the tray and picked up the knife and fork.

Aiden scowled. He should give the bastard a rash of shit for co-opting his lunch, but it was too much effort. Besides, he wasn't hungry.

"Wolf won't forget about the plane." Kait's gaze was wide and worried as she scanned Aiden's face. "He knows how important Demi is to you."

He must look even worse than he'd suspected for his sister to look so anxious.

"Before you ask, I feel fine." He could tell she was dying to ask, even though she could sense how annoying he found the question.

Partly because it was the question that everyone—from nurses, to doctors, to scientists—kept asking him, which became tedious, and partly because the simple act of having to answer that question reminded him of why they were asking it. Which reminded him of what had happened to his squad brothers. Which was a constant reminder of what he could face himself—death by insanity.

Although that possibility was lessening every day.

"So...nanobots? How the hell did you pick those up?" There was a hint of accusation in Cosky's question, like he figured Aiden had to be responsible somehow. "I mean, seriously? Nanobots?" The shake of Cosky's graying head held disbelief and disgust. "What the hell?"

The good doctors must have filled Cosky and Kait in on the *culprits* they were facing off against.

"Yeah." Aiden's headshake was just as perplexed. He still hadn't processed that disturbing news. "You know anything about those damn things?"

"Nanobots?" Cosky paused his chewing. "Not enough. We need Leonard Embray, he's Shadow Mountain's organic robotics consultant."

Aiden scowled. If Embray was the go-to man on nanobots, why the fuck hadn't someone already gone to him? Maybe they had. Except a Dr. Embray hadn't sat in on any of the medical updates he'd been given. "Haven't met him."

"He's the CEO of Dynamic Solutions." Cosky glanced at Kait. "He was instrumental in neutralizing the NRO."

Aiden's eyebrows rose. The dude they were talking about was *that* Leonard Embray? The founder of Dynamic Solutions? Fuck, the company had their fingers in most of the robotics—hell, most of the technology—the world's brainiacs were creating.

As for Embray — "Wasn't he forced into a coma? Didn't his buddy steal Dynamic Solutions from him?"

The scandal had been all over the news.

Cosky's face hardened. "Yeah. Turned out his second-in-command was NRO. When Embray fell into his handy-dandy coma, the NRO stepped in and took over the company. After we rescued and revived him, he turned all that brain power to defeating the organization that had turned him into a pawn."

Cool. Sounded like Embray was the man they needed. "When is he arriving on base?"

"He isn't. Not any time soon, anyway. He's currently up in space, on the International Space Station. His stint isn't up for another four weeks." A scowl joined the hardness on his brother-in-law's face. "And we can't contact him while he's up there. Every transmission is recorded and tracked. Even sending him a secure, coded message could expose Shadow Mountain to U.S., Russian and Chinese intelligence. Wolf won't take that chance."

"Fuck." Aiden growled. "So the plan is to sit here and hope the world doesn't disintegrate before he returns to Earth?"

That sounded like a damn shitty strategy.

"Pretty much," Cosky said, his voice as frustrated as Aiden's had been. "In the meantime, we mitigate the threat of infection, and figure out a way to shut those damn bots down if they go up for sale." He paused, his eyebrows lowering over his icy eyes. "You were wearing gloves and boots, right? How the hell did they get through the leather?"

Aiden shrugged. "No fucking clue."

"Brickey says none of us were infected." There was confidence in Kait's voice, but deep concern in her eyes, concern that was directed at Aiden.

He could sense her fear for him. Even see it in the worried brown eyes locked on his face.

Aiden smoothed his expression. "Brickenhouse and Cole *both* said I was clean. The bots never infected me."

Kait nodded, but hesitantly. Her forehead furrowed. "But what if you do have them, but they're just inactive—like with your teammates?"

"If that's the case, the docs would have found some sign of them inside me. They found them in Squirrel and the rest, after all, even though they were inactive by then. Stands to reason that they would have found them in my blood and tissue samples if I'd been infected." Aiden forced nonchalance. Was it a twin thing that Kait had voiced the exact concern that was currently tying him into knots?

Kait's brows knitted. She didn't look convinced. "I suppose."

Time to distract her.

"You were trying to cure me of any possible bot infestation up there above Karaveht, weren't you?" He didn't give her a chance to respond. "There was no reason to waste so much energy on a thigh wound. You healed that lickety-split. The rest of that scorching heat was about purging whatever infection I'd been exposed to. Maybe you roasted the suckers. Maybe that's why I wasn't infected." He paused before adding gruffly. "I appreciate it, either way."

"I didn't know what you'd been exposed to." She shrugged. "But I figured it couldn't hurt." She slid a glance toward Cosky, who was scraping the last of the potatoes up with his fork. "From what the docs have said, Benioko was right. You never posed a threat to me."

Cosky froze, then slowly set his fork down. When he looked up, his face was completely flat, but his gray eyes glittered with irritation. "We didn't know that at the time. Sue me for trying to keep you safe."

Apparently, there was still friction about how things had played out up there amid the ice and snow. Had Wolf worked things out with Cosky? He didn't ask. Wasn't his fucking business.

"Too bad your Benioko didn't bother to explain *why* I was safe to touch." Aiden raised his eyebrows. They'd been damn lucky. If Benioko had been wrong, and Kait had been infected, he'd have broken the bastard's neck.

"Sure, would have helped if he'd explained what we were dealing with." Cosky agreed with a sharp nod. But then his face went reflective. "My gut says we're facing a new weapon." While Cosky's voice remained mild, his eyes glittered with icy rage. "Drop a canister of those nanobots behind enemy lines and watch your enemy tear each other apart. They obviously tested this weapon in Karaveht." He tilted his head and stared at Aiden, his face darkening. "Do you think WARCOM knew what they were sending you boys into?"

Rage, which was at a constant simmer lately, spiked. "I don't know. Not for sure. But I suspect so."

"Wouldn't surprise me." Cosky's face twisted into bitterness.

The dude had cause for both his suspicion and his resentment. NAVSPECWARCOM had sure goat-fucked him—as well as Zane, Rawls and Mac—during that hijacking incident four years back.

His gaze narrow and distant, Cosky's expression turned thoughtful. "Hurley must wonder what happened to you and the bodies of your team-mates."

Aiden nodded. Thank Christ he'd turned off the cameras. "At least whoever's behind that damn test doesn't know about this base."

"Wolf and his boys have done a fine job of keeping Shadow Mountain off the radar." Cosky's voice sounded reluctantly admiring. "Nobody will find you here."

Aiden didn't doubt that. He'd heard no mention of Wolf's team, or the Shadow Mountain base through the years, and he had all the right connections and had been listening in all the right places. No wonder his brother was so reluctant to contact Embray.

Demi, however, wasn't nearly as well shielded. "I need to get down to Coronado, but Wolf's ignoring me."

"Demi's safe," Cosky reminded him. "Forged Security is making damn sure of that. If anyone goes after her, they'll step in and whisk her to safety."

The reminder wasn't much help. He'd been lucky nobody had gone after her already. But it was coming. He could sense it. Tag, Tram and the rest were good in a pinch, but she was safest in Aiden's care. Her presence on this earth was essential to his survival. Even if they split, just knowing she was out there, living her life, would be enough to keep him grounded.

He'd burn the world to ash to keep her safe. He couldn't ask that of Forged Security. She was just a client to them.

When Cos reached for the dish of applesauce that had accompanied the chicken fried steak and mashed potatoes, Aiden's hand shot out to grab it first. Not because he wanted it, but hell—it was his lunch, not Cosky's.

With a shrug, Cosky sat back. "Have you reached out to Hurley? Shadow Mountain is shielded. Hurley's boys won't trace the call back here."

"Not yet." The sweetness of the applesauce turned to ash in his mouth. He dropped the spoon back in the dish and stared down. "Can't quite stomach their damn questions."

He didn't know, not for sure, if WARCOM was responsible for what had happened. But he didn't know that they weren't either.

It was fucking hell not trusting your superiors.

"If SEAL Command was behind what happened," Kait said, echoing his thoughts. "If they were testing something," she continued quietly, "then you can't go back to your team—"

"My team's gone." Aiden's throat tightened. Still, he knew what she meant. She meant the SEAL community. Lead filled his chest, pressed against his heart. He waited for the loss to hit. But there was too much rage and bitterness, along with grief, over Squirrel and Lurch and the rest of his squad brothers. The thought of walking away from the teams just felt numbing, not painful.

He took a deep breath and focused on Kait, shaking off the hollowness. There was still one person out there who pierced that emptiness. "I need to get to Demi."

If Wolf didn't pony up a plane, he'd check himself out of the base and find one for himself. He was done waiting. The protective detail didn't mean she was safe. Shadow Mountain was the only place they couldn't get to her.

"I still don't get why you wouldn't let me talk to her about flying up." Kait sounded hurt.

Kait and Demi had been talking every day, but not about flying up and not about Aiden.

"If her line's tapped," which it probably was, "it's safer not to give the bastards a heads up. I'll fly down and just show up, grab her, and run." Of course, they could still try to interfere, but he was prepared for that.

His pulse jumped when his cell vibrated against the plastic tray. He picked it up and accepted the call, frowning at the lack of caller ID.

"Aiden?"

He recognized the flat voice, and it wasn't Wolf.

"Tag?" Aiden jerked up, his heart suddenly pounding. Tag wouldn't be calling unless something had happened. Something bad.

"Yeah." Tag's voice was hard. "We've got a problem."

Chapter Fifteen

Day 7
Coronado, California

Demi hissed as ten claws pierced the skin of her forearm. The furry asshole she'd agreed to adopt curled its lips back, exposing long, sharp fangs.

"Oh, *come on* you one eyed, three legged, no tailed, human-hating son of a serial killer." She crooned in a soothing—certainly not critical—tone of voice. Her new master did not tolerate criticism. "This medicine is good for you. Trust me." A low, seething growl greeted her proclamation. She winced as the claws dug in deeper. "I'm trying to help you. This stuff prevents infection. If you don't swallow it, you'll get sick and back to the vet you go. Remember how much you hated it there?"

Juggling the cat and the medicine, she dipped the eyedropper into its bottle and sucked up a dose of milky liquid. The cat writhed madly in the towel wrapped around its leg and torso. Originally, only its head had been free. Until it wiggled its front legs loose and unleashed those lethal claws.

Beads of blood oozed down the fresh scratches on her arms. The cat had neatly spaced these new scratches between the scabs from their previous battles. Administering the medicine was more of a two-person job. One to hold the cat and one to force open its stubbornly clamped jaws and squirt the medicine down its hissing gullet. Not that she had a second person available to help her. Its attack on Megan and Elise three days ago had circulated through the building. Her neighbors avoided her now.

Clamping the creature to her chest, she carefully placed the medicine bottle on the kitchen counter and lifted the stopper to the orange whiskered face with its sutured eye socket. The demon's remaining eye—which was metallic green and glittering with malice—locked with hostile intent on the eyedropper. He retracted his claws from her arm and swatted the eyedropper out of her hand.

With a soft *plink*, the eyedropper hit the tile. Demi groaned, watching it spin across the kitchen floor. Since bending to pick it up would plant her face too close to those murderous claws, which she had no doubt the ungrateful creature would put to good use, she walked over to the kitchen alcove with its gorgeous view of Princeton Park. Usually, the rolling grass, studded by majestic evergreens and banks of colorful flowers, soothed her.

Not today.

Not for the past four days, if she was honest.

"You're the most ungrateful little snot in the history of ungrateful snots." She crooned in that annoyingly sweet voice she hated. But the cat responded violently to harsh voices. "You know you're alive because of me, right? Who rushed your furry, bleeding ass to the vet when you were dying? Who paid your vet bills? Who bought your specialty food—both wet and dry—along with your bed and carrier and toys, which you won't even play with? Me. That's who. The person you keep trying to bleed dry. You could at least take your medicine without shredding me."

She eased the growling animal onto the kitchen table, towel and all, and let go, then backed away with the caution of someone expecting a bomb to go off.

The cat rolled and shook off the towel. Claws skittered against the glass table's surface as it fought to get its remaining legs beneath it. Demi winced as it leaped off the table and raced wildly across the living room, disappearing down the hall. No doubt it was diving under the guest bed, its favorite hiding place.

At least its injuries didn't look infected—which was a relief considering her failure at getting the antibiotics into him. The vet had suggested injecting the medicine into the wet food, but the wily animal refused to eat the laced meal.

She'd bought a travel cage for the cat's trip home from the clinic. But the vet had recommended keeping the animal contained to force rest and promote healing. So, she'd also bought a dog crate big enough to accommodate a cat bed, litter box, and bowls for water and food. The furry asshole destroyed the entire ensemble in under an hour. Hell's bells, there had been water, wet kitty litter, and cat food everywhere. It even broke the welding on the cage and bent the metal until it could squirm its way through the bars.

She hadn't tried to contain it after that. The effort it put into escaping the cage was more likely to cause injury than hiding under the guest room bed. At least when it was loose, it settled down. Plus, it was eating and drinking and using the litter box.

Returning to the kitchen, she retrieved the stopper from the floor and screwed it back onto the medicine bottle. She'd give the heathen some time to decompress and try again—no doubt adding to her collection of bloody scratches.

She glanced across the kitchen counter when her cell phone vibrated against the granite. *Kait* lit up the screen. Setting the bottle down, she picked up her phone.

"Hey, Kait, your timing is perfect." She lifted her still-steaming cup of Colombian coffee and breathed in the full-bodied fragrance of citrus and spice. "The furry little maniac is back in hiding. I have about an hour before I have to offer my skin and blood in sacrifice to his continued good health."

"It's not Kait." Aiden's flat baritone made that instantly clear. "*Skin and blood? Sacrifice?* What the hell...?" his voice trailed off as if he didn't know where to start with his questions.

"Aiden?" Demi straightened hard, bobbling her cup. Some of the coffee slopped over the edge, landing on her hand. She winced as the hot liquid sank into the healing scratches.

"Listen," he sounded tense. "We don't have much time."

"Time for what?" Demi narrowed her eyes, the scratches forgotten. "Why are you on Kait's phone?" Was he with Kait? He must be. That was the only way he'd have access to his sister's phone.

She didn't know where Kait lived these days. The location was a big mystery. She wondered sometimes if all the secrecy was necessary, but considering what Kait's husband had gone through with the US government along with that rogue, ultra wealthy secret society—yeah, she could see where Cosky was jittery when it came to their safety.

"I'm on Kait's phone because you pick up for her." She heard frustration in his voice, before he took an audible breath. "I'll explain everything in person." His tone was measured.

Demi's spine snapped straight in annoyance. "I told you. I'm not flying off to—"

"Two men dressed in Navy whites are headed to your door." Aiden barreled over her comment, his voice tightening. "They're *not* with the Navy. They're *not* from ST7. They're *not* who they will claim to be. They'll probably tell you I'm hurt, or dead."

Startled, she pulled the phone away to look at it, which was ridiculous. The blank screen wouldn't tell her if he was joking. "Why would they tell me you're hurt? Or dead?" She paused, her brow furrowing. He obviously wasn't dead. But... "Are you hurt?"

"No, I'm fine. They'll try to grab you and use you to flush me out." Aiden's voice went faint for a moment, as though he turned away from the phone. "You need to distract them. Delay them, but without setting them off. Keep them busy until Tag and Tram get to you. Pretend to believe everything they tell you. Don't push them. If they get antagonistic, then do whatever they say."

Her stomach tightened. "What's going on, Aiden?" Her voice rose. "Why are these people trying to flush you out?"

How much danger was he in?

How much danger was *she* in?

A beat of silence fell, and then he sighed. His slow exhale sounded weary, almost morose.

"The last op my squad was sent on was a setup," he said quietly. "I'm the only one of my team to survive. Now the bastards behind my crew's murder want to chat with me. Find out why I survived. They'll try to use you to get to me."

Demi's heart stuttered as horror gripped her. He'd lost his entire team? That couldn't be right. "Squirrel? Grub? Lur—"

"Dead. All dead." His devastation showed in his voice. The blank emptiness of it.

She choked back her sympathy. He obviously didn't want to talk about his loss. "Who set you up?"

"That's unclear." His tone tightened. "We don't have time for twenty questions. They'll be knocking on your door any minute."

Which just reminded her of another question.

"How do you know they're on their way up to my door?" Maybe he was wrong, overreacting or something—although she'd never known Aiden to overreact.

"They were sighted going into your building." Another beat of silence, followed by the most measured tone of voice yet, as though he knew she wouldn't like what he was about to say. "I've had eyes on you for the last four days. But someone reported my surveillance team to the cops and got them locked down. The point guy got a message to Tag before the whole fucking lot of them were rounded up by COPD."

The first part of that announcement hit hard. So hard, she barely heard the second part.

"You've *what*?" She rocked back on her heels, her jaw dropping in shock. "You have someone watching me?"

"Yes." He sounded impatient again. "To protect you. To keep you safe in case the bastards showed up at your door before I could get down to Coronado and protect you. When you wouldn't answer my calls, I hired Forged Security to keep an eye on you. Tag and Tram have the vampire shift, so they weren't caught in the COPD round-up."

That's why he'd been so persistent in calling her? To warn her? A commanding knock on the front door of her condo ruptured her indignation. She froze.

"Was Tag going to come up and get me?" Her voice dropped to a whisper.

"No." He didn't sound surprised by the question.

"Someone's knocking on my door," she said directly into the phone mic, keeping her voice low.

"Answer it. Pretend to believe whatever they tell you. Distract them as long as you can." He paused, his voice turning gritty. "Baby, I will get you out of this, but our best odds of getting you clear of those bastards is to wait until Tag and Tram arrive."

"What if I don't answer the door? Maybe they'll go away."

His voice gentled. "They aren't going away, sweetheart."

"But if I don't answer, maybe they'll think I'm not home."

"They'll pick the lock and let themselves into your condo."

"I could hide." Demi offered in a small voice, her mind racing to find a solution.

She did not want to answer that door. She did not want to have to distract them without alerting them to the fact she knew what they were up to. She'd never been much of an actress, which had never been a big deal in her life. She'd always found that honesty served her better. Until now. This was the first time her terrible acting skills could get her in trouble.

Another commanding knock hit the door, followed by a voice. "Demelda Barnes? We need to speak with you."

Demi's mouth went dry. "Will you stay on the line with me?"

"I can't." His voice was so gentle it made her want to cry. "We have fifteen seconds before a high intensity electronic jammer hits your building. Once it hits, cell phones won't work."

"*What?*" Her voice rose. He was taking away her only means of communication?

"Yeah. I'm sorry, but we can't chance anyone warning those bastards that Tag and Tram are on the way. Trust me, babe—I've got you—"

The phone suddenly went dead. She was not a tech expert, but it was clear the jammer Aiden had mentioned was at work. She stood there, her hand clenching the phone, as more thuds struck her door. Her heart pounded so hard she could hear it in her ears.

After a moment of heavy, panicked breathing, she squared her shoulders and methodically set the phone on the counter. Aiden had promised he'd get her out of this situation. He'd never lied to her. Men he trusted were on their way. She took a deep, even breath. She'd met Tag and Tram enough times to trust them, too. Enough times to know they'd sacrifice their lives without hesitation to keep her safe.

The thought soured her stomach and shook her hands. It took enormous effort to force her shaky legs to step toward the door.

You can do this, Demi. Breathe. Keep your fear hidden and your mind alert.

You can do this. Piece of cake.

Too bad the quick pep talk did nothing to calm the urgent slam of her heart, or the rising tide of fear.

Chapter Sixteen

Day 7
Denali, Alaska

Aiden eased his rigid grip on the cell phone when his fingers cramped. What was going on at Demi's door? Was she keeping the bastards after him occupied until Tag and Tram could get to her? Sure, Cameron Sotto was camped outside the building with the electronics jammer, but the dude was tech support, with only rudimentary training in self-defense. They'd been lucky he'd left the van to grab a coffee before COPD had swarmed Demi's surveillance team, but he wasn't trained for action.

"Relax," Cosky said from beside him. "It hasn't even been fifteen minutes since you talked to Demi."

It hadn't? Aiden glanced at the clock on the phone. Cos was right. The realization did nothing to ease his fear. He couldn't breathe properly. That must be why he was moving so slowly—like he was slogging through molasses.

He lengthened his stride, vaguely aware of light gray walls and a dark gray sidewalk. The gray on gray was disorienting, blending into an endless, monotonous tunnel. They'd opted not to grab a utility vehicle. Cosky claimed it was quicker to take the elevator.

Aiden was tempted to hijack the next vehicle that came along. It was embarrassing how much stamina those four days in isolation and the ER had cost him. Hell, his heart was pounding like a motherfucker.

Had Tag and Tram arrived yet? Had they secured the targets? Was Demi okay? If anything happened to her...

"She'll be fine." Cosky's voice was flat. Certain. "Tag and Tram won't let anything happen to her. They'll protect her like she's one of their own."

Aiden didn't doubt that. But that didn't mean the bastards at Demi's door wouldn't still prevail and whisk her away.

"Zane and Rawls are meeting us at the hangar," Cosky said, his tone even, his breathing controlled despite the rapid pace he'd set.

Cosky's calm breathing sent shame curling through Aiden. Here he was gasping like the little train that could, as he huffed and puffed his way to the elevator.

He took another quick look at the cell phone. Maybe it had rung without him noticing. Nope. The elevator doors whooshed open. He and Cos stepped inside. Cosky punched a button marked HANGAR and the doors snapped closed. The floor beneath his boots vibrated, and the lift rose.

Cosky shot him a knowing look. "Give Tag time. He's kinda busy right now. He'll call when he has something to report."

Aiden grimaced. That advice did nothing to mitigate the frustration of waiting, or the praying for good news. There were no guarantees that Tag and Tram would get to Demi in time. No guarantees that Demi could distract and stall the bastards at her door.

Cosky must have glimpsed his fear, because he squeezed his shoulder. "Relax. Trust your brothers to keep your woman safe."

That advice brought a scowl. "Yeah? Would you say that if Kait were in trouble?"

With a shrug, Cosky released his grip on Aiden's shoulder. "A redundant question. She's here on base."

Bastard.

"That scowl's not gonna make things move faster." The elevator doors snapped open, and Cosky stepped out.

Aiden followed him out, only to stop dead.

There was no corridor ahead of them, just a cavernous space filled with aircraft of every shape and size. The hangar went on and on, as far back as he could see. So did the various aircraft. Directly in front of him was a UH-1Y Venom, to the right of it a Boeing Apache, and behind that, a UH-60 Black Hawk. Further back, a Boeing Chinook and a Sikorsky Seahawk—which was weird as all shit since the Seahawk usually operated off ships.

Did Shadow Mountain have a Navy? Nah, that wasn't likely. A Navy would be impossible to keep under wraps.

Behind the choppers was a Cessna Citation X+, which was the fastest private jet available. Hell, he'd checked into that model, even come close to picking one up for himself. Thanks to his talent, which showered him with more money than he'd ever need, he could cover the twenty-three-million-dollar price tag. But explaining how he could afford a multi-million-dollar jet, while on an Uncle Sam budget, had nixed the idea.

Other than the money he periodically won through his pseudonyms, which he funneled into various charities, Demi's condo was the most expensive purchase he'd made. He'd covered his tracks well, making sure everyone, including Demi, thought the condo had been possible because of an unexpected inheritance, one Donnie had come into prior to his death.

The memory brought on a grimace. She'd certainly loved the guy. It was a constant itch that she didn't have the same depth of feeling for him. In retrospect, focusing on sex had been a poor decision. But he'd been certain the quickest path to her heart was through her bed.

Sucking back a sigh, he glanced back down at his phone. Still nothing from Tag.

Fuck. Fuck. Fuck.

He wasn't feeling Demi's fear though, not like he had three years ago when Chester had accosted her outside the elevator. He'd felt the icy bite of her fear then, even over the adrenaline and exertion of charging down a flight of stairs. This was the first time she'd been in danger since the Chester incident. Why wasn't he feeling her terror? Was it because of the distance between them? Not just physical, but emotionally as well?

Cosky had stopped next to the Citation X. The jet's ramp was down. Must be their ride. Aiden lengthened his stride. Although the color of asphalt, the ground felt strange beneath his boots. Soft, rather than hard, as though it absorbed his footsteps. Weird. What was even stranger was how close to each other the aircraft were parked. How did the crew maneuver them out of the hangar and onto the airstrip?

"How do they get anything to the runway?" He joined Cosky in front of the ramp.

"That's right, the Thunderbird doesn't have any windows." Cosky turned to face him. A slow smirk spread across his face. "You never saw the bird land, did you?" The smirk spread wider. "Hell, man," Cosky grinned. "I won't spoil the surprise."

"Flying isn't new to me." Aiden glanced back down at the phone.

Still no call. His fingers had gone white again.

"Trust me," Cosky sounded certain. "You've never flown Shadow Mountain style."

Aiden raised his eyebrows and scoffed. What the hell was the bastard yapping about?

Aiden followed Cosky up the steps. He stopped at the foot of the cabin to stare. His normal flights weren't nearly as luxurious as this. Eight plush, cream-colored seats, arranged in sets of two, faced each other. Four ran along the right side of the plane and four along the left. The rows were separated by a narrow aisle. Behind the chairs was a couch on one side of the cabin and a couch with a worktable against the other wall. Small, oval windows, with the shades drawn, accompanied each chair. The air smelled fresh and slightly floral.

Nothing about the jet indicated a military bird. Hell, even the carpet looked airbrushed and fluffy.

"Ah, hell," Cosky's voice turned sour. "What's he doing here?"

Aiden followed his brother-in-law's gaze to the last of the eight chairs. It took him a few seconds to recognize the unlikable and mouthy bastard from Wolf's exfil team. What had Rawls called him? O'Neill? The dude was slouched down in his chair, eyes closed, apparently napping. At least the asshole had taken a seat far enough away to ignore him. Aiden dropped into a chair across the aisle from Zane and scowled down at his phone.

What the hell was going on? Tag and Tram should have dispatched their targets and contacted him by now.

Forcing his frustration back, he turned to Cosky, who'd taken the seat across from him. "How long will it take the ground crew to haul us to the airstrip?"

Cosky chuckled. Leaning forward, he pulled on the bottom of the window shade next to Aiden's chair. The curtain rolled up, leaving the window bare. "Buckle up and prepare to be amazed."

"Right." Aiden rolled his eyes before turning his attention back to his phone.

"You ever hear that old adage about a watched pot never boiling? Pretty sure it applies to cell phones, too," Cosky said dryly, although his gray eyes were almost sympathetic.

Aiden clipped his seatbelt together and glanced out the window. Impatience steamed through him. He saw no ground crew arriving to move the jet to the airstrip. Talk about a staging clusterfuck. Why the hell would the Shadow Mountain ground crew park their aircraft like this? It would take hours to maneuver the planes and choppers out of the Citation's way.

He frowned as a low whine started up beneath his feet. The buzzing wasn't engine noise or vibration. Maybe the ground crew was finally clearing a path. But when he glanced out the window, the aircraft surrounding the Citation were gone.

What the hell?

He leaned into the window and peered down. The aircraft below were getting smaller with each second.

"What. The....?" There was a sense of ascension now, although it was coming from the disappearing ground, not from the plane itself. "We're on a lift?"

He craned his neck and looked up, trying to see the ceiling.

"Relax." A shit-eating grin spread across Rawls's face, who was sitting next to Zane. "We ain't gonna hit the roof. A magical portal will open and deposit us directly onto the runway."

"No shit?" Aiden pulled back, realizing for the first time that everyone in the cabin was watching him with various degrees of amusement. Except for O'Neill, who was still slumped in the back with his eyes closed.

A grating whine sounded, this time from above. He leaned against the window to look up and watched a good chunk of the ceiling split and slide to the sides. Watery streams of light brightened the dark chasm. Within seconds, they were outside; the sun beaming down on them. Blue sky and fluffy clouds were everywhere. No grass, no trees. No buildings. No rolling hills or roads. No people. Just an endless stretch of blue sky.

He leaned against the window again, looking down. Cement. Fuck, they were on the runway. A runway up in the clouds.

Still gawking, he shook his head. "Where the hell is this runway?"

"Now that," Cosky scoffed, his smirk vanishing, "is an excellent question."

Aiden absently glanced down at his cell. His fingers had loosened their desperate grip, but still no call. It was too dangerous to call Tag. A distraction at an inopportune moment could prove disastrous. Which meant he had to wait for Tag or Tram to call him.

He battened down his impatience and turned to Cosky. "You don't know where we are?"

They'd worked for Shadow Mountain for three years now. How could they not know?

"We know we're somewhere up on Denali." There was a shrug in Zane's voice, like he didn't really care. Zane projected impenetrable calm, which made him hard to read.

"The real question is how the hell they're hiding this, not just from the climbers, but from the locals...." Cosky trailed off with a perplexed shake of his head. "This is Mount Denali, for Christ's sake."

Cos was right. At least a thousand people climbed Denali every year. Some of those climbers should have noticed planes and helicopters taking off from the mountainside. Hadn't they questioned where the aircraft had come from? Plus, there were a good dozen towns surrounding the mountain. Denali wasn't hidden within a remote region of Alaska. Civilization encircled the sleeping giant.

"That's not the only...irregularity," Rawls said in that slow drawl of his. "There's also the weather up here. There's never any wind."

"Or snow, or rain," Zane broke in.

"It's like the runway sits outside all the weather systems." Cosky cocked his head, a frown pulling at his forehead. "It can snow up a blizzard in Talkeetna, yet not a flake up here."

All of which sounded like bullshit to Aiden. An invisible airstrip? Protected from wind, rain, and snow, and sitting outside the regular weather systems, like it occupied a different dimension?

Pure crazy talk.

There had to be some explanation for this mysterious airstrip, a lucid one, regardless of what his formerly rational buddies were claiming.

Chapter Seventeen

Day 7
Coronado, California

By the time Demi reached the door, her heart was racing, and her skin felt like ice. The pep talk had sped up, rather than reduced her fear. She sucked down several deep breaths, but the effort to calm herself had no effect on her racing heart or clammy skin.

Another thunderous knock sounded, followed by a loud voice. "Ms. Barnes. We need to speak to you. This is better done face-to-face."

Now, that sounded ominous.

She stirred, forcing herself to take another deep breath. Ignoring them wouldn't work if they planned to pick her lock and let themselves into her home.

"Just a second," she yelled at the door.

How was she supposed to distract them until Aiden's friends arrived? Her frantic mind locked on the primary source of her frustration over the past few days. The furry demon. The seed of an idea unfurled. The little monster would make an excellent distraction. She'd just have to make sure he didn't get hurt. Although the people caring for the feline demon were the ones who ended up bleeding, not that stinker of a cat.

Which felt like karmic justice. Let the animal slice and dice the men at her door. It would serve them right. Squaring her shoulders, she rubbed her sweaty hands against her jean-clad thighs and reached for the door handle.

You've got this, Demi. No problem. Just pretend you were distracted by the cat.

After one final deep breath, she unlocked the door. As she jerked it open, she assumed an annoyed expression. "Did you have to make so much noise? You scared Trident—" she tossed the name out. *Huh. Looks like the cat has a name now.* "—off before he swallowed his medication."

The tall, gaunt man standing directly in front of her door stared at the blood trickling down her scratched-up arms. A startled look flickered across his long, lined face. After a moment, he shook himself. Basset hound eyes rose to meet her gaze and his face folded into a mournful expression.

"Ms. Barnes?" He didn't wait for her confirmation, just plowed right into fake introductions. "I'm Lieutenant DeLeon with Coronado Naval Base, specifically SEAL Team 7, and this is Father Darien Grant, the base chaplain." He tilted his head to his left, indicating the dark-haired, muscle packed guy with dead eyes standing to his left.

That second introduction convinced Demi Aiden hadn't been exaggerating about the danger. Those empty eyes didn't belong to a priest. They belonged to a serial killer.

"May we speak with you?" The stick of a man asked, putting enough sympathy in his voice to make her teeth ache. "It's about Aiden Winchester."

She drew in an exaggerated, sharp breath and strove for a worried expression. "Is he alright?"

This seemed like the appropriate question for someone who was in a relationship with a SEAL and had a base officer and chaplain unexpectedly show up at her door.

"I'm afraid not," stick man said, his voice excreting copious amounts of saccharine sympathy.

"Oh, no! Oh, no!" she added the second exclamation for effect. "What happened? I just talked to him and—"

"When was that?" muscle man interrupted; his voice flat.

"I don't know. A week ago, I guess." Since signs of agitation were in order, she wrung her hands and rambled on, trying to sound as scattered as possible. "He Zoomed with me from some tent in God knows where. He never said where he was. He never tells me anything." A hint of genuine anger touched her voice. She forced it back. Someone in fear for their boyfriend's life wouldn't be expressing resentment. "Is he okay?" She instantly shook her head and pressed her hands to her cheeks. "He's not, is he? You already said he wasn't okay. What happened to him? How bad is he hurt?"

She didn't hide the shake in her voice or her trembling hands. They'd attribute the reaction to the bad news they'd just delivered.

"It's bad." Mr. Muscles's voice was as dead as his eyes. "He's not expected to survive. He's asking for you."

Stick man pasted on a fraudulently sympathetic smile. The sugary tinge to his fake compassion was discomforting, like fingernails raking down a chalkboard. She hoped he attributed her slight recoil to the news he'd delivered.

"Of course...of course..." She stumbled back and turned, leaving the door wide open. "Let me get my purse and phone—"

"Ms. Barnes, we don't have time—"

"Oh! No!" She stopped abruptly, filling her voice with dismay. "Trident has a vet appointment today."

"You can cancel it on the way." Impatience rang in Stick Man's voice. "Winchester could die at any moment. You don't have time to dally."

"Aiden will never forgive me if his little warrior got sick. He loves that cat. He was furious with me when Trident snuck out of the complex and he got hit by that car." She turned around and widened her eyes, hoping they looked full of entreaty instead of terror. "Can you help me get him in his carrier? He can be a little rascal sometimes." *Make that a complete asshole.* "But with your help, I'm sure we can get him corralled and into his carrier in record time." Both men's gazes dropped to her scratched up arms and widened in alarm.

"We really can't afford the time—"

"I'm not leaving without Trident. Who knows how long I'll be sitting by Aiden's bed. Trident can't be home by himself. He needs daily doses of anti-inflammatory medicine and antibiotics. We can drop him off at his vet on the way to the hospital. They'll take care of him while I'm with Aiden." When neither man looked thrilled with this prospect, she doubled down. "I'm not leaving without him."

Muscle Man's eyes turned the color of mud. Deadly threat laced the brown irises. Stick Man just looked calculating.

She forced steel into her spine and faced them down. She needed to get her overlord into his travel carrier. Trident, which appeared to be his name now, actually did need his daily medications and care. She couldn't leave him behind, nor could she imagine Aiden bringing her back to the condo to pick the animal up. But with some help from these two assholes, she'd have the demon safely locked in his travel cage by the time Tag showed up. When she escaped, the cat would come with her.

Down the hall came the murmur of voices. The fake Navy guys glanced down the corridor. Tension flashed across their faces. Muscles bunched in their arms. She tensed, certain they were about to leap at her, shove her backwards, then follow her into her condo. Which meant this charade of theirs would be over. God only knew what action they'd take then.

Acting on instinct, she leaned out the doorway and peered down the hall. Megan and Elise, her neighbors across the hall two doors down were headed her way.

"Megan! Elise!" She waved, catching their attention.

The fake priest swore beneath his breath. The guy was a terrible actor. A *real* priest wouldn't swear like a sailor. He glanced at his crony. Stick Man offered a slight shake of his head and the two men blocking her door eased back a couple steps.

Megan and Elise picked up their pace when they saw the two men dressed in Navy whites. Alarm touched their faces—which still sported scabby scratches from their encounter with Trident four days ago.

"Hey." Megan peered at Demi's face. "Is everything alright?"

"Aiden's been hurt." Demi forced the lie out. It felt wrong to lie to her friends like this, even if the lie was for a good reason.

"Actually," Stick Man turned, flashing the women behind him a mortician's smile, "Ms. Barnes is needed at Aiden Winchester's bedside, but she's worried about her cat. Apparently, it needs medication? Perhaps you two would be good enough to take care of the animal while she's gone."

The concern on Megan's face collapsed into alarm. She took a huge step back and sidled to the right.

"I'm so sorry, Demi, but we have a...a...thing. In fact, we're headed out of town ourselves." She slid a meaningful look in her wife's direction, who nodded emphatically. "If it were any other time, but—" Megan shrugged apologetically and turned, rushing down the hall like the Grim Reaper was behind her with a raised scythe.

"I hope Aiden pulls through," Elise offered, before turning and hurrying after Megan.

Demi didn't blame them for their hasty retreat. Trident had leaped for their faces, barely missing their eyes, when they'd helped her administer the medication the morning after she'd brought the cat home.

Frustration flashing across his hang-dog face, the mortician wannabe turned back to her. "We really need to leave now, Miss Barnes. I'll send one of Aiden's teammates back to care for the cat. If you'll—"

Ignoring him, Demi turned, marching down the hall between her front door and the living room. They wouldn't shoot her while Megan and Elise were within earshot. "Look, the longer you argue, the longer this will take. I'm not leaving without Trident."

A whispered conversation broke out behind her. She was halfway across the living room when she heard muffled footsteps follow her. Now that they had her alone, with no witnesses, would the two men continue with this pretense, or would they launch into threats and fists to force her to leave with them? Her head went light at the possibility.

Her heart galloping, she rushed down the hall and into the spare bedroom. She closed the bedroom door behind her, more to keep the animal contained than her would-be kidnappers out.

"Miss Barnes?" Stick Man's voice came from outside the bedroom door.

"In here," Demi shouted back.

There was no use hiding her location. She needed her would-be kidnappers' help to get Trident into his carry case. It had taken three veterinary assistants to get him into the cage when she'd retrieved him from the clinic. He was smart enough to remember that incident and do everything possible to avoid a repeat.

"Close the door so he doesn't get out," Demi said when the two killers, with their fake smiles, stepped into the room.

She grabbed the kennel by its handle, lifted it from the bed, and pushed it into Stick Man's arms. He took it reluctantly, with deep revulsion, like helping her with the cat was far below his paygrade.

"Trident is under the bed." She picked up the fleece blanket that was lying next to the cat carrier.

She shook the throw out, noting the multitude of shredded holes that hadn't been there five days prior. The cat certainly knew how to use his claws and teeth. She almost asked one of the men to crawl under the bed and toss the blanket over the furry asshole, but there was a steep learning curve to that maneuver, one that produced blood and shredded skin. These guys would go for their guns the moment Trident attacked. She didn't want the cat dead, just contained. She'd have to be the one to crawl under the bed after him.

"Get a good hold on the cage and make sure the door is open." She dropped to her knees.

"Remind me why we're doing this again?" the pretend priest asked in an empty tone. Almost like he was more curious than annoyed. "We'd have her out to the van by now, if we used some 9mm persuasion."

Stick Guy made a shushing sound. Demi pretended she hadn't heard them. Going down on her belly, she crawled under the bed while pushing the blanket in front of her. It was a tight fit, the wooden slats of the frame snagging her hair.

Trident was at the head of the bed, huddled against the wall next to one of the bedframe's legs. She lifted the fleece, holding it as far up and out to the sides as she could, while letting it droop slightly in front of her eyes so she could see.

Arrggglll! The cat warned in a low, guttural growl of doom.

"Good kitty." Demi lifted her voice into that chipper chirp she despised.

Errgggowl! Arrggggowl! Stiff bodied and vibrating with rage, the cat shifted closer to the leg of the bedframe. Demi sidled that way, too, the blanket held up and out. She'd gotten to know the animal's eccentricities and judging from its rigid body and blazing eye; it was about to attack. Sure enough, in a blur of movement, it launched itself at her head.

Demi caught the cat in the blanket. Before he could disengage his claws and escape, she rolled him over and over in the throw, until he resembled a writhing lump of fleece. Once the whirling dervish of claws and teeth was safely wrapped up like a burrito, she took a second to catch her breath. Wow, that had been the easiest capture yet.

"I've got him. That cage better be ready. He's pissed." The blanket wiggled beneath her hands as the demon she'd captured fought to escape.

"I'm coming out. Put the cage on the floor but keep the door open."

She carefully crawled backward, the blanket clamped to her chest, while the cat squirmed and wiggled and howled in fury. A paw, claws extended, reached through one of the shredded areas in the blanket and tore a new furrow into her forearm. A burning sting engulfed her arm, followed by wet warmth trickling down her skin.

"Here." Stick Man thrust the crate toward her head as she squirmed out from beneath the bed. She rolled onto her butt. Horror filled her as the blanket unraveled. A whiskered nose and glittering emerald eye peaked through a loose edge of the fleece.

Shit!

She shoved the cat, blanket and all, into the carrying case. Slamming the door shut, she engaged the locks as the blanket unraveled completely and a bomb detonated inside the cage.

Errgggowl! Arrggggowl! The plastic kennel rocked beneath the cat's fury. Claws attached themselves to the grated door and rattled the metal.

"You shouldn't have bothered catching that thing." Muscle Man's voice was laconic. "That cage ain't gonna hold it."

He was right. At its current level of ferocity, the furry demon was going to dismantle its carrier. Hopefully, a couple miles of duct tape would prevent the crate from disintegrating.

"There's duct tape in the kitchen." She shouted to be heard over the screeching and growling. "It's in the drawer to the left of the sink. Could one of you get it for me?"

Muscle Man looked toward Stick Man, who shrugged. With a roll of his eyes, the pretend priest turned and stalked out of the bedroom.

"Better grab some scissors too," Demi called after him, doing her best to keep the cage intact while keeping her fingers away from the slats along the side of the crate and the metal bars across the door. "They're in the same drawer." She held her breath as the cage rocked violently within her grasp. "Hurry!"

More yowling. More rocking of the crate. The sound of claws skittering against plastic. Demi held her breath and silently urged Muscle Man to hurry.

She caught a shimmy of movement at the bedroom door. That was quick. The dude must have raced to the kitchen and back. Stick Man was bent at the waist, peering into the rocking crate, like he was fascinated by the demon inside. She looked over his stooped shoulders, ready to grab the tape from the fake priest's hands.

Only it wasn't Muscle Man sliding into the room.

Chapter Eighteen

Day 7
Coronado, California

Demi recognized the blue eyes and brown hair. Brett Taggart. Aiden had taken her to several cookouts where the former SEAL had manned the grill. She'd sensed his lethality back then, just as she'd sensed it in Aiden and the rest of his teammates. Even off-duty and surrounded by people and things familiar to them, Aiden's friends had been watchful, their eyes constantly sweeping the landscape.

She'd wondered if that level of preparedness ever went away.

Tag's lethality wasn't masked now. It showed in each slow, precise step as he eased up behind stick man. It showed in the narrow, stony gaze locked on his target. He reminded her of a predator. All rigid focus and slow deliberation, his muscles fluid as he stalked his prey.

Dizziness hit her. The scene was so surreal. There was Trident, howling and hissing and rattling the cage with an ear piercing—wake the dead—kind of racket. And then Tag behind the cage…creeping up on Stick Man with predatory stealth. It felt like the two didn't belong in the same scene at the same time. Like they should cancel each other out.

Stick man straightened, but he was so distracted by the cage shaking and feral growling, he failed to notice the danger approaching from behind.

She expected Tag to draw his gun. One was clearly visible—its black handle poking up from the leather holster snugged beneath his armpit. Wouldn't a weapon give him an edge in the coming battle? Apparently not, since he ignored the gun. Instead, he slid behind Stick Man and wrapped his right arm around her would-be-assailant's neck. With a sharp step back and a jerk of his elbow, he yanked Stick Man off his feet. He followed that movement with a rapid twist of his torso and threw his prey to the carpet, where he landed on his stomach. Once her unwelcome visitor was down, Tag dropped onto the guy and wrenched both arms behind his back.

Just like that, the battle was over. Stick Man let loose with a couple of startled gasps and shimmied his shoulders. The muscles in Tag's arms bunched as he pressed down harder on his captive's wrists until the wiggling stopped.

Tag looked up at her, his breathing easy, his eyes calm. "We'll get you off to Aiden as soon as we offload these bastards." He scanned her, his gaze lingering on her scabby arms. "Either of these jokers hurt you?"

Demi shook her head. He must know from the condition of her scabs that those wounds were days old, acquired long before her unwelcome visitors had knocked on her door.

"Tell you what," Tag said, his voice conversational, "once we've got these two tied up, you can take a couple of whacks at them. A little punishment for the trouble they put you through."

With a slow, confused shake of her head, Demi just stared back. Was he joking? Serious? His calm, casual demeanor could point to either. She turned her attention to Stick Man, who was just lying there, his cheek pressed against her tweed carpet...like he'd completely given up.

Good God, talk about anticlimactic. Tag had taken the guy down in a second—maybe two—with absolutely no effort. He wasn't even breathing heavy. With Aiden's caution about how much danger she was in, she'd expected her unwelcome visitors to pose more of a threat.

"No?" Tag shrugged, his attention returning to his captive. "Well, let me know if you change your mind. There are flex cuffs in my back pocket. Grab two and bind this bastard's ankles."

That's when she realized she could hear again. Or at least hear things other than howling, growling, and cage rattling. She bent to peer into the cat carrier. Had her furry demon perished from a stress induced heart attack? A huge, metallic green eye glared back at her. Well, he wasn't dead. Strange that he'd gone so silent.

"Demi?" Tag's calm voice brought her eyes back up. "The cuffs?"

The cat was quiet and secure for the moment. She'd wrap the crate with duct tape after she secured Tag's prisoner. She straightened, skirted the crate, and plucked a couple of plastic cuffs from Tag's back pocket.

"There's another guy in the kitchen," Demi told him, as she zipped tied stick man's ankles.

"Tram took care of him. When you're done with the ankles, bring a couple of those ties up front."

Demi plucked two more plastic cuffs from his pocket and scooted up until she was kneeling beside Tag.

"You're doing great." Tag shot her an approving glance and shifted his knee further up Stick Man's arms, freeing his wrist. "Cuff his wrists. Be prepared. If he's gonna try anything, it will be now."

Apparently, Stick Guy didn't have the energy, or maybe the nerve, to fight for his freedom. He simply lay there, placidly, letting her cinch the plastic ties around his wrists.

Once Stick Man's wrists and ankles were bound, Tag yanked on the cuff straps until the plastic was so tight it cut into the guy's skin.

"That should do it." He straightened and rose to his feet. "We'll get you out of here as soon as our backup arrives to take charge of this bozo and his clown car associate."

"I need to get some duct tape to reinforce the cage." She glanced toward the kennel, which was silent and still. She'd better get to work before the cat recovered from his stupor and tore the crate apart.

"What the hell do you have in there?" Tag shot an absent look at the plastic cage. "It sounded like a velociraptor. It made a great distraction."

"A cat. An injured, very unhappy cat."

His gaze dropped to her scabby and scratched up arms. "Is it responsible for the condition of your arms?" He shook his head. "That won't sit well with Aiden."

"Just a miscommunication. He's stressed and scared." She kept the explanation vague. Trident didn't need an even worse reputation. Besides, it wasn't a lie. Trident was frightened and did not realize she was trying to help him.

As she turned toward the door, a grunt sounded behind her. She spun to check on Tag with such speed she almost fell over, only to find her rescuer following behind her with his captive slung over his shoulder. Good God, the amount of strength it must take to haul someone the size of Stick Man across the room without staggering.

Thank God Tag was on her side...or more like Aiden's side. Did he know she'd broken up with his former teammate? Granted, Aiden had gotten the news secondhand through Kait. But telling him over the phone that she hadn't changed her mind about calling it quits on them and then refusing his calls constituted a breakup, didn't it?

A thick, woolly numbness set in as she swung back around to pick up Trident's carrier and take it into the living room. The condo was eerily quiet. Almost hushed. Like she was divorced from reality or caught in a dream.

She found Trammel's captive in the living room, sitting on her couch. Had the fake priest been harder to subdue? She hadn't heard sounds of struggle, but she'd been in the bedroom and Trident had been making a

God-awful racket. Still, of the two men who'd showed up at her door, she suspected the muscle-bound guy was the dangerous one. Which was odd, as Stick Man appeared to call the shots.

Even bound at the ankles and wrists, the fake priest made her skin crawl. It was his eyes. The muddy, dead sheen to them, like his soul had vacated his body. She'd have to get rid of the couch now. Every time she looked at it, she'd remember him sitting there, his cold, dead eyes locked with malevolent intent on her face.

She set the cat carrier on her dining table and headed to the kitchen. The duct tape was right where she remembered it. By the time she'd finished wrapping the plastic carrier with tape, only the vents and parts of the gate showed, and low, seething growls were vibrating in the air surrounding the crate.

Tag's captive was sitting on the couch next to Trammel's. She dropped the vibrating, growling kennel in front of the pair.

Tram glanced over, his gaze stopping dead when it reached her arms. His eyebrows shot up. "What the hell happened to you?"

She considered blaming the marks on her would-be-assailants, but most of the scratches were scabs now. They'd still be bloody and raw if her unwelcome visitors had caused the damage.

Luckily, Tag presented the perfect distraction.

"They aren't talking." Tag's voice rose in competition with the growling coming from the crate. "And we don't have time for a proper interrogation. You'll have to handle that yourself. Ryker's second string will take charge of these bozos while we haul ass to meet up with you. Our priority is getting Demi out before more of the clown brigade shows up." He tilted his head and listened. "Yeah. She's right here." Tag turned to Demi and handed her his phone. "It's Aiden."

"Demi?"

Aiden's voice was barely audible above Trident's growling, and the sound of claws digging into plastic and rattling metal. Cupping her hand over her left ear allowed her to hear him better, but not by much. Turning, she headed back down the hallway toward her bedroom.

"You did great, baby. Really great."

The affirmation barely made a dent in the thick woolliness clogging her mind. She didn't feel like she'd done great. But then, she didn't feel much of anything. That weird mental fog was still blunting her thoughts.

Aiden's voice roughened. "Did they hurt you?"

"No." She forced the word out of her thick throat, which seemed to loosen her speech enough to free more words. "I distracted them, like you asked. And then Tag and Tram came."

Slipping into her bedroom, she closed the door behind her. The cat's ruckus and male voices from the living room all but disappeared.

"Thank Christ," Aiden murmured.

She thought his voice shook a bit. But probably not. Aiden wasn't the kind of man who showed emotion. No doubt the perceived tremor came from a disconnect between her brain and ears.

A shaft of anger pierced her numbness. Was it so hard for him to show he cared about her? That he was relieved she was safe and unharmed. That she meant more to him than an occasional fuck.

"What happens now, Aiden?" The question emerged sharper than she'd intended. "Now that you have your bad guys, can I return to my life?"

A long pause rocked the line. Aiden finally responded in an utterly flat voice. "No. You still aren't safe. The two Tag and Tram have in custody are guns for hire. The bastard who hired them is still out there. He's willing to kill to get what he wants. And he wants me. He obviously knows we're connected. The two bastards who came after you prove that. I don't know when we'll have the threat contained. But until we locate the asshole behind all this, you need to vanish."

"Okay." Her voice was resigned.

She wasn't stupid. Like it or not, Aiden was right. She wasn't safe on her own. The two men sitting on her couch proved it. They would have kidnapped her without Tag and Tram's intervention. She didn't like to think about that, to think about what they'd have done to her once they had her under their control.

Muscle Man's blank, dead eyes flashed through her mind, and she knew, without a doubt, she'd wouldn't have survived the kidnapping.

Chapter Nineteen

Day 7
San Bernardino, California

Three hours after following Tag and Tram out the back entrance of her condo complex and stowing Trident's carrier in the cargo area of Trammel's SUV, Demi and her cat arrived in San Bernardino. The trip to the rendezvous point should have taken two hours. Would have, if things had gone smoother on the feline front.

She'd directed Tram to the animal clinic, where she'd wasted fifteen minutes begging the clinic staff to take Trident. The receptionist and veterinarian refused, claiming they had neither the time, nor the space, to care for Trident for an extended period. She offered to prepay. She offered twice their daily fee. She would have offered a kidney if she thought it would have helped. Their refusal, she was certain, had more to do with the hissy fit spewing from Trident's carrier, rather than the lack of a definitive pickup date. Either way, the clinic's refusal meant his noisy majesty would have to accompany her on this unexpected trip.

Aiden would not be pleased.

Even less pleased than her two stoic rescuers, who'd spent the past two hours listening to Trident's howling, growling, hissing, and cage rattling. Hell's bells, the furry little demon had some lungs on him, and enough energy to flood the SUV with a near constant cacophony of his displeasure. It didn't help that they'd gotten stuck behind road work for thirty minutes and then fell victim to slow traffic syndrome. From the periodic forehead massages, not to mention the wincing, she suspected the men up front had horrendous headaches. So did she.

"We're here," Tram said during a momentary lull in Trident's hysterics. His white fingers tightened around the steering wheel. "Thank Christ."

Demi silently echoed his thankfulness, relieved that her chauffeur hadn't pulled over and ended Trident's histrionics with a well-placed bullet.

The airfield was surrounded by a chain-link fence topped with razor wire. Tag drove through the open gate. The runway was cracked and discolored, while the grass surrounding it was stringy and yellow. Clusters of rusted metal buildings followed the fence line. A white jet squatted in the middle of the runway, sunlight bouncing off its gleaming white paint.

Accompanied by the ping of kicked-up gravel, Trammel's SUV closed on the plane. The four men huddled next to the plane's lowered staircase straightened. As the SUV slowed and then stopped, one man stepped away from the group.

Aiden. She recognized him instantly. Six-plus feet of lean, sculpted sexiness. Broad shoulders that went on forever. A muscled, impressive chest. Flat abs and trim hips. Short, black hair gleaming beneath the late afternoon sun. He closed on the SUV with a powerful, fluid stride. Her breath caught as she watched him come. Lord, she could watch this man move all day, and bask in his power and strength.

Why was she breaking up with him again? It was hard to remember when the epitome of sexiness was headed her way. And then he was there, yanking open the passenger door and pulling her into his hard, muscular arms.

"Fuck, babe, it's good to see you," he whispered, his hot breath stirring the hair at her temple.

His arms tightened around her waist, sealing her against his chest. For the longest time, he simply held her, his embrace rigid and intense. Comforting.

You're breaking up with him, remember? This warmth will vanish once he leaves again. You'll be left with emptiness and anger and endless days to fill.

But the warning was lost within his arms, when he was embracing her like he never wanted to let her go, when his heart was a steady, comforting *thump* against her ear. Even the press of his gun, which was holstered just beneath his armpit, did nothing to quell the contentment. He pulled away to press a gentle kiss to her forehead. And then his mouth found hers. The kiss was tender rather than hungry. A gentle stroke against her lips, a caress brimming with relief, with the promise he'd keep her safe...that everything was going to be okay.

His gentleness, the sense of being protected...treasured...loved...melted every atom in her body. Her bones and muscles liquified. She relaxed into him. With a deep, guttural sigh, his arms tightened around her. The kiss deepened. Their tongues came out to play—teasing and stroking. His hands spread out, caressing her back, and then massaging her shoulders, before skimming down her arms.

That's when he froze, and then pushed her away.

"What. The. Fuck?" Just like that, the tenderness was gone, replaced by a deadly growl.

Her eyes opened to his thunderous glare. His gaze was locked on her scabby arms. A thunderstorm gathered over his chiseled face. Lightning flashed in his black eyes. His index finger lightly traced one of the scabby furrows crisscrossing her right arm.

"The cat? It did this to you?" Jerking his hand back, he shoved tense fingers through his thick black hair, leaving it tousled and sexy, and turned to glare at the back of Trammel's SUV.

Uh oh. She took a step back and cautiously glanced behind her, where enraged rumbling rose from the open cargo area. She winced. Demi thrust her body between Aiden—who radiated lethal intention—and the duct-taped kennel Tram was carrying around the corner of the SUV. She stopped in front of her soon-to-be-ex and braced a firm palm against his hard chest.

"You can't kill my cat." She paused as the ridiculous order hit the air. Of course he wouldn't kill Trident over some stupid scratches. Aiden wasn't unreasonable.

"Watch me." The response was clipped and flat.

Okay, maybe he wasn't as reasonable as she'd assumed.

She pushed harder against his chest. "I know you're upset about the scratches, but they aren't as bad as they look." He snorted and stepped to the side. She moved to block him. "If you're that worried about them, I'll ask Kait to heal them."

Not that she had any intention of following through on that promise. Hell, he probably hadn't even heard the comment over the noisy theatrics coming from Trident's crate. A solid thump hit the ground behind her. She turned in time to find Tram straightening and the kennel rocking and rolling before finally tipping over. She winced as the possessed howls coming from the duct-taped, plastic carrier climbed even higher.

Her hand still pressed hard against his chest; she turned back to Aiden. "Yes, he's loud. And yes, he scratched me." Bit her, too, but she left that out. "He's scared and hurting and not accustomed to people. He needs understanding and kindness—not threats."

He took a deep breath. Held it. Let it out gradually. Slowly, the muscles against her palm softened. "What the hell's that cat doing here, anyway? Tag said you were taking him to his vet."

Demi shrugged and eyed him cautiously. "They couldn't take him."

He scoffed beneath his breath. "Wouldn't take him is more like it. He's not getting on the plane." His tone hardened. "He will not hurt you again."

She stiffened and backed up several steps, her hand returning to her side. "I'm responsible for him. Where I go, he goes."

"Tram can take him back to Coronado and drop him off at an animal shelter." Aiden's voice was adamant.

"Absolutely not." Demi's voice rose, the vet's comment about special needs cats and the high risk of euthanasia still fresh in her mind. "A shelter would kill him. He needs help, Aiden, not a death sentence."

Aiden split his glare between the kennel and her scabby arms. "For Christ's sake, Demi, look what that asshole has already done to you. Cat claws are full of bacteria. You're risking an infection."

Her annoyance melted. His anger on her behalf, as well as his concern for her health, was kind of sweet. But she still wasn't abandoning Trident. "He's hurt and scared. I'm not ditching him."

"Then we have a problem." Aiden crossed his arms over his broad chest, his face implacable. "Because that kennel is not joining us on the plane."

"Fine. Then I won't be either." Her smile was full of teeth and snark. She turned to Tram. "Would you take me to the nearest car rental agency?"

"For Christ's sake, Demi." Frustration flashed across Aiden's face. "That damn cat isn't worth your life."

Before Demi could respond to that nonsensical argument, a minivan came flying through the gate. Aiden pivoted. In one smooth movement, he pulled his gun and stepped in front of her.

Tram pivoted as well, assessing the oncoming vehicle. "They're friendly." He glanced at Aiden. "Hotch's team. They're bringing the bastards who were after your girl. You wanted to..." he glanced at Demi "...chat with them." He paused, arching an eyebrow. "Remember?"

With a tight grunt, Aiden reholstered his gun.

The van stopped next to the SUV. She recognized the three men who climbed out as the same men who'd stormed her condo and taken charge of her would be assailants. There hadn't been time for introductions, since Tag had hustled her out the door and down to the street as soon as his backup had arrived.

"Hotch." Aiden offered a single nod of acknowledgement as a blond guy, with thinning hair and no neck, swaggered toward them.

"Winchester." Hotch nodded back. Halting, he planted his feet and braced his palms on his hips. "Nice." He stared at the jet. "You've traded up." After a moment of silent contemplation, he jerked a thumb toward the van. "Hope you get what you need from those bozos. They wouldn't confide in us." Grimness tightened his voice. "Do us a solid and make the bastards pay for what they did to your crew. They were our brothers too."

A muscle twitched in Aiden's cheek, but he simply nodded and turned toward the men watching from beside the plane. Cosky and the others must have hung back to give her and Aiden some privacy.

"Cos, Zane, Rawls, you want to give these boys a hand with our guests?" As the men he summoned headed toward them, Aiden turned back to her. "Our conversation isn't finished," he grated out before striding over to the van.

"Demi," Cosky held her gaze. "Kait's gathering everything you'll need for the next few weeks." He paused, his gaze dropping to the duct taped kennel. "Including cat supplies."

"Don't mind Aiden," Rawls added as he followed Cosky to the van. "Dude's had a tryin' week."

She recognized all three of the men who passed her. They'd been caught in the craziness three years ago when that strange, homeless lady had tried to kill Cosky...repeatedly...in front of Demi's coffee cart.

"*Our conversation isn't over*, my ass," Demi muttered beneath her breath as she grabbed the handle of the cat carrier.

"Let me get that for you." The voice behind her was deep, with a rough edge, as though it wasn't used often.

She turned and found herself staring into metallic green eyes. The guy was huge and ripped, with a couple days of golden scruff softening his hard jaw. Her gaze dropped to the mountain lion tattoo snarling from his muscled bicep. She'd seen him waiting alongside the plane when the SUV had arrived, although he hadn't been in that loose huddle surrounding Aiden.

"And you are?" Demi asked warily, raising her voice to be heard above the growling at her feet.

"Name's O'Neill." He reached for the handle of the crate. Demi pushed his hand away. He straightened and studied her eyes, then ran a palm down his stubbled face. "I won't hurt him."

"No? Then what are you planning to do with him?"

A slow smirk spread across his face. "Sneak him on the jet while they're distracted."

"Why would you do that?"

He shrugged, casually scratching the corner of his jaw. "To screw with them? Because I like cats?" He shrugged again. "Take your pick. If you want him on board, we need to move. Time's running out."

Demi turned to check on Aiden. The van doors were still open, and he was leaning across the back seat, fighting to drag Stick Man out. O'Neill was right. Her soon-to-be-ex was completely focused on his captive.

"Okay. Let's go." She bent to grab the handle on the top of the crate, but O'Neill reached it first.

"I've got him." He bent toward the kennel and said something she couldn't hear.

The cat's growling stopped mid-snarl.

While Demi was processing the timing of Trident's sudden blessed silence, O'Neill hefted the crate and headed for the plane's ramp in a ground-covering lope.

Chapter Twenty

Day 7
San Bernardino, California

Demi took a step toward the plane, only to remember Trident's medication. She'd stuffed the two plastic bottles into her purse just before Tag rushed her out of her condo. Tram's SUV was parked next to her, its passenger door still open, her purse in plain sight. Three long steps later, she reached into the back seat and grabbed her bag.

By the time she turned to follow O'Neill, he was already charging up the jet's staircase. The steel steps clanged and shook beneath each fall of his boots. She followed him up the stairs, pausing at the top to look behind her. Aiden and Cosky were halfway to the plane with Stick Man. They'd each wedged a shoulder beneath her would-be kidnapper's armpits and were half-dragging, half-carrying him across the gravel lot. Little puffs of dust stirred beneath their boots. Aiden's head rose, his gaze catching hers. She was too far away and at the wrong angle to see the expression in his eyes, but his face looked the opposite of friendly.

She jerked her chin up and squared her shoulders, holding his intense gaze. It was his fault she couldn't care for Trident from the comfort of her own home. So, he could suck it up and let the cat on board. She held eye contact until he scowled. Certain he'd received her mental screw you, she turned and sauntered into the jet.

She paused at the mouth of the cabin to appreciate the view. The interior of the airplane was the personification of luxury. Rows of oversized, cream-colored leather chairs, the upholstery soft as butter beneath her fingertips. Plush carpet the color of a robin's egg cradled her sneakers. The walls shimmered with a pearl sheen. Even the air smelled expensive—fresh and floral.

O'Neill had seated himself at the back of the plane. But from her position, she didn't see the cat's carrier. At least until she reached the last two seats and found he'd tucked the crate next to his chair against the wall.

"How's Trident?" She dropped into the seat across from him.

She bent to look inside the crate. The cat was curled in a tight ball at the back. No growling, howling or rocking and rolling. The duct-taped plastic looked bizarre now that the cat wasn't trying to rip the kennel apart.

"Trident?" O'Neill scoffed. "What kind of pussy name is that?" He lifted the kennel until the grated gate was directly in front of his face. "Is that what has you so cranky? You're pissed because the chosen one named you after the symbol of dirty, nasty squids? Can't say I blame you, buddy. Not one bit."

Demi's mouth fell open in surprise. The shock quickly morphed to pissed. "Excuse me! The chosen one? A dirty, nasty squid?" Her voice turned shrill. "I didn't choose any of this. And I don't appreciate being called a squid."

Let alone a dirty, nasty one.

O'Neill's head snapped up. Startled green eyes collided with hers. "I wasn't referring to you."

"No?" Demi frowned, studying his face. With his eyes so wide and horrified, he looked almost comically contrite. "Then who?"

"Aiden." He said the name with a pucker to his lips, as though it left a foul taste in his mouth.

"You call Aiden a dirty, nasty squid?" Her lips twitched.

He shrugged. "Not just him. All SEALs."

Ah. There was obvious rivalry there.

With a tired sigh, she leaned back. "Aiden didn't name him, I did. I haven't had him long and hadn't settled on a name when those two assholes pounded on my door."

O'Neill frowned over that as he settled the crate between his knees again. "How did he end up with Trident?"

"I needed a distraction to keep the assholes occupied until Tag arrived." Demi offered a wry smile. "I chose the cat, pretended he was Aiden's beloved pet. And, well...Trident seemed like something a SEAL would name his pet."

Muffled footsteps and voices at the front of the plane caught her attention. Aiden and Cosky appeared at the head of the cabin with Stick Man. They dragged him to the first chair and forced him down.

A sneer spread across O'Neill's face at her explanation. "You chose well. That's exactly the kind of ridiculous name a special operator would name their pet."

Okay. That wasn't sarcastic at all.

She glanced toward the head of the plane. Aiden was scowling—no surprise—at either her or O'Neill. Probably both. He took a step in her direction, only to stop short as Cosky's hand descended on his forearm.

"He needs a more appropriate name." O'Neill lifted the kennel from his lap and carefully swung it to the left, setting it down beside his chair again. "Something that doesn't conjure up candy-assed wannabe warriors."

Demi's lips twitched. Unlike Aiden and his three friends on board, O'Neill had *obviously* never been a SEAL. She could just imagine the amount of razzing that went on between the five men. Military dudes were notorious for hazing members of other commands. Although, she hadn't realized such intense animosity existed between them.

A horrendous clanging—much like the noise that had accompanied O'Neill and Trident up the jet's staircase—came from the front of the plane. Zane and Rawls staggered into the cabin with a writhing, struggling Muscle Man. When the fake priest tangled his legs with Rawls, tripping him, Zane hauled back his arm and drove his fist into their captive's face. Muscle Man went limp.

Seriously, hadn't anyone explained to the asshole that smart people picked their battles? Trying to free himself when he was bound by his ankles and wrists, surrounded by a horde of SEALs and stuck on a plane didn't seem particularly bright. Rawls and Zane shoved their captive into the chair in front of Stick Man and buckled him into place.

O'Neill had laid his head back and closed his eyes, the picture of relaxed insolence. Mimicking his vibe, she leaned back, too, sighing as her butter-soft chair's upholstery accepted her weight, cradling her exhausted body like a fluffy, yet supportive cloud.

Oh, my...

Before long, curiosity infiltrated the contentment. Trident was oddly silent. Had he died in there, suffered a heart attack after all his caterwauling and cage rattling? Demi leaned over, tugging the front of the crate toward her so she could check on him. A brilliant green eye glared back at her and a low, rumbling growl vibrated through the crate.

"None of that," O'Neill muttered without opening his eyes.

The growling stopped in mid rumble.

Huh. She straightened, her eyebrows rising. "What are you, the cat whisperer?"

With a heavy, put-upon sigh, O'Neill opened his eyes, which were green and bore a remarkable resemblance to the single eye glaring at her from Trident's cage. What a weird coincidence.

"Cat's like me." O'Neill shrugged.

Demi digested that before asking tentatively. "When we land, could you help me give him his medicine? He missed his morning dose. He can't afford to miss his evening one, too."

O'Neill tilted his head, looking down at the travel carrier. "What meds?" He paused before looking up. "What's wrong with him, anyway?"

Demi leaned back, sinking deeper into the cloud surrounding her. Lord, this was the most comfortable chair in the history of comfortable chairs. "He was hit by a car. The vet had to remove his back leg, tail, and eye. He's on an antibiotic and anti-inflammatory. But he's feral and hates people, which makes it hard to get him to take his medication."

O'Neill's thoughtful gaze shifted to her arms and lingered. A hint of softness touched his face. "That's where you got the scratches? From trying to give him his meds?"

Demi froze, considering the man across from her with caution. O'Neill was the best option she had for getting the meds into Trident. She couldn't afford to scare him away.

His narrowed gaze lingered on her face. He scoffed softly. "Relax. Once the Citation's in the air, I'll take him back to the head, lock us inside, and get the meds into him."

Unless the jet's bathroom was bigger than a normal airliner, there wouldn't be room for him, her, and the crate. "There won't be room for—"

"You're not invited to this party." The curve to his lips took the sting from the comment. "One more set of scratches on your arms and Aiden's gonna drop kick this old warrior out the emergency exit."

Demi wasn't sure whether the old warrior O'Neill referred to was himself or Trident. Guilt stirred. Her seatmate had no idea what he was getting himself into. "He's difficult to handle—"

"Like I said," he held her gaze, "cats like me. He'll take his meds. No problem." But then disgust crossed his face and his lips twisted. "Now, if he was a bird, we'd have a situation."

Confused, she shook her head. What did birds have to do with anything? "What do you mean?"

"Birds hate my guts." He shrugged, as though it was no big deal.

But judging by the tightness around his eyes and the furrow above his eyebrows, the avian reaction did bother him.

Weird.

But what was even weirder was how he twisted in his seat and glanced toward the front of the plane. When he turned back to her, his mouth was a thin line and frustration lit his green eyes.

Weird. Weird. Weird.

With another unconvincing shrug, he sprawled back in his seat. "Yeah, our feathered friends hate my guts."

Had she heard regret in his voice? No, that couldn't be right. Why would anyone feel regretful that birds didn't like them? Seriously, why would that even matter?

She had to be reading him wrong. Except she was almost certain she wasn't.

Chapter Twenty-One

Day 7
San Bernardino, California

"You keep grinding your teeth like that and you'll be bunking with the base dentist." Cosky shot him a derisive look from his seat across the aisle. "Trust me, O'Neill's not putting the moves on Demi."

Aiden's jaw tightened, not because of O'Neill. Even if the asshole was hitting on Demi, she wouldn't reciprocate. Not in front of him. Nor would she troll for a new dude so soon after their breakup. He forced himself to relax. Besides, that kiss they'd shared earlier had been too intense, too emotional. She wouldn't have kissed him like that if she really planned on going through with this breakup.

The teeth grinding and tension had nothing to do with O'Neill and everything to do with Demi—with the way she was ignoring him. Would it kill her to acknowledge his existence? But this wasn't the time or place to hash out their relationship. Not with an audience of assholes clustered around him who were sure to rate his reconciliation attempt in the negative and follow that up with a bombardment of unhelpful advice.

The view from his window changed as the plane rolled down the runway. Metal sheds gave way to crisp, yellow grass, then chain link fencing, and finally the rounded tips of Ponderosa Pines as the plane took to the sky.

Although he couldn't hear its demonic yowling, he knew the damn cat was on board. The duct-taped kennel had vanished when he'd dragged his captive from Hotch's van to the jet. No doubt O'Neill had facilitated the cat's boarding. It was exactly the kind of dick move the asshole would make. Aiden's argument with Demi had gotten loud. Everyone knew he didn't want the damn cat on board, didn't want it near Demi. So, of course, O'Neill—the bastard—would gleefully lug the creature on board and hide it at the back of the plane.

He rolled his shoulders to soothe the building ache in his muscles. Once Demi calmed down, she'd realize he'd simply been worried about her. Another shoulder roll was followed by a deep breath. He shifted his frustration from Demi to the long-faced, zip-tied asshole strapped to the chair in front of him.

AKA—the bastard who'd gone after his woman. Big, *BIG* mistake.

Tag and Tram hadn't interrogated the asshole back at the condo. Their priority had been getting Demi to safety. Hotch and his team, however, had been blessed with more time and lethal rage. They'd crewed with Squirrel and Lurch in the past, considered them brothers. They'd wanted answers, wanted to know who'd set up that Karaveht clusterfuck. Aiden understood their rage and their need for answers. He shared both.

The asshole across from him was showing the facial bruising and swelling of fist persuasion. Puffy, pinkish red around the eyes. The bulbous swelling, redness, and faint traces of blood from a recently broken nose. A split lip. The injuries were fresh, mere hours old. They would turn colorful and dramatic over the following days.

Hotch's team hadn't gotten even one answer to their many questions. Aiden still didn't know who'd hired them, or where they'd planned on taking Demi, or who was behind the slaughter at Karaveht and the massacre of his team.

His calculating gaze shifted back to the bastard in front of him. Fists hadn't worked, but they had other options available to them. Drugs would drag every bit of info out of them. According to Cosky, Shadow Mountain had developed the kind of kickass interrogation drugs that ripped information from unwilling minds.

The asshole wouldn't be holding onto his secrets much longer.

He made a show of studying the dude's clothes—the officer whites with the rinky-dink trident pinned to the lapel. The medals and ribbons on display outed him as a fake to anyone who knew what they were looking at.

"Where did you get your costume? Toys "R" Us?" He crossed his arms and stared at the bastard's decorated chest. Some of the red on those ribbons and metals were splotches of blood.

The asshole shrugged, then laid his head back and closed his eyes.

"Good call," Aiden taunted. "Rest up. We've got painful plans for you."

"Keep dreaming," the killer in the priest costume gloated from the row ahead. "You'll get nothing from us."

Aiden scoffed loudly. "Trust me, you'll sing like a canary during mating season."

These bastards must know who hired them. He could work his way to the bot bomb's mastermind from there. It wouldn't surprise him if the name they spilled was Grigory Kuznetsov. The Russian arms dealer had to be involved somehow.

O'Neill stood, carrying the cat carrier by its handle, and stepped into the aisle. Aiden ignored the movement until Demi followed him up and out. They headed toward the back of the plane.

What the hell were they up to? Curious, Aiden unclipped his seatbelt and rose to his feet.

"Try not to be an ass." Cosky's unsolicited advice followed Aiden down the aisle.

He shot his brother-in-law the middle finger over his shoulder. By the time he reached the pair at the back of the plane, O'Neill had set the crate down in front of the john.

"Are you sure?" Demi's face was lined with concern. "He's calm now, but he can be a handful. Once you cut the duct tape from the door, there will be nothing to stop him from attacking. Maybe we should wait—" She stopped talking as soon as O'Neill shook his head.

"Look." O'Neill opened the john's door. "There's plenty of room for me and the crate. Once I close the door, he'll be trapped. If I get his morning doses into him now, he'll only be a couple of hours late, instead of a whole dose late." He turned back to Demi and held out his hand. "His meds?" The bastard looked right at Aiden but didn't acknowledge him.

"The dosage is on each bottle." Demi pulled two small plastic bottles—one white and one light blue—from her pocket and pressed them into O'Neill's hands.

It didn't take military intelligence to piece together what was going on. O'Neill had taken over the cat's care. Perfect. The bastard's tanned arms would look just fine with bloody ribbons of skin hanging off them.

O'Neill lifted the kennel and shuffled forward, setting it on the toilet lid. The door shut behind him with a forceful click. Demi eased forward, her head—with its spiky aqua hair—tilted. Her forehead scrunched.

She was so damn cute. He rubbed at the ache spreading through his chest.

"You know I wouldn't have hurt your cat, right?" And then, just in case she hadn't connected the dots. "I was concerned, that's all. Cat claws are full of bacteria...infection. Hell, dozens of people die from infections brought on by cat scratches every year."

He pulled the number out of thin air and offered her a coaxing smile. She turned, nailing him with a glance he couldn't interpret.

"Dozens, huh?" She scoffed, then turned back to the door, this time leaning in slightly.

At least she hadn't told him to go to hell. That was progress, right? "What are you listening for?"

This time, she didn't look at him. "Growling."

He cocked his head. "From O'Neill or the cat?"

"Either. Or." She finally pulled back from the door, but the worry never left her face. "It's just...weird. To give Trident his medicine, O'Neill will have to take him out of the carrier and pry his mouth open." She grimaced, absently skimming her right fingers down the scratches on her left arm. "Trident makes it very clear—with a lot of noise—that he doesn't appreciate being handled. But I don't hear any growling. There should be lots of growling by now." She glanced at Aiden. "Do you hear anything?"

Aiden gave it a good listen. "Nope. Nothing."

Demi nodded, confusion joining the anxiety on her face. "Which is just...weird. O'Neill says cats like him, but we're talking about Trident, and that cat doesn't like *anyone.*"

Trident? That was the third time she'd called the cat that. "You named him Trident?"

Her shoulders jerked and then her spine snapped straight, but she didn't look at him. "Yes, I did." Her tone chilled. "You have a problem with that?"

He backed up a step, his eyebrows rising. "Not at all. I'm just...surprised."

If Demi hated his career as much as Kait said, why would she name her cat after the SEAL symbol of honor, courage, and commitment? Maybe she didn't detest his career as much as Kait thought.

"Yeah?" She finally glanced at him.

The skin above her nose wrinkled. He recognized the scrunch. It meant her mind was wandering. He wanted to lean in and kiss the crinkle. But such intimacy might not be welcome now. Fuck—everything was so off-kilter. So damn awkward.

"O'Neill hates the name," Demi said absently, the faintest trace of a curve to her lips. "He said it's a candy-assed, pussy name."

Aiden stiffened. *Candy-assed? Pussy?*

"Trident's a fine name," Aiden snapped. "O'Neill doesn't know what he's talking about."

Besides, it was Demi's cat. She could name it what she wanted. If O'Neill thought otherwise, Aiden would be sure to disabuse him of that misconception.

Day 7
Somewhere in the sky

When O'Neill finally opened the bathroom door and slipped into the hall next to Demi, he didn't have a mark on him. No scratches. No bites. No blood. No shredded skin. Bemused, Demi looked from O'Neill to the kennel sitting on the toilet seat. The door to the crate was closed, but the duct tape securing it had been sliced. She squatted to get a better look inside the carrier, which was just sitting there...silently. Trident was a fluffy orange ball curled at the back. His glowing green eye locked on her face. He didn't growl, but his lips curled back, exposing needle-sharp teeth.

She rose, doubt stirring. Had O'Neill actually taken the cat out of the carrier? There was no proof he'd given Trident his meds. At least none of the evidence she was used to seeing. Like scratches and blood, or smears of white liquid on clothing and skin. When he handed the plastic bottles to her, she surreptitiously weighed each against her memory. Were they lighter? She couldn't tell.

"Did he take the full doses?" She tried to keep the suspicion out of her voice. It wasn't the end of the world if he was lying about getting the meds into Trident. Worse case, the cat would miss a dose. She'd make sure he got his next one.

"Like a good little soldier." O'Neill looked far too self-satisfied. "He drank some water, too. He won't cause you any more problems."

"I heard no growling." She made a production of scanning his arms. "I don't see blood."

With a shrug, O'Neill reached for the kennel's handle. "He likes me."

As he turned, holding the kennel out in front of him, she got another look inside the carrier. This time, Trident's head was curled into his flank.

"He's sleeping!" Shock reverberated through her. "I've never seen him sleep."

O'Neill smirked, looking extremely pleased with himself. "Sleeping is a dangerous activity if you're injured, in unfamiliar territory, and don't trust the people caring for you."

Riiight. Did the dude really think that his mere presence had put Trident at such ease the cat could fall asleep in an instant? Kind of egotistical, wasn't it?

"So, he feels comfortable enough with you, after what, thirty minutes? That he can let down his guard and sleep?"

O'Neill shrugged. "Looks like it." He shrugged again. "After all, his majesty *is* sleeping."

Demi's eyebrows quirked. "His majesty?"

It was one of the less judgmental nicknames she'd given the cat, but she couldn't remember calling him that in front of O'Neill.

"He prefers that name." O'Neill's voice and face were deadpan. When he turned to face the aisle, irritation flickered in his eyes. His voice chilled. "How 'bout giving us some room?"

Demi glanced in the direction he was staring. Aiden wiped a hand down his face, his fingers lingering over his mouth like he was locking his response inside. Annoyed black eyes met irritated green ones. Neither man gave an inch. At this rate, they'd still be standing there four hours from now when the plane landed.

She turned, squeezing past O'Neill and the cat carrier. "I'm going to use the restroom. When I come out, I hope you two have moved past this juvenile impasse."

By the time she exited the bathroom, both men were sitting again. She returned to her previous seat. O'Neill was stretched back, eyes closed. All relaxed, arrogant male. It was too bad she didn't get any quivers, goosebumps, or butterflies when she looked at him. She grimaced. Sadly, Aiden was the only man who set her hormones ablaze. It was going to be hard to find someone new. She sighed and settled deeper into her chair, staring at O'Neill's closed eyes. Something told her he wasn't sleeping.

"Did Trident's wounds look okay? Was there any sign of infection?" She hadn't seen any that morning, but infection and reinjury were a constant worry. As was the fear she wasn't caring for the cat properly.

O'Neill's tawny eyebrows knit. He opened his eyes and sat forward, glancing toward the kennel with its sleeping cargo. "How long ago was his surgery?"

"Seven days. There's only three more days of the antibiotic."

She hoped there was a vet clinic where they were going. And a shopping center. Tag and Tram had rushed her out the door without letting her pack a suitcase. Fresh clothes were a priority.

A flicker of gentleness touched his hard face. "He's fine. No sign of infections. His surgical wounds are healing. Look, he's been on his own for a long time. He's used to taking care of himself. Trust me, you don't need to worry about him."

"Right." She pushed aside the worry about Trident's next dose of meds. That was something she'd worry about when she had to give them.

Apparently, he knew what she was thinking, because he shook his head slightly, his green eyes softening. "Stop worrying about him. You won't have trouble getting his medicine in him tonight. He knows you're helping him now."

He did? How?

"He hates the name you gave him, though. He wants you to change it." She laughed. "Right."

Except there was no humor on his face. Was he joking? Her smile slowly faded as his face flattened. Maybe not.

"Does he have a name in mind?" she asked, curious. What did he think the cat should be named? It had to be O'Neill objecting to the name, not the feline. The cat wouldn't care.

"Leo, Zeus, Odin, even King would work. But he likes His Majesty the best." O'Neill's voice was sincere. So was his face. There wasn't even a flicker of humor in his dark green eyes.

Seriously? He was acting like he'd held a one-on-one intimate conversation with the cat. Was he crazy or being facetious?

Still, the name didn't have to stick. She'd put no thought into it, just grabbed it because it was associated with SEAL mythos. She really should give him a different name, one that matched his personality. Besides, Trident would be a constant reminder of her poor choice of romantic partners.

She glanced down the plane, catching sight of Aiden's black hair and rugged face from behind Stick Man. Her *Dear Aiden* speech was memorized—at least when she was practicing in front of the mirror. Giving it in person, to his face, was something else entirely. Her belly was already twisting with nerves.

It was going to be a long three hours.

Chapter Twenty-Two

Day 7
Denali, Alaska

"Hey, asshole, wake up."

Something hard slammed into the side of Aiden's calf. He jolted up so fast he almost tumbled, face-first, out of his seat and into his captive's lap, which would have been humiliating times ten.

A gray, wintry landscape and misty, elongated shadows followed him into wakefulness. The murky images wavered, straining against the sunlight streaming through the open windows. His heart still pounding like a motherfucker, he blinked the images away, then rubbed his burning eyes. That damn dream again. It seemed like the hellish thing was waiting for him every time he closed his eyes.

At least he'd finally recognized why the white, twisted faces looked so familiar. With their gaping, elongated mouths and eyes, they looked like the death masks from the *Scream* movies.

"What the hell's wrong with you?" Cosky snapped from across the aisle. Annoyed eyes scanned Aiden's face. Slowly, a frown knit his forehead. "Even the rankest banana knows better than to nap while on guard duty. You're asking for a blade across the throat."

"He doesn't have a blade." Aiden's tone was indifferent, which was concerning, or should have been. But a soul thick lethargy blunted his unease.

"You have a blade." The bite left Cosky's voice, but the frown intensified. "Strapped to your ankle. Takes two seconds for your captive to grab it."

Aiden almost pointed out that his guy's arms were secured behind his back. But the excuse didn't matter, and he didn't have the energy to defend himself. He shrugged instead.

"You look like shit," Cosky said after a moment of staring. "Better hit the ER when we land."

"A good night's sleep and a couple of solid meals will fix me up." He ignored the fact he'd operated for longer stretches of time on no food or sleep and hadn't been the worse for wear.

Maybe he *should* swing by the ER and make sure those microscopic fuckers weren't taking a whack at him. Although he wasn't exhibiting any of the symptoms his brothers had shown. He checked his fingers, which were resting on his thighs. No tremors.

Turning to the window, he scanned the blue sky. "How long before we land?"

"An hour, give or take." A frown still clouded Cosky's face. "Try to stay awake."

Aiden saluted. "Aye, sir." He loaded the affirmation with sarcasm.

"Smartass." Cosky rolled his eyes before facing forward again.

An hour later, Aiden stared out the window as the Citation approached the Shadow Mountain runway. The landing was even more surreal than the lift off. The jet headed directly toward Mount Denali, only to veer hard to the east at the last possible moment. The mountain, with a vast swath of snowy cliff, greeted him before the plane dropped, touching down on a narrow runway clinging to the mountainside.

This runway was lethal. Yet according to Cosky, there had been no landing or lift off mishaps in the base's history. The fact that the Shadow Mountain pilots consistently stuck this landing, with no injuries or mangled aircraft, while clinging to the side of a fucking mountain—without hitting it—was remarkable.

Over a thousand people climbed Denali each year. Didn't any of them notice choppers or planes heading straight for the mountain, only to vanish? Granted, the meatheads climbing the slopes wouldn't see the runway. The airstrip clung to the east side of the mountain, while ninety-five percent of the climbers chose the West slope. The mountain itself stood between most of the climbers and the approaching aircraft.

But what about the five percent that climbed the other slopes, or the locals on the ground, or the tourists wandering through Denali National Park? Hell, they must see the aircraft. Didn't they wonder where the aircraft had gone? And what about radar? The Shadow Mountain aircraft must show up on radar, right? Didn't their subsequent disappearances raise questions with the local authorities?

Demi slept right through the plane's landing. A pity. He'd been looking forward to her reaction to Shadow Mountain's runway and the hydraulic lift's descent into the base hangar. Which reminded him...

"Do the lifts rotate?" He turned to Cosky as they unbuckled their seatbelts.

If the jet arrived at one end of the runway, they'd have to turn it around, so it was facing the full length of the strip for the next takeoff. There wasn't room to maneuver the plane on the runway, so the airlift must do the positioning.

"So I've been told. Though I've never seen it." Cosky stepped into the aisle and waited for Aiden to release his prisoner's seatbelt.

Aiden yanked the captive up. He'd cut the ankle ties on his guy as they approached base, to facilitate disembarkment. His prisoner seemed resigned to his fate, shuffling off the jet with subdued acceptance.

Wolf waited several feet away with a six-man security team of black-haired, hard-faced warriors. Between their tats, tactical clothing and flat, cold eyes, the six men—seven if he included his brother—emitted a badass vibe. The men took charge of the prisoners and marched them between the various aircraft to a ten-person utility cart sitting in the hangar's mouth.

"The Bell's prepped and waiting." His face impassive, Wolf turned to Cosky, handing him a plastic square the size of a baseball card. "Explain when she needs to wear it."

She? Demi was the only *she* disembarking from the plane. He leaned in for a closer look as the plastic square changed hands. Sure enough, it had Demi's name printed on it, along with a barcode. A prickle of concern stirred.

"What are you two up to?" The question was thick with hostility, far more than he'd intended. But it was too late to moderate his tone.

"I'm taking Demi back to the house. Kait's got a room ready for her." Cosky shifted to face Aiden, holding his gaze with narrow, ice-gray eyes.

Aiden set his shoulders. "Like hell you are. She's staying here. With me."

His face impassive, his gaze unreadable, Wolf shook his head. "Shadow Mountain cannot shelter her. She will do better with Kait. In The Neighborhood."

In The Neighborhood? Aiden scowled. No fucking way. She wouldn't be protected in a damned neighborhood. Demi would be safer on base, under *his* protection.

"She stays here. On base," Aiden snarled through gritted teeth. "With me."

If the bastard behind Karaveht tracked him or Demi down, the chances he could infiltrate the base were nonexistent. But penetrating a neighborhood would be easy. Aiden didn't doubt that Cosky had security at his home, but such precautions wouldn't stop the butcher of Karaveht. Judging by his bot testing operation, the bastard had the resources to hire teams of mercenaries. Cosky's neighborhood wouldn't stand a fucking chance.

"Where's your damn sense?" He stepped into Cosky's space, aggression swelling. "You shouldn't want Demi anywhere near your wife. Her mere presence puts Kait in danger, too."

Cosky froze, then methodically squared his feet and shoulders. Danger radiated from every inch of his rigid body. Ice chilled his gray eyes to crystal chips.

"Fuck you, dude. There's no way I'd *ever* leave Kait home alone with Demi, unless I was certain she was safe. Unless I was certain our home was impenetrable. Tangos have been looking for us for years, long before you showed up." Disgust replaced the icy rage. "You think Zane would leave Beth and his kids in an unsecure location? Or that Rawls would shrug off Faith's safety? We know, without doubt, that our families are safe when we're gone. Nobody can penetrate The Neighborhood's shield."

"All security systems are fallible." Folding his arms, Aiden leaned forward, refusing to back down. "Guards can be bribed. Alarms can be neutralized. You can't be certain your system is impenetrable."

"Actually, we can." Rawls ran a finger down his nose and winked. "Because *our* security system was designed by Faith, my wife, the most brilliant scientist in the history of brilliant scientists."

Aiden glanced around. Zane had joined the cluster of hard-faced and opinionated men. "Where's Demi?"

"O'Neill's taking her to the Bell. Trust us, nobody will get to her under Faith's shield," Zane said in his perennially calm voice.

He studied his former CO's unconcerned face. He'd never known Zane to ignore security concerns. Nor could he imagine the dude overlooking them now, not when it came to his wife and kids. Why were they all so certain this shield protected their families?

"What's so special about this security system you have?" He looked from former teammate to former teammate.

Rawls slapped his back and grinned, looking unnervingly proud. "Because it's a force field. Like you see on those sci-fi shows. Faith cooked it up a few years back. She re-engineered one of the NRO energy bombs into a force field, one fed by solar energy. The field envelops the entire Neighborhood. Only those with an entry chip, or—in Demi's case—a badge, can enter."

"You'll need to be chipped to enter. So will Demi, eventually," Cosky added, with an edge to his voice, like he was still pissed.

"Chipped?" Aiden grimaced. *Hell, no.*

USSOCOM had chipped most of its operators a couple years back. The chips were fancy GPS locators, which enabled leadership to pitch the technology as retrieval devices, technology that would locate missing or captured operatives. Aiden had refused to take part in the program. As had the rest of his team. Chips could be hacked, which would allow anyone to access their location at any time. Terrorists would pay top dollar for that information.

Cosky must have read his discomfort with the idea, because he scoffed. "For Christ's sake, man up. This tech didn't come from Uncle Sam. It wasn't developed to keep tabs on you. It comes from Faith, who's as wholesome as Mr. Rogers—if Mr. Rogers was a woman." His voice took on a scathing tone as he switched his glare to Wolf. "Faith's been a godsend. If she comes across any of Shadow Mountain's secrets, she passes them on to us, unlike some of the closed mouthed bastards around here."

Aiden cocked his head. "Yeah, like what?" God knew his big brother liked to hold on to his secrets.

"Like the fact this whole place is run on solar energy." Cosky shook his head, like he wasn't sure how they'd ended up down this conversational rabbit hole.

Rawls grinned, his blue eyes lazy and amused. "While my wife's a genius, she's not nearly as wholesome as Cosky believes. Mrs. Rogers, she ain't."

"How about we don't dig into your sex life, asshole?" Cosky swung his irritation toward his longtime friend.

Rawls shrugged, running a hand down his face, which did nothing to wipe away the smirk.

"I'm not the one who misidentified my Faith as wholesome." Rawls's drawl slowed to a languid crawl. He turned to Aiden. "Point is, Demi will be safe in The Neighborhood. As safe as she would be tucked inside the mountain. Accept that and mosey along."

Not so fast. It was Demi's life on the line. "How does this—" *what had they called it?* "—force field work? Do unauthorized visitors..." he paused, frowning. "Bounce off it?"

"No bouncin'." Rawls shrugged, his blond hair glinting beneath the hanger lights. "Faith calls it a holographic shield. She tried to explain the mechanics a time or two, but hell—I'm no scientist. Somethin' about particle beams and heavy matter tunnels through holo-programs or some shit." He rubbed a hand down his face and looked confused. "It's pretty remarkable, though. If you try to cross the barrier without a chip or a badge, it sends you somewhere else."

Aiden just stared at him. *What the hell did that mean?* "Where does it send you?"

Zane squinted, like the conversation was giving him a headache. "Don't ask me how it works. But somehow Faith's technology ejects you from the opposite end of the shield from where you tried to enter."

Cosky nodded, with a half grimace/half wincing twist to his face. "It's the craziest thing. You don't see any houses or people or cars. You don't even realize you've gone through...anything. The forest looks the same. You're surrounded by trees, shrubs, even birds. It feels and looks like you've only taken a couple of steps. But then you realize you're standing a couple of klicks away."

Aiden digested that. Cosky had obviously tested the technology. At least from the ground. "What if someone tries to access it from above? By chopper or parachute?"

That weird flinching look flashed across all their faces. Except for Wolf. His brother just looked bored.

"Same thing as the ground." Zane grimaced. "No access code, no getting in. You *think* you landed in the spot you targeted. Only to realize you're a couple of klicks outside the shield. Now if you're chipped, or you have a badge, or the chopper is rigged with a passcode broadcaster—like the Bell—you slip right through the force field and land where you intended."

Aiden rubbed his eyes. This scenario was easier to believe in science fiction than in the real world. Zane's explanation sounded impossibly farfetched. He needed to test this force field himself. "What happens if someone in the chopper isn't chipped or carrying a badge?"

"Everyone who arrives in the Bell has a chip or a badge," Wolf broke in.

Aiden moved on as another question hit him. "What does it look like from outside the shield? Can you see the community? The houses? Any people?"

"Nope." Zane shook his head. "Looks like virgin forest until you pierce the shield." He sighed and rubbed his eyes. "Take my advice. Don't try to figure it out. It will just give you a headache."

Aiden weighed his options. Wolf ran the Shadow Mountain base. Unless his big bro relented and allowed Demi to stay, Aiden was shit out of luck.

He couldn't sneak Demi into his assigned quarters, not when the only way to access the base was through aircraft being lowered into the air hanger.

Resigned to the inevitable, Aiden twisted to face his big brother, who'd maintained his macho, impassive, He-Man expression through the entire confrontation. "Guess I'll need one of those badges too."

"'Fraid not," Cosky interrupted without bothering to hide his satisfaction. "Space is limited in The Neighborhood. We get no visitors, so have no need for motels."

Aiden grunted. Irritation, which hadn't completely dissipated, swiftly rose again. "Your point?"

Cosky looked skyward. "The point is, you're bunking on base."

"Not happening." Despite his annoyance, he kept his voice cool. Level. "Staying with you will give Demi and I a chance to talk."

"Fuck no, dude. We only have one spare bedroom, which Demi will be occupying. We're not gonna ask her to share it with you."

Aiden planted his fists on his hips. "Don't be an ass. You got a couch, don't you? A goddamn floor? I've sacked out on worse."

"For Christ's sake, she wants to cut you loose. Your mere presence will make it awkward for her," Cosky snapped.

His brother-in-law wasn't wrong. But how was he going to patch things up with Demi if he wasn't around to talk to her?

Rawls chuckled. Ever the peacemaker, he stepped between Aiden and Cosky. "Ignore Cos's inhospitality. You can bunk with Faith and me. We got a guest room. Even better, we're next door to this clown." He shoved Cosky's shoulder so hard the bastard staggered back a couple of steps. Rawls looked incredibly pleased with that feat of strength.

"You cannot stay in The Neighborhood," Wolf interrupted. While his dark gaze was implacable, a shimmer of sympathy lit his eyes. "You are needed on base."

Scowling, Aiden turned on Wolf. "Why?"

He couldn't afford to be stuck here, not without Demi. He needed the time and proximity to prove to her that something special still existed between them.

"You have captives to interrogate. We must identify who is behind this bot weapon and prevent the weapon's launch. I have never seen Benioko so worried." An expression close to concern touched his brother's face, as though the shaman's anxiety rattled him.

Aiden forced himself to relax. He felt like he was at war with himself. Half of him wanted to dive into the interrogation and find out who was behind the slaughter of his team. The other half wanted to rescue his relationship with Demi. Both actions were essential to him, yet irreconcilable. He couldn't do both at the same time.

"I have no intention of abandoning the interrogation or the search for answers. I'm merely making bunking arrangements for when the interrogation is complete." Sudden exhaustion crashed through Aiden, making it hard to focus.

Wolf was already shaking his head. "There is more at stake than the information Demi's attackers possess. We must have a vaccine ready in case this weapon is deployed. *You* are our only hope of a vaccine. The labs need you on base, close at hand."

Dammit.

Aiden scrubbed a palm down his face, trying to think past the tiredness. He could hardly bitch about Wolf's request. If the worst happened and the bots got loose, a vaccine was essential for the survival of humanity. If Benioko's vision came true, everyone would die...including Demi.

He needed to focus on stopping the release of the weapon, and finding a cure if they were already too late to contain the threat. Which meant he needed to be on base.

Fixing his broken relationship would have to wait.

Chapter Twenty-Three

Day 7
Denali, Alaska

Wolf commandeered one of the utility carts outside the hangar's entrance. A two-seater this time, with a pickup bed. Aiden sat in silence, nursing his suddenly pounding head as his brother navigated the dark gray warren of tunnels. The confrontation with Cosky must have over-amped him, leading to an adrenaline crash—which explained his weariness—and the jackhammer breaking his brain apart.

He'd been on base for a week now, but his time had been split between the isolation chamber and emergency room. And while this wasn't his first trip through the Shadow Mountain lair, it was his first chance to take in base specifics. When he'd first arrived, Wolf had taken him along a back route, one that avoided the populated areas, so he'd seen little of what made Shadow Mountain unique.

The hanger level was nothing more than walls and two lanes of traffic. One coming, one going, with a white line separating the two. Wolf exited onto a ramp that spiraled downward. There were four exits off the ramp, with neatly stenciled signs above each exit. Level Four simply said *Enesolo*.

Level three said N-Z. Then a level down: A-M. The last exit was simply marked *Hetazenee.*

Aiden studied the unfamiliar word before the utility vehicle passed beneath the arch. "What's the language on the signs?"

Wolf slid him a flat look which triggered Aiden's hackles.

"Kalikoia." His brother's answer was short, like Aiden should have known the answer.

Facing forward again, Aiden scowled. How the hell would he know that?

Wolf might be embedded in the Kalikoia culture, but Aiden wanted no part of it. His heritage was the one his dad had taught him, the one his dad had chosen for himself. It was SEAL culture and community. Their dad had left his tribal heritage behind, forged a new life and alternative path. He'd done so for a reason: because he wanted no part of the culture he'd grown up within. Aiden was content to follow in his father's footsteps.

The main level had all the typical base stuff. Cross walks. Blinking caution lights where tunnels intersected. Signs with arrows pointing in various directions. Still, a strong science fiction vibe permeated the base. The walls looked like some kind of strange metallic mesh, with circular embedded lights. The road beneath the vehicle's wheels was black, but with hints of iridescence. Everything looked sleek and black and futuristic.

Unlike the exits, the doors along the roadway were labeled in English and Kalikoia, which was handy. He knew where the cafeteria was now. The supply and weapons depots too. His eyebrows rose as they passed by a recreational center, followed by a cinema. This place had all the comforts of home. Opaque doors embedded into the walls periodically split in the middle, whooshing to both sides as people walked through them.

"Where did you stash our detainees?" Did Shadow Mountain even have a brig? Probably. Base jails were a staple of the industry.

"Command Central," Wolf said shortly, without looking at him.

Was he still pissed about Aiden's lack of tribal knowledge? His big bro had been trying to pull him into the whole tribal schtick for years. When would Wolf get it through his thick noggin that he wasn't interested?

Wolf kept driving. And driving. And driving. The road shifted to a plain concrete webbed with cracks. Same with the walls. The doors were hinged wood, with actual doorknobs. The vibe was chipped fatigue, rather than modern futuristic. Eventually, Wolf pulled into a parking slot in front of a recessed wood door. HQ was painted in faded white letters above the door frame. Headquarters? Seemed odd that a Native American base would use military terminology.

Aiden climbed out of the cart and followed Wolf to the door. A dark-haired dude with a long, dangling braid looked up from his desk in the center of the tight foyer. Recognition flared on his face as soon as his gaze landed on Wolf. He straightened in his desk chair.

"*Betanee.*" The guard bent his head, respect in both his tone and posture.

Wolf paused before the desk. "Benioko awaits us. Let him know we are here."

The guard inclined his head. "Of course, *Betanee.*"

There was that word again, and the guard's response sounded almost ceremonial, but Aiden didn't ask for an explanation. Wouldn't want to rile big bro again.

"Your shaman is assisting us in the interrogation?" He wouldn't have considered prisoner interviews to be included in shamanistic duties.

"He wishes to speak with us before we begin."

Aiden studied the building as they walked side-by-side down the long, gray hall. Fuck, the place was dingy. Gray on gray. The floor was thinner in the middle, like thousands of boots through the years had left their mark.

Wolf stopped in front of an open door and gestured for Aiden to enter. The room beyond reminded him of the briefing rooms he'd occupied throughout his career. The same vast table, with the same rolling chairs. Only this table was oblong, rather than rectangular, and the wood was full of carved words. Hundreds upon hundreds of Kalikoia words. He skimmed over them, suspecting they were names, although he didn't recognize any of them. Neither Cosky nor the rest of his former SEAL teammates were carved into the surface. Was that because they were still alive? If so, and these names honored dead warriors, then Shadow Mountain had a monumental safety problem.

While special operators died on the job, fatalities weren't as common as most people believed. His gaze narrowed on the surface of the table. Sure as hell not this common.

The sudden burn in his chest and tightening of his throat surprised him. Flashbacks went off like fireworks in his mind.

The grotesque winking of Grub's eye. "Don't fucking move." The lift of a rifle. Twitching fingers and eyes. "Calm down, bro." Squirrel's voice, first calm, then cold. Rifles lifting. Crack. Crack. Crack. Sprays of ruby red and dull gray streaking the snow-scuffed ground.

Shuddering, Aiden shoved the memories aside.

The burn got worse. It climbed his throat and singed his mouth, then tried to rush his mind...his memory. He took a deep breath and forced the fire back.

I'll make them pay, guys. They won't get away with what they did to you.

The promise doused the flame to an ember but kept the spark alive. He'd find out who was behind Karaveht. He'd make the bastard pay. But he wouldn't allow the rage to consume him, either. He had his own life to live, which included mending his relationship with the woman he loved.

He took a seat at the back of the table. Wolf sat in the chair beside him. His mouth watered as he caught sight of a coffee pot and stacks of Styrofoam cups on a table against the wall. Perfect. He stood up and headed to the coffee stand. A strong cup of joe would fix him right up.

Someone must have recently filled the pot, as the black gold hit his cup in steaming spurts. He returned to his chair and savored the scent of fresh coffee as he sipped. Just how he liked it...strong enough to strip paint.

Wolf stood the instant an old man shuffled into the room. He greeted the elder with a bent head and shoulders. Aiden rose as well. Ah...the great Benioko, he presumed.

"*Taounaha.*" Wolf's voice was heavy and deep, and thick with respect.

Aiden silently repeated the word. He'd heard it before, but what did it mean? The word was obviously Kalikoia, but it hadn't been the shaman's name. It must represent a tribal rank or title. Not that he intended to ask. Ever. No sense in opening himself to more of his brother's snarky looks. Aiden settled for mimicking Wolf's bent posture.

Benioko offered an absent nod, and the small leather pouch dangling from a cord around his neck swished from the right to the left.

"Sit."

The word didn't carry the abrasiveness of an order or the politeness of a suggestion. It sat somewhere in between. The old man walked around the curve of the table and pulled out a chair across from them. He settled into the thick upholstery with a grimace, like his bones and joints found the transformation from walking to sitting painful.

"Your people look for you." Benioko's faded gaze lifted to Aiden's face.

Aiden wasn't surprised. WARCOM knew he'd survived the disintegration of his team. But that was all they knew. His CO didn't know if he was alive, or captured, or holed up somewhere completely insane. No doubt his superiors were shitting their shorts, wondering what had happened to him and the bodies of his murdered teammates.

"They have many questions." Benioko's voice was phlegmy, his gaze distant.

Of course WARCOM had questions. He had questions as well. Maybe they could fill those blanks in together. He should contact his CO, update him, and get an update in return. USSOCOM—hell, the entire military—needed to know about this damn nanobot weapon.

Assuming they weren't already aware of it.

Assuming they weren't the ones who'd created it.

He needed to talk to Wolf first, though, make sure his brother was good with him reaching out to SEAL command while he was tucked away in Mount Denali. He didn't want to expose the Shadow Mountain base, or his former teammates, if there were still people looking for them after that dust up a couple of years back.

He suddenly realized that the room had fallen silent, and both men were staring at him. He raised his eyebrows. "What?"

Wolf grunted.

How the fuck had he filled that animalistic rumbling with so much displeasure?

"Well?" Aiden settled back in his chair. Damned if he was going to feel shame about his lack of attention. "That mumble didn't tell me a damn thing."

Except it wasn't Wolf who answered. With a small sigh, one that sounded worried, rather than annoyed, Benioko folded his veined hands with their translucent skin and laid them on the table.

"Soon, it begins. The *jaeetce* will sweep across the face of *Hokalita* until only the *jaee* will walk free."

Aiden understood little of what the old man said. Still, his warning sounded dire. He debated, but hell, he needed to know what the shaman was talking about.

He glanced at Wolf, bracing himself for a cutting reaction. "Translation?"

"Soon this new plague will sweep across the face of our sister earth, leaving only the infected to walk free." Surprisingly, Wolf provided the translation with minimal attitude.

The sick and infected? From what Aiden had witnessed, the infected wouldn't survive for long once they succumbed to the bots. A horrible crawling sensation crept down his spine. Benioko had just outlined the extinction of humanity.

It was hard to argue with that assessment after what had happened in Karaveht, after what had happened to his team. Although, the bots in his crew were currently inactive. Did the bots shut down after the host was dead? He suspected there was more to it than that. There must be some kind of kill switch built into the weapon. Whoever had created this bot atrocity wouldn't want it to infect their own people.

"Has anyone in your lab figured out how to turn the damn things off?" Aiden took another sip of coffee. He could sure use the caffeine hit and the mental clarity it brought. "If we can identify the bots' off switch, we can mitigate its spread. If worse comes to worst, hell, an EMP blast should fry the damn things."

Aiden turned to Benioko, but the shaman didn't look relieved by the possibility of turning the bots off and saving the world. He just looked exhausted, like his visions were draining the life, and hope, from him.

"The *woohanta* does not see the dangers in his creation," Benioko said in a thin, tired voice. "He does not see that creation empty of the Shadow Warrior's and Blue Moon Mother's *Hee-nes-ce* will grow teeth and claws and turn on him." He paused, shook his head, his expression weary. "He thinks he controls these new beings. He does not. This creation will slip its leash. He cannot stop it. He cannot call it back."

New beings? Benioko made it sound like the bots were sentient. But they were simply a collection of organic computers. And computers could be deactivated.

How did Benioko know any of this, anyway? Through visions? Dreams? Aiden's own gift was prophetic in a way. He saw into the future, but only for money. Were Benioko's visions set in stone? Did what the shaman see always come true, or could the outcomes be altered? He frowned. They must be able to alter the events in Benioko's visions, otherwise Wolf wouldn't have flown out to rescue him. Otherwise, no one would scramble for an antidote or a solution.

Not that it mattered. He wasn't about to let humanity slide into obscurity without trying to stop it.

"Are your lab rats looking into turning the bots off?" Aiden turned to Wolf. "If they have electrical components, an EMP should work on them. Maybe an MRI or CT scan for those infected."

Wolf nodded, only to then shake his head. "They try. But we have no active nanobots, so there is little to work with."

Aiden released a tense expulsion of air. "You have the bots from my teammates."

His brother shrugged. "They are not active. We have identified the components used to create them. Knowing this, there are many theories on how they replicate, how they transfer to other victims, how they affect their hosts. Yes—even how they might be turned off. But with no active bots to test on, or observe, all we have is assumptions. We were unable to reactivate even a single bot, no matter the methods used. And without active bots to experiment on, there can be no tests on turning them off." Wolf rolled his neck, looking momentarily disheartened.

Aiden digested that. "There are still the two clowns your boys took control of. Let's have a go at them. See who they point us to." He pushed himself up. "We should look into Grigory Kuznetsov, too, the arms dealer we were sent into Karaveht to find. USSOCOM spooks swore the bastard was in Karaveht. If they're right, he must have headed up the testing there."

"There is another matter." Benioko straightened and set his shoulders, an implacable mask settling over his face.

Cautiously, Aiden sank back into his chair and studied the shaman's suddenly formidable aura. Benioko had gone from frail and diminished to proud and powerful in the space of a heartbeat.

"Shadow Warrior grows weary of your deliberate *eseneee*." The shaman's hooded eyes were locked on Aiden, making it clear to whom he referred. "It is time for you to cease this foolishness and learn the Kalikoia ways. Our future, indeed, the future of all *Hokalita's* children, depends on this."

There was more to this than Aiden not knowing the tribal language. A lot more. Every muscle in his body tensed in resistance. He was not Kalikoia. He did not belong to this tribe.

"I wasn't informed that staying here and working with Shadow Mountain personnel to prevent the apocalypse hinged on submitting to your tribal ways." His voice hardened. "If so, I'll pass. I have no interest in the Kalikoia. I don't believe in your Shadow Warrior, or elder gods, or any of your tribal mythology."

Wolf stirred, then went still, his gaze on the table. But disapproval emanated from him, prickling against Aiden's ire.

A sharp crack of laughter rose from Benioko. "It matters not what you believe. Or where your interests pull you. The Shadow Warrior and elder gods have chosen you. You have no say in this."

"Fuck that," Aiden drawled.

The old shaman simply smiled. A grim smile.

One that looked like a threat.

Chapter Twenty-Four

Day 7
Denali, Alaska

As soon as the helicopter landed, Cosky shoved back the cargo door and hopped to the ground. Turning, he grabbed Trident's kennel. She couldn't tell whether the cat was making a fuss. The deafening scream of the engine and *whop whop whop* of the blades spinning overhead filled her ears. Huddled in the jacket O'Neill had handed her when they'd boarded the Bell, she exited the helicopter. Instinct kept her head and shoulders curled and her hands over her hair as she hunched her way out from beneath the blades.

The helicopter had set down in the middle of a circular driveway, one that snaked toward and then away from a rectangular house bursting with windows. The road had been plowed, but there were clumps of ice scattered about. They sparkled like diamonds beneath three triangulated overhead lamps.

Once she was far enough from the chopper blades that her hair agreed to stay on her head, she stopped to stare in wonder.

The helicopter had whisked her to a Christmas paradise. The house and its surroundings looked like something ripped from a Nicky Boehme painting. The rectangular house, with bright white light streaming through its endless windows, lit the night like a flare. Icicles and jewel-toned Christmas lights dangled from the edge of the bonnet style roof. Snow-flocked trees, wrapped in jewel bright lights glittered from every direction.

"Christmas in February," Demi breathed.

She should have expected something like this. Kait loved Christmas. And God knew Alaska was the place to go hog wild with the decorations and lights.

"Christmas 24/7, 365 days a year, if Kait has anything to do with it." Cosky set Trident's carrier down next to her and rocked back on his boots, studying his home with an indulgent expression. After a few moments, his voice turned brisk. "I texted her from the bird to let her know we were on the way. I need to talk to Zane. I'll carry the cat inside in a minute."

With that, he turned and walked back to the helicopter, the ice crackling beneath his boots.

With a soft sigh, Demi tore her gaze away from the glittering beauty of Kait's home and looked down at the cat carrier. "I'm sure you're sick of that kennel, but I'll let you out soon."

According to Cosky, Kait already had a litter box, along with Trident's vet-recommended wet and dry food on hand. When she'd heard of Trident's inclusion on the trip, Kait hadn't blinked, hadn't balked. She simply stepped up to make sure Trident was taken care of.

Behind her, the roar of the helicopter intensified as it took to the sky.

"You'll love Kait," she told the cat, before taking a deep breath of mountain air. She held it, savoring the crisp pine scent. "This trip will be good for you. The fresh air will help you heal."

The smell surrounding her—fresh air, conifer needles, and wood smoke—reminded her of her childhood, of all the weekends and vacations spent hiking and camping with her parents in the Six Rivers, Redwood, and Sequoia national parks. Her mom and dad had loved the outdoors, preferring tents to motels. They immersed themselves in various forests throughout the year. The flashes of memories brought both warmth and sorrow. Even now, sixteen years after their deaths, she still missed them.

She'd often wondered about Kait's new life. After she hooked up with Cosky, Kait's life became shrouded in secrecy. Sure, they talked almost daily, and they'd met up often for mini and lengthy vacations. But the locations where they met were always a rendezvous at a beach town, or in New York city. Never at each other's homes. She hadn't even known where Kait lived until today.

The amount of secrecy had been weird, even with Kait's explanation of what had happened to Cosky and his teammates. Would the men still have a price on their heads after three years? It seemed unlikely.

Kait mentioned during one of their phone calls that she's started creating stained glass panels and windows. Demi saw some of those creations glowing in the house's windows. Like most of Kait's art, the panels were full of vivid colors and comically drawn animals. There were dramatically colored birds with excessively long legs and necks, yet with fuzzy torsos. Raccoons with elongated hands and confused faces. A mountain lion smothered in dandelion fluff.

Fifteen years ago, they'd bonded through photography. But Kait had already been making a name for herself as a blown glass artist whose work was steeped in vibrancy and color. That love of color was visible in the crimson blankets thrown over the porch swing and the bright blue cushions on the rocking chairs to the left of the front door.

Where she didn't see Kait was in the house's color—which was dark. Very dark. Even with the light streaming through the windows, she couldn't tell what color the exterior was. Maybe charcoal. Maybe navy blue. Cosky, according to Kait, was the kind of guy who surrounded himself with dark, solid colors—on his clothes, his cars, and no doubt his houses. The exterior of their house felt like all Cosky, or maybe a compromise between the two of them.

Cosky's dark exterior, protecting Kait's sunny interior.

Compromise and the merging of tastes came with time and proximity. Kait and Cosky had been living together for three years now. They shared their lives, a bed, breakfast, and dinner. Demi's eyes drifted to the swing. An ache filled her chest. Kait's man was home for the quiet moments, for the squeak of the rocking chairs, or huddling beneath blankets on the swing. It was those quiet moments that built a life...that led to a home.

This was what she'd had with Donnie. It's what she'd wanted with Aiden.

She shook her head and swallowed hard. The lump in her throat tasted like sorrow and broken dreams.

The front door flew open, banishing the unwelcome bout of melancholy. Kait flew across the porch and down the stairs. Demi took several steps forward and then they were wrapped in each other's arms.

"I can't believe you're *finally* here!" Kait half screamed, before pulling back. She grinned and flicked Demi's bangs. "I love your hair. That bluish-green suits you."

Demi laughed. "Wait until it grows out and my normal mousy color comes through. I'll look like a mess then."

"Mousy?" Kait shook her head so hard her long, golden braid almost slapped Demi across the face. "You could never look mousy. Or a mess. You're always beautiful."

Which wasn't true. Had never been true. But that was the beauty of Kait. She truly believed what she said.

"If anyone's gorgeous, it's you." Demi pushed Kait back to scan her from head to toe. "Alaska certainly agrees with you. You're glowing."

A weird, almost hesitant look lightened Kait's brown eyes. She glanced toward Cosky.

"What's wrong?" Demi glanced behind her. Cosky and his buddies were still huddled together. Nothing seemed off back there.

When Kait turned back to her, the tentative look was gone. "Nothing. I'm just so glad Wolf's finally agreed to let you come visit."

Wolf, aka Kait's half-brother, had been the one to prevent her from visiting? Demi bristled. What had she ever done to the asshat to make him so hostile toward her?

Kait must have picked up on Demi's annoyance, because she squeezed her hand. "Don't blame him. There are still people after Marcus, and they know about me. If they knew the two of us were friends, they could follow you up here. Wolf's anal about the security around this place."

"Your brother's excuses sound more paranoid than anal."

Kait grimaced and for a moment darkness stalked her face. "Trust me, he has his reasons."

"I'm sorry." Dismayed by the shadows suddenly swimming across her friend's face, Demi caught Kait's hand and squeezed. "I shouldn't have been so dismissive about Wolf's concerns. Let's change the subject. The Christmas lights and the stained-glass panels in your windows are beautiful. They're so...you." She paused before adding quietly. "You look so happy."

Or she had, until Demi had crapped all over their reunion.

A huge smile split Kait's face and filled her eyes. "I've never been happier."

Demi believed her. Kait had always been gorgeous, but she seemed to glow now. Tall and lean, with curves that caught men's attention—even grumpy ones, like her adoring husband—she'd always stood out in a crowd. And that was before people got a look at her hair. Her long, golden, Rapunzel-esque hair. Since she usually caged her thick tresses in a braid, most people never saw the full glory. But Demi had seen it loose, and hell's bells, was it ever stunning.

But truly, the most beautiful thing about Kait was the fact she was as lovely on the inside as the outside. Not a bitchy bone in her body. She was the best friend Demi had ever had. And she'd missed her so much over the past three years. Phone calls and vacations had kept them in touch, but it didn't come close to the bond they'd shared when they'd lived in the same building.

Kait linked her arm with Demi's, then pulled back to study Demi's face. "Marcus says those horrible men didn't hurt you." She scanned Demi's body next, lingering, like she was looking for signs of hidden trauma. "But knowing my big lug of a husband, he'd whitewash what happened to prevent me from worrying. So please, tell me the truth. How *are* you?"

Demi considered the question. "Honestly? I'm fine. I wasn't hurt. They never even touched me. I distracted them by convincing them to help me get Trident into his kennel." She blew out a breath and smiled ruefully. "It was rather anticlimactic to be honest. I expected a battle, maybe a gun fight, when Tag and Tram showed up. Instead, Aiden's buddies had those guys zip-tied and on the ground in seconds. No fuss, no struggle. Not even a punch thrown."

Kait considered that, her worried expression disappearing. "That's because you distracted the bad guys. You kept them occupied so the good guys could get a jump on them. Thank God you're so levelheaded and clever." She turned, scanning the driveway until her gaze fell on the kennel. "That must be your cat. Let's get him inside and out of that crate. I'm sure he needs to use the kitty facilities."

Arms linked, they started toward the cat. With each step, Demi felt her tension ease. Being with Kait felt so normal, like they hadn't been separated by thousands of miles and new relationships.

Kait was the only close friend she had. She had Aiden, of course, but not as a friend. A lover? Sure. But friend? Not so much. She'd been friends with Donnie, as well as lovers. They'd known each other inside and out. But her relationship with Aiden was different. Superficial even. There was still so much about him she didn't know. Parts of him that were closed off—at least to her. But then there were parts of her that were closed off, too. They hadn't spent enough time together to explore all the closed off spaces between them.

She used to think that love went hand-in-hand with friendship. That you couldn't have one without the other. But her experience with Aiden proved that assumption was false.

This time, the melancholy didn't set in. Not with Kait by her side.

"Hey," Kait yelled at Cosky. "Can you tear yourself away from your boy band and make yourself useful? Maybe pretend to be a good host and carry Demi's cat into the house?" She grinned as she yelled, a huge radiant smile that almost split her face in two and proved to everyone that she adored her big lug of a husband.

As Cosky broke away from his buddies, Kait turned back to Demi.

"I put your cat's litter box and food and water dishes in the basement. It's quiet down there. Plus, there's a sofa and recliners. We can sit and chat and keep him company. Maybe once he gets to know us, it will be easier to give him his medicine."

"The basement sounds perfect." Demi bent to peer in the crate. A glowing emerald eye stared back. "Although he's been surprisingly mellow since O'Neill gave him his medicine." She straightened. "It was kind of weird, actually. Trident was in full-blown murder mittens mode until O'Neill told him to shut up. After that, he settled right down. I tell you; the man has mad cat magic."

Her face full of shock, Kait stopped dead.

"O'Neill? As in this tall dude?" Kait held her hand a couple of inches above her head. "Brown, bristly hair? Tattoos everywhere?"

"You forgot his green eyes. They're identical to Trident's." Curiosity swelled at her friend's incredulous tone. "I take it you don't like him?"

"O'Neill? That's who you're yapping about?" Cosky swooped down and lifted the cat carrier. "Trust me, the dude's an ass."

Kait waited to continue the conversation until her hubby was several steps ahead.

"I've seen him around base, but I've never spoken to him." Their arms still linked, Kait and Demi swung around and followed Cosky toward the house. "But as you see, Marcus and the rest of the clones universally detest him."

"The clones?" Demi asked in a whisper.

"Zane, Mac, and Rawls." Laughter rang in Kait's voice. "Haven't you noticed that other than hair and eye color, those three and Marcus are four peas in a pod? Tall, dangerous, and seriously ripped." She fanned her face energetically. "I may be committed to my man, but I still have eyes. They all shed that swoon-worthy sexy, alpha vibe."

Demi choked on a giggle. Holy shit, Kait had totally nailed that depiction. "You'll need to broaden the clone club to include Aiden. He definitely meets all those parameters."

"Ewww." Kait made a face. "Aiden? He doesn't spew hot, sexy vibes."

Demi sputtered out a laugh. "Maybe not to you, as you're his sister. But trust me on this, Aiden spews out that vibe with every breath he takes."

Kait heaved an exaggerated sigh. "If you say so." She glanced at Demi as Cosky disappeared inside the open door. "Have you talked to Aiden yet?" She paused before adding quietly, "Assuming you haven't changed your mind."

"I haven't changed my mind," Demi said as Kait let go of her arm and stepped through the door. If anything, she was even more certain of her decision. "But I haven't talked to him yet. There was no privacy on the plane. And I never saw him again after we landed."

Although, she was certain he'd been somewhere inside the tight knot of men talking in front of the plane. O'Neill had been the one to carry Trident's kennel to the helicopter and keep her company. Aiden had been too focused on the conversation with his friends to even notice she'd left the plane.

She knew why. Understood it even. He was on a mission to find the people who'd killed his teammates. No doubt that's what that masculine huddle had been about. Of course she would be a lesser priority. As she should be. But he could have focused on her long enough to say goodbye, long enough to make sure she was okay. His lack of effort proved she was so far down his priority list she didn't even register.

Kait reached back and tugged her through the door, and into an open, airy room with a ceiling so high, and filled with so many diamond-shaped windows, it seemed to touch the starlit sky. Awe stole her breath.

"Kait," she whispered. "This room is incredible."

With her hands planted on her hips, Kait tilted back her head to look at the diamond windows above them. Moonlight crept through the panes, while thousands of stars sparkled overhead.

"I know, right?" She sighed, her braid swaying in the air, her face dreamy and soft with love. "It was Marcus's wedding gift to me. We couldn't live outside the base at first, not with a price on the guys' heads. But I was getting depressed buried inside Denali like that. No sunlight. No moonlight. No fresh breeze or clean air. And then Faith developed her shield. Finally, we could live out in the open, protected beneath the shield. This house was a true collaboration. We designed everything together—except for the ceiling. That was all Marcus. He said he wanted to give me the sun and the moon and the stars. He designed the ceiling himself, then hired some of the base tech guys to build it. After we returned from what I thought was a romantic vacation, he unveiled his gift. He called it a late wedding present." She sniffled before offering a watery smile. "I might have cried."

"I don't blame you. It's perfect." This room, with every dia-mond-shaped window, proved how well Cosky knew Kait, how much he loved her. He'd known the perfect gift to give her. One she'd treasure forever.

Kait was a lucky woman. But then Cosky was a lucky man.

"How do you keep the snow off the roof?" Demi asked, craning her head back to get a full view.

"Through the awesome work of the Shadow Mountain engineers and mechanics. The roof is metal, and slopes on all four sides, so the snow slides off easily. Plus, they wired the entire roof for heat. It's the coolest thing. You can see the snow falling, but it doesn't cover the windows. My work shed is outside. I'll introduce you to it tomorrow." Kait glanced around the living room. "It looks like Marcus already took your cat downstairs." She walked around Demi to close the front door. "What did you say you named it? Trident? What did Aiden think of that?" Curiosity brightened her eyes as she headed back to Demi and led her across the light drenched living room.

"He didn't seem to care about the name. But he sure hates the cat." Demi followed Kait across the room and into a wide, airy hallway. Halfway down, Kait opened another door and led the way down a flight of carpeted stairs.

Kait snorted. Hands on both rails, she glanced over her shoulder. "I'm not surprised. Aiden hates cats. But to be fair, they hate him right back. Aunt Issa had a cat when we were growing up. When she moved in with us after Mom died, she brought it with her. It attacked Aiden constantly. Issa said it was because Aiden teased it. But no, Aiden avoided it. It didn't like me much, either, but it never left me bloody." She grimaced and shook her head. "Kind of left a lasting impression on him."

"Well, don't get too attached to Trident—the name, I mean. That was a spur-of-the-moment choice. I'll probably be changing it." Demi reached the last step and followed Kait into the basement, which was massive and fully furnished.

Kait had already mentioned the couch and recliner, but there was also a gigantic television stretched above a rock fireplace and a thick, rustic desk tucked in the corner. She saw Trident's kennel, the door open, at the back of the room, along with a litter box and a couple of bowls.

A toilet flushed, and a door opened in the basement's back corner. Cosky stepped out. Demi had spent enough time with the pair to recognize the gleam in his light gray eyes as he closed on them. That look hit his eyes just before he pulled Kait close for a lengthy kiss.

All righty then...

To give them some privacy, she headed toward the kennel, which was empty. She crouched, peering beneath the desk, and found an orange, fluffy ball curled against the wall. His glowing emerald eye watched her with suspicion, but he didn't growl. At least that was progress. Still, the litter box hadn't been used and the food bowl didn't look touched.

By the time she straightened and turned around, Cosky was gone and Kait was sitting on the couch.

"Marcus is throwing steaks and potatoes on the barbeque, but we have some time before the grill is ready. How's your cat?"

"He seems okay." Demi sat down beside her. "He's great with the litter box and has been using it since I brought him home." She didn't want Kait to think she was okay with the cat ruining her spotless carpet.

"That's unusual with a feral cat, isn't it? I thought they were hard to litter train."

Demi had questioned that herself. "He's either very smart, or he used to be someone's pampered pet. Anyhow, I still haven't decided on a name for him."

"Why not Trident? You never said. Is it because you don't want any reminders of SEAL stuff after you break things off with Aiden?" Kait's voice was full of understanding and sympathy.

"Partly," Demi admitted, her throat aching. "But I've also been told it's a shitty name."

Kait's eyes widened. "Who told you that?"

"O'Neill." Demi's lips twitched. "He says it's a pussy name. That a badass cat deserves a badass name, not a dirty, filthy squid name."

"What?" Kait laughed. "I bet that went over well with the four clones on board. I mean, dissing SEAL culture like that. No wonder they don't like him."

"Oh, they didn't hear him," Demi assured her. "We were at the very back of the plane. The clones were sitting in the first few seats.

Kait gave her an odd look. "You sat with O'Neill instead of Aiden?"

There was no judgement on Kait's face or in her voice. No reason for Demi to feel defensive. Yet she did.

"I didn't sit with O'Neill," she stressed. "I sat with Trident. O'Neill was sitting there too."

"Hmm." Kait made a soft humming sound. "It sounds like O'Neill was hitting on you."

Demi thought back and shook her head. "No. He really wasn't. He was concerned about the cat."

There had been no appreciative glances from him. No flirting. He hadn't even tried to goad Aiden by pretending to flirt with her.

"You're sure?"

Demi nodded emphatically. "I'm positive. There were no...vibes...from him. He helped with Trident, that's all. Even got some meds into him."

Which reminded her...

"How far is the closest vet?" While beautiful, this place was out in the middle of nowhere.

"There's one in Talkeetna, which isn't far." Kait's demeanor quieted. "Getting back to O'Neill. You know I just want you to be happy, right? Sure, I'd love to have you as my sister-in-law, but we're already sisters. That will never change, even when you move on from Aiden. If you're interested in O'Neill, I'd support you."

The lump was back in Demi's throat. But this time, it tasted like affection and trust.

"Believe me," Demi worked up a smile. "I'm not interested in O'Neill, and he's not interested in me. You're barking up the wrong tree."

Which was a shame. Because O'Neill was exactly the kind of man she wanted. He was sexy enough to join the clone club. And he was kind—at least to her and Trident. Plus, he worked with Cosky, so he was home nights, weekends and holidays. And judging by Kait's comments during previous conversations, it didn't sound like Cosky and his teammates, which included O'Neill, were sent on many dangerous missions. Kait said their lives were drama free.

Too bad O'Neill didn't curl her toes like Aiden did, or make her palms sweat. But nope, her libido had given him a hard pass, and she needed the tingles and belly flops, along with the proximity. It was the only way to build a future.

Chapter Twenty-Five

Day 10
Denali, Alaska

Frustration seethed so thickly inside Aiden, he felt like he was drowning. With a low growl, he threw himself into the chair next to Rawls. This meeting was in the same room Wolf had led him to three days earlier. He was even sitting in the same damn chair, which felt a little too déjà vu for his liking after the complete blindside Benioko had pulled on him earlier.

If he'd trusted WARCOM, if he was certain they weren't behind this clusterfuck surrounding him, he'd have left Shadow Mountain on the spot and returned to his old command. Unfortunately, that wasn't an option, not until he knew for sure who was behind that damn bot weapon, and the testing on his teammates.

In the meantime, Shadow Mountain had all the tools he needed. He just had to man up and ignore the old shaman's attempts to bully him into joining the tribal cult.

The chairs circling the enormous table were filling up fast. A white noise kind of murmur filled the space thanks to the dozens of conversations taking place between the hard-faced men loitering around the room. Most of the dialogue sounded foreign. Kalikoia, he'd bet.

His gaze landed on the coffee table and froze. Christ, he could use a cup of that steaming pick-me-up. But the string of men waiting to grab and fill their cups dissuaded him. He'd wait until the line waned and hope the pump pot still had some servings left.

The decision just kicked up the frustration.

Rawls swung his chair around until it faced Aiden and did an exaggerated double take. "From that black cloud smothering your ugly mug, I'm guessin' the interrogations ain't goin' well?"

Aiden shot his buddy a seething glare and faced forward again. He should have paid more attention to where he'd sat. The last thing he needed was Rawls's inability to keep his pie hole shut.

Unfortunately, the southern asshole had good instincts. Those two fucking clowns he'd gone to the trouble to fly up to Denali knew nothing. Absolutely nothing.

Goddammit.

A frown knit Rawls's sandy eyebrows. "Seriously? You got nothin' from them? Shadow Mountain has some of the best shit available to force hostiles to sing and dance."

"Even the best shit on the market can't make someone talk if they don't know jack shit." Aiden tried to keep the snarl at a minimum. It wasn't Rawlings's fault Demi's attackers had turned out to be disappointments.

The only contact number they'd revealed was already disconnected. According to Shadow Mountain intel, their bank accounts had vanished, leaving no transfer or deposit information to track down who'd paid them. Hell, the morons didn't know who hired them. Their rambling answers to all his questions had led to nothing.

"Shit, bro," Rawls said, sympathy slowing his drawl to a crawl. "That's fucked. Your luck's all upside down, ain't it?"

Aiden scowled back. What the hell was that supposed to mean? Was it some subtle dig about Demi? Did everyone know he was on tap for a Dear Aiden letter?

"Rumor has it you got a bounty on your pretty head." A wicked gleam lit Rawls's blue eyes. "Two million, they say." A smirk joined the gleam. "Have to admit, I'm disappointed in you, son. You're slippin'. The bounty on my noggin's five mil."

Ah...

Aiden relaxed. This wasn't about Demi. This was Rawls's batshit crazy competitiveness coming out. The dude liked to bet on the most bizarre shit.

Aiden scoffed. "*Was* on your head. You boys killed everyone who had a stake in liquidating you. And that five spot was for the whole lot of you, which means I'm worth double what you were in your prime."

Rawls reeled back, like he'd been mortally injured, only to lean forward again and peer around Aiden. "You hear that, Zane? This ass here thinks we're past our prime."

"Not Zane," Aiden drawled, filling his tone with mockery. "Just you."

Zane shook his head, then lifted his eyes to the ceiling in a *lord help me* gesture. "Rawls been running his mouth again, has he?"

"Now that's just hurtful." Rawls plastered a wounded look on his face.

After another long-suffering look at the ceiling, Zane turned to Aiden. "Cos says you got hold of Devlin Russo?"

Aiden simply nodded. Dev was the only person in a leadership role at HQ1 that he trusted. Plus, a recent promotion to commander of ST4 had given him the contacts and authority to find out what Aiden needed to know.

"He come through for you?" Zane asked, raising his voice.

The dozens of conversations had edged into a rumble, although none of the warriors surrounding them appeared to be paying the SEALs in their midst any mind.

Aiden shrugged. "Still a lot of shit he doesn't know. But it sounds like an USSOCOM-wide blackout. There's no chatter about a new weapon. No whispers of nanobots." Aiden frowned. "Hurley knows I'm alive. He's got people looking for me. But no one knows where I am." He shot Zane a wry look. "Dev says the SAT images of the exfil site above Karaveht went wonky just before you boys pulled me out."

"Imagine that." Zane's face was as bland as his voice.

The lack of SAT images didn't surprise him. Wolf had the technology to keep his base and warriors hidden.

"When the exfil chopper with the CDC team didn't find me or my crew, they headed to Karaveht," Aiden continued. "They found nothing. The town had been torched. It was still burning when the evac crew arrived."

Zane rocked back in his chair, looking thoughtful. "They found nothing?"

"Nothing," Aiden confirmed. "The entire place was rubble and ash. We hit one of the houses with a M14 on our way out, but the blast wouldn't have taken out the entire town. And get this, Dev said there were no bodies on site. There should have been remains. Charred ones, at least. But the sweep team found nothing."

Zane digested that. "Someone cleaned the site before Hurley's boys arrived."

"Looks like it." Aiden squinted thoughtfully. "One other thing. They found no water. The well and pipes were dry." He frowned and shook his head. "Even after the torching, there should have been water in the well. The CDC found the well capped and the water gone."

Rawls ran his fingers through his short blond hair, leaving it sticking up in multiple places. "Sounds like the bots were dumped in the well and distributed through the water system."

Aiden nodded.

Everyone was quiet for a moment before Zane asked. "Did your team come into contact with any of that water?"

"We did not," Aiden's voice tightened. "My crew picked up the damn things some other way."

Rawls's face darkened. For the first time, his voice sharpened. "Did Dev know about the nanobots?"

"He didn't know shit." Aiden scowled. "Hell, he didn't even believe me at first. He kept asking how I could possibly know nanobots were responsible. I told him I didn't trust that USSOCOM hadn't been behind the whole fucking thing, so I hired a lab to run Squirrel's and Grub's blood and tissue samples, and they found the bots." Which was true to an extent. "Dev was not happy I'd run to a lab." And was that ever an understatement. The dude had been livid. "He's insisting I return my crew's bodies to HQ1 so they can run their own tests." Aiden broke off with a grimace and a shake of his head. "I told him as much as I could, without exposing Shadow Mountain. At least Dev knows we're dealing with nanobots now. He knows the bots target the brain, and that they can scrape—" Aiden paused before shrugging, "elements from the human body to reproduce themselves."

"Dev's not wrong," Zane offered quietly. "Those bodies should be returned to Coronado. They're not infectious, or so the Shadow Mountain labs claim, so their families deserve to lay them to rest. Plus, with both Shadow Mountain and USSOCOM dissecting the bots, there's a better chance of understanding and countering the weapon." He frowned, studying Aiden's face. "Has Wolf said when they plan to release the bodies?"

Aiden released a tight breath and rolled his shoulders. Zane was right. His squad's families deserved closure. They deserved to know what had happened to their sons, husbands, and fathers. They deserved a casket draped in the red, white, and blue of their sacrifice. They deserved a physical location to lay down flowers.

It was too damn bad he couldn't give that to them. "Benioko won't release them from isolation. He says they're still a danger."

Zane's brows furrowed. He straightened abruptly. "Wait a sec—he claimed they weren't dangerous when we swooped in to save your ass." His frown deepened. "And the bots, are they still inactive?"

Aiden didn't understand the shaman's sudden caution, either. "That's what the lab rats say."

"Then why are they suddenly a danger?" Rawls asked.

An excellent question for which he had no answer.

With a shake of his head, he scrubbed his hands down his face, wincing at the scrape of stubble against his palms. He needed to shave before he choppered down to see Demi. Although when that would happen was anyone's guess. Flying down to The Neighborhood kept getting pushed further and further away.

"What about those new cameras you boys were modeling?" Zane asked, taking a sip from his coffee cup. "Cosky seems to think they're connected to the Karaveht clusterfuck."

"Yeah..." Aiden squinted at Zane's coffee cup and suppressed a yawn. A quick look at the coffee stand showed the line had vanished. Time to grab a cup. "The cameras were purchased from Nantz Technology. Nantz is a peripheral weapons contractor out of D.C. According to Dev, the cameras weren't meant to be tested during our op. They were supposed to undergo testing months ago, but the battery packs went missing. A new shipment of batteries coincided with our insertion, so we were stuck with them. And that drone we were sent into Karaveht to recover? It was a prototype from Nantz too."

Rawls grunted, his face hardening. "Easy enough to make batteries disappear."

True, which was why Aiden hadn't crossed Nantz off his suspect list.

He'd pushed back his chair, ready to rise to his feet and assault the coffee table, when Benioko shuffled into the room. Wolf followed. The room went quiet. Heads bowed.

Aiden sat back down, his gaze skipping from dark-haired warrior to dark-haired warrior. They all had leather cords hanging from their necks. With some, the cords were attached to small, hand sewn leather pouches resting against their BDU shirts. For others, the cords disappeared beneath their necklines, but the lumps beneath the fabric of their BDUs clearly showed where the pouches lay.

He'd noticed before that Wolf wore a pouch. Sometimes below his shirt, sometimes swinging free. Benioko had worn one, too, the day before. To his left, half a dozen spots down, O'Neill was kicked back in his chair, apparently napping.

There was no leather cord around his neck. Nor were pouches hanging off the former SEALs surrounding him. Those pouches must be a Kalikoia tribal thing. Which meant that O'Neill wasn't part of the tribe. No surprise, considering his light brown hair and green eyes.

His gaze drifted back to Wolf's pouch. What were those things? Some kind of voodoo magic?

Wrong culture, asshole.

Kalikoia culture wasn't into voodoo. Although, how the fuck would he know? He knew nothing of Kali culture. For all he knew, those pouches could carry the ashes of their dead enemies.

"Aiden." Wolf's flat voice cut through the silent room, as effective as an RPG blast at drawing every eye. "Join me."

The request froze Aiden in his chair. Did Wolf intend to ambush him with another request to join the Kalikoia tribe? Only this time in front of Shadow Mountain's top warriors? Was Aiden's inclusion in his brother's plans to stop the apocalypse pursuant on bending to Benioko's will?

"Your ears quit workin'?" Rawls asked. "Your big bro's callin' you to the head of the class."

He sure was.

The question was why?

Chapter Twenty-Six

Day 10
Denali, Alaska

The coffee line had dwindled to one warrior when Benioko turned to Wolf. "Your *javaanee* must lead this meeting.

"Aiden?" Wolf's voice rose until the name was more question than identification. Foolishness there. The Old One could be speaking of no other. Wolf had only one brother.

"*Taounaha...*" Wolf's voice trailed off.

Kali tradition called for obedience to the Shadow Warrior's mouthpiece. One who communed with the elder gods could not be wrong. Yet, tradition also called for tribal choice, and accepting the Kalikoia customs was at the heart of every tribe member's choice. Such a decision should never be forced. One offered to show the *eseneee* the ways of the *Hee'woo'nee*. But one did not force the joining.

Yet, three rotations earlier, in this very room, Benioko had done just that.

Wolf still had trouble believing it.

"Your *javaanee* was there. He witnessed the *wanatesa* in its infancy." Benioko's cloudy gaze turned inward. "He has seen how it begins. He senses its ending. There is no other more qualified to speak to its danger. He must lead this discussion."

Wolf relaxed, inclining his head in agreement. Perhaps he had overreacted to the Old One's insistence on Aiden leading this meeting. The shaman's explanation made sense.

He still didn't understand *why* the Old One had been so demanding earlier. He'd never seen the *Taounaha* so...unyielding. Although, Benioko insisted often, that Wolf needed an official *Caetanee*. One eagle chosen.

Perhaps this was behind the *Taounaha's* unexpected behavior.

Tradition called for a male chosen by the eagle spirit to lead the warrior clan. As Jude had been, and now Wolf. But the *thae-hrata* had selected few during Wolf's lifetime. Indeed, he, Aiden, and Kait were the only eagles chosen within the past forty cycles. Female claimings by the *thae-hrata* came from the Blue Moon Mother, not the Shadow Warrior. As such, Kait could not assume the weight of *Betanee*.

Which meant when the elder gods called Wolf to the web of his ancestors, there would be no one to take his place.

His gaze skipped to Aiden, who was speaking with Zane Winters. From Kait's description of their spirit claiming, they had been chosen by the *thae-hrata* at the same time. Although neither had realized it. Instead of celebrating their claimings, they'd dismissed the *thae-hrata* as an abnormality—a sick or injured bird.

The pair had not even known to search for their claiming totem after the *thae-hrata* took to the air, so the spirit eagle's gifts had been left behind. The knowledge burned through Wolf's chest like fire. To abandon the spirit gift was unheard of among the Kalikoia. The most heretical act conceivable. That their *anestoo* had left his children so unprepared was unforgivable.

Benioko claimed the *thae-hrata* favored both the maternal and paternal sides of Wolf's lineage. But it must run deep in the Winchester lineage for all three of his *anvaat* to be eagle chosen.

Had the elder Winchester been eagle chosen as well? Had he hated his Kalikoia heritage so much he had rejected the claiming? Left the totem behind? Such a thing was inconceivable to Wolf—but his *anestoo* had rejected everything concerning his tribal heritage in favor of the *woohanta's* ways.

Perhaps he'd rejected the *thae-hrata* as well.

Time to move this meeting along. Wolf rose to his feet.

"Aiden." His voice brought immediate silence. All his warriors' eyes turned toward him. "Join me."

His *javaanee* had half-risen from his chair when Wolf called to him. Yet he did not join Wolf as requested. Instead, he sank back down with narrowed eyes and suspicion on his face. Wolf could not fault his reaction. Not after what had last happened in this room.

A stir went through the assembled warriors when Aiden didn't move. Wolf scanned the room and smoothly continued, using the same words Benioko had spoken.

"Aiden was in Karaveht. He saw the results of the weapon *Taounaha* foresaw. He lost his SEAL team to this weapon. He witnessed the symptoms of the infection." His gaze returned to Aiden, pleased to see his *javaanee* had relaxed. "There is no other more qualified to speak to its danger."

Wolf sensed rather than saw the old one's satisfaction as Aiden rose and made his way around the table. Benioko still held hope that Aiden would give in and learn the ways of the Kalikoia, thus making him eligible to step in as Wolf's *Caetanee*. Wolf had long since lost this expectation.

There would be no eagle chosen to serve as his second.

But then, he didn't need one. One could not ask for a better *Caetanee* than the warrior currently filling that position. Samuel may not have been chosen by the *thae-hrata,* having been chosen by the raven spirit instead, but in every way imaginable, his old friend was doing an admirable job as Wolf's temporary second in command.

Perhaps traditions needed to evolve, and Samuel's temporary status should turn permanent. Samuel, at least, was favored by the Shadow Warrior and gifted a spirit animal clan. Unlike some sitting at this table.

His gaze drifted to O'Neill and hardened. The *jie'van* was kicked back in his chair, boots on the table, eyes closed. No surprise such an insolent man was shunned by the elder gods.

"How much of a sitrep do you want?" Aiden asked as he stopped next to Wolf. His gaze flickered toward Benioko and hardened before looking away.

"A full account." Wolf scanned the room and frowned. "My warriors have been briefed, but perhaps something you say will spark a strategy to defeat this new weapon." He handed Aiden a remote to the overhead monitors and showed him how to work it.

Originally, his *Caetanee* had intended to do the briefing. As such, Samuel had prepared a full slide complement to accompany his sitrep.

Aiden scrolled back through the PowerPoint presentation. When he reached the slide with a map of Tajikistan, he started talking. "We were sent into Karaveht to recover the schematics and prototype of a revolutionary drone technology."

Wolf had heard the specifics of what Aiden was outlining many times by now. His attention wandered, returning to O'Neill's sprawled figure.

The *jie'van*'s boots were still on the table, his head back and eyes closed. The longer Wolf stared, the harder it was to rein in his ire. To show such disrespect in the *Taounaha's* presence. This should not be tolerated. It would not be accepted from any other warrior.

Why did Benioko allow such disrespect from O'Neill? What did the *Taounaha* even see in the *jie'van*? A man shunned by both the elder gods and the spirit animals.

"Calm yourself, *Ho'cee*," Benioko murmured with amusement in his voice. "He acts as a defiant *anvaa*. One who lashes out to prove he doesn't care."

"He cares for nothing." Wolf's voice was low, but seething. O'Neill's mere presence triggered his irritation.

Benioko shook his head and sighed. "Soon, Shadow Warrior will reveal why we have need of his gifts." His voice was tired, yet sure.

Gifts? What gifts?

Wolf frowned, his displeasure spiking. "If the Shadow Warrior favors him so, why did he not gift him with a spirit animal? Why does he have no totem?"

With a slow turn of his head, Benioko stared straight at him, then lifted his eyebrows. "The *heschrmal* claimed him. You doubt this?"

Wolf froze, shock burning through his lungs. "He lied. He showed no proof of the claiming."

Benioko scoffed. "Did *you* show proof of *your* claiming?" He turned his head in O'Neill's direction and regret settled over his lined face. "Claimings are sacred and private among the *Hee'woo'nee*. He should not have been questioned or judged." He turned back to Wolf. "You know this, *Ho'cee*."

Wolf opened his mouth, only to snap it shut. He could not argue with this. No, he had not been asked to show proof. His claiming had been accepted as fact.

The Old One was right. The spirit animal claiming was an intensely private moment within the tribe. It was never shared, other than an announcement of when the event had happened and what animal had appeared. One never shared the totem they'd received.

Yet the only way to prove a claiming, as O'Neill had been asked to prove, would be to share the totem the spirit animal left behind.

His gaze sought O'Neil and lingered.

But this...this *jie'van*? The one sprawled so tauntingly across from him? He had been chosen by the lion spirit after hundreds upon hundreds upon hundreds of cycles of no claimings?

Every part of Wolf—physical, mental, and spiritual—resisted the possibility. Why would the elder gods gift such a man—a complete ass of a man—with such a powerful animal spirit? The last representative of the *heschrmal* had followed the Shadow Warrior to the web of the ancestors a hundred cycles before the first *woohanta* had set foot on Kalikoia lands. Nobody even remembered who the last lion chosen had been. And the knowledge of what ability the *heschrmal* gifted to their chosen had long since disappeared into the currents of time.

Why would the lion spirit appear now? Why would it choose O'Neill?

Perhaps it hadn't. Perhaps O'Neill had lied about the claiming, as everyone believed.

But...if the Old One spoke the truth, then the *Hee'woo'nee's* conduct toward O'Neill would explain the bite to his tongue. He seemed to deliberately antagonize Wolf and the rest of the warriors. Even Mackenzie and his men had had enough of the *jie'van*.

Except this was O'Neill. His grating attitude had started long before he'd made the *heschrmal* claim and been shunned. He'd been a thief and a bully through middle, junior, and high school. Stealing lunches. Stealing answers to homework and tests. Starting fight after fight, most of them with Wolf. Then, a couple rotations before graduation, after the supposed claiming, he'd disappeared. Nobody had questioned his absence.

The timing of his alleged claiming had added to the suspicion O'Neill had faced. He'd been seventeen. All other spirit animal claimings happened during puberty. O'Neill had long left puberty behind when he announced his induction into the lion clan.

And then he was gone.

Wolf had forgotten the *jie'van* existed until Benioko had returned to base a cycle ago with O'Neill in tow.

Wolf was still watching, perhaps even glaring at O'Neill, when the *jie'van's* eyes suddenly opened. O'Neill straightened, his boots hitting the floor. His off-putting green gaze latched onto Aiden. Something must have caught his attention.

"You believe these continuous feed cameras are linked to the test of this weapon?" O'Neill's voice was thoughtful rather than arrogant, snide, or smug, his three most common tones. "Who did WARCOM contract with for the cameras?"

Aiden's gaze narrowed. Surprise flickered across his face. He studied O'Neill closely. "Nantz Technology. Same contractor who developed the drone prototype we were sent into Karaveht to recover."

O'Neill settled back in his chair. This time, his boots remained flat on the floor. His gaze went distant, his face thoughtful. "Nantz Technology is a peripheral weapons supplier. They've never developed core weapons." He sounded reflective though, rather than dismissive, like he was connecting dots in his head. "Nor do they have a medical or nanobot focus," O'Neill added absently. "The timing between the cameras and test could be a coincidence."

"It's possible." There was surprise on Aiden's face. But then there was surprise on all the warriors' faces.

A whispered conversation broke out between Zane and Rawls. Both men's gazes, along with the warriors surrounding them, were locked on O'Neill. So many questions in dozens of eyes. How did O'Neill know this information?

Wolf wondered as well. He turned to Benioko, who stared back with a bland expression. The Old One knew. He was not surprised by O'Neill's knowledge.

Where had O'Neill gone after he'd left the *Brenahiilo?* Neither the shaman nor O'Neill had explained where he'd gained his impressive warrior skills. Wolf had hoped the *jie'van's* induction into the warrior clan, which came through the *Neealaho* binding ceremony, would take care of his O'Neill problem. To join Shadow Mountain, a Kalikoia warrior had to merge with the *Neealaho,* the neural net that connected all as one. But the blending ceremony required great strength—both tribal and personal. Many could not receive the merging of so many minds and spirits. O'Neill had little tribal blood, less than a third. Nor had he been blessed with an animal clan. His tribal strength was so weak, merging with the *Neealaho* should have been impossible for him.

Yet merge he had. Which left Wolf no choice but to accept him into the warrior clan. One could not reject one of the Shadow Warrior's chosen fighters.

O'Neill suddenly frowned and glanced around the table. His face went blank, his eyes flat. He sprawled back out in his chair, his boots thudding as they hit the surface of the table.

But he'd already revealed more than he'd intended. Shadow Mountain warriors were too perceptive to miss what had just happened—how the one they least respected had proved he was more than he pretended. More than they'd assumed.

"As of now, our best bet of finding this bot weapon is through Grigory Kuznetsov, the Russian arms dealer we were deployed to find," Aiden continued; his gaze still locked on O'Neill's face.

"You're certain this man is involved," Samuel asked, his question quiet.

Aiden shrugged. "According to my contact at HQ1, Navy intelligence is certain Kuznetsov was the point man behind what happened in Karaveht. Am I certain the bastard was behind the slaughter of my team? No. But the spook assigned to the op is certain Kuznetsov was in Karaveht prior to the weapon's deployment. And his name is the only one I have. We should start with him."

"So, your current intel on Kuznetsov is based on squid intelligence? The same squid intelligence that sent you into a hot spot after an arms dealer and drone prototype that wasn't on site?" O'Neill's voice, sharp with mockery, filled the room. "Sounds like you're headed for a repeat of your earlier clusterfuck."

Aiden cocked his head, his face assessing rather than angry. He saw O'Neill's mockery for what it was. An attempt, a weak one at that, to shore up his asshole reputation.

"Squid?" Aiden repeated quietly, his gaze searching as it scanned O'Neill's face. "Where did you come up with that? It's a MARSOC diss."

O'Neill's mouth snapped shut. After a moment, he shrugged and resumed his indolent posture—kicked back in his chair, eyes closed, boots on the table. But the exchange gave Wolf his first insight into his childhood bully, and where'd he'd disappeared after high school.

O'Neill, the scourge of Shadow Mountain, was a former Marine Raider.

Chapter
Twenty-Seven

Day 10
Denali, Alaska

Aiden weaved his way through the milling warriors, hoping to escape from
the conference room before Benioko accosted him. Since the shaman's private attempt to persuade Aiden to join his cult had failed, Aiden expected
the old man to give public hounding a try. So far, he'd evaded the shaman,
who was still at the back of the room with Wolf and a reverential cluster of
warriors.

He'd just stepped through the door when talons latched onto his biceps. His brother's Kalikoia warriors wouldn't be so familiar, and he'd left
Benioko behind, which meant the iron fingers had to belong to one of
his former teammates. Probably Cosky. Rude and assertive described his
sister's husband well.

But when he turned to glare, the hawkish face that greeted him was
Mackenzie rather than Cos. It didn't surprise him. Mackenzie wasn't
known for his manners, or temperament either. He'd seen his former commander slip into the conference room and take the wall behind Zane and

Rawls during the middle of his TED Talk. The wall lean had surprised him. He'd expected the dude to take Aiden's abandoned chair.

"Come," Mackenzie barked, letting go of Aiden's arm. He pivoted, his shoulders leading the way, and stalked to an open door ten feet to the left.

Aiden followed Mackenzie down the hall and through the open door. Zane, Cosky, and Rawls stood in a loose huddle near another table. A smaller one with no Kalikoia words carved into its surface.

He turned, scanning the room for a coffee stand and found...nothing. Fuck.

This impromptu meeting was going to be unbearable without a caffeine punch to stabilize his patience and temper.

He sighed, exhaustion suddenly crashing over him. "Can this wait? I need..." His voice trailed off. He could hardly admit he needed a damn nap. Before he could backpedal, his commander—or former commander—stepped into him, standing almost chest to chest.

"Hell no, this can't wait!" Mackenzie snapped, a thunder cloud rolling across his lean face. He jutted his chin out. "You got a problem with that?"

A crackle of irritation flickered beneath Aiden's fatigue. It was just like Mackenzie to turn this into a confrontation. While the bastard's short black hair carried more gray, and his face more lines, his black eyes still flashed with temper. The commander's disposition hadn't softened since he'd been booted from ST7.

"We're not questioning what you said back there," Zane broke in, calmly smoothing the tension riding the aftermath of Mackenzie's outburst.

It looked like those old team dynamics were still in play. Zane was still smoothing the choppy waters following hurricane Mackenzie, and the commander still needed a fucking filter.

"We have questions about O'Neill," Zane continued.

O'Neill? Not Kuznetsov? Not the two clowns who'd gone after Demi? Not Aiden's detailed account of what he'd seen in Karaveht or experienced with his own team?

"What about him?" Aiden's eyebrows lifted.

"This was the first time he's asked questions in a briefin'. Before today, he just sits there, boots on the table, eyes closed, actin' like his shit's too grand for the rest of us." Rawls squinted, then shook his head. "But now? Hell, the dude's obviously piped in. He knew of Nantz Technology. He knew what they manufacture. Hell, he even used USSOCOM lingo."

Zane nodded and used his index finger to scratch the middle of his furrowed forehead.

"And he called us *squids*," Mackenzie practically snarled, as if that was the missing rivet that sank the ship. "Straight out of the marine raider field book." He gritted his teeth before adding in an angry rumble. "Asshole."

Aiden glanced between his former teammates. Seriously? They were worked up because of O'Neill's SEAL insult? Was life so slow under Wolf's leadership they had to generate drama to feel alive?

"He didn't get the insult quite right," Aiden drawled, loading his voice with mockery. "It's dirty, nasty squids."

"The point is," Zane glanced at the opaque glass window in the door Mackenzie had closed, as if ensuring nobody was outside listening to them, "he's obviously got contacts. Non-USSOCOM contacts. We can use that."

Aiden cocked his head, considering that. Fair enough. "I don't know the guy. But then I'm not the one who's been crewing with him. That would be you boys. Why the hell would you think I'd know more about him than you do?"

Rawls shrugged. "Didn't that brother of yours fill you in on the Shadow Mountain crew?"

That question brought a scoff and an eye roll. "Big bro hasn't told me shit about anyone on this base. That goes double for O'Neill." He frowned before adding, "That said, I get the strong impression he'd like to toss O'Neill out on his ass."

Cosky nodded, curiosity flickering in his silver eyes. "We get the same impression. Why hasn't he? What does O'Neill have on him?"

"No clue," Aiden drawled.

O'Neill's history was the least of his concerns. Although, if the dude had contacts outside of USSOCOM, they could be downright helpful. Assuming the bastard would admit to having any contacts.

"The guy's got to be a former raider," Rawls said, his brows creased in thought. "That would explain his hand-to-hand and close quarters skills."

"Nah," Cosky's eyes narrowed. "My money's on intelligence. One of the stateside alphabet soups. CIA or DIA, maybe AMI. Special ops soldiers wouldn't know about Nantz Technology or the shit they develop."

Mackenzie grunted. "Intelligence makes sense, explains how Wolf always has up-to-date SAT images and resource reports."

"Agreed." Zane nodded. His voice turned thoughtful. "If O'Neill has contacts in the CIA or NSA, it makes sense why Wolf hasn't canned his ass, even though he clearly wants to."

Rawls shook his head, his face doubtful. "Don't think so, skipper. Wolf's crew was already piped in—intelligence wise—long before O'Neill planted his boots on base."

Aiden barely caught a yawn. Man, he could sure use some damn coffee. Those nightmares were playing hell with his sleep. "What's O'Neill's full name? I'll have Dev check him out."

Cosky's eyebrows bunched. He shook his head and shrugged. "Never heard another name. Just O'Neill."

Aiden glanced at the others, receiving head shakes or shrugs. "Is O'Neill his last name?"

More shrugs greeted his eyes.

Hell, he'd have to ask Wolf. His brother must know O'Neill's full name. Maybe he even knew where the dude had crewed prior to arriving at Shadow Mountain.

"I'll see what Wolf and Dev know," Aiden promised, wiping a hand down his face to hide a yawn. "Now if that's all—"

Zane immediately broke in. "Anything new from the lab tests?

"Not that I'm aware of."

Did Zane honestly think he wouldn't have mentioned it in the meeting, or while they'd been having their little chat earlier?

"You haven't asked?" Mackenzie snapped, turning the question into an accusation.

"Of course, I asked." Aiden snapped back. *You jackass.* "They have nothing new to share."

Mackenzie grunted his version of an acknowledgement and swung toward the door. "Keep me in the loop."

Aiden grabbed the edge of his tactical pants to keep his fingers at his side. He wasn't sure exactly what his hand had in mind—a salute or the middle finger. Both were possible. Neither were appropriate.

If Mackenzie hadn't had the back of every operator under his command, and went to bat for them repeatedly, someone would have killed him years ago.

He waited for Zane and Rawls to follow the commander out of the room before blocking Cosky's access to the door.

"How's Demi?"

"Haven't talked to her much." Cosky stopped within inches of ramming into Aiden. He took a long step back. And then another. "Don't see that she's missing your face, if that's what you're asking."

Like the asshole would know if she was missing him. His brother-in-law wasn't nearly as perceptive as he assumed.

"She eating? Sleeping?" He needed to free up time to hop on the Bell and fly down to visit her.

Cosky scoffed. "Do I look like her dietitian or sleep therapist? Get off your ass and visit her. Wolf will give you a badge and the Bell."

"I'm working on it. The lab has me pretty tied up."

Cosky's face softened. He glanced at the inside of Aiden's elbow. "No shit. They turned you into a pincushion. You sure the lab's not overrun by vampires? Christ knows they've sucked enough blood from you."

Aiden grimaced. He'd been asking himself the same question. Which reminded him...

"Is that damn cat still ripping Demi to shreds?" Even more importantly. "Tell me Kait healed those scratches."

With a yawn, Cosky ran a palm down his face. Looked like Cos needed a coffee boost as much as Aiden.

"Demi wouldn't let Kait heal her. Claimed the scratches were healing fine. As for the cat, they say he's an angel. Taking his medicine twice a day. No scratching. No biting. Demi's calling it a miracle." He dropped his hand and scowled. "You know she named the damn thing Trident? For Christ's sake, convince her to name it something else. It's blasphemy to name a passive little shit like that after a symbol of power and courage."

Aiden couldn't tell if he was kidding. Probably not. Cosky took the symbolism inherent in the Trident seriously. Kait said he still had his, even after all the bullshit WARCOM had put him through.

"Tell her to name him something pampered and precious," Cosky continued. "Like Prince, or some shit."

Aiden zipped his lips. No way was he telling Demi what to name her cat. But it was interesting that both O'Neill and Cosky felt the cat was misnamed. Yet for opposite reasons. Cosky said the animal was too delicate for the symbol. O'Neill said the symbol was too delicate for the cat.

Strange. But interesting.

Day 10
Washington, D.C.

The man on the other end of the line had no name. What he had were excuses. Endless excuses. None of which were acceptable. How hard was it to grab one solitary woman?

Impossible, apparently, when one hired incompetent hacks.

"Explain to me how you can lose a plane." Clark's voice remained mild, even as his fingers dug into the arm of the elephant chair with such force they left imprints in the tough leather. "The FAA requires the registration number to be visible on the aircraft. They also required aircraft to file flight plans. This Citation is not a ghost. It exists."

"Of course it exists." The man with no name's voice erupted down the phone line. "My guy followed the girl and her guards to the airfield. He saw her board the jet. He texted me the registration number. I ran it. Nothing came up in the search."

"Then your goon misread the numbers," Clark's voice sharpened. He collected himself. When he spoke again, his tone had returned to its normal, mild octave. "It would appear that all three of the men you hired for my needs were second rate, at best."

According to No Name's own account, Aiden Winchester had been waiting at the airfield. He'd been right there, and this *asshole's* hired goon had let him fly off into the sunset—with the very woman he'd been sent to kidnap. What a complete moron.

"I don't hire second-rate." No Name's voice hardened. "This fuckup was not because of employee failure. There is no record of that jet landing or taking off from San Bernardino. It didn't even show up on radar. Someone disappeared that plane, which requires money. Lots of money. A luxury your target doesn't have."

Clark pondered that. Who had Winchester hooked up with? Someone with enough resources to hide a plane, apparently.

He could concede that the disappearing plane was out of his hired gun's control. But what about the girl he'd hired them to grab? They'd lost her, too, even though they'd been right there in her building. And then they'd gone and got themselves caught.

Amateurs.

He hadn't paid a fortune for amateur hour.

Clark reined in his frustration. "I'm disappointed. You assured me this would be simple. You assured me your men were the best."

"They are. This was a unique situation." Mr. No Name's tone tightened. The pompous ass clearly didn't appreciate having his failures laid at his feet.

Too damn bad.

Clark's fingers dug deeper into the arm of the elephant chair. He'd paid an exorbitant amount of money to acquire Winchester or his girlfriend. And this...this failure was unacceptable. Not because of the money. Because of Winchester.

He had to get hold of Winchester.

"I'm disappointed." Despite his best efforts, his voice thinned. "I require Winchester, his woman, or my money back."

"I'm working on it. Just let me do my fucking job." The line went dead.

Clark scowled. He'd be happy to comply if the bastard wasn't so goddamn awful at fulfilling the terms of his contracts. The bounty he'd put on Winchester's head was fortuitous. His original reasoning had been math based. The more contract killers looking for the SEAL, the better the chance of acquiring him.

At least he had other options now that Mr. No Name had proved his incompetence.

Pushing himself up, he wandered over to the enormous window looking out over the glittering lights of Washington, D.C. For the first time, his touchstone view didn't soothe him. His heart was pounding way too fast. His muscles were so tense they ached. Lightning bolts of pain periodically shot through his jaw thanks to the latest round of teeth grinding.

No Name's news had not been the worst of the day. That honor would go to his eyes and ears in Hurley's command.

The admiral—indeed, the entire United States military by now—knew about his NNB26 nanobots. They knew how his bot weapon had affected the citizens of Karaveht and why Winchester's SEAL teammates had killed each other.

They knew *everything*. Except who created the weapon.

Since Winchester and his teammates were still missing, and Hurley's evacuation team had found no bodies in Karaveht, the only way they could have found out about his little prodigies was through Winchester. Or more precisely, through the SEAL's dead teammates.

Someone must have autopsied them and discovered the nanobots and Winchester had passed the information on. His contact in Hurley's office had said they were in contact with Winchester, although the SEAL refused to tell them where he was, or who he was with.

Winchester had hooked up with someone powerful, though. Someone with a full lab—one equipped with AFM, NMRs, SEMs, STMs and SPMs. All of which were required to work with nanotechnology and all of which were expensive as hell. It reminded him of the ghost jet that had landed and taken off in San Bernardino. But there was also Winchester and his dead teammates' disappearance from the evacuation site in the hills above

Karaveht. Something must have dropped in to pick them up before Clark's crew had arrived, yet there was nothing on the SAT pictures during that timeframe. Nothing on radar either. No flight plans.

A ghost chopper, if you will, rather like Mr. No Name's ghost plane. No doubt both were owned by the same organization that had discovered the nanobots.

Which was terrible news.

He'd prayed—actually prayed—that No Name's phone call had been to inform him they had the Barnes woman under wraps. At least he'd have had a bargaining chip to get Winchester into his lab.

But no...*dammit*.

Clark took a deep breath, forcing air into his lungs. For the first time in, well, forever, he was on the verge of panic.

Whoever Winchester was working with was well-funded. So well-funded they'd discovered his nanobots. But even worse, they had access to Winchester—who was apparently immune to the nanobots.

If they figured out why Winchester was immune, and figured out how to replicate that and make others immune, they'd render his weapon inert. His retirement plan would self-destruct.

The only thing in his favor was the fact the weapon would never be traced back to him. He'd covered his tracks and his identity completely, hid himself through endless shell companies and aliases.

He was safe.

When his cell started buzzing, he picked it up, hoping the call was from Mr. No Name saying he'd tracked down Winchester, or someone claiming Winchester's bounty, which would mean they'd captured the cagey bastard.

Basically, just hoping for a ray of sunshine on this shitty day.

But nope—the call was from Doctor Lovett, his nanobot miracle worker.

"Christopher," Clark forced a jovial tone. "I was just thinking about you! How does a raise sound?"

He should present him with a BMW, too, or a car of equal status and value. It was simply good practice to keep your top performers well rewarded. Such generosity was one of the first things he'd learned as an entrepreneur whose success often depended on the brilliant creations of others.

"Clark!"

There was a harried note to Clark's name. And Lovett hadn't responded to the offer of a raise.

"What's wrong?" Clark's tension, which had barely faded, returned with tornado force gales.

"It's the NNB26 prototype." Lovett sounded stunned. "They're active again."

Perplexed, Clark frowned. "That is not possible. I haven't reactivated them."

"That's the point," Lovett said in a rush. "I checked the program. Nobody reactivated them. Yet they *are* active again. Scurrying around like ants in their maze."

Instinctively, Clark shook his head. "That's simply not possible."

"Possible or not," Lovett's voice rose and edged into shrill, "the NNB26 prototype nanobots are active. Come down and see for yourself."

Chapter Twenty-Eight

Day 11
Denali, Alaska

"Everything's so pretty!" Demi stared out the window, soaking in the thick flock of snow weighing down the tree branches along the road. "You really do live in a winter wonderland."

"I remind myself of that every December and January when the sun refuses to rise until 10:30 a.m. and then disappears again at 3:00 p.m." Kait leaned forward in the driver's seat, staring intently at the snow packed road before them. "Or when I'm stuck at home for days on end because of an endless round of blizzards."

"Like the storm that rolled in the day after I arrived." Demi's voice sounded sleepy to her own ears. The tall, thick snow berm that streamed past the car was hypnotizing. Did Alaskans imagine snow berms rather than sheep when they had trouble sleeping?

"Yeah. That's why I rushed you into town so early the next morning, before the storm was due to hit. You needed clothes ASAP. Sure, you could have borrowed jeans and sweaters from me—but secondhand underwear and bras?" Kait shuddered, and then shot her a chiding glance. "And if you thank me again for funding that shopping expedition, I swear I'm gonna smack you."

Demi made a zipping motion across her lips, even though she still felt uncomfortable with Kait paying for everything. As in *everything*.

The biggest challenge that accompanied running for your life—other than having no luggage, thus no change of clothes—was not being able to use debit or credit cards. Electronic transactions were easy to track. To avoid detection, she had to use cash. Which she couldn't get without using her debit card.

Enter her best friend, who'd stepped in to cover all of Demi's expenses.

"Just so you know," Demi said. "I'm keeping track of every single penny you spend on me, and I *will* pay you back once I can access my bank accounts again." She caught the frown pulling at Kait's face and hurriedly added. "But that's not me saying thank you or anything like that."

"Right." Kait rolled her eyes.

When they reached a fork in the road, they kept to the left.

Demi twisted to look behind her. "Isn't that other fork the one we took when we went to Talkeetna the other day?"

As soon as Demi had awakened this morning, Kait had insisted on taking her out for breakfast, so she'd expected another trip to Talkeetna. Which, apparently, was the closest city.

"Yes. But we're not headed to Talkeetna. The best breakfast in the universe is served at The Neighborhood's Breakfast Bar." She sent Demi a conspiratorial grin.

Kait had mentioned The Neighborhood several times, but Demi had assumed she was referring to the people and houses surrounding her and Cosky's home.

"We're almost there." Kait's voice vibrated with anticipation. "It's around this next bend."

Demi faced front again. Her chauffeur took the curve, straightened the Expedition out and rolled into an adorable, picture-perfect little village. The place was tiny, encompassing barely a block's worth of buildings, all of which were made from whole logs. Some shops were bigger—like the grocery-hardware store at the end of the block and some smaller—like the bakery and bookstore. But they were all log cabins. They all had steep, A-frame roofs topped in a fluffy white cap of snow, and they all sported garish, blinking lights proclaiming the name of the establishment in exuberant flashing letters.

The blinking neon signs should have been ugly and out-of-place amid the village's rustic charm. Yet they weren't. Instead, they added an avant-garde kind of winkity-wink charm. Like the garish signs were a local joke, and everyone was having a good laugh at them.

The entire block looked adorable, like something pulled straight from a fairy tale.

"I wish you could see your face!" Kait crowed. "I knew you'd love it."

They parked in front of The Breakfast Bar, which matched the log cabin theme. But with an extra twist of charm thanks to the painted windows that traveled the length of the building. Each window featured wilderness themes of mountains, rivers, and forests, along with the animals that called Alaska home. Demi recognized the impressionist touch of the landscapes along with the whimsical flair of the wildlife. But the random bursts of color were an artistic signature too.

"When did you find time to paint the windows?" Still staring at the colorful glass panes, Demi unbuckled her seatbelt. New images kept jumping out at her the longer she looked. Like the lynx lurking within the boughs of a spruce tree in the bottom corner of the first window, or the owl tucked behind a cluster of pinecones.

"It was a long, slow process. I had to fit the painting around my commissioned pieces, or when a project just wasn't gelling, and I needed to rethink the design." Kait pushed open the driver's door and inhaled deeply. "My God, I never get tired of that smell."

Demi could smell it, too, now that the door was open. She took a deep breath and groaned at the yeasty, buttery scents. Drool pooled in her mouth. "That's got to be fresh bread. No wonder you've labeled this place as the best breakfast spot in the universe."

Kait slid out of the SUV on a laugh. "That heavenly scent isn't coming from Olivia's kitchen. It's coming from Mary's." She tilted her head toward the cabin to their left with its neon sign blinking *BAKERY.* "We'll stop there after we've eaten. If we go now, we'll be too stuffed for breakfast."

Demi followed her out of the SUV. They gingerly stepped up onto a plank sidewalk that had been scraped of snow and sprinkled with rock salt. The boards were surprisingly sturdy beneath her feet, with a light coat of grit. No slipping at all.

A bell pealed as they pushed open the solid wood door to The Breakfast Bar and stepped inside.

"I can't believe you all named this cute little town The Neighborhood," Demi said after they slid into a rustic-looking booth at the back of the restaurant. "That name has such an ominous vibe. Like *The Stepford Wives* or *Get Out.*"

With a rueful shake of her head, Kait turned *her* coffee cup over. "I wouldn't say we named it, unless the naming came about because of indecision and apathy." She shrugged. "Nobody could agree what to call our little slice of heaven. And while everyone was arguing, the shops started naming themselves. The Neighborhood this—or The Neighborhood that. By the time the fourth or fifth shop went in, The Neighborhood just stuck."

Kait straightened, smiling as a tall, Native American woman with long black hair, two menus, and a coffee pot approached their table. "Demi, this is Olivia Holden, the best cook in the known universe. Olivia, this is Demi Barnes. She's my best friend and visiting from California."

Surprise widened Olivia's mahogany brown eyes.

After a hesitation and an apologetic look across the table at Demi, Kait continued. "Demi's been dating my brother. Aiden's recent trouble found its way to her door, so he flew down to Coronado and brought her up here. Wolf approved her to stay until the danger passes."

"Ah, I see." Their hostess's face cleared. "It's nice to meet you, Demi. Whatever trouble Kait's brother brought to your door won't find you up here. You can count on that." The smile that lit Olivia's face turned her from beautiful to stunning. She placed a thick, one-page paper menu in front of each of them and filled the ceramic cups with coffee. "Holler when you're ready to order."

"Why was she so surprised to hear I was visiting?" Demi waited until their hostess had disappeared through the swinging door that led into the kitchen.

Kait toyed with her spoon, her face lined with conflict, as if she didn't know what to say. She finally blew out a breath and raised her eyes, holding Demi's gaze. "Remember how I told you Wolf was extra cautious about the security around Shadow Mountain, and by extension, The Neighborhood?"

Demi nodded. She would have described the precautions Wolf took as paranoidly anal, but what did she know?

"Well, there are reasons behind his caution." Kait stirred cream and sugar into her coffee cup and set her spoon down. "Shadow Mountain and its warriors have been involved in dozens of global conflicts, few of which most people have even heard about. Like the situation Marcus and his teammates found themselves in three years ago. If the NRO had gotten their way, a good chunk of the world would have died. Shadow Mountain, along with the clones, stopped the massacre from happening."

"What's the NRO?" Demi lifted her cup, the ceramic warmth sinking into her palms, and took a small sip. The coffee was surprisingly smooth and flavorful for restaurant fare.

"They don't exist anymore, but back then, they called themselves the New Ruling Order." Kait grimaced. "In reality, they were just a bunch of one percenters who wanted to rule the world. The clones, along with Wolf and his warriors, neutralized them."

Demi could almost hear Cosky's tone and inflection in the word neutralized.

Kait picked her cup up and sighed. "The point is, Shadow Mountain has made some nasty enemies in the past. Chances are they'll make even more in the future. Wolf's men fight the kind of people who'd kill everyone on base and in The Neighborhood without a second thought. Wolf's precautions are in place to keep his people safe. The only visitors allowed are close family members of Shadow Mountain personnel. Wolf and his team vet everyone. Nobody can access the base or The Neighborhood without authorization."

Demi took another sip of coffee as she studied Kait's shadowed face. What a strange and secretive world her friend had fallen into. Kait had told her about the force-field that supposedly encapsulated the entire community and prevented unauthorized visitors from entering. It sounded farfetched. But the concept certainly fit with the extreme security measures Wolf appeared to have implemented.

Olivia returned to the table, so Demi put her questions on hold. On Kait's recommendation, she ordered the seafood omelet. Once Olivia had refilled their coffee cups and disappeared back into the kitchen, Demi launched her next question.

"Does everyone who lives in The Neighborhood have family on base?" She'd only seen the air hangar when she'd arrived, but Kait said over a thousand people worked there.

"Yes. Well, both base employees and their families. Or those with significant others, like Olivia." She nodded toward the kitchen. "She's Samuel's fiancée. Samuel is Wolf's second in command. Olivia is part of The Neighborhood's book brigade—where we discuss romance novels and drink loads of wine. I think you'll love her as much as the rest of us do."

A twinge of jealousy shot through Demi upon hearing the affection in Kait's voice. Kait's circle of close friends had obviously widened after moving to Denali, while her own had dwindled to zero. At least locally.

Still, the book brigade club sounded like a blast. She'd happily join in while she was here. An evening spent discussing favorite books while drinking gallons of wine? Not much could beat that.

"Anyway," Kait cleared her throat. "Everyone who lives here is connected to someone working at the base. Even the shopkeepers. When the stores first went in, I didn't think they could survive. But they're doing okay. Shadow Mountain supplements them, and we all shop locally. The owners will never get rich, but they don't seem to care. I think they just want something to keep them busy. Olivia, for example, is only open for breakfast—and even then, only on weekdays, while Samuel is at base. She takes evenings and weekends off. Her schedule is perfect for me. You know how much I hate cooking. And Marcus leaves for the base so stinking early, I barely get to kiss him goodbye, let alone cook breakfast for him."

"Still not a morning person, I see." Demi's lips twitched at the disgust in Kait's voice. It was nice to see that some things hadn't changed. "And you've told me dozens of times that Cosky took over all the cooking since you kept getting distracted by a new idea and leaving for your workshop while the oven or burner was on."

Kait tried to look offended but collapsed into giggles. "Marcus forbids me from cooking if I'm by myself. He says I'm dangerous in the kitchen."

A man forbidding his wife to do anything would normally raise Demi's hackles. But she didn't want to lose her best friend to a home fire any more than Cosky did.

"Ah...he knows you well." Demi sent her a teasing smile, but it slowly died. Aiden still didn't know her routines. But then, they hadn't spent enough time together to settle into habits.

"It must be nice having Cosky home nights, weekends, and holidays. But from what you said earlier about Shadow Mountain's enemies, his job must still be dangerous." Demi stopped to sniff. Some delicious scents were drifting out of the kitchen. Her stomach rumbled. "How do you handle that?"

Kait was silent, her gaze intense as it searched Demi's face. "Things have been pretty quiet since they defeated the NRO. He's been gone on training missions, mostly. But it looks like things are about to heat up again, if this weapon Aiden stumbled into gets loose in the world." Her face pinched with anxiety, only to smooth again.

Demi shifted uneasily in her chair. If the weapon used on Aiden's team was behind things heating up, then Aiden would be in danger too. He'd go after the people who'd killed his teammates.

"But won't you be scared for Cosky while he's off fighting this weapon?" She'd be a nervous wreck when Aiden went after it.

"Of course, but I'll do what I did with Dad and Aiden. I'll keep busy, distract myself with work. It helps that I trust Marcus to do everything possible to stay safe and return to me. He's well-trained. He's smart. And he has dozens of well-trained, smart men surrounding him. He won't be alone out there. And I won't be alone back here, either. It helps to have Faith, Beth, Amy, Olivia and Mary around. When the guys are gone, we'll band together, form our own little posse."

"It would be nice to have a posse." Demi's voice turned wistful.

"You know..." Kait's voice was careful, her face cautious. "Marcus says Aiden can't go back to the SEALs. He lost trust in the command structure. He suspects they're behind what happened in Karaveht." She searched Demi's face, then leaned across the table, reaching for her hand. "Maybe you should wait to break things off with him. If Marcus is right, those long deployments might be in Aiden's past."

Demi thought about that, only to shake her head. "He'll just move on to another career, one just as dangerous. I think he thrives on the adrenaline." She shook her head again. "Besides, I'm not as brave as you and the other women in your posse. Waiting at home for news would kill me. The stress. The fear. I couldn't do it. I don't want to do it."

Kait accepted her answer with a small sigh. "Well, it was just a thought. I keep hoping he'll join Shadow Mountain. If he did, he'd be home most nights and weekends after this new danger has passed. And if you two stayed together, we could be neighbors again. Only this time, forever."

Demi's smile was wobbly. That sounded wonderful, and completely unrealistic. According to Kait, Aiden had known about the Shadow Mountain base for years. Yet he'd shown no interest in joining his brother's team. She doubted that would change anytime soon.

And even if it did, she hated the thought of him going off to war. Shadow Mountain might not be SEALs, but according to Kait, the men who manned it were still soldiers. They had enemies. They left their homes to fight evil. And evil fought back. Every time they left base, there was a chance someone's husband or father or fiancé wouldn't make it back home.

She refused to spend the rest of her life agonizing over Aiden. Whether he was alive. Whether he was dead. Whether he'd been one of the many sacrificed to keep evil in check.

Chapter Twenty-Nine

Day 14
Denali, Alaska

"How many spooks did you speak to?" The question was interspersed with panting, which was ridiculous. A stroll through the base corridors on his way to the elevator should not get his lungs so worked up.

It figured that Russo would call with a Kuznetsov update now, while Aiden was headed to the air hangar. The lab had finally called it quits on the bloodletting and given him the greenlight to jump base. Wolf had even okayed his ride on the Bell and allowed him to visit Cosky's precious *Neighborhood*.

He stopped at the elevator, welcoming the delay to catch his breath. Time to hit the gym again. His lack of PT was showing.

"I'm on the move, so if I go silent, hold the line until I hit a signal again." Aiden didn't quite believe Cosky's reassurances that cell phone reception was exceptional. For Christ's sake, they were buried beneath tons of concrete, dirt, and rock. He punched the UP button for the elevator. "So, none of the spooks or soups know where Kuznetsov is?"

"Depends on which soup I spoke with," Russo said. "They're all reporting different locations."

The elevator bell chimed, and the doors slid open. He stepped in and pressed the button to the air hanger. With luck, the Bell would be prepped and waiting. If he was extra lucky, Cosky would have one of those handy-dandy Neighborhood badges waiting for him. Having to cool his heels while someone rustled one up was going to strain his patience—which was already as thin as day old ice.

"The CIA and NSA put him in Sevastopol." Devlin's voice was a staticky rumble on the line. "But INTCEN, DGSI, and CNRLT claim the bastard's in Seltso, along the Desna River. Mossad claims he's in Istaravshan, Tajikistan."

"Istaravshan?" Aiden straightened from his slouch against the elevator wall. His instincts lit up with a low grade buzz the instant Dev mentioned the town. "That's only one hundred and fifty klicks from Vahdat."

"One-fifty-one, if we're going to be precise. Plus—it came from our Israeli friends. Mossad has some damn fine intelligence gatherers."

True. "What's your gut say? Did Kuznetsov go to ground in Istaravshan?"

Dev's grunt carried ambivalence. "My gut ain't talking. Besides, what we think doesn't matter. USSOCOM won't move on it. They'll need a solid sighting before they'll do anything. Nobody wants a repeat of what happened in Karaveht. They won't greenlight another op until they have Kuznetsov's location double and triple checked, with clear, identifiable photos. Which won't happen anytime soon, with all the soups focusing on different locales." He paused before adding quietly, "Feels like a scattershot op to me. My guess is that Kuznetsov, or someone connected to him, is setting off false identification after false identification to keep everyone guessing."

"Fuck." A scowl heated Aiden's face. He'd hoped for more. A lot more. They didn't have time for patience and prayers.

"I hear you, brother." Sympathy practically dripped down the line.

Aiden's scowl grew. He didn't want sympathy. He wanted—hell, needed—results.

"One more thing, about that name you gave me," Dev added, his voice sharpening.

"You mean O'Neill?" Aiden asked, waiting with barely leashed patience as the elevator slowed and the bell chimed.

"That's the name. Singular, like Madonna," Russo said. "Looked into him like you asked. You sure that's the right name?"

"That's all I have," Aiden said. Not even Wolf knew the dude's full name. Or if he even had one.

"Nobody got a look at his birth certificate?"

"My brother did." The elevator doors snapped open. Aiden stepped out and into the air hanger. "Said the only thing listed was a first name. O'Neill. No last name given."

"Hmm..." Russo paused. "No parents listed?"

"The mother was. Mary Beacher. No father. Nobody knew who knocked his mother up." Aiden wove his way between the various aircraft, and damned if his legs weren't getting heavier with every step. "I take it you didn't get anything off the name?"

He hadn't expected Russo to uncover anything. The ask had been a long shot.

"On O'Neill? No." Russo hesitated before continuing with a what-the-hell tone of voice. "But my friendly neighborhood NSA spook is a big sci-fi fan, so he tossed Jack O'Neill in for the hell of it."

"Jack O'Neill?" Aiden shook his head. "Doesn't ring any bells."

"It wouldn't, if you aren't a Stargate fan. It was a sci-fi hit during the late 1990s to the late 2000s—partly because of Richard Dean Anderson, who portrayed Colonel Jack O'Neill, an Air Force Special Operations Veteran. Anyhow, my spook is a big Stargate fan and has far too much imagination, so he tossed Jack O'Neill into his search criteria—and damned if he didn't get a hit. A big one. Adding Jack to the search triggered a hit on a classified file, codename Stargate. Restricted access. No information available."

Aiden stopped short between a Cessna and a Black Hawk. "That makes no sense."

"Codenames aren't supposed to make sense." Russo's voice was dry. "That's why they're codenames. Wouldn't want anyone to follow the breadcrumbs to an actual identification."

"You think Stargate is O'Neill? How can you be certain the file doesn't spell out some highly classified op or something?"

"I'm not certain," Russo said with the verbal equivalent of a shrug in his voice. "A coded file could be about anything—operations, operators, hell, even snitches. No way to tell what it contains without gaining access to it. And according to my spook, this file is impenetrable. I'm not saying it's your guy. I just find it interesting, that's all."

"Any info on which of the soups classified the file?"

Russo paused. When he continued, his voice was more cautious than ever. "Looks like ODNI."

"Fuck me," Aiden breathed. "I hope your spook has some serious hacking skills, and that hit didn't register, or if it did—" *which it probably had*, "it can't be traced back to him."

Nobody in their right mind wanted the Office of the Director of National Intelligence crawling up their ass.

"No shit," Russo said, his voice hushed, like he was worried the ODNI had already traced the search back to him and was listening in on him from space or some shit.

"That file can't have anything to do with O'Neill," Aiden said, shaking his head. "No way."

"Not saying it does." Russo paused again. "You're going to ask him about it, aren't you?" The question came with a clear, *"you stupid fuck"* attached to it.

"Maybe." Russo knew him too well to believe an outright denial.

He groaned. "You are! Jesus. You know if he is ODNI, asking him about Stargate could put an extra bounty on your head."

"What's another couple of million?" Aiden started walking again. "Maybe I can push the bounty above five mil." Which was what the combined bounty had been for his former ST7 leadership.

Dev snorted. "You took Rawlings up on one of his batshit crazy bets, didn't you?"

Aiden could almost feel Russo's eye roll through the line.

"That's classified." He rounded a Sky Hawk, and the Bell came into view. "You got anything else for me? I'm about to go skids up. I got somewhere I need to be."

"That's it. I'll call if I hear anything more." The line went dead.

Aiden closed on the Bell, and the tall, dark-haired asshole pacing beside it. Cosky stopped his pacing when he saw Aiden, waited for him to get close enough, and drove a plastic badge into his chest. Aiden came to a sudden hard stop, most of the air vacating his lungs beneath the plastic punch.

He grunted, grabbing the badge before it hit the ground. "Fuck, dude, what was that for?"

"Your slow ass is making me late for date night." Cosky turned, hopping through the open cargo door and into the belly of the Bell. "And here I thought you were in an almighty hurry to get your love life squared away."

"Date night?" Aiden jeered, following his brother-in-law into the chopper. "Does Kait know you're seeing other women already?"

"Trust me, Kait is all the woman I need. No way I'd risk what I have with her by screwing around."

"You're telling me you made a date with your wife?" Aiden put so much effort into his eye rolls they stung. "Isn't that like closing the coop after the chickens have escaped?" He turned, sliding the cargo door shut. He picked up the headsets sitting on the seat next to Cosky, and sat down, handing one headset to his brother-in-law, and adjusting the other over his head, so the mic was pointing in the right direction. "You're supposed to date 'em before you marry them, not after."

"You're mixing your metaphors, jackass." Cosky adjusted his own head-set before shooting him a get-real look. "And forgive me if I don't take relationship advice from the dude who's about to get served with the verbal equivalent of a Dear John letter."

Aiden set his jaw. Not if he could help it. At least it sounded like Cosky and Kait would be gone, which gave him the time and privacy to talk to Demi and convince her to give him another go.

"Where are you taking Kait?" *Translation: How long are you two going to be gone?*

"Talkeetna. They've got a kickass seafood and steak place." Cosky shot him a knowing look. "You'll have two hours, or close enough, to make your case. But I wasn't busting your ass earlier. You can't stay with us. I'm not putting Demi in that position. If she's uncomfortable, Kait will be caught between the two of you and miserable as hell. You'll need to take Rawls up on his offer to stay with him and Faith." He paused, studying Aiden's face with an *I'm-not-shitting-you* look. "After you're done talking with Demi, call him. He'll pick you up."

Aiden raised his eyebrows. "Doesn't he live next door to you? I can walk to his door."

Cosky shook his head, a long-suffering expression on his face. "In the dark? With no NVDs? Through four feet of snow? Don't be an ass. Call him. Kait would never forgive me if I let you kill yourself during your first trip up to visit us."

Aiden made kissing sounds and batted his eyelashes. "I didn't know you cared, bro."

Before Cosky came back with a brutal and probably amusing retort, a low, deep whine surrounded them. The Bell's floor vibrated beneath their feet. The chopper's hold held no windows, but even without seeing the ground getting smaller, Aiden could tell they were rising.

From what Rawls had told him earlier, the flight to Shadow Mountain's Neighborhood took twenty minutes, which meant the distance between the base and the township was somewhere around one hundred and thirteen klicks. Quite a distance to sink roots.

"Why build your Neighborhood so far out? You could have cut your commute by half if you'd set up camp just outside of Denali." Aiden adjusted the headset mic, which kept trying to migrate beneath his chin.

Cosky, who was slouched down in his seat, head against the wall, looking half asleep, didn't bother opening his eyes. "We wanted distance between the two in case the base was ever targeted. Besides, twenty minutes is perfect decompression time. By the time we set down, base pressures are behind us, and family time is ahead. We try to separate the two."

Aiden could see that. By the time the Bell circled and dropped, worries about Kuznetsov and nanobots had given way to worries about Demi and their future. Or lack thereof. Frowning, he organized the points he wanted to make into punchy sound bites.

What we've got together is great.

We can build on what we've already created.

I can give you a home and a family.

The sex is fantastic. We can build on that.

"Don't think about it so hard." Cosky sounded reluctant, like he didn't want to get drawn into the drama but was finding it impossible to remain neutral. "Thinking too much when it comes to women never ends well. Use your instincts. Speak from your gut."

Easy for him to say. The dude already had his woman roped and tied. Aiden rolled his shoulders and tried to relax.

You've got this. This isn't rocket science. You're not locked down, cut off from your brothers, with RPG strikes raining down all around you. This isn't life and death, no matter how much it feels like it.

With a light rocking motion, the Bell settled on the ground. The engine's roar decreased. So did the beat of the rotors. Aidan took his headset off, rose to his feet and dropped it on the empty seat. Cosky followed suit.

"Home sweet home."

Without the buffering of the headset, the beat of the Bell's rotors drowned most of Cosky's voice out. But Aiden was certain that the words he caught carried relief. No doubt Cosky was thrilled that the opportunity to dispense relationship advice had ended.

Cosky dragged the cargo hold door back, motioned Aiden out and followed him to the ground, dragging the door shut behind him again. They ducked and shuffled their way out from under the rotors. Once they'd cleared the icy backwash of the rotors, the winter chill felt lazier, even warmer.

Aiden took the scene in with a slow, focused scan. Emerald trees, with Christmas lights vaguely visible through clouds of fresh snow. It figured that Kait would go batshit crazy with the whole Christmas theme, and that her besotted husband would let her. He took another longer look around. Christ, there were trees everywhere. Dozens of boughs surrounded the house for unfriendlies to hide beneath. What the hell was Cosky thinking?

He shifted his attention to the house. It was full of windows and bright light. The whole place was lit up like a bullseye. He scowled. Had Cos lost his ever-loving fucking mind? All that light would lead the unfriendlies right to their door and those windows would make the place impossible to secure.

"We need to have a serious conversation about these trees and windows," he told Cosky, as the Bell took to the sky.

"If you can talk some sense into your sister about that, be my guest," Cosky muttered back as he brushed past Aiden.

The front door, with its festive holiday wreath, opened, and Kait stepped onto the porch. He could barely make out the crown of Demi's aqua-colored head behind his sister's shoulder.

Kait rushed down the steps, heading directly toward him. Aiden got a quick glimpse of Demi in the doorway, huddled in a thick tweed sweater jacket of blocky greens and blues. And then his sister blocked his view. He enveloped her in a hard hug, then pushed her back to give her a narrow eyed, leisurely, face to toe examination. Things had been in such an upheaval the last few times he'd seen her, which had been in the clinic. He'd paid little attention to how she looked. Cosky better be taking care of her, otherwise they'd be having a serious conversation—probably spelled out with knuckles and bruises.

His sister looked great, though. Much more relaxed than the last time he'd seen her, when anxiety and stress had drained the glow from her face.

He let her go and stepped back. "Looking good, sis. Denali agrees with you."

"Right?" Kait laughed, her voice exuberant. "Who would have guessed? I always thought I was a sun and sand kind of girl." She linked her arm with his and they lazily followed Cosky toward the porch. "I can't believe this is the first time you've been here. You know Wolf would have made an exception for you to visit, right?"

"No offense, but I wanted to spend what little downtime I had with my girl." He glanced at the open door, but Demi had disappeared.

"Yeah..." Her voice went quiet for a moment. She shot a quick glance toward the empty doorway, and the exuberance faded from her face. "Did Cosky tell you we're going out to dinner? He and I, I mean. You'll have privacy to talk to her."

From the sympathetic look that had replaced the joy, she didn't expect the convo to go well. Aiden's stomach tightened. Regardless of that gut shot expression his sister was wearing; he still had a chance to patch things up with Demi. He knew she had feelings for him. He had feelings for her, too—strong ones. Sure, there were problems they needed to work out. But every relationship had rocky moments.

Emotions held couples together during the rough patches, and they had those emotions in spades. They just needed to explore compromises, ones they could both live with.

He wasn't giving up on her.

He wasn't giving up on them.

Chapter Thirty

Day 14
Denali, Alaska

A cursory glance when Aiden walked through his sister's front door showed Kait's personality all over the place. The open floor plan, the endless windows, the red and green color scheme, even the high ceiling with the dozens of tiny, diamond-shaped windows. He didn't see Cosky anywhere in the design or decorating of their home. But then he wasn't looking for his brother-in-law's artistic stamp. He was far more focused on the aqua-haired beauty across the room.

She was standing so still and stiff, with such wariness on her face. His chest tightened and ached. He hated seeing her so uncomfortable around him. They'd never been uneasy around each other—not before they dove into bed, not while they were doing the dirty, and sure as hell not after. Until today. Until now.

"Have you heard anything about those nanobot things?" Kait asked, looking almost as uncomfortable as Demi.

Her eyes were bouncing between him and Demi so often, she was going to sprain them if she wasn't careful.

"Not yet," Aiden said. *Dammit.*

"Have you talked to your teammates' families? Explained to them what happened?" Kait shot a worried look toward Demi.

Aiden tensed. "Not yet."

He clipped the words out, hoping she'd get the message. SEAL deaths and family bereavement were not subjects he wanted to discuss in front of Demi, who was already skittish about such things. Relief hit when Cosky appeared from the other side of the kitchen.

"Babe," Cosky walked across the living room to the front door and pulled a crimson coat off the coat tree. He held it out to Kait. "We need to get on the road."

For the first time, Aiden realized Kait was dressed to kill. Hip-hugging black stretchy pants. A patchwork crimson and black jacket over a deep burgundy blouse. Her boots were crimson too, matching the jacket. Cosky looked like a bum by comparison. Although he had showered back at base before hopping on the Bell, and changed out of his BDUs into charcoal slacks and a light gray dress shirt since returning home. The accompanying jacket was—surprise, surprise—dark gray.

Cosky stuck to gray or black. Probably came from a life spent operating in the shadows, a life where standing out could get you and your brothers killed. No doubt, Kait was the only spot of color in his brother-in-law's drab life.

Which was another touchy subject, one he mentally added to his list of things not to talk about in front of Demi. Because his life mirrored Cosky's in every way, except for the woman by his side and the organizations they worked for. Although it was a tossup, whether Aiden even worked for WARCOM anymore. HQ1 might have declared him AWOL by now and sent the master-of-arms after him. Although, if that were the case, Dev would have mentioned it. Probably.

After a round of goodbyes, Kait and Cosky disappeared down the hallway next to the kitchen. The silence in the living room grew deeper and wider until the opening and closing of a door down the kitchen hall sounded as loud as an M14 blast.

"Their garage is through the utility room, which is down that hall," Demi offered awkwardly.

The heavy silence must have been getting to her too.

"Good to know." Aiden already knew how to access the garage in case they needed to escape the house through a secondary access point.

Earlier that afternoon, at the base, Cosky had unrolled a set of house plans across their cafeteria table and marked the access and escape points with a red marker. The more the dude talked about entrances and exits, the more obvious it became that while he might profess confidence in The Neighborhood's shield, he wasn't taking chances with Kait's safety.

"How's your cat?" What he really wanted to know was whether the damn thing was still scratching her to hell and back every time she got close to it. But asking that would just remind her of their last argument.

"He's doing great." Her dark eyebrows rose, and she nailed him with a knowing look. "Taking his meds like a little trooper. Hasn't scratched or bit me since we arrived."

Huh. That verified what Cosky had said, but such a dramatic shift in behavior seemed odd.

"But we both know you don't give a shit about the cat." There was a hint of challenge in Demi's voice.

Aiden kept his face flat. No, he didn't care about the damn cat. He only cared that it had hurt her. He added her cat to the list of topics to avoid discussing.

The silence grew to astronomical levels—until it resembled an emotional black hole, sucking the peace from the room and filling the space with unbearable tension. Driven to break the silence, he said the first thing that came to mind.

"How are you settling in?" Christ. He cringed. Talk about stupid questions.

"Fine." Demi's arms tightened around her waist. "What did Kait mean when she asked about nanobots?"

Ah, hell. Aiden groaned beneath his breath. Another subject he didn't want to get into. "I'm afraid that's classified."

Demi's lips pressed tight. "Kait knows about them."

"Because she works at Shadow Mountain. She was there when Wolf's crew found me." And had been blessed with several days in isolation because of it.

She just looked at him, her stance still, her face watchful. "Aiden, I'm tired of all your secrets, of being locked out of your life.

Ah, Fuck. Fuck. Fuck.

He scrubbed his palms down his face. This was a fucked if he did, fucked if he didn't conversation. Explaining what had happened would illustrate how dangerous his job was, which could drive her away. But refusing to explain could—probably would—push her away too.

Before he could respond, her shoulders slumped.

"Never mind." She sounded tired. Beaten.

He didn't make the mistake of assuming he was off the hook, not with that determined expression plastered across her face. She was just refocusing her mental energy.

She took a deep breath and began. "I know we talked over the phone about the fact I intend to break things off with you. I was just waiting until I could tell you in person. I didn't want to distract you during one of your missions."

"Yeah." The acknowledgement burned up his chest and throat and through his mouth. "I want to talk to you about that."

She shook her head. Sorrow flashed across her face before it hardened with resolve. "There's nothing to talk about. I haven't changed my mind."

Aiden's heart took off, pumping like he needed the oxygen and energy to stave off a life or death threat. "Look, I know now that you want more than I realized. But I can give you everything you need. The wedding. The kids. The white picket fence. A home. I can give you all of that."

"Can you?" A look of longing flared in her eyes, then died. "Because honestly... I don't think you can."

"I can." He inserted confidence into his voice. But his heart kept racing faster and faster, and his chest was getting tighter and tighter. And the certainty grew that he'd already lost her.

"The wedding, the white picket fence, the kids, those are just symbols. You can't give me the two things that turn those symbols into a home."

The look of sorrow on her face churned like ground glass in his gut—tearing him apart. He could feel the emotional distance between them expanding, pushing her further and further away.

"I'll give you everything, everything I can give." It came out as a promise. A hoarse, raspy promise that edged into a plea.

She nodded and wiped her cheeks, even though she wasn't crying. "That's the whole point, Aiden. You can't give me what I need. What I want. You're not wired for it."

Heat exploded in his chest. He felt like he was drowning in flames, like someone had dropped a lit napalm canister into his gut. "Demi, what we have is good. We can build on it."

"What we have is sex. Fantastic sex, true, but it's still just sex."

That stopped him cold. What? There was more than sex between them. His voice sharpened as anger lit. "You know damn well there's more than sex between us."

"Really? What else?" Her voice sharpened as well. "We haven't spent enough time together to build anything more. You're never home! We don't share a living space. We don't have a routine together. We haven't merged our tastes, discovered a favorite song, found a favorite restaurant, or even bought furniture or pictures together. We aren't a couple, not even close. All we do during those rare days you're in town is hop into bed. Sex. Sex. Sex. With periodic breaks for food—or for you to head off with your SEAL buddies for target practice. Even when you're in Coronado, half the time you're off with your teammates." She took a deep breath before adding quietly. "All of which would be fine—if all I wanted was sex, because yes, the sex is out of this world—but I want more. I want someone I can share my life with."

Aiden took a step back and regrouped. There had to be a way to make her see he could give her that life. "When we first hooked up, you told me you weren't looking for anything but a fuck buddy," he reminded her, keeping his voice calm, non-confrontational. "Friends with benefits—that's what you said you wanted. So that's what I gave you."

Even though he'd wanted everything she was asking for now. They were finally on the same page, wanting the same things. So why did she seem to be slipping further and further away?

"I know." Her voice trembled, but her shoulders were straight. Rock solid. Unbending. "But that's not what I want now. I want a husband. A home. A family. I want what Kait has."

"Which is what I wanted from the beginning with you. I only went with the fuck buddy arrangement to keep you close, to make sure I was the one sleeping next to you when you realized you wanted more than sex, when you realized you were ready to start over again, to move on from Donnie."

She didn't look convinced. But then why would she? He'd never shown her what she meant to him. He'd been too afraid it would send her running. Hell, he'd never even told her he loved her.

He needed to rectify that ASAP.

"Look..." He braced himself and leaped. "I've always wanted a life with you. I fell in love with you when Kait first introduced us, back when you were still married. I've been in love with you for God damned forever." The look on her face shifted. But not to joy. Not to disbelief. She looked...shattered. Fear kindled. He doubled down on his reassurances, desperate to make her believe him. "Demi, I want that house with you. I want the wedding and the kids. I want a family with you. I want what Cosky has."

Her face crumpled and huge, fat tears silently spilled down her cheeks. His chest burned. He drew her into his arms like she was priceless and fragile. But fear gnawed at him. Her expression was not one of relief. Her tears were the opposite of joy.

Something was wrong, but what? He'd told her he loved her. He'd told her they shared the same dream. Yet his love hadn't changed her mind. "Tell me what you're thinking."

"Do you know how Kait and Cosky turned this house into a home?" she asked into his shoulder, her voice thick.

He frowned; the question was so simple—there had to be a catch to it. "Because they love each other."

"No. Well, yes, that too." Her laugh was raw, and so sad it made his entire body clench. "But there's more to a home, to a life together than love. They share their lives, Aiden. They share themselves with each other."

His frown dug deeper. "Demi, nothing is stopping us from sharing our lives too. We can have what Kait and Cosky have."

She withdrew from his arms with a sigh and used her palms to scrub the tears from her cheeks. "When I said they share their lives, I meant they're together almost all the time." Squaring her shoulders, she looked him straight in the eye. "What's your plan, Aiden? Kait says she's not sure you're going to return to the SEALs. Is that true?"

He watched her cautiously. "I'm not sure. Things are up in the air at the moment."

She nodded, unsurprised by his confession. "If you don't remain with the SEALs, are you going to join Wolf and Cosky and your other friends here at Shadow Mountain?"

He instinctively shook his head. "I don't belong here."

"No? Then where do you belong? What will you do?"

Scowling, he backed up, creating space between them. There was an undercurrent to her question that scratched at him. Instinctively, he realized she was finally getting to the reason she was breaking up with him, and he wouldn't like it.

"Are you asking what I'm qualified to do for a living?" Although he sensed that wasn't what she was asking—it was something more. Something deeper. "Former SEALs are in high demand once they leave their teams. Trust me, I won't have trouble finding an alternative career path."

"I know you won't." Except...she didn't look relieved. "But whatever you do next will mimic your life as a SEAL, won't it? Saving people, protecting people, rescuing people. Going after bad guys. Racing all over the world being a hero." She paused, and her voice dropped to a whisper. "How often would you be home?"

And there it was. His throat tightened. "Demi—"

"I don't want an absent husband, Aiden." The resolve on her face was rock solid. Her voice strengthened. "I want a man who is home every night. Someone who eats dinner and breakfast with me. I want a man who's around to play with our kids, to teach them baseball and basketball, to take them camping on weekends. I want a husband who is embedded in our lives, not lurking in the periphery." Her voice thickened. "I want a husband who trusts me enough to share his secrets." Her voice turned watery. "Who trusts me enough to talk about his nightmares. I want what Kait has, a committed, present husband."

Aiden took another step back, his mind spinning.

"I trust you," he protested. But the thought of revealing his nightmares knotted his gut. He needed to protect her from what he'd seen...what he'd done. He needed to keep his personal life with her separate from his job.

If he left WARCOM, his new career would probably be in private security. There wouldn't be as much blood, or as much death in that line of work. The nightmares were bound to ease, maybe even vanish. At least he wouldn't disturb her sleep anymore.

Except a foggy, elongated face tried to push its way into his mind. He shoved it back. He had no clue what mission had spawned that freaky nightmare. But he'd had enough of it. Time to put it to rest.

He refocused, trying to find an argument that would appease her. If he joined a private security firm, he wouldn't be gone as long, or as often, as during his career with the SEALs. Although the job would still call him away. Even something as simple as protecting the rich and famous would involve traveling with the client—living with them when necessary. And rescue operations would involve even more time away from home—the planning, the scouting, the actual operation.

Unable to remain still, he circled the living room, his mind flipping through everything she'd said. He needed to buy some time to come up with a compromise that would convince her to give him another chance.

"Everything is fluid right now. I have no idea what I'll be doing tomorrow, let alone a month from now." He paused his pacing and turned to her, skimming a tired hand over his head. The exhaustion was back, sucking the ability to rationalize from his brain. "How about we pause this discussion until we have a better idea of where I'm headed and what I'll be doing?"

The only thing he knew for certain was that he'd be going after Kuznetsov as soon as he had a location. And yeah, that would involve several days away from Demi. But it was critical that they lock the bastard and his weapon down. Of course, bagging and interrogating Kuznetsov was just the beginning. They'd still need to identify the party responsible for developing the nanobot weapon and passing it off to Kuznetsov. Taking down the weapon's developer would mean even more time away from

Demi. But he wasn't willing to sit out on either operation. Demi would just have to accept that.

"But we know one thing already, don't we?" Demi's voice was too quiet and knowing for Aiden's peace of mind. "You won't be taking a nine-to-five desk job pushing papers around, will you? Anything you choose to do will be full of adrenaline and risk. It will be hero stuff. And heroes die." Her voice dropped to a whisper. "That's the other problem, Aiden. Death already took one man I loved. Losing him almost destroyed me...did destroy a part of me."

His breath caught. He took a shaky step toward her, suddenly seeing the chasm in front of them. "Demi—"

She held up her palm. "No. Let me finish. Before I met Donnie, before his death, I could have sent you off into danger, because part of me would have been certain you'd always come back. Part of me would have been certain that death would never happen to us, that we'd be spared. Donnie's death cured me of such foolish thinking." She took a deep breath and shook her head. "I'm sorry, but I won't sit around waiting for a knock on my door telling me I've lost you. I won't open myself—or my children—to that kind of pain." She sucked in a deep, raw breath and continued quietly. "I know what you do is important. I know the world needs men like you, men willing to sacrifice themselves to keep the world safe. But having to wait on the sidelines while you're off fighting the evil in the world, uncertain whether you're alive or dead, uncertain if I'll ever see you again... I can't do it. I won't do it. A life like that, full of uncertainty and fear, would destroy me."

Aiden reeled back, his hope that they could find a compromise extinguished by her explanation.

She'd been right. He couldn't give her what she needed. He was incapable of taking a pencil pusher job so she could have her safe husband.

If waiting on the sidelines, constantly fearing that knock on the door would destroy her, then sitting back, and letting others risk their lives to keep the world safe, would destroy him.

Numbness crashed into exhaustion, freezing him from the inside out, until nothing but emptiness remained. There was no compromise here. No way they could work their way through this. No way they could remain together.

Not without destroying each other.

Chapter Thirty-One

Day 15
Washington, D.C.

Clark leaned over his laptop and punched the execute key. A new screen popped up.

NNB26 prototype: Deactivate YES. NO.

Clark clicked on the YES square and slumped against the backrest of the computer chair.

Processing...

"It's done." Clark picked up his cell phone from the table in front of him and scanned the call log. No incoming call from Kuznetsov. Grimacing, he set it back down.

The stainless steel table his laptop sat on was a blur in front of his burning eyes as he swiveled his chair to face the lanky, thick-boned man in the white lab coat. Lovett was hunched over the desk that contained the computer and screen that monitored the Atomic Force Microscope that was mounted to the top of the NNB26 tank. Clark could access the AFM screen himself, but he'd have to close out of the programming window, navigate to the AFM sequencer, enter a slew of passwords and—he yawned. He was too damn tired for that. It was easier to let the good doctor monitor the AFM while he kept the programming window open. Although, if this last programming patch didn't work, he was all out of fixes.

"Well?" Clark flinched at the sharpness in his voice as the question hit the purified air.

It had been five long days, with very little sleep, and his head was giving him hell, so were his spine and shoulders. The human body was not built to hunch over a laptop for days on end. A steady dose of aspirin wasn't even easing the pain anymore.

"Nothing. They're still scrambling around like ants on their mound." Dr. Lovett rolled back his chair and straightened, arching his spine. His hands migrated to the small of his back. "No disruption at all this time."

"Damn." Clark was too tired to put any effort into his frustration. "They're circumventing my new programming faster each time."

It had taken his NNB26 prodigies half an hour to reactivate after his first round of programming. By his fourth attempt to shut them down, they hadn't deactivated at all. They'd followed the same pattern through each of his reprogramming attempts. His nanobots were fabricated to allow a complete reset, followed by multiple reprogrammings. After all, each batch of bots sold would need their own kill switch. Customers would not be pleased if their multi-million-dollar weapon was unexpectedly shut down because a different customer activated their weapon's off button. Before a batch of bots were sent off to their new owners, they'd be reset, then reprogramed to a specific code triggering deactivation.

Or at least that had been his intention.

But he'd also expected that resetting the prototype would wipe their programming and memory clean. But that wasn't what appeared to be happening. Resetting and deactivating them didn't wipe their memory. They simply never reset.

They were adapting to and circumventing his new programming faster than he could create the codes. A wave of exhaustion swept over him. If he were lucky—very, very lucky—a fresh approach to the kill switch problem would hit him after he got some sleep. Until then, there was nothing more he could do.

He picked his cell up again. Still no call from Kuznetsov. Which was strange. The Russian had been insistent about putting the bot prototype up for sale ASAP. At the very least, he'd expected the arms dealer to return his call and attempt to bully Clark into releasing their cash cow into the world prematurely, regardless of the consequences.

Kuznetsov wasn't big on thinking things through.

"It's time to consider implementing the fail-safe. This prototype is too dangerous to lose control of." His thumbs still pressed into the small of his back, Dr. Lovett swiveled his chair to stare at the osmium tank across the room. "Since the kill switches no longer work..." The worry on his face clearly spoke of his reservations. "It's my opinion we should hit NNB26 with the hydrofluoric acid."

Clark cast a tired glance around the lab. White walls, glass windows, and endless stainless-steel countertops surrounded him. Half a dozen stainless steel desks, facing each other in units of two, were spread throughout the room, supporting everything from computers to monitors to various types of electron microscopes, to piles of reference materials, along with pencils, pens, legal pads, loose sheaves of handwritten notes and electronic tablets.

His lab and the power grid supplying Nantz Technology were hardened against electromagnetic pulses. The NNB26 prototype was as well. He hadn't wanted his bots disabled if someone chose an EMP burst to shut his microscopic prodigies down. Dousing the tank with the acid was simple and would effectively dissolve the little bastards. They'd threaded silicon molecules through the bot structure to enable the fail-safe. The acid would dissolve the silicon, as well as most of the organic components. His little prodigies would cease to exist.

Dammit.

Five years of development, and hundreds of millions of dollars down the drain.

Dammit.

But Lovett was right. The weapon was too dangerous without the kill switch. It was also worthless. Nobody would buy it if they couldn't control it.

Still, he wasn't quite ready to give up on the prototype yet. Not when he was too tired to think clearly, so tired he might be missing a simple solution. A couple more days wouldn't hurt anything.

"Wait on the fail-safe for now." Clark's tired gaze traveled to the osmium tank. "NNB26 isn't going anywhere."

At least the bastards were contained. Osmium was the densest metal available. Not even his little prodigies could chew their way through it. Plus, the sheer weight of the tank, several tons at least, would prevent theft. Nobody was getting that sucker out of the lab. He'd had to use a lighter metal for Kuznetsov's carrying case—but then his microscopic soldiers hadn't needed to be contained for long during the testing period. Just long enough to drop them in the well.

"I need to get some sleep." He stretched. "My brain isn't functioning at full capacity. Once I've had some sleep, I'll reassess the situation."

If he had to scrap this iteration of the weapon and move on, they'd be looking at years of more work and millions more dollars.

He scrubbed his palms down his face, feeling the stubble of five days of frenetic activity against his palms. Sleep wasn't the only item on the agenda, so was a shower and a shave. "Get the fail-safe ready, but don't implement it yet."

"As you will." Lovett didn't sound happy with the decision.

"What of the cadavers from Karaveht?" Clark asked, his mind shifting to other complications.

"Still no evidence of nanobot activation in their samples," Lovett replied.

"Thank God for that," Clark muttered beneath his breath.

If the nanobots reactivated in the samples, or the cadavers, they'd be looking at a disaster. Sure, the room was off limits and password protected, and they were monitoring the samples remotely, but hell, all it would take was one person breaking protocol to infect everyone on site.

It hadn't occurred to him that the kill switch would quit working, or the bots could get out of control. If it wasn't crucial that the samples and cadavers be under constant observation, he'd incinerate everything as he'd done with most of the bodies they'd recovered from Karaveht. The few he'd kept for testing were currently frozen in the morgue on the lowest level of the Nantz building, as were the tissue, blood, and brain samples they'd pulled from the bodies they'd collected.

He frowned as Lovett went to work preparing the hydrofluoric fail-safe. It wouldn't hurt to dose the ashes of his test subjects from Karaveht with acid, too, make sure the bots couldn't reactivate amid the charred ashes of their hosts. It would mean digging up the pit they'd buried the ashes in, but better to err on the side of caution.

He picked up his phone as he rose to his feet. Still nothing from Kuznetsov. He'd left multiple messages telling the Russian to call. They could hardly proceed with the sale of NNB26 now, not with the weapon in such an uncertain state.

Kuznetsov wouldn't like the postponement of the sale. But there was nothing he could do about it.

Day 15
Denali, Alaska

"Mary, these cinnamon sticky buns are dangerous." Beth Winters, one of the clones' wives, refilled Demi's wine glass from the bottle on the coffee table and sat back down on the couch on the other side of Kait. "Zane's obsessed with them and he's usually not a pastry kind of guy."

Beth was an elegant blonde with the most unusual violet eyes, the kind of eyes Demi had always thought were myth rather than reality.

"Rawls will swear to his last breath that he doesn't like Mary's sticky buns better than mine." A smile softened Faith's deep blue eyes as she brushed a strand of dark hair back. "But we both know he's lying."

"I doubt that, honey." Mary's smile carried a hint of raunchiness, signaling what was to come. "He's never been privy to my sticky bun."

A beat of silence fell before raucous laughter filled the room and comparisons to sticky buns and other sexual innuendos took flight.

The bookstore felt like it was bursting with women, although there were only seven in attendance; she, Kait, and Beth sharing the comfy couch, two on the loveseat on the other side of the coffee table, and one in each of the armchairs that flanked the couch. The bookstore's sitting area was arranged to facilitate conversation, and the chatter hadn't stopped since she'd followed Kait into the store.

The owner of the Book Nook, a petite redhead with hazel eyes, round glasses, and a mop of curly red hair, had opened her store at 7:00 p.m. to host the book brigade. Mary brought an assortment of pastries. Everyone brought a bottle or two of their favorite wine. The conversation and laughter flowed smoothly. So did the wine. The atmosphere was vibrant and joyful.

She shouldn't have come.

While Kait's posse had welcomed her with warmth and generosity, including her in their conversations and laughter, Demi felt like she was sleepwalking. Her body might sit on this couch beside Kait, but her spirit was drifting, grieving, mourning an unbearable loss.

She thought she'd prepared herself to let Aiden go. She hadn't. Not even close.

It made no sense why it hurt so much to cut ties with a man who was barely in her life. Why each breath without him felt dipped in flames. The world suddenly felt empty and leaden. His deployments had been bad, but this...this was even worse. Why? She'd spent far more time without him than with him. She'd gotten used to the loneliness when he was gone. But this didn't feel the same. It was deeper, darker, emptier.

Permanent.

She'd heard people compare losing someone they loved to losing an appendage—the severing of an arm or a leg. But that wasn't what it felt like to her. Not with her parents, or Donnie, or even Aiden. Instead, it felt like a never-ending hollowness inside her, an emptiness so deep and vast she felt like she was drowning.

From experience, she knew that the emptiness would eventually fill in, become less deep, less wide, more bearable. But for now, there was only pain and barrenness.

Another burst of laughter swept the room. She fought to focus on the present, on the women, the conversation, and her surroundings. Books were everywhere. Colorful or somber covers were in every corner of the room—stacked on bookshelves, on tables, even perched in the built-in nooks climbing the rustic walls.

Which felt appropriate as the Book Brigade was discussing books, or, at least, one book. Their choice for this week's discussion was *The Ex I'd love to Hate*, a billionaire romantic comedy, by an author named Nadia Lee.

Judging by the laughter and excited chatter, everyone loved it. And the book did sound delightful. Who didn't love a grumpy hero out for revenge and a snarky heroine who gave as good as she got? Kait offered her a copy to read before the meeting, but Demi passed. A romance, no matter how funny, just wasn't appealing. Not at the moment, not after ripping her heart out and tossing it into the frigid Alaskan night.

"Oh. My. God!" Olivia Holden squealed. An honest to God squeal. "Did any of you read *Baby for the Bosshole*? The first book in Nadia's Lasker Brothers series? It's just as funny as the one we read for tonight."

Mary, another brunette with glowing skin, long inky hair, and soft brown eyes, laughed back. "The way Emmett kept ruining her dates by making her work late—"

Kait snickered. "And how he thought he was doing her a favor, because redoing spreadsheets was so much fun—"

"I just love her sense of humor," Beth added. "Like what she named the hamster in *My Grumpy Billionaire*."

Demi absently listened. While she loved the idea of a book club, a thriller novel would suit her current mood better. One where everyone died...except for the dog or the cat.

Not that she blamed Kait for dragging her to this meeting. They'd agreed that a couple of hours spent discussing books and drinking wine was a better alternative than staying home and brooding. The laughter, conversation, and wine should provide the distraction she needed. Yet it didn't. Her mind kept flipping back to the night before.

She'd spent the last twenty-four hours replaying the conversation with Aiden in her head. What she'd said, what he'd said. The defeated look on his face when he realized there could be no compromise between them.

He said he loved her. And she believed him. Aiden wouldn't lie about that. Not even to keep her in his life. Her stomach clenched, the wine sloshing sourly before trying to climb her tight throat.

If only love made a difference.

But love wouldn't bridge this gulf between them. It wouldn't keep him content in a safe 9 to 5 job. If they married, it wouldn't keep the anxiety from ripping her soul to shreds while he was gone, doing whatever he ended up doing. For her, love just made the fear worse.

Eventually, their love would turn to resentment, and then to anger. They needed to break things off now, before their love grew claws and teeth and started to rend and tear. Eventually, these feelings would wither and die, leaving them both free to find new partners, new loves, a new life with someone else. Someone who was on the same page, someone who wanted the same things.

An image flashed through her mind; Aiden with his arms around a faceless woman, her belly round with child. Another flash; a dark-haired toddler cradled in Aiden's muscled arms.

She flinched. Her stomach rolled again. Sourness burned up her throat. She choked the bile down and shook the images away.

Don't think about that. Not that. It will get easier. Each day will be easier.

The promise rang hollow in her mind, like a lie.

To distract herself, she focused back on the conversation, anything to avoid the expanding rift in her soul.

"Cosky isn't saying," Kait said. "But it's coming. That's obvious."

The tension in Kait's voice caught Demi's attention. She frowned, wishing she'd paid more attention. The book discussion was apparently over. Whatever they were talking about now was upsetting everyone. She could see the effect it was having on Kait. The skin at the corners of her eyes looked pinched, and her eyes were too wide, the whites showing. Clear signs of anxiety.

"Zane isn't talking either." Beth's voice was tight. "But we know they'll go after whoever attacked Aiden. They crewed with Aiden's teammates. They won't let their deaths slide." She turned her head toward the left armchair where Olivia was sitting. "What about Samuel? Has he said anything to you?"

Aiden? What did this conversation have to do with Aiden? Demi's gaze shifted from tense face to tense face.

"All Samuel will say is that this new weapon, the one that was used against Kait's brother and his SEAL team, cannot go up for sale," Olivia said. "He says if it deploys, it will be catastrophic."

Silence fell over the room. A thick, tense silence. Kait was the one who broke it.

"Samuel's right. I can't...I can't go into detail." Kait sent a fleeting glance at Faith. "But this new weapon, the one used on Karaveht, then on Aiden and his team..." She shook her head, her eyes going shiny and blind. "If someone were to use this on the general population, it could sweep the globe faster than anyone could stop it."

So, only Kait and, from that sidelong glance, probably Faith, knew what their men were facing. Which made sense as both women worked at Shadow Mountain. At least Aiden hadn't been lying when he said the situation was classified.

"We're working on countermeasures." Faith's voice was quiet. Steady. But her face had gone so pale, the hundreds of freckles stretching across her cheeks and nose stood out like flecks of gold. "Methods to stop the weapon from spreading and to protect the population from its effects."

"Kait, Faith, I know you can't tell us what happened to Aiden and his men, nor what this new threat is. Zane says the information is restricted." Beth's voice was as tight as her face. "And I know the clones all think that keeping us in the dark will make things easier on us, that if we don't know what they're up against, we'll worry less." She blew out a breath and blindly reached for Kait's hand. Their fingers curled and clung. "But they're wrong. Knowing the enemy makes the danger less scary. I wish they'd just tell us what's going on."

A murmur of agreement went around the couches and armchairs. Still, neither Kait nor Faith broke their silence. Demi wondered how much of their tight-lipped reticence was because of the confidentiality of their jobs versus promises to their husbands.

What was it about this new weapon that had the clones so rattled? Her mind flashed back to the night before, and the brief exchange between Kait and Aiden. She'd asked him about nanobots.

Was that what this weapon was? Some kind of nanobot plague?

She almost asked Kait but withheld the question at the last moment. She didn't want to put her friend in an awkward position when it was clear Kait didn't have permission to divulge anything.

"I just wish..." Kait's voice faltered. "...that it wasn't Shadow Mountain and our guys who end up fighting the evil assholes of the world. I thought things would be safer after they brought down the New Ruling Order."

"It has been safer," Beth said. "Ever since they joined Shadow Mountain, they've been home almost every night. They've been sent on more training, rescue, and good Samaritan missions than battles. But we knew that wouldn't last. We knew the NRO wasn't the only greedy, evil organization out there. Eventually, they were bound to get sucked into another save the world situation."

Kait sighed, offering a slow nod. "Benioko even said as much when he asked the clones to join Shadow Mountain."

Faith swallowed hard, her face still white and drawn, her freckles a blazing band across her cheeks. "We've been lucky so far. But we need to prepare for what's coming, for when they leave."

Demi tensed. Aiden would join the Shadow Mountain forces when they went after the men behind this new weapon. She knew that, without a doubt. Her heart picked up speed, slamming against her ribs. Chills prickled her spine. He wouldn't stand aside and let the clones and his half-brother's soldiers take down the monsters who'd killed his team. Instead, he'd do everything possible to shut down this deadly new weapon and the men who'd developed it.

Her stomach churned at the thought. It didn't matter that she'd broken things off with him. There hadn't been enough time for her feelings to die. She still loved him. That hadn't changed. How ironic. The fear and anxiety she'd tried to avoid were already rolling around inside her.

"How in the world do you handle something like this?" she asked out loud, her gaze skimming the tense faces of the women surrounding her. "Knowing someone you love is in danger. How do you stop the fear from eating you alive?"

A few seconds of weighty silence fell before multiple sighs broke the silence.

"By keeping busy," Kait finally said, with a glance at Beth and then Faith. "At least that's how we handled it when the guys were fighting the NRO. It helps to have someone to talk to, someone who's in the same boat, experiencing the same fear."

Beth nodded. "We stayed busy, and we had each other." Her lavender eyes darkened and went distant. "While the guys were off fighting, we'd get together. We'd talk, binge Netflix, play cards or board games, discuss books. That's where the book club idea came from."

"And wine." Kait's lips twisted. She looked half amused and half terrified. "I remember us drinking loads and loads of wine."

Olivia sighed and rubbed at her furrowed eyebrows. "The worst thing we can do is sit around and obsess about what's happening to them, worry about the danger they're in. That's a surefire way to crazy town."

Nods of agreement went around the room.

"So, we hang together and stay busy." Kait squared her shoulders and forced a smile. "We'll get through this together. Book by book, movie by movie, wine bottle by wine bottle."

Demi's swallow got stuck in her throat. She wanted to believe it was as simple as that. She really did. But she could already see the flaws to that approach. Here they were, together, talking books, drinking wine. Their men weren't even gone yet.

And yet, fear and anxiety were stamped across every one of their faces.

Chapter Thirty-Two

Day 16
Denali, Alaska

Aiden lowered the barbell to the rack, the heavy clang of metal hitting metal echoing in his ears. Sitting up on the padded bench, he sucked air in and blew it out of his laboring lungs. His heart was pounding hard enough to rattle his ribs. His pulse thundered in his ears. Sweat slicked his hair and trickled down his face. Christ, his t-shirt and shorts were already sticking to his damp skin. Grimacing, he used the bottom of his shirt to mop his streaming face.

It was embarrassing how out of shape he was. He'd barely been working out for thirty minutes, and at a weight set to half of normal, yet he couldn't catch his breath. Hell, his legs and arms felt like pudding. He shouldn't tap out so easily, or so soon. He couldn't even blame the exhaustion on blood loss. The vamps in the lab had ignored him for the past three days.

Thank Christ, the weight room was empty. He could do without the taunts his so-called buddies would pile on him at this lackluster performance.

It was 4:00 a.m., two days after talking to Demi. He'd hit the gym early this morning, well before Wolf's warriors would start arriving. Some alone time, that's what he'd been looking for. A quiet space away from his quarters and the four walls he was climbing, a peaceful place to work his body, which always focused his mind.

He needed to launch a hard pivot in his quest to locate Kuznetsov. Devlin was still coming up empty, as were Wolf's intelligence operatives. Nobody knew where the Russian was holed up and time was ticking down. That fucking weapon could go up for sale at any minute, and they had no intel on who'd developed it, or where it was located. They needed a break, and fast.

The urgency to take action kept ramming into his inability to act. He couldn't even work up a strategy until they located the asshole and knew the terrain they'd be inserting into. The frustration was enough to drive him to drink, particularly when combined with the sucker punch Demi had delivered to his heart.

Concentrating fiercely on his heavy breathing, he backed away from thoughts of Demi, and locked down the loss and regret. She wasn't his future anymore. He had to accept that and move on. He needed to focus on Kuznetsov.

The door to the gym squeaked open and then banged shut. Aiden scowled and glanced over. His scowl gained strength at the sight of O'Neill standing in front of the door, his hand bunched inside the pocket of his sweats. Of all the guys who could have joined him so early in the morning, did it have to be this asshole? The one with a boulder sized chip on his shoulder?

But then Dev's voice echoed through his mind.

The spook got a hit on a coded file...Stargate...classified by ODNI.

Aiden's scowl faded. He eyed O'Neill thoughtfully. It was unlikely there was a connection between O'Neill and the super-secret file Dev had unearthed. But if Stargate had something to do with O'Neill, then the dude had connections. The kind of connections that might get a lock on Kuznetsov.

Of course, ODNI could—probably would—target him if the conversation got back to them. Those boys didn't appreciate anyone nosing into their classified operations. He weighed the risk and shrugged. So far nothing was working, Kuznetsov was still in the wind. To take the Russian down, he needed to think outside the box. Asking O'Neill for help wasn't just outside the box—it was outside the entire building. He pushed himself up from the bench. Praying that his mushy legs would keep him upright, he headed across the room.

His hand still bunched inside his pocket; O'Neill watched him approach. The closer Aiden got, the flatter the dude's face became. Those eerie eyes turned cold and calculating.

"Winchester," O'Neill drawled once Aiden stopped in front of him. He scanned Aiden from head to sneakers, looking supremely unimpressed. "You're up early."

His tone implied Aiden looked so awful he should have stayed in bed. Aiden couldn't fault the dude for the disparagement. He suspected he looked every bit as shitty as the dude had implied.

"Could say the same about you." At least when it came to the up early part of the greeting. Aiden studied O'Neill's face. It looked shuttered and unwelcoming.

Someone wasn't happy to have company this morning. Maybe O'Neill used early morning gym hours as his alone time too. This was the first time Aiden had hit the benches so early. He didn't know when O'Neill worked out.

There was no non-confrontational approach to this conversation. The fact he'd asked someone to run a search on the dude through the soups network was already confrontational. If O'Neill was a spook, he wouldn't be pleased to find an inquiry had hit his name—assuming he hadn't already been alerted to the probe.

There was no sense in tiptoeing around the subject, so he went in with all weapons firing.

"I had a buddy run you through the soups and spooks network and fuck if he didn't get a hit."

O'Neill's eyebrows climbed. Amusement touched his face. "I highly doubt that."

Aiden let nothing show on his face. Internally, though, he was one big grimace.

Sure, he'd hoped for some reaction to the news. But amusement? Not so much that. A reaction more guarded would be nice. Maybe a flicker of tension or sudden stillness. Mockery and sarcasm were not on his list of obvious tells.

But then, if the dude was ODNI, he wouldn't give a damn thing away. Those boys were machines. Trained to kill. Trained to deceive. Trained for non-reaction to reactionary events. Aiden frowned. They were also trained to subvert, to disarm, to use whatever they could to muddy the waters.

Like mockery and sarcasm? Probably. But then, that could just be an O'Neill thing. Christ knew the guy was an asshole.

Aiden's mind rewound to the meeting where he'd briefed the Shadow Mountain warriors on what had happened in Karaveht. O'Neill's questions had been thoughtful, even surprising. Maybe there was more to the bastard than he let on. Maybe there wasn't. Neither possibility mattered. He couldn't afford to leave any stone unturned. If O'Neill was or had been ODNI, he'd have contacts, contacts Dev didn't have access to, contacts that could prove invaluable.

He needed to ask the bastard for a favor.

Fuck, did that burn.

Scrubbing a hand through his hair, Aiden yawned and wobbled slightly as a sudden, bone deep exhaustion crashed over him. Again. *What the hell?* He'd gotten some actual sleep over the past two days. Plenty of it. He shouldn't be so damn tired. Nor should those bench reps from earlier have drained him, not to this extent.

Maybe he should swing by the clinic when he left the gym, have the docs check him out.

"You okay?" O'Neill asked, the two words drawn out with obvious reluctance.

Hell, he must look even worse than he felt if O'Neill was expressing concern.

"Just peachy." He grimaced and ran a hand down his face, hesitating several beats too long. Yeah, he was stalling. He dropped his hand and focused on O'Neill's blank face and sharp eyes.

"Look, I don't know if my contact's info is square. No clue if you're Stargate, or with ODNI. What I do know is that we've got a big problem. None of my or Wolf's contacts are zeroing in on Kuznetsov or the nanobot weapon. We can't afford to wait, not anymore. Not when that damn thing could go off at any moment."

O'Neill was silent for one...two...seconds. "I'm listening."

Well, that was something, at least.

Aiden nodded, taking a tired breath. Chills suddenly swept across his hot skin, leaving goosebumps and shivers in their wake. Damn, maybe he was getting sick. Which would make it the first time in... He tried to think back but couldn't remember the last time he'd picked up a cold.

O'Neill, he abruptly noticed, was watching him with narrowed eyes and a wrinkled forehead. Much more of this silence and the dude was going to express concern again.

What had he been saying? Oh, yeah—contacts.

"I know we didn't get off to the best start. But these bots are above us—above all of us. If they get loose—" he sucked in a sharp breath, the livid, raging faces of his dead brothers swelling in his mind. "We won't be the only ones to pay the price. The entire world will blow up alongside us." He broke off to massage the ache spreading through his temples. "I'm not asking for confirmation about your background. But if you are, or were a spook, then, for God's sake, reach out to your contacts. Nobody will question where the intel came from. I'll make sure of it. I'll keep this conversation private. But we need a break. If you can provide that break, then for Christ's sake, make some calls."

He didn't wait for a response, just brushed past O'Neill's frozen form and headed for the door. Exhaustion dogged every step. A hammer chiseled at his skull. Chills coursed through him with increasing intensity. He didn't have anywhere to be, anything to do. For all of two seconds, he considered swinging by the clinic, having them run more tests—make sure those damn nanobots weren't rocking and rolling in his noggin.

Except they'd run every test known to the medical field and given him a clean bill of health. Plus, these new symptoms didn't match the ones he'd witnessed in his team brothers. He checked his hand. No twitching. Nor was he feeling particularly enraged and paranoid. It was probably just a cold, which sleep, fluids, and some healthy chow would cure.

He followed the sidewalk to the elevator and pushed the button for the third level, where his quarters were located. A couple hours of shuteye, followed by a good breakfast were in order. If that didn't curb the exhaustion, headache, and chills, he'd pay the clinic a visit.

Day 16
Denali, Alaska

His fingers fiddling with the small leather pouch tucked in his pocket, O'Neill watched the Shadow Warrior's chosen one stagger out the door. The squid looked wrecked, like he'd just climbed off a hell of a bender. The gray face. The stumbling. The obvious fatigue. The sweats. Okay, maybe not the sweats. Wolf's younger bro had been working out, after all. But Winchester was ripped, a sure sign of someone who'd turned exercise into an obsession. Guys who zealously worked out didn't sweat so copiously.

Except Winchester didn't have that telltale stink of boozy toxins seeping from his pores. Nor had Winchester's eyes been red or sensitive to the light, which ruled out the hangover theory.

Something else must have been ailing the chosen one. Woman trouble, perhaps? There had been obvious friction between the bright-haired woman on the plane and Wolf's little bro. O'Neill considered that for longer than he should have. It made no difference if Winchester and the woman on the plane were splitting. He had no iron in that fire.

Except for the cat. He liked the cat.

Still, it was hard to imagine that breaking up with some chick would hit Winchester like a hangover. Whatever was going on with the dude had to be something else. Something more. Not that it was any of his business. Not that he cared, even if the bastard had the balls to ask him for a favor, which brought up something else entirely.

Annoyance rippled through him. Did the asshole really think O'Neill had to be *asked* to reach out to his contacts? That he hadn't done so immediately when it became clear how dangerous this new weapon was? Did Winchester and the rest of them *really* think he'd let the world go insane and all the people in it slaughter each other unless someone asked him *nicely* to stop it?

He huffed a disgusted breath, bitterness rising. What the hell was wrong with him? Why was he still here, skulking around this motherfucking base, where nobody bothered to talk to him, but everyone thought the worst of him? He scowled, his fingers clamping over the *heschrmal* totem in his pocket. He should slide back into the shadows and do his part to keep the world safe all by his lonesome.

Except he couldn't leave. Not now, not when everything the *Taounaha* had shown him was coming true.

The ability the *heschrmal* had given him was more curse than gift. He'd used it three times since the spirit lion had appeared before him. Its use the first time had been accidental and drove him from the *Brenahiilo*. The second time, it had been used against him deliberately, and forced him back among those who despised him. This last time, when he'd attempted to use it on the prisoners from California, the gift had proved useless. But then none of Winchester's fancy drugs had pulled info from them either. Maybe his *heschrmal* talent hadn't failed. Maybe those two assholes had nothing useful to share.

He'd spent a full year hanging around base because of what the *Taounaha* had shown him. What a waste of time and tolerance. The mouthpiece had advised patience, had told him his presence was required early, even though the apocalypse hadn't yet tiptoed into view.

Benioko stressed building rapport and trust with Wolf and his warriors. O'Neill grimaced, every synapse in his brain vibrating with irritation. Yeah, that hadn't gone well. He was still *jie'van*. The unwanted one.

Outcast.

He would have left months ago if those damn visions Benioko had shoved into his mind didn't still haunt his dreams, if the knowledge of what was coming didn't fill him with dread.

O'Neill hadn't asked to see it, hadn't asked to be involved, didn't want to be a part of this Herculean attempt to save the world—and all the people in it. But he couldn't turn his back on it either, and he sure as hell hadn't asked to witness his own death or the irony surrounding it.

And the kicker—the greatest irony of all—was that the only person he'd trusted way back when, the one person he'd exposed his true self to, would never know that despite her betrayal, he'd still knowingly sacrificed himself to save her life along with everyone else on the planet.

He scoffed beneath his breath. She'd done him a favor, really. Taught him to trust no one, count on no one. Her betrayal had driven him from the *Brenahiilo* and stung a promise from him. The promise that he'd never return, never let anyone betray him again.

Yet wasn't that exactly what he was doing? Setting himself up for the ultimate betrayal? None of the warriors on this base gave a shit about his ass. When the situation went sideways, which it would, he'd be left out in the cold.

He never should have let Benioko talk him into joining Shadow Mountain. He should have stayed put and fought against the end of humanity from the shadows where he worked best. He'd still end up dead, but on his own terms, watching his own back instead of sacrificing himself to keep other warriors alive.

Grimacing, he turned toward the door. Aiden Winchester was right about one thing, though. It was time to reach out to his people—again. His real people. The ones he could count on. Find out if they'd pinpointed who was behind this apocalyptic weapon and if they had a location on Kuznetsov yet. But most of all, he needed to brace himself, because the storm was coming and about to swallow him whole.

The *Taounaha* and the Shadow Warrior owed him one. A big one. Like fucking everything. When he joined the web of his ancestors, he had better live like a king.

Chapter Thirty-Three

Day 16
Denali, Alaska

Five hours after his embarrassingly wimpy workout, Aiden awoke to a banging on his door. He grabbed his tactical pants from beside the bed and fumbled into them with shaking hands and legs. Fuck, he felt worse—a lot worse—than he'd felt prior to shucking his clothes and falling asleep. He wrenched the door open and twisted left to avoid Cosky's fist, which—since the door was out of the way—was headed straight for Aiden's face.

"Jesus H. Christ." Aiden added a long step back to the torso twist, hoping to avoid a broken nose. Cosky's summons sailed harmlessly by. "Be careful with that thing."

"Why aren't you answering your phone?" After a quick head-to-toe scan, Cosky frowned. "You look like shit, bro."

"So I've been told." Aiden yawned. His five-hour nap obviously hadn't done him any favors. Time to stop by the clinic.

Still frowning, Cosky stepped back. "Get your ass into some clothes. We've got a location on your arms dealer. Wolf has called a briefing." A pair of black eyebrows climbed, almost disappearing into Cosky's hairline. "I assume you want to join us?"

Aiden didn't waste time confirming that ridiculous question. Instead, he slammed the door in his brother-in-law's face. The clinic would have to wait. He had a briefing to go to.

He threw on a loose t-shirt, pulled on socks and his shitkicker boots, and headed for the door. Each stride felt heavy, achy. His scalp tightened beneath the pounding inside his skull. His gut gave a small but obvious heave. Just one more annoying symptom to add to his growing list of ailments. He was hot, too. Way too hot. Fever hot.

His memory rewound to those minutes on the hills above Karaveht, to the raging, insane eyes of his brothers, to rifle fire and obliterated faces.

Could these sudden symptoms be nanobot related?

The question stopped him in his tracks. No fucking way. He was sick, that was all. A flu or a cold. Maybe food poisoning. He rarely got sick—but hell—it happened every once in a triple blue moon.

The docs had found no sign of nanobot activity inside him during their endless rounds of testing. Besides, why would the bots affect him now? It was over two weeks post-Karaveht. If he'd been infected, the signs would have shown before now. Plus, these symptoms—the shakes, the queasy gut, the headache—they weren't the ones his teammates had shown.

Still, he scowled. He'd better swing by the clinic instead of joining the rest of the boys in the conference room. If he was contagious—with *anything*—he couldn't afford to infect the entire Shadow Mountain force, sure as hell not now, when they finally had a location on Kuznetsov.

"Son of a bitch!" he snarled beneath his breath.

Frustration and disgust swelled until he felt like he was about to explode. *goddammit*. Things were finally moving, and he was sidelined by this shit. If he knew for certain he wouldn't infect the entire base, he'd join the briefing, regardless of how shitty he felt.

It royally sucked being responsible.

He yanked open the door again. Cosky was gone, thank Christ. Hopefully that five second conversation hadn't transferred the crud currently ruining Aiden's day to his brother-in-law.

Some dude in grease-stained overalls was waiting for the elevator. Aiden took the stairs, giving the guy plenty of room to avoid infecting him. As he stomped his way down the stairs, he pulled his cell phone from the pocket of his tactical pants. Missed call after missed call lit up the call log. He thumbed the number that belonged to Wolf. His big bro answered before the second ring.

"I'm headed to the clinic. I've either picked up some kind of crud, or those damn nanobots are late to the party. I'm not taking the chance of infecting anyone—whether I'm carrying the flu or the bots." He grimaced at the surge of fear that accompanied the bot part of the statement.

Don't panic…don't think about it…it could be nothing.

Too bad his overactive heart and adrenal system refused to listen to his brain. He hesitated, then forced himself to ask the obvious question.

"You have any of those visions? One that might concern me?" Aiden asked, trying like hell to keep his voice casual.

Wolf's silence ate the line. And then— "There have been no visions from the Shadow Warrior. Not as of recent."

Which must mean that no, Wolf had not seen Aiden's imminent demise. The admission would have been reassuring, except it hadn't been Wolf who'd dreamed of that clusterfuck above Karaveht. According to Wolf and Cosky, that lucky save had come courtesy of Benioko's warning from the elder gods.

Maybe he should have called Benioko instead of Wolf. Nah.

One level down, two more to go. He headed down the second stairwell, his head throbbing in earnest, his boot strikes a muffled thud in his ringing ears. This line of questioning wasn't doing his headache any favors. Time to move on. "What's the sitrep with Kuznetsov?"

"The *Taounaha* has located him."

Aiden's eyebrows flew up. He recognized the Kalikoia title for the shaman. Perhaps he hadn't heard correctly through his ringing ears. "Benioko? He supplied the location?"

He suspected he'd heard the name just fine, though. Dammit. Now that was a surprise. An unwelcome one. Call him suspicious, but how the hell had the old man picked up the arms dealer's scent? Did the shaman have contacts, those not godlike? Maybe everyday ordinary spooks that provided photo evidence and GPS locations?

"Yes." The confirmation was flat. Like big bro was expecting push back. As he should.

"How the hell did he suss that out? A vision straight from the Shadow Warrior?" Aiden winced at how antagonistic he sounded. Judging by the icy silence thickening between them, his big bro didn't appreciate the mockery. Better dial his tone back.

On the second-floor landing, bent almost double beneath the wheezing of his lungs and cramping of his muscles, he paused to catch his breath. All this agony from walking down two flights of stairs. Stairs, for Christ's sake.

What had they been talking about? Oh, right. Benioko and his visions. Fuck, he hoped Wolf knew what he was doing, trusting the shaman's intel like this.

After using the bottom of his t-shirt to swipe at the sweat trickling into his eyes, he opened the stairway door to the first floor. The blood whooshed through his head in a rapid, sickening throb. The corridor in front of him was empty. Thank Christ. He turned right, the gray walls and floor bleeding into an endless, shimmering tunnel.

His head went light and started spinning. He stopped, leaning against the wall for stability, vaguely aware of Wolf's demanding voice calling his name. He swallowed hard, fought to force the vomit back into his lurching gut, and pressed the phone harder against his ear.

"You sound like a dying buffalo. Do I need to send medical to you?"

Even with the phone pressed tight to his ear, Wolf's voice sounded tinny and distant. "It wouldn't hurt."

The next wave of nausea hit so hard and fast he couldn't keep it down. He leaned over and vomited, twice, in quick succession. After a few seconds of nothing, he straightened and used the sleeve of his shirt to wipe his mouth. When he slumped back against the wall again, his legs gave out. Slowly, his t-shirt rasping against the wall, he slid down until his ass hit the hot floor. Of course, floors weren't hot. The heat was coming from him.

Was Wolf still on the line? He didn't ask, just started talking.

"I'm in the main corridor, twenty feet from the stairs." So far, he hadn't run into anyone, but that was pure dumb luck. "Tell everyone to steer clear of me. No clue what I have. But it hits hard and fast. If this shit goes through your boys..."

Out of breath, he let the warning trail off. Wolf would've gotten the message. His big bro wasn't stupid. Distantly, he heard the rumble of his brother's voice, although he couldn't decipher the words, just the tone. A comforting rumble of worry. It sounded like his dad's voice, which was strange. Until now, he'd never thought Wolf and Dad sounded the same.

He latched onto that familiar, comforting rumble as the gray tunnel sucked him in and swallowed him whole.

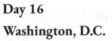

Day 16
Washington, D.C.

With a heavy sigh and slumped shoulders, Lovett rolled his chair away from the computer monitor. "It's clear that an acid bath does not render the NNB26 prototype inert." His white hair a crazy, tousled mess thanks to the countless times he'd raked his fingers through it, he swiveled to stare at Clark. "It's time to explore other options."

"Agreed." Clark dragged his gaze from the magnified view inside the NNB26 tank. The bots were scurrying around like an angry colony of ants. The last acid bath had pissed them off rather than destroying them. It had also mutated them. They were no longer black and round, they were almost translucent and oval.

So far, all acid options had failed. Yet their other fail-safe options were a logistical nightmare. An EMP blast wouldn't affect them. An MRI was questionable. Still, it was hard to argue against Lovett's advice when every acid they'd dumped over the bots had failed to permanently dissolve them.

He stood, arched his back, and wandered over to the small Osmium tank sitting on the stainless-steel table. The container, which had been specially designed and manufactured to hold the prototype, while withstanding an acid wash, currently housed millions of the nanobots—somewhere around ten percent of his supply. The bots had been transferred to the chamber before he'd programmed them, when they'd been safe to handle. A larger vat made of osmium housed the rest in a secure clean room down the hall.

On paper, hydrofluoric acid should have dissolved the nanobots. And dousing them with the acid had worked...at first. They'd been a melted, charred mess for a couple of hours. But then some had revived. Then more. Then the rest of them. The damn things had used the acid as material to rebuild themselves. Lovett hit them with more hydrofluoric acid. The bots were active again within the hour. On the third dose, they didn't dissolve at all. That same pattern had followed with each acid they'd tried. Except the revival times shortened with each test.

It was the damnedest thing. His organic prodigies were learning how to protect themselves. Clark felt simultaneously impressed with their ingenuity—like a proud papa—and thoroughly terrified.

If they couldn't deactivate the damn things with the kill switch or destroy them with acid, how would they stop them if they escaped their tanks?

Not gonna happen...those tanks are bot proof. Acid proof. Disaster proof. They've held the little bastards for years. They'll hold them for an eternity. You need to focus on matters of more concern.

The silent reassurance might have been comforting if the bots weren't changing. Evolving. Who knew what trouble the microscopic monsters were heading toward?

"Look into alternative methods to shut them down." Clark returned to the desk his laptop was on and picked up his phone. The nanobots weren't the only uncertainty plaguing him.

Kuznetsov still hadn't returned his phone calls. The silence from the arms dealer was almost as unnerving as the situation with the NNB26 prototype.

"As you wish," Lovett frowned, fingering his chin. His mouth pursed—which gave him the look of an overly thoughtful bass. "Perhaps liquid nitrogen would do the trick."

In other words, the fool didn't know what would kill the bots for good.

"Keep me apprised." Before he said something he'd regret, Clark stuffed his phone in his pocket, tucked his laptop under his arm and headed across the cold, white tile to the cold, white door. All this white on white was giving him a headache.

"Of course." Lovett sounded appropriately chagrined.

As he rode the elevator back up to his office, Clark turned his attention to his other problem. Five days now with no return call.

Something was wrong.

There were plenty of reasons Kuznetsov might not be answering his phone. But only two of them concerned him. Someone had captured the bastard, or, hell, the arms dealer had double-crossed him.

Had Hurley's men captured the Russian? His spy in the admiral's office claimed they hadn't located Kuznetsov, but someone else could have. Still, there could be a simpler reason behind the lack of return phone calls.

Kuznetsov was ignoring him.

The very traits for which Clark had hired the Russian—shrewdness, cunning, and ruthlessness were a concern now. What if the bastard had double-crossed him? Kuznetsov could set up a sale on the nanobots without Clark's permission or knowledge. He could cut Clark out of the deal entirely.

He'd sent the Russian five vials of NNB26 with strict instructions to use all five vials in the well at Karaveht. Kuznetsov could have ignored that order and held a vial or two back. Clark had known this was a possibility, but it hadn't mattered. Not back then.

Upon activation of the kill switch, the bots in the extra vials would become inert. They wouldn't activate again without additional programming. Kuznetsov knew this. The Russian's customers were every bit as ruthless and deadly as the arms dealer himself. Selling any of them an inert weapon was a death sentence. Kuznetsov wouldn't be that stupid...would he?

But if the Russian *was* that stupid, if he'd sold a vial or two of NNB26, and if those bots reactivated, well, then humanity was in trouble. The NNB26 prototype had been created to replicate themselves. With no kill switch, they'd just keep creating more and more of themselves. The more people they infected, the more building materials they'd have available. They'd just keep replicating themselves, infecting as they went, until they blanketed the entire world and killed every person on earth.

Chapter Thirty-Four

Day 16
Denali, Alaska

O'Neill paused in the doorway to the war room and looked for a place to park his ass. It wouldn't be in a chair, that was obvious. Wolf's Alpha and Beta teams were in attendance, which pushed the constraints of the space. The room was overflowing with huge, muscled bodies, some with long hair, some with short. All with impassive, flat faces and watchful eyes. A good chunk of those eyes had turned toward him as he stepped through the door. He could almost hear the internal groans as they caught sight of him.

He was still *jie'van*. Unwelcome. His gaze skipped from hard face to hard face, all so righteous in their moral superiority. His muscles seized beneath the ever-familiar rise of frustrated irritation. Nobody in this room knew a damn thing about him. None had given him the chance to prove himself. He was still caught in the same fucking riptide of his childhood, held to a standard nobody had bothered to explain.

He glimpsed the crown of the *Taounaha's* head with its gray, braided hair. Perhaps there was one in the room who knew him well, even too well.

The chairs surrounding the table were occupied. Those warriors who hadn't grabbed a chair leaned against the walls. The scent of coffee overshadowed the smell of sweat and male musk. Testosterone amped the air. He'd never seen so many warriors in attendance at a strategy meeting. Hell, even the *woohanta* were here. Except for Winchester.

That realization brought him up short. Where the hell was the Shadow Warrior's favorite squid? Apprehending Kuznetsov was at the top of Winchester's wish list. Hell, the bastard was obsessed with bringing the Russian in. Understandable, sure, but that obsession should have propelled him front and center for this meeting.

He glanced toward the three former SEALs propping up the wall beside him. Winchester wasn't the only one missing. So was his brother by marriage. Their absences had to be connected. Then again, Wolf's little bro had looked like shit earlier this morning in the gym. Complete and utter shit, as a matter of fact. Like he'd had a hell of a hangover, or he was coming down with a nasty bug. Was that why he was missing this mandatory meeting?

Not that he was going to ask.

"Hey, asshole," Mackenzie snarled from O'Neill's right. "How about you move your ass so we can close the damn door?"

That was Mackenzie for you, snarling rather than asking, referring to everyone as *asshole* rather than by their names, constantly exhibiting his generally shitty disposition. No wonder Wolf called him *umbretan*. The former commander *was* best described as the human personification of a thundercloud. How the hell did the bastard's wife put up with him?

"Since you asked so nicely..." O'Neill sent him a saccharine smile. Ignoring the stiffening of Mackenzie's body, he pushed into the bastard's personal space, then turned around and parked his ass against the wall—shoulder to shoulder with the *umbretan* himself. "That better?" Another saccharine smile, this one with lots of teeth.

Shock seized the dude's muscles. His hawkish face darkened past his habitual thunder cloud mimicry. Lightning flashed in his black eyes. Commander Squid was not pleased with O'Neill's intrusion into his coveted personal space.

Too damn bad.

He snared the edge of the door and swung it shut, ignoring the ominous vibrations seething in the air to his left.

"Now simmer down there, skipper." A soothing drawl started up as Rawlings tried to intercept the brewing explosion. "Man's got to stand somewhere. Not much space left, as you can see."

O'Neill suppressed a grin. Mackenzie was so damn easy to detonate.

It was amazing the guy had ever passed BUD/S, earned himself a spot on the teams, and then climbed all the way to Commander of ST7. Explosive personalities didn't fare well in WARCOM. They burned through their allies and contacts quickly. Mackenzie certainly fell into that category. After all, nobody had stepped up to save his ass when his career had gone up in flames.

He'd heard about the guy long before the commander and his men had hit the skids with USSOCOM. Discovering they'd joined Shadow Mountain had been a surprise. Nobody in SEAL Command or among the soups knew where they'd disappeared. Some believed they'd been killed, although Zane Winters remained in contact with his family and Simcosky in contact with his mother. Mackenzie and Rawlings, they didn't have family and hadn't reached out to anyone. Hell, the whole lot of them had simply vanished.

It all made sense once he found them tucked away in Wolf's Mountain. Shadow Mountain might just be the biggest military secret of the century. Nobody would have found them here.

"It don't seem natural, Aiden missin' out on this and all," Rawlings said from the other side of Mackenzie. "He's been the one gunnin' for Kuznetsov. After what happened to his team, this takedown is personal. He'd want to be here."

O'Neill tuned into the conversation. Mackenzie's internal vibrations had eased. At least he wasn't vibrating with the intensity of an off balance, fully loaded missile that was about to self-destruct.

"Nothing to be done about it." Winters's voice was matter of fact. "Can't do much when you're out cold in the ER. Cos says the docs don't know when he'll wake up, or even *if* he'll wake up. Hell, they don't even know what's wrong with him."

"It's those damn bots." Rawlings sounded certain. "The ones that took down his team. They got into him, somehow, and now they're creatin' havoc."

"Maybe, but there's still no sign of them in his blood or brain, which is where the damn things congregated in Squirrel and the others." Winters sounded more cautious, like he wasn't ready to jump on the bot train with no evidence. "Plus, Aiden's symptoms are different. His crew didn't run a fever and fall into a coma."

In a coma?

Well, that explained why the chosen one was missing the meeting. Too bad. The fact they were even having this strategy briefing was because of Winchester's relentless pushing.

At the front of the room, Wolf rose to his feet, with the television remote in his hand. He pressed a button and both the monitors filled with color, then images.

"What you're looking at is Petropavlovsk-Kamchatsky, a Russian city in the far east Russian corridor. The city sits along the Pacific Ocean, against the shores of Avacha Bay, which is also home to Rybachiy Nuclear Submarine Base." He clicked the button again and another image swallowed the screen—a man, barrel chested, light on neck, with massive arms. His head was shaved. His eyes were small and mean. "Our mark is Grigory Kuznetsov, a Russian arms dealer. He's believed to be involved in the testing of the *wanatesa* weapon that decimated Karaveht and Aiden Winchester's

SEAL team. Our intel indicates he's hiding within this fenced, monitored, and guarded compound along the eastern corner of Petropavlovsk."

A moment of shocked silence fell, followed by a cascade of voices blurting *what the hell* and *you have to be fucking kidding me*, all of which came from MacKenzie and his two SEAL henchmen. Okay, henchmen might be a bit bombastic. But Mackenzie, Winters, Rawlings and Simcosky stuck together.

Wolf ignored the raised voices at the back of the room. Of course he did. The big bad Wolf showed rare talent in ignoring those he didn't wish to acknowledge. Usually, it was O'Neill.

It tickled O'Neill immensely that Wolf's invisibility spotlight was centered on others for a change.

"The terrain surrounding our quarry is snowy, mountainous, and ringed by volcanoes. It's also prone to blizzards during this time of the cycle. The snowpack is currently estimated at thirty-eight inches. To avoid detection, we'll have to snowshoe to our attack points. The Thunderbird can exfil us directly from the compound once we've secured the target and package, but we don't want to alert Kuznetsov or his guards to our presence on *aggress*."

"Wait a mother fucking minute!" Mackenzie pushed off from the wall, his shoulders pulled back, his face hard, tendons standing out on his neck. "You're telling us this is where Kuznetsov went to ground? In the ass crack of Russia? Right next to a submarine base?"

"Yes."

Wolf shifted to face Mackenzie, his expression impassive, but O'Neill sensed the annoyance beneath the simple acknowledgement.

Zane Winters stepped away from the wall. "Where's this intel coming from? Our sources pinpointed several likely locations." He frowned before shaking his head. "Petropavlovsk-Kamchatsky is not on the list."

O'Neill almost rolled his eyes. Like the squids' contacts had an exclusive lock on where Kuznetsov had gone to ground. Talk about ego.

On the other hand...

"The man's got a point," O'Neill drawled. Who could blame him for seizing on such a prime opportunity to needle Wolf? Honest to shit, he couldn't help himself. Even though he knew with absolute certainty that Kuznetsov was indeed bunkered down in Petropavlovsk-Kamchatsky, right next to the Rybachiy Nuclear Submarine Base. He, too, had been surprised when his spook had told him that. But the intel was square. Not that he intended to admit it. "It seems mighty foolish of the guy to hunker down in the beast's belly, so to speak. Didn't Winchester say he was a Russian defector? Why the hell would he go to ground in the heart of Russia?" He paused and lazily scratch at the corner of his eye, before moving in for the kill shot. "Where did this intel come from, anyway?"

Fuck, would Wolf's answer ever set the squids off. He swallowed an unholy grin, ignoring the reproachful look Benioko sent him. Hell, under the circumstances, with his looming sacrifice and all, the Old One should let him have some fun.

The skin across Wolf's broad forehead tightened. But before he addressed his hecklers, the Old One struggled to his feet. He turned to face Mackenzie and the other squids, but his gaze sought and held O'Neill's eyes.

"This information came from me," the *Taounaha* informed the room, his face and voice full of dignity.

His gaze flitted to Mackenzie and back to O'Neill, where it lingered, silently reminding him who'd supplied the intel, and that the tip had been accepted without question. A sliver of shame went through him, eroding his enjoyment of the situation. O'Neill looked away.

He grimaced. The Old One was spoiling his fun.

"*You* supplied the intelligence?" Mackenzie's thick eyebrows flew up in surprised outrage. "How the hell did you manage that? Through a—"

Rawlings's hand shot out. His palm slapped over Mackenzie's mouth, muffling the next word, but O'Neill was close enough to hear it.

"*Vision.*"

The derision in the gritty voice, muffled as it was, sucked the last of the enjoyment from O'Neill. That was the trouble with the three *woohanta* beside him. They had no respect for other cultures or other perspectives. Even if they didn't put stock in the Shadow Warrior or the *Tabenetha,* they could still be respectful of the *Taounaha* and other belief systems.

"No. Not a vision."

Wolf's voice was as close to a snap as O'Neill had ever heard it. Mackenzie's final, derogatory question had obviously been audible to everyone, even through Rawlings's palm.

Wolf leveled an icy gaze on the cluster of *Woohanta* near the door, O'Neill included. "Benioko was approached by a source, one who remains anonymous. This contact provided the intel, along with photos, charts, and video. Our own intel techs verified the data provided. Our target *is* in Petropavlovsk. The video footage and photos are proof of this."

He clicked the remote again, and an image of a fenced area, full of steel sheds and wood houses, edged by huge mounds of snow, filled the screen. A flagpole—from which flapped the white, blue, and red stripes of the Russian flag—rose above the fence line. Next to the flagpole stood an equally tall power pole. Wolf cast one more disdainful glance toward Mackenzie before turning back to the mounted television screens.

Another click of the remote and a grainy black and white video rolled across the screen. A thick set man stomped down the steps of a two-story house with an A-frame metal roof. The camera zoomed in until the man's fleshy face and mean eyes were clearly visible. There was no question it was Kuznetsov. Same bald head. Same tiny eyes and muddy expression. His burly body was buried in a wool coat, which was plastered against his barrel chest. The jacket sleeves slapped his thick wrists.

Kuznetsov stood there for a moment, his small eyes scanning the fenced compound. Another man came into view, this one wearing a camouflage parka with the hood pulled up. His gloved hands cradled an AK-74M assault rifle against his chest. Kuznetsov shouted something at the other guy and moved to intercept in a combination stomp/strut.

"Through photos and video footage, we've identified eight guards split between two twelve-hour shifts. We've also identified multiple surveillance cameras. The grounds are being monitored from virtually every angle." Wolf nodded toward a smaller wood house with a flat roof. "The guards—both shifts—are based out of here." He paused the video as the man Kuznetsov had accosted escaped into the flat-roofed house. "At all times, there are two guards patrolling the grounds, while two remain inside this house. We believe they monitor the camera feeds from the inside."

"Those camera feeds will need to be cut," someone toward the front of the room said. Nods and indistinct murmurs of agreement swept the room.

From beside him, O'Neill heard mutterings about disinformation and photoshopping techniques. Rawlings stepped forward and raised his hand. O'Neill almost rolled his eyes. The squid had probably been a teacher's pet in school.

"With the technology available these days, it's easy to Photoshop images. Have you sent these photos and videos through photo forensics?" Rawlings's tone was borderline apologetic, like he knew it was an asshole question.

O'Neill kept his face straight. *Why yes, yes he had.* Which the *Taounaha* knew. When the Old One turned to stare at him, his dark eyes more scolding than ever, O'Neill pretended not to notice.

Wolf's face tightened. He answered the question with a truncated nod and gritted his response out. "They have. However, if you have reservations about this mission, you are welcome to sit it out."

O'Neill shot the former squids huddled to his left a quick glance. How were they taking that obvious dismissal? Not well, judging by the flat, sour looks spreading across their faces.

"The five men stowed in your morgue crewed with us." Mackenzie's tight voice sounded like gravel, with a generous dose of *fuck you.* "They were brothers. This mission is ours more than yours."

His face tranquil, Benioko stared Mackenzie down. "Your words are ignorant. Like an *eseneee anvaa,* you do not see the full picture. This battle belongs to all of us. You will not be the only ones affected by what comes."

More scowls and frowns emerged from his left. Obviously, Mackenzie hadn't bothered to learn the language of the *Hee'woo'nee* during his years at Shadow Mountain, otherwise he'd object more strenuously to being compared—unfavorably—to an ignorant child.

Rawlings raised his palms towards Wolf and Benioko in a placating gesture. "We meant no offense. It's just that Aiden's contact gave him very different potential locations."

"Did Aiden's contact establish that Kuznetsov was in any of those locations? Did he provide photo or video evidence?" Wolf's voice remained flat, which somehow increased the bite.

O'Neill suppressed a laugh. It did his heart good to see Wolf's teeth directed elsewhere for a change.

"No." MacKenzie looked like he'd chewed on a lemon. "We've been waiting for an update."

His face set, Wolf stared back. "The *Taounaha's* source has provided all the information we need to act. Kuznetsov *is* in Petropavlovsk-Kamchatsky. This is where we will apprehend him. Join us or not. Your company is of little consequence to us."

Wow! Wolfie had his canines bared. O'Neill didn't remember ever seeing him so short with someone. Of course, Mackenzie had it coming, so there was that.

After that bit of drama, the conversation moved on to logistics.

"Those cameras need to go." Samuel's voice was matter-of-fact. "A scrambler would take them out but leave our target wondering why the electricity didn't go down too. We need to cut the power to the whole compound."

Wolf clicked a button and an image of the gated entrance with its towering power pole lit up the television screen. "We take down the power here," he said. "This region of Russia is known for its unstable electrical grid. Particularly during the windy season, which is in full swing now." He paused. "We're monitoring a complication. The latest weather projections call for a low-pressure ridge to settle over the area within the next thirty-six hours. If the forecasts are accurate, we'd be *aggressing* into snowy, windy, even blizzard conditions."

O'Neill frowned, surprised that Wolf and the Old One would take such risks with their warriors' lives. While grabbing Kuznetsov and containing this nanobot weapon was imperative, they still had time before the situation went critical. His contacts had heard nothing about this nanobot weapon. No mention of it was circling the dark web. There was no sign it was up for sale.

They could afford to wait out this low-pressure ridge.

Apparently, he wasn't the only one questioning the wisdom of attacking during unsettled weather. A warrior on the left side of the table questioned the decision.

Wolf looked at Benioko and then back at the warrior who'd asked the question. "There's reason to believe the weapon is up for sale. We must secure it immediately."

O'Neill straightened. He'd just spoken with his contacts. Someone would have told him if the weapon was up for sale. The only way Wolf could have received that information was directly from the Shadow Warrior via the earthside mouthpiece.

Benioko had been in touch with the elder gods.

While he was trying to assimilate the knowledge that they'd apparently jumped straight to DEFCON 2, one of the intel techs scurried into the room and joined Wolf. An intense conversation broke out. The room was dead silent. He was too far away to catch the exchange, but it was bad news. Wolf was facing the other direction, so he couldn't see his face, but the way his shoulders bunched looked ominous. And then there was the other dude, the one who'd interrupted the meeting. He was facing O'Neill, and hell, he looked unnerved, like he'd watched the world die in front of his eyes.

Yep, bad news had walked through the door.

After a few more moments of conversation, the tech guy scurried back out the door. Wolf stood there for several seconds, staring after him, his shoulders still bunched, the back of his neck tense. O'Neill's pulse picked up. So did his breathing. This was bad. Very, very bad. He'd never seen anything affect Wolf like this.

With obvious effort, Benioko struggled to his feet and settled a claw-like hand over Wolf's forearm.

With a deep breath and a shake of his head, Wolf turned to address the roomful of warriors. "The weapon used against the people of Karaveht, as well as Aiden's SEAL team, has gone up for sale. Those selling it have posted videos to prove its effectiveness. The footage is of the villagers in Karaveht, and Aiden's SEAL team slaughtering each other. The bidding is strong." His jaw bunched. "The Thunderbird will fly within the hour."

Chapter Thirty-Five

Day 16
Denali, Alaska

Trident's thick, ominous growls frayed Demi's nerves, even though the cat hadn't drawn blood since their flight to Alaska nine days ago. Whatever mad cat magic O'Neill had cast over the feline was long-lasting—at least when it came to scratches and bites. The cat's unfriendliness, growling, and bad temper? Sadly, there was no improvement there.

Kait gently lifted Trident's stump of a back leg and leaned in closer. The growling intensified until deep-chested rumbles vibrated across Demi's thighs. She tensed, bracing herself for a display of claws or fangs, both of which were free. They hadn't wrapped him in the towel like usual since they needed to see his wounds.

"Just a few seconds more," Demi soothed in that soft, sweet voice she didn't hate nearly as much as she had prior to climbing aboard the jet.

Kait straightened from where she was kneeling in front of Demi's lapful of pissed off cat. "Everything looks great. The surgical areas are all healed. Or at least the flesh looks like it knit well. I still see stitches though. Didn't your vet say those would dissolve, or fall out by two weeks? Are we supposed to do something about them if they don't disappear?"

"She said it could take several weeks for them to dissolve." Leaning forward, Demi carefully set Trident on his three legs, next to the paper plate with a generous load of tuna. She waited to make sure he was stable, then slowly released her hold. "At least he doesn't show signs of infection or inflammation."

She'd used the last of the antibiotics days ago, and the anti-inflammatory meds before that.

For a second, it looked like Trident was going to race off and hide, as usual. Instead, he hesitated, glancing back at Demi. After another hesitation, he turned and crept toward the dish of tuna. She'd discovered tuna was his favorite food, so she'd been using it as a reward for his good behavior—as in no drawing of blood.

"If he would have allowed me to get my hands around his wounds, maybe I could have healed him completely, or at least sped up his natural healing." There was frustration in Kait's voice.

Demi nodded agreement, even though Kait had managed to get her hands on Trident several times. She suspected her friend's lack of success in healing Trident's wounds was because the cat fell into the seventy percent of patients Kait's ability didn't work on. When it came to her healing ability, Kait should just count herself lucky that the people she cared about—Aiden, Cosky, and Demi—all fell into the thirty percent she could heal.

Kait's phone rang. Cautiously, Demi leaned over and ran her fingers down the cat's spine. It arched beneath her fingertips. She wasn't sure whether the movement was from pleasure, or annoyance. But he didn't flee or growl. The fact he was allowing her to pet him while he ate was a major step forward. He'd never let her get so close before.

"What happened?"

Kait's shrill voice was Demi's first clue something was wrong. Trident flinched and fled, diving beneath the recliner across the room. Her heart suddenly pounding way too hard and fast, Demi straightened. Kait had gone rigid. Her face blanched. Her fingers were pale talons clamped around her phone.

Had something happened to Cosky?

"But that makes no sense. He was just here. He was fine." Kait's voice shook. Her throat trembled. "Do his doctors think this sudden sickness is related to those nanobots? Was he infected, after all?"

Sudden sickness? Nanobots? Infected?

Kait had asked Aiden about nanobots the evening he'd come to see her. He'd changed the subject. When Demi had asked him about them, he'd claimed the topic was classified and wouldn't tell her a damn thing. She'd thought his refusal to explain was another one of his secrets.

She should have pressed him on the matter.

Demi's chest tightened. So did her scalp. Instinctively, she knew this call wasn't about Cosky. It was about Aiden. Fear tightened her belly into an icy knot.

"No. Send the chopper. I'm coming." Kait glanced at Demi. "Demi and I are both coming." She fell silent, listening. "I know that." Another distracted glance at Demi. "She deserves to be there beside him." She paused and added, "I need her with me. She's coming." Although she didn't say it, the words, *end of discussion,* rang in her voice. She paused, listening. "I don't care. I know he's in the percentage I can heal. I've healed him before, I'll do it again." She paused once more, then responded with a snap in her voice. "You have no right to make that decision for me. I'm coming. Send the damn chopper!" Another pause, a longer one. This time when she responded, her voice had gone icy. Deadly. "I'm not messing with you, Marcus. If that chopper isn't here in twenty minutes, I will never forgive you. I'm not fucking stupid. I know it's dangerous but he's my brother. I'm not going to sit around and let him die."

Demi jolted, Kait's words hitting her like an electric shock.

Die!

Aiden was dying?

Her head went light. How could Aiden be dying? She'd just seen him. He'd been perfectly healthy. None of this made sense. What had caused him to get so sick, so fast? The question froze in her mind and started echoing. The answer hit her like a gunshot.

The bots. His sudden illness must have something to do with the nanobots Kait had asked him about. She took a deep breath, released it slowly, and watched as Kait threw the phone on the couch. It bounced off the backrest and fell into the indent between the seat cushions.

"How bad is it?" Demi fought to keep her voice even.

She'd been expecting this call for years or a visit from someone in dress whites delivering the terrible news. But not like this, not because of a sudden inexplicable illness. Not while he was on downtime. She took another breath and tried to regulate her shallow breathing.

"Bad. He's unconscious." Kait ran shaky fingers through her hair. Her face looked more gray than white now. The shock was hitting her eyes, turning them shiny and blind. "Marcus says he's running a fever. His blood pressure and pulse are unstable."

Demi tried to swallow the lump in her throat. It wouldn't budge. "Do the doctors know what's wrong with him?"

Kait shook her head. The blind look slowly easing in her eyes was replaced by resolution. "Not for sure. They're running more of their damn tests. He's going to be fine, though." The resolution on her face hardened. "You can be sure of that. I'll make certain of it."

Demi hesitated. She didn't want to put Kait in a difficult position, and Aiden had said the nanobot discussion was classified. But her need to know—to prepare—won out over the urge to maintain boundaries. "Does Aiden's sickness have anything to do with nanobots?"

Kait sighed and turned to face her. "Yeah, about that, I'll explain everything while we're on the chopper. You'll find out anyway once we reach base. But right now—" She glanced at the slim, silver watch strapped to her right arm. "We should pack a change of clothing. God knows how long we'll be camped out beside his bed."

Trident emerged from his hiding spot and crept his way toward the dish of tuna. "Do you think one of your friends would check on Trident while we're gone? To make sure his food and water dishes are full?"

Kait gave a decisive nod, as though grateful for something mundane to concentrate on, something besides her fear. "I'll call Beth. I'm sure she'll be willing."

The next twenty minutes went by in a daze, her thoughts fragmented and frantic. Fear was an ever-present swelling pressure in her chest. Everything around her felt too loud, too bright, as though her senses were overstimulated. If her reaction was so strong now, after she'd broken things off with him, how much worse would it be if they were still together? Or if it was years down the road, when there was longevity and children involved?

But then again, she frowned. How much more terrified could she possibly get? There must be a threshold to fear, like once you hit a certain level, it didn't get any worse. Was she at that threshold already? Could the fear get any worse?

Before heading upstairs, she refilled Trident's water and kibble dishes and cleaned his litter box. She paid little attention to what she stuffed in the huge, quilted bag Kait had dropped on the guest bed, but the bag was bulging and heavy by the time she carried it down to the living room and dropped it next to the front door. Kait arrived moments later with a quilted bag almost identical to the one Demi was using.

"Beth will watch Trident," Kait said as she dropped her bag next to Demi's at the front door.

Demi watched her friend pace to the window and peer through the glass. The movement was a nervous tic rather than a scan for their ride. They'd hear the chopper the instant it arrived. Kait had regained some color in her face, but her shoulders were still tense, her spine rigid, and her fingers were twitching against her thighs. Demi knew without a doubt that her friend was itching to get her hands on Aiden to start healing him.

Please...please let Kait's hands heal him.

She's done it before. She can do it again.

She has to do it again.

By the time they climbed into the chopper, Demi's muscles were in knots. Her chest was so tight it hurt to breathe. It was ironic, really, the intensity of her reaction to this news. She cut Aiden out of her life so she wouldn't go through this kind of fear and pain. And yet here she was, facing the fear and uncertainty she'd tried to avoid.

Day 16
Denali, Alaska

Demi was still processing everything Kait had told her when the chopper landed. Nanobots had infected Aiden's team and turned them crazy. Not just crazy, but homicidally crazy. They'd turned on each other. They'd murdered each other. It was unbelievable...and terrifying. No wonder everyone was so concerned about this new weapon.

Had his teammates turned on Aiden, too, tried to kill him? Had Aiden killed some of his men to protect himself? She flinched, her stomach souring. Kait hadn't mentioned that, but Aiden wouldn't have told her. He'd take that secret to his grave. And it would haunt him for the rest of his life.

Cosky was waiting for them in the air hangar, his face tense, his body rigid.

"How is he?" Kait asked as she hopped out of the chopper.

Cosky simply shook his head, a grim expression on his face. Demi followed Kait to the ground, vaguely aware of asphalt, planes, and helicopters surrounding her. The smell of oil and fuel fumes hung heavy in the air.

"Do they know what's wrong? Have they found any bots?" Kait's questions came hard and fast. Cosky glanced at Demi and his face hardened. "Yes. I told her everything," Kait snapped. "Has One Bird or Eldon tried to heal him?"

Demi twitched at the last question. Kait had mentioned earlier that she wasn't the only healer that worked on the Shadow Mountain base, although she was by far the strongest.

Cosky shook his head again, the grim look turning ominous. With Kait beside him and Demi on their heels, he started weaving his way between the planes and helicopters.

"The docs think it's an autoimmune response but they don't know what's causing it. They've pulled more blood and taken more biopsies. They've scheduled ultrasound, CAT and MRI scans. The results won't be back for hours yet."

Kait grabbed Cosky's wrist. She didn't stop him, just kept pace with him. "What about One Bird? Eldon? Joseph? Why haven't they tried to heal him?"

Cosky's jaw bunched. "Wolf won't allow it."

Kait sucked in a sharp breath. "Why not?" She sucked in another breath and bit her lip. "Never mind. I'll be able to heal him. I've done it before. I can do it again." There was a belligerent edge to her voice, like she was daring Cosky to try to stop her.

When they reached the door to the hangar, Cosky led them to a golf cart type vehicle with four seats. They climbed inside and Cosky guided the vehicle down a corridor and into a spiraling, downward ramp. Demi was so caught up in her fear that her surroundings didn't quite register, just a vague impression of a tunnel with two lanes divided by a white line, endless smooth walls, glass doors that occasionally whooshed apart and disgorged people. The cart pulled into a recessed parking slot in front of a rectangular glass door. A bright red sign above the glass read *Emergency Room*. Demi's heart jittered like a jackhammer as she followed Kait and Cosky through the door. Just because Aiden was still alive didn't mean she couldn't still lose him.

You've already lost him, remember? You sent him away. He isn't yours anymore.

The reminder didn't lessen the dread.

The clinic was sparkling clean—yet smelled like antiseptic, blood, vomit and desperation. The smell had to be something her mind had pulled up from long ago, from back when she'd sat beside Donnie's emergency room bed. The Coronado ER and this one couldn't smell identical. Yet somehow, they did.

While her parents had already been dead when she'd gotten the call, Donnie had died in the emergency room. She'd sat there beside him, holding his limp hand, urging him to return to her. He hadn't. He died without ever opening his eyes, without saying goodbye. In truth, he died before they'd made it to the ER. He died in the stands when that baseball had shattered his skull. Her heart and hope had died in the ER that day, too. It had taken years for her heart to awaken, for hope to return.

She wasn't ready for another bedside vigil. She wasn't ready to pray over another man she loved. If only this moment was a nightmare and she'd jolt awake to find Aiden stretched out beside her in bed.

Except he wouldn't be in your bed, a voice in her mind jeered. *You sent him away. Remember?*

As if she'd ever forget. As if the reality of that wasn't constantly sucker punching her in the heart.

Cosky led them through an empty waiting room, to a nurse's station beside a dark blue door. The nurse looked up. Her face softened when she saw Kait. "I'm so sorry about your brother, sweetie."

"I need to see him," Kait said, her voice shaking.

"I'm afraid that's not possible. He's in isolation." The nurse's voice was as gentle as her face.

"He's infected?" Kait grabbed Cosky's hand.

The nurse reached for a black, corded phone at the edge of her desk. "Hang on, let me get Dr. Brickenhouse. He'll fill you in on your brother's condition."

Demi fought to focus on the nurse's conversation with Kait and Cosky, but that damn phantom ER smell kept invading her senses and hijacking her mind.

We're not visiting Donnie. This is Aiden. He is not dead. He's not dead!

Her chest throbbed to the beat of each word.

After what seemed like forever, but according to the white clock above the nurse's head was only five minutes, a man in a white coat, with a long, silver braid, pushed through the blue door to their left.

"Kait. Marcus." The doctor solemnly shook each of their hands. A somber expression lined his face.

His gravity sent electric flares of fear up Demi's spine.

"Why is Aiden in isolation? Is he infected with those bots? Is that why he's sick?" The questions burst from Kait.

"He's in isolation as a precaution." The doctor sighed and pushed his glasses up to massage his eyes. "I wish I had more information to impart. But we don't know why he's sick. We believe he's having an autoimmune response, but we aren't sure why, or what it's in response to. We're hopeful the tests, when they come in, will give us a direction. For now, all we can do is treat his symptoms and keep him stable. Our immediate concern is his blood pressure and increased heart rate, both signs of shock. We're treating these symptoms with medications."

"I can heal him." Kait tossed the comment out like a dare.

The doctor's concerns devoured Demi's mind.

What if Aiden's blood pressure plummets, leading to the suffocation of his internal organs? What if his fever climbs so high it fries his brain? What if his heart quits beating? What if...

With each what if, her own internal temperature spiked. Her heart raced faster and faster still. The fear rolled through her in waves. She shut the what ifs down and focused on the here...the now. It was the only way to remain sane. She'd learned that after Donnie's accident.

Cosky's voice caught her attention, or rather the tense, frustrated edge to it. It was a tone she'd never heard him use on Kait.

"They aren't saying you can't heal him," he stressed, his voice gritty. "They're telling you to wait until the tests come back, until the docs can say with certainty that he isn't contagious."

"Why hasn't anyone asked the *Taounaha* if Aiden's infected? Benioko knew he wasn't a danger to me in the hills above Karaveht."

"Wolf says Benioko is weak from his last shadow walk. He must recover before crossing the veil again. Benioko doesn't know if Aiden is a danger to others. We'll have to look to science to clear him." Cosky looked half frustrated, half relieved. "We'll have to wait for all the tests they've done to come back."

Kait squared off against her husband, every muscle in her body tense, her eyes on fire. She drove her fingers into Cosky's chest and yanked them loose when he grabbed them. "He's dying, Marcus. It might be too late if I wait for the test results. I need to heal him now!"

Cosky stepped back, his face hardening. "We're barreling down on the most dangerous op in years. We're risking massive injuries. If you touch Aiden, Wolf will lock you in isolation alongside your brother until he knows for certain you're not infected. He can't chance you picking up the bots from Aiden and infecting the entire base. If you touch Aiden, you won't be allowed to heal anyone else. For Christ's sake, you're the strongest healer the base has. What happens if I take a hit? Or Zane? Rawls? Mac? Fuck, what if Wolf goes down?"

Kait froze, her face twisting. She looked torn. "You said there would be no mission until you had a location on Aiden's arms dealer."

"Yeah...fuck." Cosky ran a tense hand down his face. "The location came in this morning. Our strategy is set. The Thunderbird is fueled and the teams are decked out." He swore again. "I was about to call you when Aiden went down."

Kait's face was so tight it looked skeletal. Her eyes turned glassy. "When do you leave?"

Cosky reached for her hand and lifted it to his lips. "I'm sorry, babe. I wish I could stay, but I'm needed. We can't allow this weapon to deploy. We spin up at zero thirty."

Kait swallowed hard and squared her shoulders. "Aiden would want you to go. He'd want you to stop what happened to his team from happening to anyone else." Her face twisted. "Just make sure you come back. Promise me you'll come back."

Demi turned away, giving them privacy.

Poor Kait, she was facing losses in every direction. Her husband and both her brothers were at risk now. Because Wolf would be right there beside Cosky and the rest of his warriors, putting himself in danger to protect the world. The whole lot of them were heroes. It was hard to love a hero, let alone three of them.

Demi's heart would have ached for her if it wasn't numb with fear.

Chapter Thirty-Six

Day 17
Petropavlovsk, Russia

The *Heemitia,* full and round in her silver finery, glowed down on Wolf as he and his warriors snowshoed through skeletal thickets of birch and alder. The air was cold and dry. It burned down his throat and into his lungs. He and *Aggress* One were snowshoeing around the northeastern edge of Petropavlovsk. Thirty minutes earlier, *Aggress* Two had split off and headed north to the electrical pole at the entrance to their prey's compound. There, they would cut the power. Then both teams would strike.

When the backup generator rumbled to life and the perimeter cameras came on, the *aggress* would be over, and their quarry, along with his ominous new weapon, would be theirs.

So stood the plan.

Their abrupt departure for the far east of Russia had proven beneficial. The Thunderbird had landed in the hills above Petropavlovsk-Kamchatsky before the low-pressure ridge arrived. If the Shadow Warrior smiled upon them, they'd lift off with their quarry before the escalating winds and heavy snow settled over the area.

Petropavlovsk-Kamchatsky was in the badlands of Russia. Why, in *Hee-nes's* glory, would Kuznetsov hide out here in this remote town where he was sandwiched between the volcanoes of Kamchatka and Russia's largest naval base? Where the only way in and out was by boat, plane, or helicopter.

Mackenzie wasn't the only one who'd questioned Benioko's knowledge. The elder gods in the Shadow Realm were the *Taounaha's* standard source of information, and they did not offer physical proof. Yet the photos and videos provided by the Old One were physical. Concrete. And accurate.

Still, the location Kuznetsov had chosen seemed irrational. Why would the world's most hunted arms dealer hide within the country of his exile? Perhaps because it was unlikely USSOCOM would risk the sleeping giant's ire by sending a special ops team so deep into Russian territory. Besides, their prey had two means of escape. A chopper squatting in his bluff-side compound, and a massive, opulent yacht moored in Avacha Bay below. It was Wolf's job to ensure Kuznetsov didn't reach either.

At the edge of the tree line, next to the chain-link fence that surrounded Kuznetsov's snow scraped compound, Wolf and his warriors shucked their snowshoes. They didn't bother hooking them to their kits. They wouldn't need them again as the thunderbird would lift them from the Russian's doorstep.

On his belly beneath the scratchy, sparse branches of a dwarf Siberian pine, Wolf scanned the dark compound through his rifle's scope. The wind had picked up. It howled through the trees, flinging needles and dead branches in every direction.

"*Aggress* Two, countdown to first mark?" Wolf asked into his comm.

"Five minutes to strike," Tomas Beck, the team two leader, said over the comm.

Mark one was the electricity. They needed to bring down the security cameras. Beneath the infrared cameras, Wolf and his warriors would stand out like pulsing red flames on the camera feeds.

"Gotta say, boys," a low, southern drawl whispered through Wolf's headset. "It's a damn good thing we included snowshoein' in our PT. That would have been brutal if we weren't used to it."

Low grunts of agreement hit Wolf's headset.

"The wind's a bitch, though. Could do without that," one of the former SEALs added softly, either Zane or Cosky. Wolf couldn't tell them apart through the headset.

"Like I told y'all, this place is the ass crack of Russia," that slow, southern drawl said. "Cold as a witch's tit during a blizzard."

A what?

The puzzled inquiry came from Samuel, who was often baffled by Rawlings's idioms. But the query didn't come over the comm, or through the mouth. It came through the *Neealaho,* the neural web that linked all his warriors' thoughts. All except for the former SEALs.

The four *woohanta* had not been invited to submit to the merging ceremony. They would not have survived. Thus, they were not bound to the *Neealaho*, and unable to communicate telepathically with the rest of his warriors. This put them at a distinct disadvantage, although they were unaware of it. The headsets he and his men reluctantly wore were for the benefit of the former SEALs, since there was no way to communicate with them outside of modern technology.

Wolf absently listened to the *woohanta*'s complaints as he scanned the compound again. He almost told them to hold their tongues, but it was unnecessary. His scope held no one in sight. Between the wind and whispering voices, the guards would hear nothing spoken here.

Samuel. Fence. Wolf instinctively sent the order through the *Neealaho*, but on Samuel's neural path.

It was easy to send an overall message through the neural web. But it took concentration to identify and follow an individual warrior's mental pathway and link with them privately. Of all his warriors, Samuel was the easiest to reach. They'd been *hee-javaanee* since grade school, joined Shadow Mountain together, even been linked to the *Neealaho* through Jude at the same time. Touching Samuel's mind was akin to touching his own. His second eased up to the chain-link fence and started cutting the links.

"Once through the fence, spread out. Stay low. Strike on my command," Wolf said softly into the comm and through the *Neealaho*.

"Don't seem right without Aiden beside us." The southern twang gave the speaker away.

A grunt of agreement came through the comm. It sounded tense. Worried. Probably Cosky, then. Kait, Cosky's *anistino*, was waiting in front of Aiden's isolation chamber, desperate to heal him. Wolf had forbidden this until the final medical results came in. She had not been pleased, but they could not have their strongest healer compromised when they might have need of her gift.

Wolf agreed with Rawlings, though. It felt wrong not to have his *javaanee* beside him. But the elder gods had reasons for the paths their chosen's feet took. In Aiden's case, to the ER instead of Petropavlovsk.

It was not for Wolf to question the path taken.

Samuel cut the last link, stuffed the bolt cutters into his kit, and pulled it back on. Crouching, Wolf shuffled to the hole and shimmied through as Samuel peeled the chain link to the side. The snow was thigh deep on the other side. He waded through it alongside the chain-link until he was out of the way. Dropping belly-flat again, he scanned the compound through his rifle scope as the rest of his warriors wiggled through the hole and spread out across the snow. The north end of the compound was higher than the south, so even with the berm of ice and snow fifty feet ahead, he still had an excellent view of the compound and the houses it contained. The wind was gentler this close to the ground, stroking instead of buffeting. He scanned again. Still no movement.

With the weight of his body spread across the snowpack and the top layer beneath him more ice than snow, Wolf didn't sink far into the layers below him. But that wouldn't hold true once he moved.

Finally, the last man crawled through the hole in the fence—which must be Mackenzie because of all the *motherfucker this* and *motherfucker that's*.

"*Aggress* Two, countdown?" he asked into the comm as he continued scanning the compound with his scope.

One minute. The update came through the *Neealaho*.

"One minute to strike," Wolf said into the comm for the *woohantas'* sake.

A flicker of movement at the guard's shack froze his scope in place. The door opened, and a parka clad guard with his hood pulled up, stepped out the door with his rifle hanging.

"*Aggress* Two, we have movement at mark three. Repeat. Movement at M3. Guard turning south."

"Understood." The affirmative was cool, almost casual.

Mark one was the electricity. Mark two, Kuznetsov and the weapon. Three, the guards.

Wolf watched the guard, the edges of his parka flapping, stagger directly into the savage wind. The door opened again. A second guard, dressed like the first, stepped onto the house's porch. This one turned north, away from the wind.

"Second guard headed north," Wolf whispered.

"Understood," Tomas said with his habitual calmness. "Thirty seconds to strike. Repeat. Thirty to strike."

One...two...three...

Wolf counted the seconds off in his head while monitoring their mark's house through the scope pressed to his right eye.

When the electricity went down, the guards might return to their shelter. *Eight...nine...ten...* Or they might not. *Fifteen...sixteen...seventeen.* Professionals would immediately head toward their *betanei,* their boss, determined to protect their paycheck.

He shifted his scope in the direction the first guard had taken. *Nothing. Twenty-five...twenty-six...twenty-seven...*

The compound went dark.

"*Aggress*!" Wolf said through the comm and the *Neealaho.*

With his men beside him, he bolted up. The thigh deep snow sucked at his legs, turning the charge across the snow into a slog. It only took seconds to force their way through the boot sucking snow to the berm of ice and snow that separated them from the plowed parking lot.

Teddy reached the top of the mound and dropped to his belly. With the infrared scope attached to his rifle sweeping the compound, he'd knock down any guard who presented a problem.

The snow and ice squeaking beneath his boots, Wolf and the rest of *Aggress* One flipped their NVDs down and scrambled up and over the ridge, then advanced steadily along the huge snow pile that flanked the east fence.

If the Shadow Warrior favored them, they'd blend into the snowbank, camouflaged as they were with their white kits and winter fatigues. Still, his heart and pulse hammered in his ears, the combination as loud as the roar of the Thunderbird on lift off. The lack of Teddy's rifle fire assured him the guards hadn't returned from their walkabout...yet.

The electricity was still down as they reached the edge of the east snow pile. Twenty feet to their quarry. One by one, they darted to the back of the house and spread out along the rear wall. They'd employ a double breach, assaulting into the house from the front and rear, where they'd pinch Kuznetsov between the two *aggress* teams. The four SEALs, along with O'Neill, would breach the rear entrance, while Wolf and his warriors would strike from the front.

Winters presented his kit to Simcosky, who untied it and pulled out one of the pneumatic door breachers.

"Blades, not rifles," Wolf reminded them through his comm, keeping his voice to a low, toneless whisper. Even suppressed, a rifle blast would alert Kuznetsov to their presence. "Breach on my command."

Samuel pulled another breacher from Wolf's kit and followed Wolf around the side of the cabin to the front entrance. *Aggress* Two should have surrounded the guard's shack by now.

Still no shots hitting the air. Not from Teddy. Not from the guards. Only the static cry of the wind. He took a second to listen...to scan the compound through the green wash of his NVDs.

A-2, countdown to breach? Wolf sent the question through the neural web.

Their plan called for all doors to open simultaneously, followed by immediate *aggress*.

Ready. Tomas's confident voice filled Wolf's mind.

"*Aggress* in ten," Wolf said softly through the *Neealaho* and the comm.

He kept watch for unwelcome eyes and ears, as Samuel inserted the thin ledge of the breacher into the gap between the door and the frame. The sound of the pneumatic thrust, and the ripping of the bolt from the frame was barely audible and masked by the rattle of the cabin's windows as Sister Wind picked at the glass. The door hung open, listing forward. Samuel dropped the door breacher next to the wall and unsheathed his knife.

As one unmatched in knife work, Samuel went in first—low, fast, and silent—his knife pinched between his thumb and index fingers. Wolf followed, the rest of his warriors sliding in behind him.

A green-tinted guard slouched in an armchair next to a crackling fire. The guard jackknifed up as they burst through the door. Lifting his rifle, he swung the muzzle in Samuel's direction. The knife was a blur as it left his *Caetanee's* fingers.

The blade sank deep and true, silencing the shout rounding the guard's stubbled mouth. Samuel's victim dropped his rifle to claw at his throat, where the black of the knife handle bristled against a stream of red. Wolf launched himself across the room as the dying man yanked the blade free and the trickle of red became a fountain. If the guard grabbed the rifle and pulled the trigger before he died, their advantage would be lost, a dangerous position to be in when a mind-rending weapon was possibly on the premises.

He snatched the rifle from the guard's lax grip and turned to scan the room. A saggy couch. A couple of recliners that listed to the side. Another armchair. But no other guards. He half turned toward the stairway in the middle of the room. It rose sharply and curved to the right. No rail, just plank walls.

Daniel, Samuel's *jenaaee*, took position with his back against the wall beside the door. This was the young one's first *aggress*, but he already showed the sharp instincts, intelligence, and steady nature that made his *anisbecco* such a lethal warrior. Samuel had done well in shaping him.

Wolf scanned the living room again. So far, the interior of the house matched the plans the *Taounaha's* contact had dug up. There should be four bedrooms and a bathroom on the second floor. Kuznetsov was likely up there.

"We're clear back here," Mackenzie said through the comm.

Kitchen secure. Dining room secure. The updates came through the *Neealaho* as his warriors search the lower level of the house. Wolf relaxed as the *clears* hit his ears or mind.

The silence was holding. Their success looked certain.

His thoughts proved a reckless dare.

From outside, rifle fire lit the night. Loud and continuous, it easily caught Wolf's ear. It caught another ear, too. On the floor above, high-pitched maniacal barking challenged the gun fire.

Small. Trivial teeth. No jaw strength or size to cause damage.

He dismissed the danger the dog presented, although if the rifle fire hadn't woken Kuznetsov, the noise the ankle biter was making would. Concern for his outside warriors slid through his mind. He shut it down. His own battle stood before him. Pivoting, he launched himself at the stairs.

Success rode the back of silence, but their silence had fled and alerted their quarry to the hunt.

Chapter Thirty-Seven

Day 17
Petropavlovsk, Russia

His short-barreled assault rifle in hand, Wolf took the stairs two at a time.
The dog's frantic barking was audible but muffled now. He reached the
bend in the staircase in seconds. There he stopped and crouched, listening.
The dog had fallen silent. No sound came from above, but he knew by
primal instinct their mark was up there, waiting for him. Sticking his head
around the corner was not an option—unless he wished to join Jude in the
web of their ancestors. Instead, he thrust his MK18 rifle around the corner.

Crack...crack...crack... came from above. The dog broke into another fit
of barking.

The gunshots sounded close—just up the stairs close. The blasts echoed
and deafened in the tight space, making it impossible to tell how many
weapons were in play.

He compressed his rifle's trigger. The weapon spit out a dozen rounds,
for distraction more than anything. He needed to see what awaited him at
the top of the stairs. One man? Two? More? Spraying the stairs with bullets
would force the mark or marks to drop and cover.

Surrounded by the acrid smell of spent ammunition and hot metal, he
leaned around, taking a quick peek up the stairs. A blur of green straight-

ened from its crouch against the landing wall above. He ducked back around the corner as multiple rounds splintered the wood where his head had once been.

One shooter then, crouched at the top of the stairs.

He was facing a stalemate. Death awaited anyone who climbed those stairs. Time to deploy Shadow labs' latest gift, or—gifts—in this case.

"Masks on," he said through the comm and *Neealaho* simultaneously.

He shifted, presenting his kit to Samuel while firing consistently up the stairs to keep their mark busy. The smell of spent propellant and burning metal grew stronger.

His *Caetanee* opened Wolf's kit and handed him a thin rubber gas mask. The mask was new, a recent addition to their war-ware from the Shadow Mountain labs. Still firing up the stairs to keep their shooter engaged, he removed his helmet with one hand and pulled on the mask, then donned his helmet again.

"Release in five," Wolf said through the neural net and comm as he plucked a silver canister from the front pocket of his equipment belt.

This, too, was developed and produced in the Shadow Mountain labs. A fast acting, quickly dispersing vapor, the gas would render anyone unconscious within seconds of contact, all without harming them. Regular gas masks would not blunt the effects of this vapor, only the masks his warriors currently wore.

If the Shadow Warrior favored them, the gas would knock the ankle biter out, too, and save them from its incessant barking.

He twisted the canister's cap, which started the five second countdown to the vapor's release, then thrust his arm around the corner, tossing the can up the stairs. More bullets splintered the wall next to him. Pain seared his biceps. He yanked his arm back. Red was already dampening the white fabric of his winter tactical jacket.

He grunted in disgust.

How bad? Samuel asked through their private neural link.

Wolf assessed the wound. It was bleeding, but not bad. He flexed his biceps and hissed in pain. That hurt. But the arm was mobile. *Good enough.* He sent the assessment through the link. He'd have a healer tend to it once they had their quarry in hand.

He counted the five seconds off in his head. It didn't matter where the can landed. The dispersal system would propel the gas outward. The colorless and scentless vapor would quickly spread, knocking out every living creature in its path. Except cockroaches. During the testing phase, the vapor had not affected cockroaches.

After five seconds came and went, Wolf stuck his rifle around the corner again and fired off a couple more rounds. No return fire this time. He took a quick look up the stairs. The landing was empty. Time to move. His arm burning, tension gripping his muscles and chilling his gut, Wolf swung around the corner and charged up the stairs. Muffled barking greeted him, but no gunfire.

No shooter either.

The house lights flickered as he reached the top of the stairs. They flickered a second time and stayed on. He flipped his NVDs up and leaped onto the second-floor landing, Samuel right behind him.

The gas canister was on the floor against the wall, opposite from where their adversary had crouched, but no shooter. They advanced forward, rifles up. The barking rose and fell ahead of them, as if someone was having limited success shutting the dog up. They found their mark unconscious and naked, half in/half out of the first door to the left. They rolled him over.

Kuznetsov.

Wolf recognized the bulbous nose, fleshy face, and barrel-chested torso from the pictures and video the *Taounaha* had provided. They had their arms dealer.

He scanned the room as Samuel secured their naked, unconscious captive's ankles and cuffed his hands behind his back. That high-pitched, frantic barking was louder than ever, but there was no dog in the room. His gaze slid to the closet in the corner, where the barking and snarls seemed to originate. Had Kuznetsov locked the dog in the closet before converging on the stairs?

Doubtful. The smell of sex hung heavy in the room. Benioko's source had mentioned Kuznetsov was hiding out with his mistress, a big-breasted and shallow-brained Australian woman. Judging by the condom discarded on the wood floor, the sex this room reeked of hadn't been one-handed. The mistress must be hiding. Probably with the dog.

He helped Samuel drag their captive across the room. They tossed him on the bed. The gas in the canister was fast-acting but fled quickly. Still, it would be several minutes until their captive was alert enough to answer their questions.

In teams of two, the rest of his warriors from *Aggress* One advanced down the hall to clear the remaining bedrooms. After which they'd search the rooms for anything weapon-related.

Had the vapor from the canister reached into this room? The dog was still alert, which meant the woman probably was too. There was no room beneath the bedframe for the woman to hide. She must be in the closet with the dog.

Their mark was unconscious and cuffed. Time to find the woman.

As they advanced on the closet, Samuel called for One Bird through the *Neealaho*. Since his *Caetanee* wasn't bleeding, the request must have been on Wolf's behalf. Ironically, he'd pushed the injury so far from his mind, he'd forgotten about it. It didn't even burn anymore. But when he glanced down, he found the fabric covering the wound soaked and dripping.

They took position on the left side of the door, Wolf in front, Samuel behind. Wolf jerked the door open.

An explosion of ferocious barking greeted them, but the dog didn't attack. It didn't show itself at all. But the row of dresses and coats dangling from the wooden rod shivered. And then the dog's barking snapped off with a squeal.

"Hush, Muffin. Hush. They'll hear you," a thick Australian accent said from behind the curtain of dresses. Although the words were more sobbed than spoken.

Judging by the dog's previous barking, and the woman's heavy, sobby breathing, the gas had never reached back here. It was likely inert now, anyway. Which meant their gas masks were unnecessary. He removed his helmet and took his mask off. He waited a couple of seconds for any ill effects. When he felt no dizziness, he tossed it to the side and pulled his helmet back on. He'd stow the gas mask in his pack after their targets were secure.

The woman's sobs gained strength. She was crying so hard, the clothes surrounding her trembled. The dog, on the other hand, had dropped from barking to whining.

Wolf stifled a sigh. "We know you're in there." Of course they did. Her escalating sobs were a dead giveaway. "Leash your dog and come out. You will not be harmed."

The sobs shifted to shrieks, and the dog started barking like a banshee again. "I have...I have a gun...I know how to use it."

Wolf barely heard her. Were the two competing for who could cause the worst headache?

"As do we." He waited. No movement from inside. Even the clothes were still. "Your provider is bound. He cannot rescue you. Toss your weapon out. You will not be harmed."

The shrieks turned into screams, the barks into one long, shrill howl. Wolf winced. A miniature gun with a gold handle came flying out. Apparently, Kuznetsov's mistress hadn't been lying about that, if one could call this toy a gun.

"I'm...I'm not wearing...any...any clothes," the woman said between sobbing shrieks.

Wolf shook his head, frowning at the rack of clothes above the disembodied voice. "Lady, there's an entire closet of clothes above your head."

Benioko's contact hadn't been lying about the woman's mental acuity.

"*Ho'cee,*" One Bird said from behind him. "Allow me to attend to your arm."

Knowing Samuel could handle the woman and dog, Wolf turned to greet *Aggress* One's spirit healer. *Aggress* Two had their own healer...which reminded him. "Those shots from earlier, how bad?"

One Bird shook his head. His square face placid, he followed Wolf over to the bed. "Those who required it have received the *Hee-Hee-Thae.*"

Wolf frowned. "How many?"

"Two." One Bird glanced over at Kuznetsov, who was still unconscious. "Roberto was thigh shot. He recovers."

Wolf frowned. They had their mark, but the battle was far from over. A healer's energy was limited. His wound was minor. Best to save the *Hee-Hee-Thae* blessing for the flight home, when the risk of additional wounds was in the past.

"Stitch it for now." Wolf sat on the bed, facing their captive.

Samuel escorted Kuznetsov's woman from the closet as One Bird finished stitching Wolf's arm. She'd pulled on a blue, clingy, thigh length dress. Tight arms, with red-tipped fingernails, clutched a mop of white against her impressive breasts. The mop bared a set of small fangs at him. A low growl vibrated out of its open mouth. How did it know where to look? Its eyes were completely covered by fluffy white fleece.

The Australian wobbled toward him on impractical, six-inch stilettos. Even someone with the brains of a wild turnip should know better than wearing shoes she could not run in. The woman stopped dead at the sight of Kuznetsov's naked body on the bed. Her shrieks, which had subsided, rose again.

"Oh, fuck! Fuck! You killed him!" The dog emphasized her accusation with a round of barking so rabid its forehead fleece bounced along with its cries. Round, dark eyes were periodically revealed, only to disappear again.

The shrillness of the dog's barking along with the woman's shrieking pierced Wolf's head like a poker of fire. One Bird's, too, as witnessed by his wince. Kuznetsov even responded by shifting on the bed.

"Enough!" Wolf bellowed. "Sit down, shut up, and keep that dog quiet, or one of us will quiet it for you."

Not that he'd kill a dog because of its instinctive urge to bark. But Kuznetsov's mistress didn't know that, as proven by the ashen tone that edged out the white in her face and the way she urgently shushed and jiggled the dog. Her movement stopped the animal's barking, but a queasy look settled over its furry face, like the woman's relentless rocking was making it seasick.

Since the woman had forgotten how to move, Samuel dragged her across the floor and shoved her against the wall without bothering to secure her arms or legs. "Sit."

The very curtness of Samuel's order told Wolf his *Caetanee* had lost patience with the woman and her pet.

Kuznetsov lifted his head, his muddy brown eyes muddier. He used his cuffed hands to push himself up, only to collapse back on the mattress. The Russian was still too out of it to interrogate.

Wolf turned his attention to the arms dealer's mistress. "Check her pockets."

She'd had one gun. Perhaps she had another.

"Nothing but lipstick," Samuel said.

One Bird finished bandaging Wolf's wound and repacked his med-kit. As the healer left the room, Wolf walked around the bed. The right pillow had the imprint of a head on it. So did the left. He tossed both pillows to the floor and collected the guns beneath them. The comforter joined the pillows on the floor. No guns under it. But the smell of sex grew stronger.

With the bed devoid of weapons, Wolf returned to Kuznetsov. The Russian's eyes were clearer and getting more hostile now.

"We're good down here, in case anyone was wondering," Mackenzie growled over the comm. "You find the target?"

Wolf already knew his downstairs crew was unharmed. O'Neill would have warned him otherwise. Although, Wolf frowned, perhaps not. That was the disadvantage of having the *jie'van* on his crew. Even though he was linked to the *Neealaho*, he rarely used it.

"We have our mark," Wolf confirmed quietly.

"The butcher or the weapon?" Cosky asked immediately.

"The butcher." Wolf studied their captive, who'd rolled over onto his back. He hadn't reacted to his nickname. Frowning, he glanced toward the woman. Neither had she.

"Take all captives to the living room," Wolf said into his comm.

With their hostages in one place, it would take fewer men to guard them. The rest of his warriors would tear this place apart. They'd collect all the hard drives and electronic devices. If the weapon had been sold, they needed information on its buyers.

Wolf sent a silent plea to the elder gods that the doomsday device was still on the premises and not headed off to be deployed against an unsuspecting population.

Aggress Two, update. Wolf sent the request through the *Neealaho*.

All guards are secure, Tomas responded.

Wolf relaxed. They had time to attend to their captive, then. He turned back to the bed. The woman had finally stopped her phlegmy crying and sat huddled with her dog against the wall.

From the awareness in the Russian's eyes, his body had absorbed most of the vapor. What was left would not react with the truth serum. It was time to get their answers.

"I tell you nothing," Kuznetsov suddenly said. "You not break me. I take..." he frowned slightly, his gaze turning vague, then shrugged. "Instruction to guard mind."

Interesting. Their captive obviously knew they'd come looking for information and expected them to beat the answers out of him. But torture was messy, sweaty, and protracted work. The Shadow Mountain truth serum would provide answers within minutes.

"Samuel, prepare the syringe." Wolf took a step toward their captive, ready to hold him still while his *Caetanee* injected the serum.

The woman started a sobbing ramble. Her thin, pitchy voice hovered on the edge of hysterics. "Please don't hurt me. Or Muffin." Her voice rose even higher. "Take everything, if you want..." her voice broke as the sobs escaped. "But don't hurt Muffy. There's jewelry and cash in the safe. You can have it all..." She sobbed harder, her face white and terrified. "Just don't...don't hurt us."

Muffy whined and twisted in her arms, frantically licking her wet cheeks. Kuznetsov turned his head and glared at her. He said something thick and guttural in Russian.

He told her not to tell us anything, Samuel said through the *Neealaho*.

Wolf's eyebrows rose. The woman hadn't included Kuznetsov in her pleas for safety. Nor had the Russian demanded they leave her alone. There was no loyalty between the pair. This would make interrogating her easier. The fact she'd already volunteered the information about the safe was a good sign. She could be useful.

"Where is this safe?" Wolf asked, his voice mild. No need to terrify her further.

Her sobs escalated, as did Muffin's licking. "In...in...the closet over there." She nodded toward the closet they'd pulled her from. "Beneath...the floor."

"You know the combination?"

Kuznetsov shouted something to her in Russian.

Samuel shrugged. *He tells her to shut up.*

"Don't shout at me!" the woman screamed back, shooting Kuznetsov a blind, terrified look. "They have guns! They're going to kill us!"

Muffin, picking up on her mistress's panic, started growling again.

Wolf sighed. "The combination?"

Perhaps there was more than jewelry and money in this safe she spoke of. The Russian seemed determined to prevent her from giving out the combination. If they were lucky—very lucky—perhaps they'd find the nanoweapon inside.

Assuming he could hear the combination between her sobs, screams, and the dog's growling.

"E-5-9-A-2-7-F." She sobbed the combination of letters and numbers out.

Wolf made her repeat the combination, then turned to Samuel, who already had the syringe out of his pack. With the needle pointed up, Samuel flicked the barrel and compressed the plunger until the air bubbles were expelled.

Wolf leaned forward and pinned the Russian to the mattress. He tilted his chin toward Samuel, who stepped up to the bed and grasped the Russian's arm. Kuznetsov rolled his head toward Samuel, his gaze falling on the syringe. He paled. "Nyet! Nyet! Is illegal!"

The response startled a laugh from Wolf. Illegal? This from the butcher of Karaveht? Did he think infecting dozens of innocent people with his insanity bug had been fair play?

"Nyet! Nyet—how you say? Nyet needles!" The Russian tried to jerk his arm away from Samuel's grasp, but Wolf pressed it into the mattress, holding it still as Samuel plunged the needle into the muscled arm. Thirty seconds later, the drug hit his brain, and the Russian fell unconscious. Wolf let him go and stepped back from the bed.

Unlike sodium thiopental, which required intravenous injection, the drug the Shadow Mountain lab techs had developed could be injected into the muscle instead of the vein, but with the same metabolism rate of thirty to forty-five seconds for the drug to reach the brain. But this Shadow Mountain drug left the brain and distributed to the rest of the body faster. Instead of five to ten minutes for the concentration in the brain to drop to levels compatible with consciousness, the Shadow Mountain drug brought a return to consciousness—or at least, the moonlight state of consciousness—within three minutes.

Leaving Samuel to watch the woman, Wolf turned his attention to the closet. Dim light spilled down from the overhead light fixture. He made several trips in and out, dumping armfuls of colorful dresses, sweaters, cardigans, pants, and coats onto the bedroom floor. It took him several minutes to shove the endless pairs of stiletto heels to the very back of the space. *Hee-nes-ce,* did this female like her tall shoes. There were no flats to be found.

Once most of the floor was clear, he crouched to study the wood planks. The light was too weak to see the flooring well, so he pulled his flashlight from his equipment belt, clicked it on, and glided the beam along the boards. The grain and slats matched up perfectly. No gaps or signs of scuffs or scratches hinted the boards had been pried up.

Crouching, he ran his fingertips across the boards' seams. A slight variation in height between the planks gave the safe compartment away. There must be a mechanism that pushed up the false floor when activated. He ran his fingertips along the edges. When he found a slightly raised, two-inch patch along the seam that had some give to it, he pressed down progressively harder until a subtle *snick* sounded. A two-by-two-foot section of the floor popped up.

A safe was tucked in the space below.

Chapter Thirty-Eight

Day 17
Petropavlovsk, Russia

The safe was made of black metal that blended into the darkness below. Almost two feet wide, it sat back from the front of the compartment, which allowed room for its door to swing open.

He leaned down and dialed in the combination Kuznetsov's woman had recited. A soft snick sounded. He pulled back the handle and the door silently swung open.

The *woohanna* hadn't been exaggerating when she'd said the safe was full of jewelry. The entire right side of the interior was stacked from bottom to top with velvet-wrapped boxes. Stacks of money took up the left side of the safe.

He swept his flashlight beam from corner to corner, making sure Kuznetsov hadn't booby-trapped the interior, but saw nothing of concern. He removed the money first, flipping through each of the banded stacks. There were a variety of currencies—the US dollar, the Australian dollar, the Russian ruble, the Chinese yuan.

He reached for the jewelry boxes next. The *wanatesa* weapon was microscopic. The vessel that contained it could be equally small. Perhaps the Russian had attempted to conceal it inside a jewelry box.

But case after velvet-lined case contained nothing but jewelry. Necklaces, bracelets, watches, earrings, rubies, sapphires, diamonds. Each piece was gaudier than the last. Unless the nanobots had been infused in the jewelry, which seemed unlikely—how would you deploy it?—the jewelry collection was of no use to them.

When the compartment was empty, he laid on his side, clamped the torch between his teeth and eased his head into the space, angling it until he could see into the safe. His flashlight beam reflected off a silver-gray rectangular case pressed up against the back wall. Leaning further down, he worked his arm into the safe, and wedged the tips of his fingers into the space between the back of the case and the wall. He pulled, but it didn't budge.

He forced his arm in further, ignoring his burning shoulder, which was wedged against the corner of the safe. Even with his fingers shoved deeper behind the case, the object didn't move when he tried to pull it forward. Was it bolted to the safe? His shoulder *and* his fingers burned as he forced his fingers fully into the space and pulled hard.

This time, the case wiggled forward a bit. Apparently, it wasn't bolted to the floor, just incredibly heavy. It was also cold, almost icy, numbing his hands.

Inch by inch, he dragged the box closer. A heavy, scraping sound accompanied its progress to the front of the safe. He kept pulling until the box sat half on the lip of the safe and half on the floor beneath it. There was just enough room to get his hands under it. He shifted onto his stomach and reached for his prize with both hands. Once he had a good grip on the box, he lifted it, while simultaneously scooting backwards.

Astonishing, how heavy the thing was. At least fifty pounds.

His heart rate doubled as he got his first good look at the rectangular container. The fact it had been hidden so deep in the safe, along with its appearance, hinted he might have found what they'd come for. The case was metal and narrow, maybe five inches wide, but long—at least eighteen inches in length. Two thick hasps with rotating clasps secured the lid in place.

Setting it on the floor, he rotated the clasps, freeing the hasps. After a quick prayer to the Shadow Warrior that the lid wasn't booby trapped, he cautiously lifted the top. The interior contained a cushioned bottom. The lid was cushioned, too. Five indented slots ran along the bottom cushion. Four of the slots were empty. The fifth held a metal container of the same silver gray as the case. It was small—maybe two by three inches, narrow at the top and bottom, with a flat bottom and bulging sides. It looked like a miniature hand grenade, complete with a metal ring and pin. Although this thing had a smooth exterior and was a third the size of a normal grenade.

He frowned at the lone metal object resting in the case. There were no labels or lettering, but this thing sure looked like a containment device that might hold nanobots. Even the grenade design was relevant. The nanoweapon hit the brain like a bomb, bringing insanity and murderous aggression.

Of course, it could be something else entirely. Maybe a prototype for a new type of explosive.

He touched nothing in the case. What if it was the nanoweapon? What if the pin had slipped and some of those brain eating microscopic bugs had escaped their prison? Wolf shuddered and carefully closed the lid, re-clasping the hasps.

He carried the metal case out of the closet and over to the bed. Kuznetsov glanced over as Wolf set it down on the mattress next to him. The Russian's face went ashen, and he lunged to the side, away from the silver box. He would have fallen off the bed if Samuel hadn't grabbed him. An urgent stream of Russian exploded from him. Their captive's recoil was another sign that they had found what they were seeking. This time, Muffin didn't react from where she'd relaxed into her mistress's arms.

Samuel translated the spate of Russian. "No. Take away. No open. Is dangerous."

More confirmation. Wolf grunted, his skin crawling at what the case likely contained. "Ask how many canisters he used at the well in Karaveht."

If he'd used four of the canisters in Karaveht, then the one left was the weapon posted for sale on the dark web. If he'd used less than four, Wolf grimaced, then they faced more trouble.

After a few seconds of back and forth in Russian, where Samuel's face grew progressively grimmer, his second finally turned to face Wolf. From the tension radiating across Samuel's face, Wolf already knew what his *Caetanee* was about to say.

"They were given five vials. Three were used during the testing in Karaveht. One was sold privately. This is the one currently up for sale on the web."

Wolf absorbed the information with silence and stillness. But frustration and rage warred beneath that calm. One of the doomsday devices was still out there.

Samuel was talking again. "He says the purchaser was anonymous. An exchange was made in Tajikistan. Money for the vial.

Is he being truthful? Wolf asked, studying their hostage.

Kuznetsov's face was slack. His eyes were vague, his words slurred. He didn't look like he could keep this secret to himself. Still, it was possible the Russian had instinctively recognized the dangers associated with Samuel's questions and was resisting answering. While the truth serum made it difficult for a subject to prevaricate, it didn't make it impossible.

Samuel shrugged. *Unknown. I will keep questioning.*

Frowning, Wolf turned to the woman. Perhaps she could answer his remaining questions. Her knees drawn up to her pillowy chest, she rocked back and forth on the floor with her eyes down. Her short pixie hair was a tousled mess, her face wet with tears.

Crossing to her, he squared his feet and crossed his arms. "What do you know of Kuznetsov's business dealings?"

Her forehead wrinkled as she peeked up at him. She clutched Muffin closer, and confusion touched her wet eyes. "Business? What business?"

"His weapons." A scowl touched Wolf's face. "Specifically, this new weapon." Wolf nodded toward the silver case. "Is he hiding more vials elsewhere?"

The confusion deepened on her face. She reached up with trembling fingers to scratch Muffin behind her floppy ears. The dog sighed and relaxed into her chest even more. "Weapons? The only weapons I have seen are the ones he kept under our pillows and the ones his guards carry."

"Not those weapons." Wolf tempered his tone when she flinched. "I speak of the silver one inside this case." He nodded toward the bed and the metal container sitting on it.

Another round of sobs broke from her. "I don't know anything about that." The sobbing sped up. "He said...he said...he was an international banker. I know...of...of...no weapons."

Muffy suddenly jackknifed up, her head swiveling toward the door. A high-pitched warning bark broke from her. Wolf turned as the Australian woman went to work, shushing and jiggling the dog again. He frowned at the sight of O'Neill in the middle of the doorframe. What was the *jie'van* doing up here? If there was a problem downstairs, Mackenzie would have let him know.

"Is there a reason you are here?" Wolf kept his voice flat. No doubt whatever reason the *jie'van* gave was secondary to his real reason—to act the fly, buzzing around and annoying everyone around him. He should have stuck him with *Aggress* Two. At least he'd be outside the house and out of Wolf's hair.

O'Neill's gaze shifted from Wolf to the bed and locked on the silver case. His green eyes narrowed. "Is that what we came for?"

Wolf shrugged. "So it would seem."

O'Neill shifted his focus to the Russian, and then to the syringe sitting on the bedside table. There was an infinitesimal relaxation to his facial muscles. "He talked then? Told you everything we need to know?"

Was that relief Wolf heard in his voice? Impossible.

"He did." Wolf crossed his arms and quirked an eyebrow. He wouldn't say their mark had told them everything. The interrogation was still ongoing. But O'Neill had no part in the questioning and no reason for his interest. "Why are you here?"

A flash of something almost like guilt crossed O'Neill's face, but it was gone so quickly Wolf dismissed it. "Just wanted to make sure we got what we came for," he drawled, mockery lighting his eyes and vibrating in his voice. "Wouldn't want this whole shebang to be for nothing."

Before Wolf responded, his pilot's grim voice came through the *Neeala-ho*.

"An alert for an unidentified aircraft just went out through Rybachiy. They're scrambling stealth checkmates. We need to get airborne."

O'Neill disappeared from the door. Wolf pivoted. The rest of their questions for the Russian would have to wait. He glanced at Samuel. "Get him dressed."

The *aggress* had gone perfectly so far, which prickled at the back of his neck. Perfect *aggresses* often ended in catastrophe. He sensed they were headed in that direction.

"Prepare for evac," he barked into the comm and through the neural net.

"I need my jewelry and money." The woman's voice broke as sobs struck again. Tears slid faster down her cheeks. "Please. I need them to pay for my way home. They will be stolen if I leave them behind."

Wolf grabbed the cell phone from the nightstand on the side of the bed that Kuznetsov had been sleeping on, then leaned across the bed to grab the phone off the woman's side of the bed.

"Lady, stop the damn crying. You can grab your things after we leave," he growled as he slipped the phones beneath the webbing of his equipment belt.

The sobbing stopped like someone had turned off a faucet. He turned to stare at her. Her skin had turned ashen. Horror swam in her eyes.

"You can't leave me here with them, with Grigory's guards." She shuddered, her arms tightening so hard around her dog, Muffy squealed and squirmed. A queasy look settled over her face. "They're awful...rapists and murderers. They constantly watch me with the most disgusting, lewd expressions. The minute you leave, they'll be on me like a pack of animals. The only thing that's kept me safe from them is that they knew Grigory would kill anyone who touched me." Her voice dropped to a thin whisper. "But once you take Grigory ..."

Wolf tilted his head back and glared up at the ceiling.

Fuck...fuck...fuck.

Sometimes the *woohanta's* favorite word was the only thing that described the situation. He ground his teeth.

The woman was right. After the Thunderbird took to the sky with Kuznetsov and the guards were discovered and freed, they'd turn on her. Gang rape was a certainty, and something he could not allow. Not when he could prevent it.

Lowering his head, he sighed and scrubbed a weary hand down his face. "Fine. You will come with us...for now. We will drop you off somewhere safe."

Where that would be, he knew not. Shadow Mountain intel would have to locate a safe place to offload her, one that wouldn't risk their chances of making it safely home. His gaze fell to her ridiculous shoes.

Those she could not wear outside this house. He did not want to explain how One Bird had healed her broken ankle with only his hands.

Women. They complicated everything.

Chapter Thirty-Nine

Day 17
Petropavlovsk, Russia

Eloise Carmichael added a round of blubbery sniffles to her whinging as she clutched her bulging satchel to her belly and watched the hard-faced fucker across the room stuff Grigory into his clothes.

Muffy was relaxing in her doggie backpack, which was strapped to Eloise's chest beneath her coat. Her theatrical performance—which was ongoing—had accomplished exactly what she intended and handed her the advantage. Although the soldiers surrounding her didn't realize it yet. Men were so easy to manipulate. Mostly through sex. But if sex wasn't achievable, sobs and screams worked almost as well.

Real men, those that defined themselves as heroic, cowered before sobbing, screaming, terrified women.

Her sobbing and screaming had served their purpose. They'd shielded her from a closer look. They'd manipulated the big, tough asshole who led these soldiers into granting her a satchel full of jewelry, cash, and her special six-inch stilettos. They'd even given her the opportunity to engineer an excuse to climb onboard their aircraft, thus granting her the opportunity to kill Grigory with her lipstick syringe before he told them anything important.

So far, these assholes didn't know enough about her operation to cause her trouble. To keep them in the dark, Grigory had to die.

She suspected the soldiers who'd stormed her sanctuary were a yank Special Ops team. Maybe SEALs, like the ones they'd tested the nanobots on in Karaveht. They wore similar uniforms and helmets, complete with night vision goggles and communication mics.

With an exaggerated shiver, Eloise hugged the satchel harder against her belly and flipped up the collar of her cashmere coat. Muffy squirmed against her chest in protest. Eloise loosened her arms. Her baby didn't like being squished.

The leader of this band of soldiers had allowed her to change into a warm pair of trackies, along with her warmest coat and Muffy's pup pack. But the boots she was wearing had come from him. One of his soldiers had appeared in the bedroom and dropped them at her feet.

The boots were another sign this team was military. A mercenary wouldn't be so accommodating. Rather than seeing to her comfort and protecting her from Grigory's guards, he would have stolen her jewelry and money, then taken her for himself before sharing her with his men.

Of course, her screaming and crying didn't account for *all* the leader's goodwill. Some of his kindness was undoubtedly because of her divulging the location and combination of the safe. He'd been pleased with that information.

Offering him the information had been a calculated risk. Once they interrogated him, Grigory would give up the safe's location and combination, anyway. Odds were, he'd give up more than the safe at that point. But if she offered the safe to the assholes right off the bat, and they found what they were looking for, maybe they wouldn't interrogate Grigory here. Maybe they'd wait until they hauled him back to wherever they came from. These Americans were deep in enemy territory, right next to a heavily patrolled Russian submarine base. They must be nervous, itching to get home.

Besides, losing this last nanobot bomb wasn't important. Clark Nantz had plenty more where it came from. The fucker thought he'd kept his identity secret through his false personas and dummy corporations. He hadn't.

Nantz wasn't as clever as he thought. None of the men she dealt with were.

While her efforts to delay the questioning hadn't worked, so far Grigory hadn't told them anything that would hurt her.

Widening her eyes until they watered, Eloise added a quiver to her jaw and another round of heavy sniffles. She needed to keep up the theatrics until they dropped her off at this haven they'd promised her. Then she could get back to running her business. If she worked them right, maybe they'd sit her next to Grigory on their ride out, and she could use the spring-loaded syringe on her former partner.

That would take care of her Grigory problem.

Too bad she only had one of her lipstick syringes. But her guard would have questioned why she was riffling through the pockets of her clothes. And she'd been distracted with keeping Muffy under control. If her baby got loose and attacked one of these assholes, they probably would shoot her.

At least she'd been able to transfer the tube from her dress pocket to her coat when she changed clothes. Plus, she'd stuffed several pairs of shoes into the satchel. She'd chosen the highest of heels, the ones with the five-inch stiletto blades spring-loaded into the six-inch heels.

What she wouldn't give to stab the big asshole with one of her fancy shoes. He'd been so condescending when she'd walked out of the closet with her favorite blades strapped to her feet. A smirk touched her mouth before she turned it into a lip wobble.

Like most men, once she'd presented him with what he expected, he didn't bother to look any deeper.

Doubling down on her trembling lips and teary eyes, she studied the two assholes hauling Grigory to his feet. They wore white and black speckled fatigues with matching backpacks. Even their helmets and boots were white. They'd certainly color coordinated with the weather. An aura of lethality surrounded them, like they knew a thousand ways to kill without breaking a sweat.

While she hadn't expected anyone to track them to this far-flung compound in the middle of Russia, she'd still taken precautions in case they were found. Since the Americans were the ones determined to find her, she'd chosen the least likely place they'd infiltrate: Russia, next to a nuclear submarine base. If they were caught, their presence in Petropavlovsk would spark an international incident and set relations with Russia back by decades. She'd been confident the yanks wouldn't chance that.

Even so, she ordered Grigory to triple their guard. Which he had. Not that the increased protection had done them any good. The big asshole and his fucking soldiers had slipped through all the guards and accessed the house—hell, the bedroom—entirely too easily,

She sighed, absently scratching the underside of Muffy's chin, taking comfort in the cool, silky texture of her fur. Even if the leader let her go, like he'd promised—she'd have to start over, find another male partner to act as the face of her operation. Setting up a new partner as the face and voice of her business would take some time—most of it spent locating the right guy to work with.

Ruthless men with pliable dispositions were impossible to find. Nor did such men take orders from women. Instead of finding such a man, she'd have to create the appearance of one, like she'd done with Grigory. Her former partner had been a two-cent thug when she'd stumbled across him. He looked the part, though, acted it, too. But more crucially, he'd been willing to take orders from her. He'd been quite the find. It was a shame she had to let him go.

After she set up shop again, she'd reach out to Clark Nantz and threaten to expose him if he didn't send her more nanobot weapons. Hell, maybe she could even convince him to work with her. She'd blame the stolen bots and the unauthorized sale on Grigory.

But no matter what happened going forward, she'd be okay. So far, Grigory had spilled nothing detrimental during the interrogation. Even if she couldn't get close enough to kill him before they threw her off their transport, she'd be long gone by the time they realized she was behind the weapons dealing. And there was nothing Grigory could tell them that would affect her return to business.

While he knew which city her weapons cache was stored, he didn't know the exact location. She moved the depot after each sale. Nor did her former lover know any of the company's banking information—or at least the real banking information.

Sure, he knew what account number to give for payment during an arms deal. But as soon as the money hit the account, she transferred most of it out. She'd hired the best computer hacker in existence to cover the transfer tracks and create a mirror account for Grigory's benefit, one that allowed him the illusion of a true financial partnership, without allowing him control over the account itself—beyond transferring a few hundred thousand. He'd never tested the upper limit of his financial freedom, satisfied with the withdrawals the account permitted him to make.

But the mirror account would cease to exist as soon as she missed the second check in. She was confident nobody would find the actual accounts. Lord knew she'd spent a lot of money to make sure of that.

As soon as these soldiers released her, she and Muffy would disappear, find a new partner, and return to business.

In the meantime, she'd already received two million euros from the sale of the fourth vial. This influx of cash, along with what was already in her accounts, would float her for a very long time if things didn't go as planned.

Day 17
Denali, Alaska

"Would you ladies like another cup of coffee?" the nurse manning the ER desk asked.

Demi's belly gurgled sourly at the prospect. "Nothing for me, thank you."

"I'll pass, too. But thanks for the offer," Kait echoed politely, her face blank, her eyes unfocused.

There had already been too many cups of coffee on an empty stomach. What Demi really needed was food. Solid food. Something to soak up the acid from all those cups of coffee. But the thought of walking down to the cafeteria and forcing herself to eat felt like too much effort.

They hadn't been allowed into the isolation unit, so Demi and Kait were camped out in the ER's waiting room. Before he'd left for Russia, Wolf had offered them the use of a base apartment. They'd declined, opting to remain close to the clinic doctors and any news they might bring.

Twenty-four hours later, the muscles of Demi's neck, shoulders, and back protested that decision. After so many hours of sitting, it was impossible to find a comfortable position. Judging by Kait's countless laps around the waiting room, her muscles weren't faring any better. Demi had taken just as many laps, but the benefits of moving were fleeting.

This too, she remembered from the vigil beside Donnie's bed. The cramping muscles and coffee-soured stomach. The combination of fear and hope every time a doctor approached.

Kait stirred, a frown knitting the furrowed skin of her forehead. "Cosky said it's a four-and-a-half-hour trip to this compound they're attacking. They left at twelve-thirty last night, which would put them on site around 05:00 a.m. Even with their hike into where that rat bastard is hiding out, they should have arrived hours ago. Their mission should be over. They should be on their way home." She bit her lip before adding, "If things had gone wrong, and they'd taken casualties, the doctors here would know about it, don't you think? They'd have been warned about incoming wounded, right?"

"I would think so," Demi agreed. Although, while the clinic would need to prepare for incoming casualties, would anyone tell them what was going on?

For Kait, yeah, they probably would. As the base's strongest healer, she'd be on the need-to-know list. The only reason Kait hadn't been on the helicopter with Cosky was because she'd wanted to be around to heal Aiden if given the chance. The rest of the base's healers had accompanied Wolf and his men. They'd keep the injured alive long enough to return to base. Once home, Kait could heal the catastrophic injuries.

They hadn't spoken much over the past twenty-four hours. They were locked in their own thoughts. Kait was caught between anxiety over Cosky and fear for her brother. And Demi was caught between memories of Donnie's final moments and fear for Aiden's current condition. Plus, there was the constant memory of Aiden's expression when she'd broken things off with him; the realization and pain spreading across his face and the gut-wrenching emptiness in his eyes. His reaction still haunted her.

That memory might be the last one she had of him. The knowledge of that sat like a lead weight in her chest.

When the door next to the nurse's station opened and the tall, lean frame of Dr. Brickenhouse walked through, Demi and Kait rose to their feet. The muscles in Demi's face and arms tightened as she'd braced for bad news.

"Ladies." The doctor stopped before them. "Aiden remains uncon-scious, but he's responding well to the medications we've started him on. His fever has come down and his heart and respiration have stabilized." He let them absorb that before continuing. "We still don't know what the autoimmune reaction is in response to, nor do we know whether his earlier symptoms will return as soon as we stop the medications."

The breath Kait released sounded choked. "What about all the tests you've been running? You looked for nanobots, right? Did you find any?"

They had found nothing in the earlier tests they'd run. But they had run even more tests since then. The nanobot question was of utmost importance to everyone. Kait wouldn't be allowed to touch him if there was any sign of bot activity. If she couldn't touch him, she couldn't heal him.

The doctor's hesitation was enough to catch Demi's breath and tighten every muscle in her body. Kait noticed his reaction as well.

"Doctor?" Kait's voice tightened into hoarseness.

"Yes...well." He sighed and peered at Kait over the frames of his glasses. "We're not quite certain what we found in his blood beneath the electron microscope." Removing his glasses, he methodically polished the lenses with the hem of his white coat. "The EM picked up fragments of...some-thing. But we're uncertain what they are. While they have some of the organic markers of what we found in his teammate's blood, they aren't fully developed nanobots. These fragments are somewhere around a hundredth of the size of what we found in his teammate's bodies, which were micro-scopic to begin with. We're testing them, but we're uncertain what they are." He paused and added quietly, "Or what we're dealing with."

"Where did you find them?" Demi twisted her fingers together. Did this mean Aiden was infected, after all?

"In his blood," the doctor said as he put his glasses back on and adjust-ed the frames. "These fragments are too microscopic to show up on the brain scans. To get a look there, we'd have to biopsy his brain and look at the sample through the electron microscope—which we aren't willing to consider at this point."

"What about his skin?" Kait asked, holding the doctor's gaze. "Did you find any of these fragments on his skin?"

From the knowing look that settled across the doctor's face, he knew exactly why she was asking. "We did not. But that doesn't mean he's been cleared for a healing. Caution is in order. We simply don't know what we're dealing with yet."

Demi's knees joined her fingers in shaking. "How many fragments did you find?"

The doctor shrugged. "Three."

Three fragments, at least that they'd found. Aiden could be loaded with those things.

"Are you trying to get rid of them?" Demi asked.

If those fragments had some of the organic markers that infected Aiden's teammates, they were dangerous. They had to be purged from his body. What if they grew into full nanobots? What if they multiplied?

Brickenhouse sighed, looking momentarily exhausted. "We don't know what they are. We don't know what they'll react to, or if they'll react to anything at all. They're not mobile. They're not alive." He shook his head. "We're assessing them. Once we have more information, we'll reevaluate the situation."

Which wasn't reassuring. By the time they figured out what they were dealing with, it could be too late to save Aiden.

The doctor turned away. Kait started and took off after him. "Doctor, hang on a minute."

Demi tuned out Kait's voice as she questioned the man about Wolf and his men, and whether the clinic had received news of casualties. She was too focused on other questions.

Like what if these fragments they'd found in Aiden's blood were the reason he was so sick? If the docs couldn't flush them out of his body, could he survive with them inside him? Or would the autoimmune response eventually overwhelm his system?

Would the damn things kill him before the doctors could figure out what they were and how to get rid of them?

Chapter Forty

Day 17
Petropavlovsk, Russia

Coming in hot, the pilot said through the *Neealaho. Two minutes to skids down.*

Wolf grunted an acknowledgement. Time to shift focus and get everyone outside to catch their ride home.

"Daniel, to me." He sent the message through the comm as the young one had not yet gone through the binding ceremony and been connected to the neural net.

"Copy," came Daniel's quiet, confident voice over the comm.

Prior to taking part in the binding ceremony, a fledgling seeking induction into the warrior clans had to prove their spirit and skill in the heat of a true *aggress.* After skill testing, Daniel had been deemed worthy and allowed to join *Aggress* Two.

They stuffed Kuznetsov into his clothes as they awaited Daniel's arrival. It seemed to take forever. But with his *Caetanee* stuffing one half of Kuznetsov's body into his clothing while Wolf stuffed the other half, they finally got him ready to head outside.

"*Betanee.*" Daniel stepped into the room with confident strides. "You called for me?"

Wolf nodded toward Kuznetsov's mistress. "She accompanies us. Take her to the Thunderbird."

As Daniel escorted the weeping woman from the room and Samuel force-marched the Russian out into the hall, Wolf hefted the silver box. It was heavier than he remembered, with sharp corners. His pulse sped up at the thought of what was inside the crate.

He addressed the four SEALs through the comm as he exited the room. "Prepare for evac. One minute to skids down."

With the silver case cradled against his chest, he took the stairs down almost as fast as he'd taken them up. The hostages were lined up neatly along the wall, their arms and legs bound, butts on the floor. There were ten men total, most from the guard shed, all alive, mostly untouched. Although one had a white bandage around his forearm. Rawlings's work. His healers saved their *Hee-Hee-Thae* gift for those they fought beside.

Outside, above the roar of the wind, came the shriek of the Thunderbird. For her to scream so shrilly, rather than chirp, meant Sky Warrior, their pilot, had dropped her hard. Wolf tensed at the realization. This was a man who babied their aircraft. To treat his newest toy so harshly meant their situation was grave and speed was essential.

"Load up," Wolf ordered.

Daniel went out first, with Kuznetsov's woman walking meekly beside him. Her bulging satchel was clutched to her chest, as though she were terrified of losing it, but at least she wasn't tottering on those ridiculous heels. The woman was still sniffling, flinching, and teary-eyed. Wolf was pleased to see that the young warrior was unimpressed by her beauty or tears.

Samuel was at the front of the pack, half-dragging, half-carrying a staggering Kuznetsov out the door. The Russian was off-balance, still feeling the effects of the truth serum.

Wolf held back, keeping the weapon he carried as far from the others as possible. He'd wait until everyone was on board before approaching the Thunderbird and stowing the silver case in the metal box attached to the top of the skids. The outside box was new, an addition to the Thunderbird for just this purpose, to keep this weapon away from his warriors.

Once their captives and the last of his men had exited the house, he joined the exodus. As he stepped through the door, O'Neill emerged from the shadows and fell into step beside him.

"What?" he growled, irritation rising at the ever-present smirk on the *jie'van's* face.

"Thought you could use some help with that box." O'Neill's gaze dropped, skimming over the silver case Wolf cradled against his chest. The smirk deepened. "You seem to be struggling with it."

No way in *Tabenetha* was he struggling with the case, but Wolf sucked the retort back. Reaction was exactly what the *jie'van* was hoping for.

When Wolf didn't answer, a frown flickered across O'Neill's face. The smugness dissolved. He scanned the case again, only this time, thoughtfulness echoed in his voice. "You're certain that's the nanobot weapon?"

Wolf shrugged. "So Kuznetsov says."

O'Neill seemed leery of the weapon. On this, Wolf did not blame him. After what had happened to Aiden's team, and the visions the *Taounaha* had shared, Wolf was uneasy with the weapon as well.

"Did he spill all his secrets, tell you who created and manufactured this monstrosity?" O'Neill asked, his voice oddly intense.

Wolf shrugged the intensity off. The world itself was in danger, after all.

"No. We did not get that information, nor who he sold the missing nanobot canister to." Wolf lifted his gaze to the sky, which was foolish, as his pilot would have warned him if the checkmates were within range. "We will interrogate him in depth when we reach home."

"Fuck." The word hissed through O'Neill's lips as if he couldn't hold it back. "You didn't find out who made the damn thing? And there's a missing canister?"

"No, and yes. You'd best board," Wolf said tightly. "It is not wise to linger near me."

While he clung to Benioko's assurance that the weapon was safe, he had no intention of allowing his men, any of his men, close to the case or the contents it held. This was simply common sense.

O'Neill cast him an unreadable look. With an exaggerated shrug, he lengthened his stride and pulled ahead.

Wolf slowed his pace, allowing O'Neill to gain distance. Overhead, a cloud swept across *Heemitia's* face, obscuring her shine. Wolf picked up his pace again. With the clouds came snow—and the low pressure ridge they'd been warned about. They needed to get in the air before the bad weather and the Russian fighters arrived.

Thanks to the Russian's staggering, wandering, drug-induced state, Samuel and Kuznetsov had dropped from first out the door, to two of the last to board. Only O'Neill and Wolf walked behind them. If Wolf had been in charge, he would have grabbed Kuznetsov and tossed him into the cargo hold by now. His second was far too gentle.

The vision hit when he least expected it, as always.

It started with a loud, electrical buzz in his head. Not his ears...his head. The visions always announced themselves with an intense hum. Several seconds of blindness followed the buzz. When he could see again, it wasn't through his eyes, it was through his mind, like a dream. A waking dream.

Everything looked...the same, yet different.

The same vista surrounded him, but not in color, in shades of black and white. The Thunderbird crouched before him, the view partially blocked by O'Neill's broad, chrome colored back. *Heemitia* was a bright silver sphere in the sky, the tail of a cloud drifting off to her left. The snow-scraped ground beneath his boots writhed with shadows and light. The vicinity surrounding the Thunderbird was clear of warriors—except for Samuel and O'Neill, who was partially turned.

Whatever was about to happen would happen here. And soon. The Thunderbird, the moon, the incoming clouds, O'Neill—they were all things he'd just seen through his eyes, in color and true life.

He turned in a slow circle, scanning the night as seen through the vision for imminent death. Visions always heralded danger. Disaster. Death. Always.

What was this one warning of?

Off to the right, next to one of the small sheds strewn throughout the compound, a silver flare lit the night. A thick, percussive cough followed. He recognized both the flare and the cough. Although in true life, the flare was red, not silver.

An RPG launch.

The recognition had barely registered when O'Neill was swallowed by fire.

The vision vanished as suddenly as it had hit. Wolf released a choppy breath. It gusted out on the tail of a name.

O'Neill.

A quick look up revealed the *Heemitia* was clear, the cloud that wreathed her earlier drifting off to the left. His gaze shot to O'Neill, who was turning. He must have heard Wolf gust out his name.

The RPG was about to strike. O'Neill was about to die. Wolf launched himself forward. Shouting would do no good. It would take a second or two for O'Neill to react, to drop to the ground. And those seconds carried his death.

With the silver case anchored to his chest, he slammed into O'Neill, driving them both to the ground. The percussive cough sounded behind them. Beneath him, O'Neill lay still as the RPG whistled over their heads, striking the ground ahead. Wolf lifted his gaze and blinked grit from his eyes.

Fire clawed at the sky where Samuel and Kuznetsov had once walked.

Chapter Forty-One

Day 17
Petropavlovsk, Russia

He was supposed to be dead.

His unfocused gaze locked on his boots, O'Neill sat perfectly still in the chair closest to the cargo hold door. The vibrations from the Thunderbird's engines skimmed through the aircraft's walls and floor, aggravating the ache in his shoulder and the band of pain across his torso. If he kept still, the throb in his shoulder and the agony around his chest let him breathe.

But the injuries he was trying to ignore were nothing when compared to death, and he should be dead.

If the ton of bricks called Wolf hadn't slammed into him and knocked him to the ground, he would be dead.

His gaze tried to stray toward the back of the Thunderbird where the spirit healers were trying to prevent Samuel from crossing into the web of his ancestors. There could be no healing of his or Wolf's injuries while the *Hee-Hee-Thae* were struggling to keep Samuel's spirit and body tied.

But then, O'Neill's and Wolf's injuries were not life threatening. Samuel's were.

He hoped that the *wanatesa* weapon, within its silver case, had not broken open as they'd hit the ground. He thought not. The case had been crushed between his and Wolf's bodies—indeed, it had caused a fair share of their injuries. But they hadn't opened it to check on the weapon. Instead, Wolf had locked the case in the outside box on the Thunderbird's skids.

No good came from worrying over things he did not control. There was nothing to do but wait and see if the container inside the case had broken open and infected him.

Just as there was nothing to do for his broken ribs, other than wrapping them. Rawlings, the southerner, had splinted Wolf's arm and wrapped O'Neill's chest. He'd relocated O'Neill's shoulder joint as well. *Relocation.* That's what the southerner called the process of manipulating his shoulder joint back in place. Even then, beneath the excruciating burn consuming his shoulder, the term had struck him as funny. He hadn't lost his damn shoulder. It was still there.

His eyes tried to stray back to Samuel again. He forced them front and center. Had the *Hee-Hee-Thae* healers kept Wolf's *Caetanee* in the physical realm? His injuries had been—O'Neill flinched—catastrophic. Samuel would have died instantly when the RPG struck if Kuznetsov hadn't caught the brunt of the blast, and if the healers hadn't converged on him en masse as he and Wolf drug what was left of him from the fiery impact zone.

They'd left Kuznetsov behind. Nobody, not even Kait Winchester, could heal those pieces of charred flesh. Even the best healer couldn't regenerate a missing body.

Now Kuznetsov was gone, and with him all the information Wolf hadn't yet pried from him. Yes, they'd found one of the nanobot weapons, but the other was still out there, along with the psychopath who'd created it.

Both failures fell on O'Neill's shoulders.

He flinched again, the guilt sinking like sludge to the very core of his soul. Losing this information should never have happened. It wouldn't have happened if he'd done as the *Taounaha* had directed and used his *heschrmal* gift to pull the information from the Russian's mind.

Sifting through Kuznetsov's mind to find out who the nanobot bomb had been sold to and who was behind the creation of the *wanatesa* weapon was the only reason O'Neill was on this mission. It was the only thing he'd been tasked with doing.

Yet it meant using his curse of a gift. Not just using it, but using it in front of others. In front of Wolf and Samuel, the two warriors least likely to believe he could do what he claimed. Even then, he would have done as the *Taounaha* directed. Indeed, he'd trudged reluctantly upstairs to do just that. But when he arrived, Wolf had already found the silver case with the *wanatesa* weapon tucked inside, and the Russian was spilling his guts as they questioned him.

Certain he'd been given a reprieve, O'Neill had backed away.

The *heschrmal* gift wasn't needed. Wolf's truth serum and interrogation were prying everything they needed to know from Kuznetsov. He could afford to wait and use his talent on the Russian once they returned to base, where he could delve into the Russian's mind in privacy, like he'd done with those two hired guns Winchester had hauled back to base. Although his gift had proved useless there. You could not pull information from minds that knew nothing.

Benioko would just have to exercise patience. They had the Russian. They had time.

Or so he'd thought.

Except Wolf hadn't gotten everything they needed before he'd ordered everyone to evac. Then Kuznetsov had died and the information he'd carried was lost forever.

The mouthpiece would not be pleased.

O'Neill started to lift his arms to scrub his face, only to freeze as pain ripped through his shoulder. *Fuck!*

"You should let me sling that thing, so you don't move it accidentally," Rawlings said, leaning across the space between their seats.

O'Neill glanced over, ignoring Rawlings's comment. "Did someone take out the asshole who RPG'd us?"

He'd heard a whole cacophony of rifle fire coming from the Thunderbird as they'd hauled Samuel onboard. Hopefully, someone had dropped the bastard.

"Think so." Rawls shrugged. "That was the only round we got hit with."

Yeah...one round too many. O'Neill scowled. "Who the hell was it, anyway? According to Tomas, the guards were all locked down."

Rawls shrugged again. "Only the ones we knew about. Must have been another guard out there we never saw."

True. O'Neill sighed. He shifted in his seat, accidentally bumping his wrist against his knee, which moved his arm, which launched the dull ache in his shoulder back into a vicious throb.

Fuck.

"You should let me sling that thing," Rawlings said again, maybe for the fourth or fifth time.

"It's fine." O'Neill didn't bother to smooth the snap from his voice. It obviously wasn't fine, but he welcomed the pain. It distracted him from his thoughts, from his guilt. The throb and the burn reminded him he had all his limbs intact. Unlike the warrior fighting for his life in the back of the Thunderbird.

Did Wolf regret slamming him to the ground and letting his best friend take the rocket? How could he not? Muriel would blame him, too. Of that, he was sure. He'd avoid her when she arrived at Samuel's side.

Why the fuck had he done it? There was no love lost between them. Never had been. Why had the bastard saved him, instead of his *Caetanee* and *hee-javaanee*? The two warriors had been one spirit in two bodies since they'd been younglings, long before they'd reached warrior status.

It was inconceivable that Wolf had let the rocket take Samuel rather than O'Neill.

Jesus.

That should be him lying armless, legless, and eyeless back there. Although, if the rocket had hit him instead of Samuel, he'd be dead, not maimed. Its trajectory would have hit him square in the back. He wouldn't have had Kuznetsov to block most of the blast.

"Ya know," Rawlings drawled, his shrewd eyes settling on O'Neill's face. "Refusin' to sling that arm and let it rest ain't gonna assuage your guilt. And it ain't helpin' Samuel, that's for damn sure."

"Fuck you." O'Neill leaned back and closed his eyes.

A few minutes later, the Thunderbird slowed. The drop in his stomach told him the bird was descending. They hadn't been in the air long enough to arrive at the base or the refueling station. The only reason to be landing early was to let off Kuznetsov's mistress. He frowned at the realization. With the Russian gone, they needed to hang onto the woman.

When the Thunderbird set down, and the engines slowed enough that the vibrations were barely noticeable through the walls and floor, Wolf appeared from the back of the craft. O'Neill stood to intercept him.

Ignoring the burn screaming through his shoulder, and the band of agony cinched across his chest, he stepped in front of Wolf, only to hesitate. "How is he?"

A slow exhale lifted Wolf's chest, but his eyes remained unfocused, his face exhausted. "Alive. For now."

O'Neill mirrored Wolf's deep exhale but added a nod. "Good. That's good."

When Wolf moved to the side, clearly intending to step around him, O'Neill moved to block him again.

The Shadow Warrior's favorite stopped, a thick, black eyebrow lifting. Some of the vagueness left his eyes. "What?"

But there was no sharpness to the question. No chill either.

O'Neill hesitated. Questioning the *Betanee's* decision would set off an avalanche of antagonism—from all directions—but someone had to remind Wolf that this woman might have the knowledge they needed. Once she stepped off the Thunderbird, she'd disappear, and they'd lose the chance to question her.

Keeping his face calm and his voice level, he did what he had to do. He challenged Shadow Mountain's commanding officer.

"We cannot let this woman go. With Kuznetsov gone, she is the only one who might know the information we need. She may know more than we think...even more than she thinks." He braced himself for blowback. "We must hold on to her and question her thoroughly."

And this time he would not hesitate to use his *beschrmal* gift on her, no matter how many warriors shared the room with them.

One could hear a pin drop in the cargo hold as everyone awaited Wolf's eruption. O'Neill kept his eyes locked on Wolf's dirt-and-ice-scoured face. But he could feel the heat of two dozen gazes locked on them. It was rare for anyone to challenge Wolf. Hell, the elder gods' favorite rarely needed challenging. But the few times he'd stepped off course, Samuel had course-corrected him.

Only, Samuel was not here. And this path needed correcting.

Like a fog had lifted, the vagueness cleared from Wolf's eyes. He cocked his head, his gaze shifting as he looked over O'Neill's shoulder toward the woman.

"You are right. I was not thinking clearly. Samuel would have—" He broke off to draw a shuddering breath, shook his head and continued past O'Neill toward the cockpit.

Surprised by Wolf's calm reaction, O'Neill turned, watching his *Betanee* shake off the beseeching hand Kuznetsov's former mistress had wrapped around his skinned forearm. Seconds later, the engines ramped up their whine and the telltale vibrations shimmied through the floor and walls again and the Thunderbird rose back into the air, carrying its maimed cargo and grieving warriors to their base.

Chapter Forty-Two

Day 17
Petropavlovsk, Russia

The black metallic walls of the machine carrying her to God knew where vibrated against Eloise's back, rattling the chair beneath her and numbing her bum. While the vibrations were uncomfortable to her, they seemed to calm Muffy. Her angel had fallen asleep as soon as the helicopter lifted off. Comforted by the warm, heavy weight pressed against her chest, Eloise lowered the zipper on her coat so Muffy could breathe fresh air. Or at least as fresh as air could get on this eyesore of a helicopter.

Huddled in her metal seat, she fiddled with her lipstick tube while she surreptitiously studied the hard-faced men sitting alongside her.

They sounded like Americans, but with an unusual cadence to their speech. And this chopper—or whatever the bloody hell it was—didn't look American at all. It didn't look like anything she'd seen before. Fuck, the exterior of the craft was downright daft. What with the way its wings pointed straight up, and its oblong body squatted on the ground. It looked like a mechanical cross between a bird and a dragonfly. Kinda like those Transformers cartoons she'd loved as a kid.

She rolled the red tube between her fingers again, and wistfully daydreamed about driving the concealed syringe into the asshole who called the shots among these lethal men. Sure, the ratbag had shown her kindness. He'd let her change into her trackies and gave her some cash and her jewelry from the safe. But none of that made up for what he'd taken from her. And she wasn't talking about Grigory.

The fucker had ruined everything. He'd set her business back by years.

With a pained sigh, she settled back against the wall of her vibrating prison. She'd simply have to adapt. Pivot. Hadn't she built her business from the ground up once already? And with nothing but brains and guile? Why, yes, she had. At least this time, she had a hefty bank account, a warehouse full of the most sought-after weapons on the black market, and a robust client list—even if they didn't know they were her clients.

But first things first. She needed to escape this fucking helicopter—or whatever it was.

She was almost certain these bastards no longer intended to let her go. Not after that conversation between the black-haired and brown-haired assholes last time they'd landed and then took off again.

The RPG blast had left her in a dire predicament. Sure, she'd expected Grigory to die. But not so soon. She'd planned to embrace and inject her former partner just before she stepped off the aircraft. She'd be gone by the time the poison took effect. If she couldn't get close to him, at least she'd be well hidden and out of danger by the time Grigory implicated her in their business venture.

She'd been lucky her former partner hadn't admitted she was the brains of the operation during his drugged rambling. But now that he was out of the picture, the soldiers surrounding her had no one to interrogate—except her. As the brown-haired soldier had stressed.

So, no, they wouldn't let her go. Not now.

Once they interrogated her and discovered she was the brains behind the testing and deaths in Karaveht, and the meltdown of their special forces team... She shuddered. Her being a woman wouldn't save her, that was for sure. If they allowed her to live, she'd do so in some dank prison, never again to see the light of day.

Her heart rate escalated. So did her breathing. She suppressed another shudder. She had to escape this aircraft. That's all there was to it.

They'd been in the air for at least two hours when the chopper suddenly slowed and dropped. It continued dropping. Eloise tensed, recognizing the subtle rocking as the craft settled on the ground.

Had they arrived at the soldiers' base? The vibrations and roar of the engine subsided. Muffy stirred in her pup pack. Several men rose to their feet as their leader pulled back the cargo door. Eloise stared out the open door. Snow fell in a soft, lazy veil, illuminating the night. No artificial lights surrounded them. No shouts or hails. They must not be at the soldiers' base.

She relaxed. There was still time to escape then. This stop might even give her the opportunity she was looking for. Distantly, a truck engine roared to life. Since her motto had always been to carry on as she meant to go on, she hauled her satchel up and rose to her feet. Muffy sat up, poking her fluffy head through the opening in the top of the pup pack.

Several of the broad-shouldered soldiers surrounding her turned to stare, including the one who called the shots. He turned from his position next to the open cargo door. Two strides across the cargo bay, and he stopped in front of her.

"We stop to fuel," he told her without preamble, ignoring the flash of Muffy's bared teeth. "You will not be released here."

The roar of a diesel engine and the grit of gravel against tires came from the dark.

"But...but...why? I've told you everything I know." She forced a lip tremble and let the tears well. The news didn't surprise her, but she couldn't afford to change her tactics now. A sudden absence of whinging would bring scrutiny. He turned away. She touched his forearm and raised her voice to stop him. "I need to use the loo. Do you have one on board this...thing?"

She was almost certain the answer would be no. She'd never seen a chopper with a bathroom. And the interior of this bloody craft was close enough to a chopper layout to make a loo unlikely.

He turned back to her with a flat face. "You'll have to wait."

"For how long?" she asked, fidgeting.

He studied her and then said with great reluctance. "Three hours."

The roar of the truck and the scraping of tires against gravel were much closer. This was her opportunity to escape. But she couldn't use that opportunity unless she was on the ground.

"I can't wait that long." She turned the comment into a whine and squeezed her thighs together like she was barely holding the piss in. "I really need to wee. Like now." When a frown touched his face, she doubled down. "Look, if there isn't a loo around here, just let me out so I can do my business behind a shed or something. Trust me, I won't last half an hour, let alone three, and I really don't want to piss my pants." She forced a visible recoil. "That's just...disgusting. Plus, Muffy will need to go soon too. The last time I took her out was before we went to bed last night."

The fucker studied her face for way too long. She tried to look like someone in the midst of a bladder emergency. A few more tears and fidgeting seemed to do the trick. A sigh shook his big frame. With an eye roll and a *"why me"* shake of his head, he turned to the open cargo door and hopped out.

He disappeared into the falling snow without saying a word. She scratched Muffin behind her fluffy ears and considered following him, but the dozen eyes watching her kept her feet still. It was imperative she act cowed and harmless. Following him out that door was not the act of an intimidated woman.

Hoping he was off finding her a bathroom, Eloise remained standing and tried to think of a good excuse to bring her tote with her. Nothing came to mind. The lead bastard had watched her pack the damn thing. He knew what was in it, knew she didn't need it for a quick trip to wee. She'd have to leave it behind.

At least she'd transferred several stacks of cash from the tote to her coat pocket while everyone was so focused on their dying mate. She had what she needed. A deep, slow breath settled her nerves.

When he returned to the aircraft, his long, dark hair sparkled with melting snow. He beckoned to the soldier who'd escorted her out of the house in Russia and tossed her into the chopper. "Take her to the metal building behind us. It has a bathroom."

Eloise's fingers tightened around the tube in her pocket. The syringe was in play after all, although not on the asshole who deserved it. She forced a shaky "thank you" and allowed her guard to help her off the aircraft. Her little angel didn't like the soldier being so close and warned him off with a combination of barks, growls, and snarls. All of which her young guard ignored.

"Look at you being all guard doggie," Eloise cooed, with another gentle scratch behind the floppy ears.

Muffy had great instincts. It wasn't a surprise her princess hated these assholes. Of course, Muffin hated most men, which just illustrated her good sense. Men were nothing but lying, cheating, bullying harbingers of misfortune.

The night was warmer and gentler than two hours earlier in Petropavlovsk. The snow fell in thick, fluffy flakes that melted as soon as they landed. Without the wind, the temperature was downright pleasant. The snow hitting her face was even refreshing.

As they crossed the compound toward the building with the toilet, she studied the landscape. Visibility was good as the snow's radiance illuminated everything. There were no vehicles around or soldiers other than those tending to the petrol needs of their daft chopper. The property appeared deserted. There wasn't even a fence protecting it, which seemed odd. At the very least, wouldn't they want to protect their petrol?

Escape, as of now, was impossible. Too many of the soldiers were watching her. They'd overtake her before she got away. She'd have to enter the building and hope there was a door or window in the back. She sent a quick plea to the universe to help her escape.

Through the falling snow, she saw the blurry impression of trees. The forest would allow her to elude anyone pursuing her. Her gaze fell on the mounds of snow around the shed. Slogging through all that white stuff was going to be a problem, and she'd leave tracks. But the fuckers chasing her would have to wade through it, too, which evened the playing field.

She unzipped her coat and Muffin's pup pack when they reached the shed and eased her little angel onto the scraped pavement so she could do her business. Muffy whined in distress as soon as her paws touched the icy ground, but squatted immediately, peed, and danced back over to paw at Eloise's calves. Within seconds, her baby was zipped back in her pup pack.

Their guard opened the wood door and found the light switch against the wall. Bright, white light flooded the building. She followed him inside, only to stop short just inside the doorway. A snowmobile sat directly in front of a large roll-up door. The machine was fluorescent green—which would stand out like a flame in the night. But it looked like it was built for speed. It rose high and blocky in the front, low and sleek through the rear. For the first time, she offered thanks for Grigory's penchant for fast toys. Snowmobiles had been a favorite of his. The newer and faster, the better.

The sheer luck of the find took her breath away. The machine sat right in front of a roll-up door at the very back of the building. She'd asked the universe for help, and good God, had the universe come through for her. The soldiers out front wouldn't see her exit the building.

If the snowmobile didn't have the keys in the ignition, she'd hotwire it. One of her first jobs as a child had been stealing utes for a chop shop in the bowels of Sydney. She scanned the area as they headed toward the back left corner of the building. Long, narrow benches ran along both sides of the building. The middle was open. A patchwork of oily stains sprawled across the cement. The smell of oil and petrol tickled her nose.

Her gaze fell on a short-handled axe lying on the right work bench. That would make an excellent weapon. The blade looked razor sharp, and it was short enough to tuck in front of her on the snowmobile. She shot a quick glance at the machine as they approached the back of the building and a door marked bathroom.

The keys were in the ignition.

A gloating smile partially engulfed her face before she banished it. Sometimes the universe was incredibly generous. She'd give extra thanks for this unexpected gift in her daily gratitudes.

The soldier escorting her opened the bathroom door, then turned, parking his shoulders and back against the wall. The bathroom was surprisingly clean and well-stocked. She pulled the door closed behind her, locked it, and took a deep, calming breath, only to choke on the noxious smell of bleach and air freshener. A fit of coughing overwhelmed her. A few seconds later, a sturdy knock hit the door.

"You okay in there?" her escort asked.

"Fine." She choked the reassurance out through her spasming throat and watering eyes. She didn't want him barging in to check on her, so she added an explanation. "Someone went a little aggro with the bleach and air freshener in here. Makes it hard to breathe is all."

A grunt of acknowledgement came through the door.

Eloise forced the coughing back. Before getting to work, she dropped her sweatpants and used the toilet. Who knew how long it would be before she found another clean, well-stocked loo. As soon as she was finished, she flushed the toilet and zipped the pup pack up until Muffy was completely enclosed inside. Then she zipped her coat up to her chin for an extra layer of protection. Best to keep multiple layers of fabric between Muffin and the syringe when it popped out.

She turned the faucet on to cover any suspicious sounds as she converted the tube in her pocket from lipstick to syringe. The false front was easy to pry loose. She heard nothing as the insert popped out, so her guard wouldn't either. She pressed the button at the bottom of the tube to pop the syringe up. Gingerly, she slid the cylinder between her index and middle finger, until the tube was hidden by her palm and the needle was sticking out between her fingers. She couldn't afford to prick herself. That would be a lethal mistake.

With a deep breath, she turned the faucet off and reached for the door handle. Her guard turned to her as the door swung open.

Not yet. Not while he's watching and can deflect the syringe.

"All good?" he asked, the question polite rather than interested. His gaze dropped to her throat and the zipped-up coat.

"Much better." She sent him a sunny smile. "Muffy was cold, so I tucked her in nice and tight," she embellished when his gaze lingered on her coat.

She slowed as they headed back across the building so she could jab him from behind. But her guard glanced over his shoulder and frowned, his pace slowing to match hers. Fuck, she needed a distraction.

"Oh, hell no! What's that?" She stopped walking and pointed at random with her non-syringe fingers and tried for a horrified expression. A muffled bark came from beneath her coat as Muffin went into guard dog mode.

As he turned to look where she was pointing, she plunged the needle into the back of his neck. The syringe was spring-loaded. It injected the poison instantly. She jerked the needle out and tossed the tube over her shoulder as his hand reached for the back of his neck.

"What the—" He spun toward her. His hand clamped over the injection site.

Created in a laboratory, this synthetic version of tetrodotoxin was fast-acting, with lightning-quick absorption rates. Paralysis occurred within minutes. Death in five. She didn't need him dead, just incapable of calling for help. But there was still a minute or two before that would happen.

Until then—distract, distract, distract.

"Oh, fuck!" She swung around behind him and brushed frantically at his neck, trying to ignore her princess's barking, which had become louder and shriller. "There's a gigantic spider on your neck." She brushed some more. "Uh oh. I think it went down the back of your shirt. It must have bitten you. The back of your neck is turning red and swelling. You better take off your shirt so we can get it out. Wouldn't want it to bite you again."

He tilted his head back and frowned at the ceiling. "Spiders aren't active in the cold."

Fuck, she'd hoped he wouldn't realize that. His hand reached for the back of his neck again. His fingertips gently grazed the skin. "I don't feel any swelling."

"It's very slight," she said earnestly.

He studied her face intently, then scanned her from head to toe, obviously looking for something that would explain the pinch he'd felt, something that wasn't spider-related. His eyes were narrow and full of suspicion when they rose back to meet hers.

She widened her eyes and strove for an innocent expression. "You really should remove your t-shirt, make sure that spider isn't beneath it."

"I'd feel it moving. There's no spider under my shirt." The suspicion deepened on his face. He reached for her arm. "Let's go." He froze, staring at his hand. His fingers were shaking. "What the hell?"

"What's wrong?" She forced patience instead of racing for the snowmobile and rolling the door up. The toxin hadn't fully hit him yet. He could still make it to the door, yell for help. She needed to distract him.

"My hand is tingling."

"The spider—"

"I didn't get bitten by a spider," he snapped.

His gaze dropped to the ground and slid back. She hadn't seen the lipstick tube land. How far back had she thrown it? Was it hidden from view?

Apparently not, judging by the hiss that broke from him and the way he staggered back.

"Wat...ya...ject...?" The words were slurred and slow. The venom was already at work.

He staggered again, caught himself, and turned toward the door. Stepping in front of him, she made a fist—thumb on the outside—and slammed it into his Adam's apple. She didn't have enough strength in her arm to collapse his trachea, but there was enough force in the blow to stun his larynx and keep him quiet until the poison silenced him.

He made a choking-huffing sound and teetered on his feet. All it took was a two-handed shove to push him over backwards. A dull *crack* sounded as the back of his head connected with the cement. For a moment, he simply laid there, then weakly struggled to get up. Since she had nothing to attack him with, she did the next best thing. She shoved him back down, turned around, and plopped her bum down on his face.

Muffin didn't like being sloshed around in her pup pack. Her barking went ballistic. Eloise prayed to the universe that the soldiers outside didn't hear the barking through the two layers of fabric and the metal shed. Or—if they did—they'd become immune to her barking and shrugged it off.

After a couple of weak attempts to throw her off, which she easily rode out, her guard went still beneath her. She eased to the side cautiously, ready to sit on him again if his stillness was a trick.

It wasn't. He lay there, frozen, his pupils dilated.

Muffin was still barking like a maniac. She needed to get out of here before her kidnappers came to investigate. With her angel still double zipped below her coat, she collected the hand axe and raced to the roll-up door. Her fingers shook as she pressed the top button on the silver panel next to the roll-up door.

Please...please...let this be the button that raises the door.

The door grumbled, then slowly rose beneath the press of her thumb. Her heart slammed harder and harder as she waited for it to rise enough to get the snowmobile out. If those fuckers outside heard the door rising, if they caught her before she made it out the door, she was toast. Double toast once they discovered their dead mate.

Finally! The door was high enough. She lifted her thumb from the up button and raced to the snowmobile. Straddling the seat, she twisted the keys in the ignition and asked the universe for one last favor. To her immense relief, the machine instantly growled to life. Lightheaded with fear and adrenaline, she guided it out the door. Once clear of the building, with acres of snow stretching in front of her, and Muffy's ferocious barking accompanying her, she gunned it and raced for the tree line.

She offered a victorious *woop-woop,* a fist pump, and a heartfelt thank you to the universe as she disappeared among the trees.

And just like that, her life was back on track.

Chapter Forty-Three

Day 19
Denali, Alaska

"I'm going to check on Livvy—" Her voice a dull, monotone, Kait broke off with an enormous yawn and a slow stretch before rising from the visitors' chair beside Aiden's bed.

"What you should do instead," Demi offered quietly, her voice thick with concern, "is get some sleep. You're exhausted. It won't help Aiden or Olivia if you make yourself sick."

Kait's face was so white and tight it looked like bleached parchment. Grooves of tension and fatigue spiderwebbed out from the corners of her eyes and bracketed her nose and mouth. Even her hair had lost its golden shine and hung greasy and limp over her shoulder.

"Right," Kait snorted, then rolled her neck. "And if that isn't the perfect example of the pot calling the kettle black..." she sighed, scrubbing absently at her forehead. "I wouldn't be able to sleep, anyway."

"You might if you tried," Demi retorted, although she had to admit she looked like death warmed over too. There were mirrors in the restrooms, after all. She knew exactly how tired and stressed she looked.

But she wasn't spending her energy reserves on healing others. The constant healings that Kait had done since Aiden was released from isolation, and the Thunderbird crew returned to base, had driven her to the edge of collapse. Demi had tried to convince her to get some food and sleep—so had Cosky—but she still ignored her own health in favor of helping others. Demi held her tongue as Kait wobbled toward the door of Aiden's room. Exhaustion had turned her normal athletic stride choppy and weak. But pointing that out would do no good. Her friend would simply ignore the observation.

On the tail of her own tired sigh, Demi turned back to the hospital bed beside her. Her shoulders relaxed as she studied Aiden.

At least he looked better. The tightness and furrows had vanished from his face. While his skin looked pale, it was no longer flushed from fever. And those horrible, rasping—almost gasping—breaths had faded into deep, even breathing. The doctors said he was responding well to the medicine they were giving him. And Kait's healings over the past two days had helped, too. But he wasn't out of the woods yet. They still didn't know what his body was reacting to, or whether he'd crash again once the doctors weaned him off the meds.

Demi stretched and yawned, absently listening to the *beep...beep...beep* coming from the machines surrounding Aiden's bed. The rhythmic beeps reinforced an ugly echo in her mind, one that stretched back six years. These same beeps had accompanied her vigil beside Donnie's bed. They'd only ceased when he'd died.

Aiden isn't dead. He's just sleeping.

She constantly reminded herself of that. Particularly, after waking from one of the short, uncomfortable naps in this chair. Sometimes, to convince herself she hadn't lost him, too, she'd rest her hand on his chest, so she could feel each inhale and exhale as they lifted her palm. His heat against her skin eased the fear, brought her back from those terrible memories of her vigil beside Donnie's bed as he lay dying.

After a slow stretch, Demi settled back in her chair. Through the wall surrounding Aiden's room came the murmur of voices. Samuel's fiancée was holding her own vigil next door.

While there had been multiple injuries during the mission to apprehend the criminal responsible for the nanobot testing on Aiden and his teammates, only two had been serious. One had resulted in death and the other in catastrophic injuries. It felt cruel that the same family who had suffered the death of one member were now facing the potential death of another.

Daniel, Samuel's nephew, had been killed during the mission, and Samuel himself, Livvy's fiancé, had been caught in some kind of blast. He'd lost an arm, a leg, an eye, and suffered a subdural hematoma.

Cosky suddenly stepped into the open doorway. His gaze swept the room and landed on her face. "Where's Kait?"

"Next door, keeping Olivia company."

"She's about to get some sleep." *Whether or not she likes it*, Cosky's determined face added. His gaze lifted, touching on Aiden. "If you need her, call my cell."

He disappeared from the doorway. Seconds later, arguing came from next door. One hard, gritty voice and a vehement, sharp one. A muffled squeal pierced the retractable wall separating the two rooms. By the time she'd reached the door, Cosky was halfway down the hall, Kait's ass and legs hanging over his shoulders.

Wow. Kait's hubby really wasn't accepting no this time. Good for him. Was he planning on walking all the way to the base apartment they were using? He'd have to. If he dumped her into a utility vehicle, she'd just jump off and haul ass back to Aiden's bedside.

"Do you think he's gonna tie her to the bed?"

She turned toward the amused voice. Olivia was standing in front of Samuel's room, watching Cosky haul Kait away.

Demi huffed out a laugh. "Probably. She's not gonna stay put otherwise."

Olivia laughed, an honest-to-God belly laugh. The wink she sent Demi was full of innuendo. "A pity. Bondage is so sexy when it's not about sleep."

Demi smiled back, although she suspected her expression carried surprise as well as humor.

What an amazing woman. Livvy could still laugh, even with Daniel dead and her man lying comatose behind her. How did she maintain such a positive attitude under the circumstances?

Demi took a tentative step in Livvy's direction. "How's Samuel?"

"He's still in a coma. Which is the best thing for him. He's putting all his energy into healing. No pain or worry to distract him." Her smile was genuine. So was her optimism. "He'll wake up when he's ready."

Lord, Olivia had turned a coma into a good thing, something to celebrate, not something to be feared. The woman was quite remarkable.

"I'm so sorry about Daniel," Demi offered. "I can't even imagine what his mother is going through. Does she live in The Neighborhood?"

Olivia's smile dimmed. Grief darkened her eyes and shadowed her face. "No, Muriel lives on the *Brenahiilo*—the Kalikoia Pinch Point reservation. She arrived yesterday and spent the night beside Samuel's bed. Today, she's with Wolf and Benioko making...arrangements."

She must have meant funeral arrangements, or whatever the equivalent was in the Kalikoia culture.

"How's Aiden? Kait said he's doing better?" Olivia asked.

"Yes. His condition's improved." Demi tried to manufacture the same optimism Livvy had exhibited earlier. She just wished her positivity was genuine. "His fever's gone. His heart rate and pulse have stabilized. He's even breathing easier."

Livvy smiled. "That's wonderful." She glanced over her shoulder into the room behind her. When she turned back to Demi, her smile was back. This time it looked tired, but sincere. "That must be such a relief for you."

"It is. Although it would be even more of a relief if the doctors knew why he got so sick," Demi admitted tightly.

Her chest tightened as worry assailed her again. How were they going to combat the illness if they didn't know what it was? Treating the symptoms wasn't a long-term strategy. Sure, the medication was keeping Aiden stable...for now. But many medicines lost their effectiveness after a while. Viruses and bacteria were always adapting, mutating, throwing off the shackles trying to keep them in check.

What if the nanobots did the same thing?

Livvy grabbed Demi's fingers and gave them a squeeze. "He's in the best possible hands. Between Kait and the rest of the base healers, along with the doctors on staff, he's got top-notch care."

"I know." Demi's throat tightened. She just hoped that was enough.

Olivia studied her face for a moment before offering a gentle smile. "Samuel said Aiden is instrumental in preventing this bot plague from taking over the world. This comes directly from the *Taounaha*, the mouthpiece of the Shadow Warrior. Benioko says Aiden is the arrow of our people, the warrior at the front of this charge. The Shadow Warrior would not let his arrow break before it has found its mark."

Demi forced a wobbly smile. "Aiden doesn't believe in the Shadow Realm or the Shadow Warrior."

A shrug lifted Livvy's shoulders. "This does not matter. The Shadow Realm believes in him." She paused, wisdom resonating in her serene gaze. "Perhaps this sickness is the Shadow Realm's doing, their maneuvering to defeat this bot weapon."

"You mean like the lab finding something in his blood they can use to create a vaccine?" Faith had mentioned they hoped Aiden's apparent immunity to the bots would help them develop an antidote.

Olivia shrugged. "We must trust that the elder gods will hold their children safe. The Shadow Warrior and Blue Moon Mother have watched over us since the first star lit the sky. They birthed the *Hee'woo'nee*. They will not let their children die now. If Aiden is tasked with preventing such a catastrophe, they will not allow him to pierce the veil and join the web of his ancestors until his task is complete."

Livvy's optimism and serenity were obviously because of her trust in this Shadow Realm and the shadow deities she spoke of. Demi found it impossible to put her faith in such an intangible belief system.

"Aiden will be fine." Livvy squeezed her hand again. "He'll wake up soon, I'm sure of it."

Demi's throat closed around a huge lump. Olivia was trying so hard to comfort her when she had even more to be worried about than Demi did. Olivia was in a committed relationship with the man lying in the hospital bed behind her. Unlike Demi, who'd broken things off with Aiden prior to him getting so sick.

"You know we're not together, right?" Demi asked. "Aiden and I, I mean. We broke up the day before your book club meeting."

"I don't think your heart got the message," Olivia said gently. Her gaze was knowing. "You're too worried about him to have no feelings."

"Feelings weren't the problem." The twisted, tight look on Aiden's face when he'd said he loved her burst into Demi's mind. She choked on a breath, tears welling. She was too tired to hold the sorrow inside. "Lack of compatibility...that's what drove us apart." She swiped at her wet eyes, her heart breaking all over again. "If we stayed together, over time, we'd end up hating each other for what the other couldn't or wouldn't give up."

Olivia cocked her head, her gaze steady on Demi's face. "I hesitate to contradict you, but I fear you are making a mistake. One you will regret. From your questions during book club, when you asked how we lived with the constant fear of our men being in danger, I suspect you're making this decision out of fear. Fear of what the future holds while Aiden walks this dangerous path." Her face softened. "But there is more to consider. There is something you are not aware of."

Demi's eyebrows rose. What could Olivia possibly know about the situation that Demi didn't? This time, Olivia hesitated before speaking, uncertainty flitting across her face.

"You are not *Hee'woo'nee*, so you would not know of the Kalikoia's ways, or of the animal spirits and their gifts, which are given to us by the elder gods." That earlier wisdom, along with a deepening intensity, radiated from her eyes.

Well, that was an odd segue, but Demi went with it. "You mean like Kait's ability to heal and Wolf's flashes of the future?"

Did Aiden have a gift? He'd never mentioned having a special ability. Besides, since he didn't believe in the Shadow Realm and the shadow gods, maybe he couldn't access their gifts. Although that didn't quite fit, as Kait had manifested her healing ability before learning of her Kalikoia heritage.

Olivia nodded, the intensity in her eyes strengthening. "Yes. Like those. Wolf's flashes come from the Shadow Warrior—his gifts strengthen and protect the *Hee'woo'nee*. But Kait's healing ability comes from our Blue Moon Mother, who provides her chosen children with nurturing gifts to cement the tribal ties."

Demi frowned at that. "But Kait said there are several male healers here on base. And she's the only female healer. Did the male healers' gifts come from your Blue Moon Mother too?"

Livvy shook her head before Demi finished speaking. "No. One Bird and Eldon received their *Hee-Hee-Thae* gift from the Shadow Warrior, to be used during battle to keep our warriors strong. Many of the *Hee'woo'nee's* animal spirit gifts—such as the ability to heal, or the gift of future sight—are gender neutral." She hesitated again, longer this time. It didn't seem like she was going to continue, but then she added, "Our great mother gifted me with the ability to see heartmates—to know when people are destined to be together." Her voice gentled. "The moment I saw you sitting by Aiden's bed, I knew you and he were gifted to each other. You two are fated to be together."

Demi's eyebrows lifted. While it was hard to refute Kait's gift, as she'd experienced it herself, it was much harder to convince herself that Olivia could see some mythical connection between her and Aiden.

Olivia's laugh was soft and understanding. "You don't believe me."

"I believe you believe—" Demi broke off, wincing. Her resistance to the idea must be plastered all over her face.

After another soft laugh, Olivia shrugged. "I understand. You weren't born to the *Hee'woo'nee*. Of course, you wouldn't believe in our ways. But this needs saying because heartmates are quite rare. The deep, internal connection you have with Aiden is prized by the Kalikoia. It is a bond that will grow and expand through each cycle. It will provide comfort and strength in times of need. It is not replaceable, nor should it be cast aside because of fear."

Demi frowned. There was no question she'd felt a connection to Aiden from the moment she met him, even back when she was married to Donnie. But she'd loved Donnie, too.

"So, you only get one heartmate—" which sounded an awful lot like a soulmate to her "and if things don't work out with them, you'll never find happiness with anyone else?" She could hear the skepticism in her question.

Livvy shook her head. "Not at all. There are multiple heartmates cre-ated for each person, but few people find even one. Amid the billions of people walking this world, the odds of encountering even one of your destined heartmates are astronomical. Most people find love and happiness with someone other than the heart intended for them. But their connection—indeed their happiness—is thin and pale compared to what they would have with one of their intended heartmates."

Demi tried hard to keep her disbelief off her face. But seriously? Everyone was given a couple of soulmates, but nobody could find them? How messed up was that? What a shitty job on destiny's part.

Livvy turned to look into Samuel's room. "The instant I saw him, I knew Samuel was my heartmate, although it took him much longer to recognize that fact. Like you, he didn't believe in such things. Not at first. But we've had three joyous cycles together. We share a connection that binds our hearts, minds and souls. I am never alone, as I sense him there with me, wherever he might be. Even now, while he sleeps, I can sense him. Am I afraid of losing him when he takes to the air with the rest of Shadow Mountain's warriors? Of course."

"Cycles?" Demi asked.

"The Kalikoia word for your year." For a moment, Olivia's face twisted, before serenity smoothed it again. "Even if Samuel had died during that last mission, even if I'd lost him, I'd still take these three cycles I've spent with him over not having known him at all. The pain of losing him would eventually subside, but the memories of him, of us, they will last forever. Anxiety and fear go hand in hand with loving men like Aiden and Samuel. But those emotions are nothing when compared to the memories we create with them beside us."

Her gaze became even more intense, and she reached out, brushing Demi's tense arm with her fingertips. "Don't let fear of the unknown, of future possibilities, sour what you could have with Aiden now. What if nothing happens to him? What if he lives into twilight age? Think of all the memories you will have lost because of what *might* happen." She fell silent, her gaze turning distant and dark, before adding softly, "Even if Samuel dies today, I will always be grateful for the cycles we had together."

As Olivia returned to her chair beside Samuel's bed, what she'd said echoed through Demi's mind. And she realized she felt the same way about her years with Donnie. Yes, the agony of losing him had gutted her for a while. But the pain had eventually subsided. These days, memories of him mostly brought peace or smiles. She also knew, wholeheartedly, that she'd take the pain of losing him over not having loved him, not having married him, not having shared those seven years with him. Hell, she'd even go one step further and admit that if she could go back in time and have a do-over, she'd still marry him, even knowing what was coming.

Besides, could the fear of losing Aiden get any worse than it had been over the past three days? She doubted it. Eventually, she'd hit a plateau, and the fear level would freeze.

No, she didn't believe in soulmates, but she couldn't deny there was a powerful attraction between her and Aiden. An attraction that had been there from the very beginning, while she'd been married and happy with Donnie. Even back then, what she'd felt for Aiden had been incredibly strong, unlike anything she'd felt before. She felt tied to Aiden in a way she hadn't felt with Donnie. Which was part of the reason it was so difficult to walk away from him.

That connection kept pulling her back.

But what if there was another reason it was so hard to call it quits and walk away from him? Oh, not the mythical soulmate connection. Something else. Something tangible. What if her instincts were telling her she'd regret leaving him, that she'd regret not giving them a chance to explore this connection between them?

They loved each other. She was certain of that now. Didn't she owe it to herself, and Aiden, to give their love a chance? To see where it led?

Livvy was right. Aiden was one in a million. And if Cosky read the situation right and Aiden couldn't return to the SEALs, any job he took would be less dangerous, easier to live with, easier to compromise on.

That's what they needed. A compromise.

A solution they could both live with.

Chapter Forty-Four

Day 20
Washington, D.C.

Clark snatched up the cell phone before the first ring faded. Hope crashed and burned when he saw the caller ID. *Christopher Lovett.*

Not Kuznetsov, then. Dammit. The Russian was still ghosting him. This shouldn't surprise him, not after finding his nanobot weapon for sale on the dark web. But it didn't look like the weapon had been sold. Or if it had, it hadn't been deployed. There were no reports of people going crazy and killing each other. So, there was still an outside chance Kuznetsov had listed the nanobots for sale in the expectation that Clark would turn the weapon over to him soon.

But if that was the case, why wasn't the Russian returning his calls? Time to admit his pet arms dealer had gone rogue or been captured. His eyes and ears in Admiral Hurley's office swore they didn't have the Russian. But that didn't mean much. Someone else could have got to him.

It was bad enough Kuznetsov wasn't the one calling, but the name on the caller ID sent tendrils of tension through his chest. His head started pounding. He clenched his hand around the phone and fought the impulse to ignore the summons.

The *only* reason Lovett would call was with more bot-related bad news. They were long past any bot-related good news. The kill switch programing still wasn't working and nothing they'd dropped into the tank had killed the NNB26 prototype. Not for long, anyway.

He forced himself to punch the talk button and lifted the cell to his ear. "Tell me you've finally discovered a method that will kill the damn things."

They'd had high hopes a liquid nitrogen dump would freeze and shatter the bots. Which it had. Except they'd reformed and reassembled once they'd thawed. The portable MRI hadn't phased them. And as he'd feared, a localized EMP burst hadn't affected the hardened technology. It hadn't even slowed the fucking things down.

What the hell did they have to do to destroy them?

This was the first time in his long, money-making career he regretted being so good at his job.

"You better get down here," Lovett said, his voice so tight Clark didn't recognize it.

"What's wrong now?"

Nothing had gone right with the damn things since they'd reactivated. They were microscopic organic robots, for God's sake. Regardless of the hundreds of sci-fi and horror shows portraying robots running amok, in reality, robots were engineered to be turned off, to be controlled. So why couldn't he regulate the fucking things?

"They seem to be...vibrating." Lovett's voice tightened even further. He sounded terrified.

"Vibrating?" His eyebrows rose. That was new.

"Yes, vibrating. And the vibrations are getting stronger, sliding in and out of various frequencies. They're able to move their tank through the vibrations. A very slight amount, to be sure—but my God, that tank weighs a couple of tons—for them to move it at all is...." He paused and took an obvious breath. When he continued, his voice shook. "Quite disturbing."

"Yes. Quite." Clark tensed, his heart suddenly racing. Why did this news feel so ominous? "I'm on my way."

For the first time, as he descended inside the bright elevator, the car seemed to close around him with claustrophobic pressure, intensifying his feeling of dread.

For fuck's sake! What the hell were the damn things up to now? These vibrations Lovett spoke of, they were deliberate. He instinctively knew that. They served a purpose. What purpose, he didn't know, not yet. But his little robots were adapting, mutating in response to their environment. After each attempt to eradicate them, their ridges expanded, thickened, turned into some kind of fucking armor.

Currently, the only thing in his favor was that the prototype was contained.

The observation went through him like an electric shock. Was that the purpose behind the vibrations? Were they trying to free themselves? Lovett had said the five-ton containment tank had moved. Impossible to believe, yet everything the nanobots were doing was supposed to be impossible. What if they were trying to vibrate it off its table, hoping to crack it open and escape? Was that even possible?

Were his NNB26 prototype nanobots that intelligent?

At the lab's security panel, he punched in his code and bent for a retinal scan. The door unlocked with a pressurized hiss. The lab seemed colder, more sterile and eye-poppingly brighter than he remembered, even though he'd visited two days earlier. It was also empty—other than Lovett. Clark had transferred the rest of the lab personnel to other projects in other buildings.

The heavy, silver door closed behind him, sealing him inside the room with acres of stainless steel and bright white light. He heard the vibration Lovett had mentioned the instant he stepped inside. The humming emanated from the center of the room, where the silver tank sat on its thick, stainless steel table. The vibration reverberated throughout the lab, alternating between a deep, guttural buzz and a high-pitched hum. Even from a distance, he could see the tank shiver.

The sound reminded him of a hive of *extremely* pissed off bees.

He'd left his laptop in his office, so Clark crossed to the computer terminal across from the tank. The interior of the tank, magnified by 1,00,000x through the AFM, was already displayed on the screen.

"Any idea what they're doing?" Clark asked, studying the NNB26 bots.

"Not even an inkling," Lovett said, watching the trembling tank with an uneasy grimace.

Clark frowned, staring at the screen. The bots had mutated on the heels of the liquid nitrogen bath. They looked tick-like now, with triangular bodies, multiple legs—or appendages that resembled legs—and a turquoise-colored shell. Currently, they were clustered on top of each other in an oblong ball. The sphere shivered and churned, which had to be what was causing the vibrations.

He'd read that bees shivered their flight muscles and wings during winter. The combined shivering of thousands of bees generated enough heat to keep the hive warm during cold weather. Was that what the NNB26 bots were doing? Were they generating heat with their vibrations?

Clark lowered himself into the chair in front of the terminal and rolled it closer to the screen. Were his eyes playing tricks on him, or was the ball of bots getting bigger...rounder? "When did the vibration start?"

"As soon as they reformed after I dosed them with liquid helium. The intensity of the vibrations has grown throughout the day."

Hmm...interesting. If their vibrations were about creating warmth, they could be reacting to the minus 269 degree Celsius temperature of their recent bath. Not to mention the temperatures of their earlier liquid nitrogen dosing. Perhaps they were still recovering and mutating from the extreme cold temperatures they'd been subjected to. He accessed the saved video and backed through the footage.

After several minutes of scrolling through the tapes, he leaned back in his chair and stared at the computer screen. There was no doubt—the bot swarm was getting bigger. The ball was markedly smaller in previous footage.

What the hell were they doing?

"What about the bots in the clean room vat? Are they vibrating too?"

"Not that I'm aware of. I've been checking the big tank periodically. So far, no vibrations in there."

The buzzing in the testing tank suddenly deepened to a roar. Clark shot a look at the computer screen and froze in shock. What the fuck? The bot ball had tripled in size. How had they done that so quickly and with no new components to replicate themselves?

The five-ton tank shook.

Jesus Christ!

Clark stared in shock as the tank slid closer to the edge by a solid inch. The roar increased. The NNB26 prototype cluster tripled again.

Good God! Clark gasped.

"Watch out!" Clark shouted as the container shot forward, straight toward Lovett.

Instead of ducking to the side, as Clark had expected, the doctor shot out a hand, as if to stop the tank from flying off the table. Which was instinctive and insane. The tank weighed ten thousand pounds. Lovett couldn't stop it.

Except the tank lurched to a stop at the exact moment Lovett's palm hit the exterior. A static crackle joined the roar.

Lovett seized, his entire body twitching. His eyes bulged. His mouth contorted into a silent scream. His hand and arm blackened, smoke curling up from his clothes and the charred flesh beneath. Urine soaked Lovett's crotch. Then he dropped like a sack of bones, hitting the tile floor with a weighty thud.

Clark gagged as the smell of burning flesh and cloth filled the lab. His legs shook as he rose to his feet and stumbled over to the smoking bundle of cooked meat. It was instantly obvious there was nothing anyone could do for the man. His eyes weren't even fixed. Or staring. They were just puddles of white goo.

Surprised that his legs were holding him up, he backed his way to the computer chair without taking his gaze off the tank. The bot container was still now. And silent. Ominously silent. He collapsed into his chair and stared in dumfounded disbelief at Lovett's smoking body.

That's what the fucking things had been doing, electrifying their prison, making it impossible for Lovett to douse them again. Clark swiveled his chair and stared at the computer screen. The bot ball had shrunk to its normal size and spread out across the bottom of the tank.

The evolutionary leap he'd just witnessed was inconceivable. The NNB26 prototype had gone from passively restoring themselves to actively protecting themselves.

In the process, they'd deliberately taken their first human life.

Chapter Forty-Five

Day 23
Denali, Alaska

His fingers drumming against his jean clad thigh, Cosky's eyes narrowed on Aiden's clenched jaw as he finished his sitrep. "So, yeah, we're fucked. Back to square one."

Aiden grunted an acknowledgement and rolled his tense shoulders. Fucked described them alright.

"Kuznetsov's mistress," Aiden said. It took effort to keep his tone even. "She's obviously more involved than you boys suspected."

According to Cosky, they'd found multiple concealed weapons in the bag she'd left on the Thunderbird, including knives hidden in the heels of her shoes. And then there was the syringe she'd used to kill Daniel and make her escape. One didn't carry concealed weapons unless they were worried about their safety. Had she felt in danger because of her proximity to Kuznetsov? Or had she been involved in her lover's weapons dealings? The fact she'd killed Daniel so easily showed she had the same psychopathic tendencies as her lover.

"Did the lab isolate what was in that syringe?" His mouth tightened beneath a surge of guilt. He should have been there. He should have been that bitch's assigned guard, not Daniel. This was his battle. It hadn't been Daniel's.

"Yeah, about that..." Cosky scrubbed his palms down his face. He followed that with a sudden, hard yawn. "Faith says the residue they found inside the syringe was tetrodotoxin—or at least a pumped-up version of it. Tetrodotoxin is found in the Blue-Ringed Octopus. One bite can kill an adult human in minutes. Only the shit in the syringe was synthetically modified for quicker absorption." His face darkened. "Daniel didn't have a fucking chance."

"When we run into her again—" and they would, he'd make sure of it— "we need to be prepared for her toxic tricks. Has the lab come up with an antidote?"

Cosky shrugged. "They're working on it."

Aiden simply nodded. The lab had a lot on their plate. Right now, they were focused on the nanobots Wolf had returned with.

The active nanobots.

The tension of that news still made Aiden's jaw ache.

"I hope the lab rats know what they're doing." He stirred uneasily, his skin crawling. "One slip up and those damn things could infect everyone on base."

Twitching fingers...twitching faces...blind, enraged eyes...the spray of blood across snow.

With a deep breath and a masked shudder, he took a mental trip around the memory.

"Faith says there's been no contact between the lab personnel and the bots since they transferred them to the tank with the atomic force microscope." Cosky didn't look relieved, though. Fuck, he looked as uneasy as Aiden felt. "They've sealed the fuckers inside a leak proof, specially designed container made from the same alloy as the ones that Wolf brought back. As an extra precaution, the tank they sealed them in is enclosed inside a specially designed air-vacuumed room. They've got a bunch of those high magnification microscopes looking inside the tank and monitoring the room surrounding it. The images are then beamed to computers on the outside." He paused, looking queasy. "So far, their precautions seem to hold them."

Aiden shied away from thinking about that too hard. They were damn lucky none of the lab rats had been infected when they'd transferred the bots to their new home. Plus, those fucking bots were microscopic. How the hell could the lab rats be so sure they wouldn't find some tiny crack in their tank and sneak out? Same with their specially designed room.

The damn things shouldn't be kept anywhere near people. It was too fucking dangerous. But it didn't sound like there was any other choice. It would take months to set up a remote lab that could monitor and experiment on the fuckers. They didn't have months. They needed answers and ways to deactivate them ASAP.

"How the hell can they do any testing if nobody can get close to them?" Aiden asked, trying hard not to let his doomsday imagination go wild.

From Cosky's wince, he was going through the same disaster scenarios. "Robotics. Faith says everything is done through robotics. From itty bitty microscopic ones inside the tank, to big ones outside." His face turned grim. "Your brother was damn lucky. He hit O'Neill and then the ground hard enough to break some ribs along with his arm. If the bot case had cracked..." He shook his head, his face grimmer than ever.

It had been six days since the Thunderbird had returned to base, and it looked like they'd gotten lucky. No signs of bot infection. Cosky, Wolf and the rest of the Thunderbird's crew had been released from isolation the day before, a day after Aiden had awakened.

He still couldn't believe he'd slept through the whole damn thing. Instead of joining forces with Wolf and his men, he'd left them to shoulder his fight, his responsibility. He'd pushed to get the Shadow Mountain warriors involved, and then he'd abandoned them. Not by choice, but the results were the same. Other men had paid the price because of his obsession. One man had died because of him. Another lay in the bed next door, fighting for his life.

The guilt of that sank deep, burned like acid in his gut.

"I know what you're thinking." Cosky's voice went hard.

"Yeah? What's that?" Cosky had no fucking clue what was going on in his head.

His brother-in-law's voice turned to steel. "You're blaming yourself, thinking you let the rest of us fight your battle, that one man is dead and another dying because of you. And that's bullshit. This bot weapon affects all of us. If it gets loose, it will threaten everyone, including the people we love. We didn't go after Kuznetsov because of you. We did it because it had to be done, because it was the first step in the fight to stop the bots from eradicating humanity. Benioko knew about this weapon and the danger it posed before we pulled your ass out of Karaveht, before your teammates were even infected. He would have approved the mission to bring in Kuznetsov even if you hadn't been involved."

Well, fuck. Apparently, Cosky *did* know what he was thinking. A long, uncomfortable silence fell between them. Cosky broke it by clearing his throat.

"Just so you know." Cosky hesitated, watching him with an odd expression on his face—partially reluctant, partially resigned. He finally released a *what-the-hell* sigh. "Demi spent nearly every second while you were getting your beauty sleep sitting beside your bed."

"So I've heard." Aiden stiffened; this was not a conversational jaunt he wanted to take.

Her bedside vigil didn't mean shit, other than she had a good heart. It sure as hell didn't mean she'd changed her mind about getting back together with him. Hell, she hadn't visited him since he woke up. Sure, she'd been sitting beside him when he'd first cracked his eyes open and broke free from those weird-ass dreams, but she hadn't been back since.

Cosky grimaced, reluctance heavy on his face. "Kait thinks she's willing to reopen the conversation about your deadass love life."

A spark of hope lit. It immediately guttered. Demi had made it crystal clear that she wasn't willing to hook up with a guy whose entire career involved risking his life. Nothing about that had changed between closing his eyes and opening them. Hell, all she had to do was peek into the room next door and look at the grieving woman sitting by Samuel's bed to realize she'd made the right decision.

Not that he wanted to talk about that. He searched for a change of subject. "Where's Kait, anyway?"

For a moment it looked like Cosky wasn't going to answer, but then he shrugged and squared his shoulders as though expecting pushback. "She's talking to your doctors."

Aiden stiffened. "What the—"

"Before you go off half-cocked," Cosky broke in with a long-suffering sigh, "the meeting wasn't Kait's idea. Your doctors asked to meet with her."

That stopped Aiden cold. His doctors had requested a meeting with his sister. "Why?"

Cosky shrugged, looking baffled himself. "Something about the healings she's done on you."

"That makes no sense," Aiden growled. "Why would they need to know that?"

"I'm sure Kait will fill you in when she gets back."

As if on cue, the accordion-style door slid back and his sister walked into his room.

She'd barely taken two steps before Aiden launched his first question. "What did my doctors want with you?"

She shot Cosky an annoyed look, but the dude just shrugged.

"They're his doctors. He's got a right to know."

The nape of Aiden's neck prickled. Was there something the doctors weren't telling him? "What's wrong? What did they say?"

She frowned, her forehead wrinkling, looking confused herself. "It's not so much what they said, as much as all the questions they asked."

"What the hell did they ask?" The tension in his neck crawled up to the base of his head, which started to pound.

"They wanted to know about all the times I've healed you over the years and what injuries you sustained that caused the healings."

Aiden cocked his head, puzzled by the explanation. "Like when I damaged my spine?"

"That and others, going all the way back to our childhood." She lifted her eyebrows. "I didn't realize until I started listing them how many times I've healed you. Turns out you're incredibly accident-prone."

Aiden crossed his ankles and settled back against the pillows. "Why would they want to know any of that?"

A thoughtful look entered her eyes. She absently scraped her thumbnail along the bottom of her lower lip. "I don't know, but the questions weren't just about my healings on you. They asked other things too. Like how often you were sick, whether you'd had any major or minor illnesses over the years. Then they moved on to Dad and Mom. All sorts of questions about their health, too."

"Like a family health history questionnaire?" Cosky asked, his eyebrows rising.

"I filled one of those out when I first arrived," Aiden said. "Back when I was in isolation." He frowned across the room at the pleats on the accordion door.

"They must be double checking." Kait settled into the chair beside Cosky. "I'd tell you to ask the doctors yourself, but I'm a thousand percent sure you're already planning on that."

"Damn right," Aiden muttered. "They say anything about when they're going to release me?"

"No. But it can't be long now. You seem like you're back to normal." Kait smiled at him, relief shining in her eyes. "You don't seem nearly as tired as you did before you woke up, either. You're never sleeping when I visit. Not like you were before."

Aiden grimaced. He wasn't sleeping because he was afraid to shut his damn eyes. He was tired of the fucking nightmares messing with his mind. Dread carved a hole in his gut. If he could figure out what the dreams were trying to tell him, maybe he could address the problem. But those damn twisted people, with their elongated eyes and mouths, never said a damn thing. They just stared at him with their slanted, hollow eyes, like they expected him to know what they wanted.

Like they were waiting for something from him.

Chapter Forty-Six

Day 23
Denali, Alaska

Dr. Brickenhouse walked into Aiden's hospital room within minutes of Kait and Cosky leaving. The doctor's arrival was both a blessing and a frustration. Finally, Aiden would get his questions answered. But dammit, he'd planned to sneak off to the cafeteria for some real food. He was fucking tired of bed rest and namby-pamby meals.

"Let me get this straight," Aiden said once Dr. Brickenhouse finished his update. "All the healings Kait did on me through the years supercharged my immune system and that's why the bots weren't able to infect me?"

"That's our working theory," Brickenhouse nodded. His face looked less lined and gray, as though he'd gotten some actual sleep. "Although, realistically, the last two healings your sister did prior to your illness probably had the most impact. Your immune system was already supercharged by those healings, which aided your body in resisting the foreign invasion, which in turn prevented the nanobots from replicating and attacking."

Aiden frowned at that. "You said you found none of those fuckers in me."

It gave him the creeps to think of the little bastards crawling around inside him, even if his immune system had squashed them.

"True. Initially, we didn't find any evidence of them in your tissue and blood work. But the samples we took were limited, and there was no way to check your brain other than the CT and MRI scans. The nanobots only showed up on your teammates' brain scans because of the size of the clusters. However, there was no indication—and still isn't—of bot clusters in any of your brain scans." He pursed his mouth before continuing. "As for the rest of your test results, there were no abnormalities in them either...until recently. And even then, only three of the slides showed abnormalities. Three out of hundreds."

"Abnormalities." Aiden's laugh bordered on grim. "Guess that's one way of describing them. Are you sure the fragments you found are from the nanobots?"

"No. We can't be certain." The doctor shrugged. "But they carry some of the nanobot markers. So, realistically, the most likely scenario is that they're fragments of bots your immune system destroyed."

Aiden grunted and thumped his head against the pillow. "So, my immune system, which Kait supercharged, just...dissolved them? That's what you're saying?"

If Brickenhouse was right, this news put a big damper on the whole inoculate the world idea. If Kait's repeated healing was why he'd survived the infestation, while his teammates had all perished, then the world was fucked.

Brickenhouse looked tired again, as though the weight of the world was on his shoulders. Which it kind of was. "It's unclear how your body eradicated the nanobots. We're still figuring that out."

Great. The docs and lab rats didn't have a clue how his body had defeated the killer bots. Which meant they couldn't manufacture a cure. Not from Aiden, anyway. He sighed. They needed a fucking miracle. But he'd take that miracle from his quarters, not this damn hospital bed. He swung his legs over the side and stood. Time to facilitate his own release from the clinic.

"Now that you've given me a clean bill of health," which Brickenhouse had done before the conversation morphed into supercharged immune systems, "it's time for me to bid you *adieu*. If you need me, you've got my cell number."

To his shock, Brickenhouse didn't protest. Guess he really was back to normal.

Afraid the doctor would change his mind before Aiden could escape, he hurriedly dressed in the clothes Kait had left him and stuffed his cell in the back pocket of his jeans. He grabbed a vehicle from the charging station in front of the clinic and drove it to the alcove in front of the corridor that led to his quarters.

He was restless when he reached his apartment. Unsettled. A long, hot shower helped some, but he was too wired to sleep. Hell—he didn't *want* to sleep. He didn't want to face those damn stretchy-faced people until he absolutely had to. Besides, he'd slept for days. He didn't need more shuteye.

What he needed was food. He was hungry enough to eat an elephant. He paced to the tiny kitchen and yanked open the refrigerator. Kait had stocked it with his favorite foods. The space came equipped with a two-burner stove and a microwave, along with a cabinet of pots and pans, and another full of dishes, glasses and cups. He could cook himself something, although that seemed like too much work. It would be easier to head to the cafeteria and grab something there. He called in his order of a double-meat, double-cheese, double-bacon burger with a double order of fries, and smiled in satisfaction when the cook promised it would be ready on his arrival.

After he'd filled his belly, he'd hunt down his big bro and find out what Shadow Mountain intel was doing to locate Kuznetsov's mistress. He'd check in with Dev too. Maybe Dev's soups and spooks network could find the woman. Although Dev's contacts had been wrong about where the Russian had holed up.

Benioko's informant, on the other hand, had been Johnny-on-the-spot with his information. Aiden had a theory about who that informant was. Kuznetsov's location had come within hours of his plea to O'Neill in the gym. Hell, maybe the Shadow Mountain outcast really *was* Stargate. Either way, it wouldn't hurt to meet with the dude and see if he had more helpful info to pass along. It was time to take a closer look at Nantz Technology, too. The whole fucking camera thing still bugged the shit out of him.

With newfound energy buzzing through his mind, he started for the door. First lunch. Followed by some head rattling. The door buzzer sounded as he crossed the room. Kait, probably, or maybe Wolf. Although Rawlings was a good bet, too. His former CO was a momma hen.

As it turned out, the one person he hadn't expected was standing at his door.

"Demi?" He stared at her in shock, drinking her in, as he absently raked his fingers through his still wet hair.

She looked thinner. Her face was pale. Her brown eyes were wide and anxious. He sucked in a breath along with the scent of roses from her shiny hair, which looked freshly washed. The scent, so full of memories and emotions, almost drove him to his knees.

For a moment, hope burst hot and wild inside of him. It surged through his veins as powerful as an adrenaline rush. Was Cosky right? Did she— He snapped the reaction off. There were multiple reasons Demi could be standing in front of his door. None of them meant she wanted to take him back.

Hell, maybe she'd dropped by to say goodbye. With Kuznetsov dead, she might think it was safe to head home. His hand lifted, clamping around the edge of the door.

He swore beneath his breath. Yeah, a goodbye was the likely scenario here. His fingers pressed harder against the edge of the door. Dammit, his refusal to let her leave would not help his case—not that he had much of a case to begin with. Or any case at all, to be truthful. But he didn't want her thinking he was holding her hostage, either.

She couldn't leave.

Not yet.

It wasn't safe.

Day 23

Denali, Alaska

"Hey." Demi stared at Aiden's hand, which he'd wrapped around the edge of the door. His fingers were turning white. "I hope... I hope I'm not interrupting anything."

She tried for a smile, but felt it tremble and then fade from her lips. He didn't look happy to see her. His face was tight. His black eyes were flat. And she'd heard him swear beneath his breath when he opened the door.

Was she seeing anger or frustration on his face? In the flat darkness of his eyes? Was he annoyed with her? But why? They hadn't seen each other since the night they'd spoken and parted ways. Maybe that was it. Maybe he was mad at her for breaking up with him, then sitting beside his bed as he slept, when he couldn't kick her out of his room.

It was odd, though. She would have sworn relief flashed across his face when he'd opened the door and saw her standing there. But it was gone now. She must have imagined it. Her gaze returned to his hand, studying the way it clenched the edge of the door. His fingers were bleached and rigid. Yep. Sure looked like anger to her. She hovered there, the urge to flee strong. She should leave. He obviously didn't want to see her.

But she couldn't. Something, possibly foolish optimism, or perhaps stubbornness, held her feet to the floor.

Olivia's comment about compromises and heartmates and rare connections had burrowed into her mind like a bunch of ticks and refused to let go. She still didn't believe in soulmates. But she believed in regrets, and some regrets could eat at a person, whittle away at them year by year. Walking away from him, without talking to him first, without trying to find a compromise, would haunt her for the rest of her life.

"Can I come in?" She forced the question out and braced herself in case he said no.

He stirred and stepped back. Without saying a word, he pulled the door all the way open. A physical, but not a verbal, invitation. Hardly an enthusiastic welcome.

She slipped past him. His apartment was identical to the one Wolf had given her to use. Same galley-style kitchen and combination dining-living room. Same bland, off-white walls with a total lack of prints or paintings. She glanced to the left, where a short hallway disappeared into darkness, and knew she'd find a bathroom and bedroom back there, both bland, both boring. Functional, but with less personality than your average motel room.

Apparently, Shadow Mountain put all their resources into fast planes and top-of-the-line equipment—military and medical—rather than sprucing up their employee's quarters.

Typical.

"You'll have to postpone the goodbye," Aiden said from behind her, a hard edge chilling his voice.

She turned, cocking her head in confusion. He stood facing her with his feet squared, his shoulders back, and a challenge in the tilt of his chin. The steel was in his eyes now, too. Cold. Hard. Adamant. Pure black steel.

"Goodbye? Are you going somewhere?" She took a step back before forcing herself to stillness.

"You're leaving. Isn't that why you're here? To say goodbye?" He didn't move, yet his body seemed to tighten.

"No, I—"

"Just because Kuznetsov's dead doesn't mean you're safe. Whoever created the nanobot weapon is still out there, still after me. You're still in danger. You can't go back to Coronado yet."

That's why he was so tense? So cold? "I'm not going anywhere. I didn't come to say goodbye."

The news loosened his shoulders. The black ice melted from his eyes. "No? Then why are you here?"

Right. She searched for an explanation that wouldn't leave her vulnerable. But the only thing that came to mind was what Livvy had told her. Maybe she could use that as a lead-in.

"Olivia was telling me about the gifts the Shadow Warrior and Blue Moon Mother give to their tribal children. She said Kait's healing came from the mother creator to strengthen tribal ties and that Wolf's premonitions came from the Shadow Warrior to protect the tribe."

Olivia's self-proclaimed gift was on the tip of her tongue, but she shied away from mentioning it. She didn't want him to think the only reason she was here was because Olivia had convinced her they were soulmates. But avoiding Olivia's gift left her with no transition into what she'd come here to say, and he was waiting for an explanation. She could see it in the furrow of his brow and the narrowing of his eyes.

Rattled, she threw the first question out that occurred to her. "Do you have a gift like Kait or Wolf?"

The question was supposed to be a throwaway, a means to ease her into a discussion about Olivia's self-proclaimed gift. And from there, into a serious conversation about whether he felt there was an unusually strong connection between them, which would naturally lead to a discussion about whether they should resume their relationship.

She'd assumed through the years that he didn't have a talent like Kait or Wolf, because he would have told her. Hell's bells, it didn't even occur to her that his answer would be yes, because surely...surely, he would have shared such an integral part of himself with her. Surely, he wouldn't have hidden something so huge from her.

While he didn't respond with a verbal affirmative, he didn't need to. His reaction gave him away and told her everything she needed to know—all of it unwelcome. His gaze widened, then narrowed. Caution touched his face and sank into his eyes. He took a step back.

"Why do you ask?" His words were cautious. And he didn't deny it.

Her mouth fell open as the painful realization struck that he did, indeed, have a gift. "Oh. My. God. You do."

He'd always held his secrets close, locked them inside. She'd known that, had known he didn't share everything, or even most things with her. But she'd thought those secrets were SEAL-related. That they had to do with the secrecy inherent in his career. Missions, locations, targets, timeframes—things that could get him and his teammates killed if they leaked out. She'd accepted all those secrets. She'd even made allowances for the nightmares he refused to talk about since he'd said they were related to his missions.

But this...this...this secret was not related to his SEAL career. This was not something he was forbidden to share. This was a *personal* secret, something he'd deliberately kept from her.

He knew she knew about Kait's and Wolf's abilities. He knew she'd kept those secrets safe. He knew his secret would be safe with her, too. There was no reason for him to hold this revelation back. No reason except for one. He didn't want to share such a fundamental part of himself. Not with her.

He'd claimed to love her, but he couldn't. Not when he'd kept her in the dark about this. Trust was tangled with love. You couldn't have love without trust.

And this secret was such a blazing example of lack of trust.

Chapter Forty-Seven

Day 23
Denali, Alaska

Demi reeled back. Aiden had an extra ability, too. One he'd never told her about.

"Why didn't you tell me? Why—" Her throat closed and started to ache. The why was obvious. He didn't trust her. Not with the important stuff. Not with the core of him. Her lungs struggled to find breath. The connection she'd thought stretched between them didn't exist. It couldn't. Not when he'd withheld something so vital from her.

"Never mind." Her voice sounded breathless. "I need to go."

"Demi..." His voice was rough, his face conflicted.

About what? He'd made his decision years ago. Three years. He'd had three years to tell her about this and dozens of opportunities. All those times Kait had healed him in front of her. All those times they'd marveled at Kait's incredible ability. It hadn't even occurred to her he might have an extraordinary gift, too. Because he would have told her if he had one.

"Coming here was a mistake." She stared at the door. He backed up against it, blocking her way. "Move. Please."

The breathlessness in her voice gave way to dullness, to numbness. The numbness spread to her chest before engulfing her entire body from head to foot. It felt good, this detachment; something to burrow into, to curl up and grieve inside.

Aiden didn't budge from his position against the door. "Look, you came here for a reason, right? Let's talk about it."

A spontaneous laugh burst from her—sharp and humorless. "Why bother? When have you ever shared anything important with me? What a fool I've been. I thought you shut me out because of your job. Because of the secrecy required to keep you and your teammates safe. I thought you held your secrets so close because you had to, because you were forbidden to share." Another sharp laugh splintered the room. "How about this for irony? While you were sick, I convinced myself that we had some kind of connection, something special, like what Kait found with Cosky, or Olivia found with Samuel." She paused long enough to draw in a shaky breath. "But Cosky knows about Kait's healing ability. Samuel knows about Olivia's gift. But you...you never trusted me enough to tell me you even had an ability." Her voice cracked and then simply stopped working.

The numbness waned, pain prickling through the detachment. Her skin felt on fire. Her chest burned.

"Trust has nothing to do with it." Aiden's face twisted. He scrubbed a hand through his damp hair and took a small step forward. "I trust you. I've always trusted you."

"Sure." Demi eyed the door. He was still in the way. "You trust me? Got it. So, tell me, what's your ability?"

His face went flat and locked down. She laughed again, only this time it held far too much pain for her comfort. The fire in her chest exploded outward, consuming her entire body. Her face burned. So did her eyes.

"Can't even bring yourself to tell me now, can you?" She steadied her breathing and hardened her voice. "Move away from the door, Aiden."

His hand went from his hair to his face, covering it completely. He pushed back against the door, using it like a brace. "It wasn't because I didn't trust you that I didn't tell you about my *gift*." He loaded the last word with derision. His hand dropped. He shook his head, disgust thick on his face. "I didn't tell you because it's fucking embarrassing."

The unexpectedness of that admission snapped her from her emotional tailspin. Embarrassing? "How so?"

He drew a deep breath and grimaced. "My ability doesn't save lives. Hell, it doesn't benefit anyone but me."

There was something lurking beneath the disgust on his face, something hollow, but honest. Pained sincerity radiated from him.

"I don't understand." Her voice was quiet now. The fire receded until she could think again. He seemed to mean what he was saying. His frustration rang clearly in his voice, was alive on his face.

"Kait's gift allows her to heal. She takes away people's pain, heals their injuries...she can save lives. Her gift's a fucking miracle."

Demi nodded her agreement.

Aiden started pacing back and forth, from wall to wall, in front of the door. "And Wolf's gift... Fuck, it saves lives too. He's saved mine twice now with those forward flashes he gets. He's saved Kait too. Hell, his premonition even saved O'Neill on that last mission."

Demi nodded again and waited for him to continue.

He took another trip to the wall and back. When he spoke again, his voice had dropped to a gritty snarl.

"My gift, in comparison, is a fucking farce." There was more than disgust on his face now. There was loss and emptiness, like what he'd been given was worthless. A slap in the face, even.

But a farce? Surely not. They were talking about extraordinary abilities. How could anything that was outside the normal human range be a farce?

"That can't be true, Aiden." She gentled her voice.

"Yeah?" He stopped abruptly and spun to face her. His hands curled into fists and slammed down on his hips. He looked frustrated and...ashamed?

"You want to know what my great gift is? Well, here it is. I have the Midas touch. My gift results in money. Lots and lots of money. It doesn't save lives or prevent tragedies. It just makes me richer and richer."

She let that sink in. His gift made him rich? How was that deserving of such anger and shame? Most people would love to have such an awesome ability. She kept the observation to herself, though, because Aiden obviously was disgusted with his ability.

She swallowed her confusion and tried to see his perspective. He made money off his extraordinary ability rather than saving people's lives? How was that a bad thing? One could do great things with a constant influx of cash. Maybe it didn't directly save lives like Kait's and Wolf's gifts—but helping people financially could indirectly enhance their situations, sometimes even save their lives.

Did he not see that?

Maybe there was more to his gift than what he was telling her. She needed more information.

"When you say you have the Midas touch, what does that mean?" She chose her words carefully.

His shoulders curling forward, he scrubbed both hands down his face. When he dropped them again, he looked defeated. "If I look at an article or a television report of an upcoming horse race, I'll know what horses are going to win. I know what baseball or football teams are going to win. When I walk through a casino, I'll know what machines are about to drop a big payout. I know what stocks are about to surge. Fuck—" he drew a deep breath. "I even know the weekly lottery numbers. I could win every single fucking time if I wanted to."

Woah.

Although Demi never said the word, she must have mouthed it, because he flinched and looked away. Which was so weird. Why was he so ashamed of this ability?

"I don't understand why you find this such a problem, Aiden." She couldn't hold the comment back. He wasn't putting on an act. He was too vulnerable and raw.

"Because it's a fucking ridiculous ability. It helps no one other than me," he snapped, his eyebrows furrowing and pulling down.

"But you could use it to help others." She stepped forward to touch his arm. "There is so much good you could do with the kind of money you're talking about." She waited until his gaze focused on her face before continuing. "There are thousands of people out there waiting on experimental treatments or surgeries they can't afford. People with no insurance and no money who can't even get on the transplant list unless they come up with the procedure costs." She was surprised he hadn't already thought of this. "Or what about all the people who've hit hard times and need help with rent or house payments, even food...lunches for kids?" She stroked his arm. "You could help a lot of people by giving that money to various charities."

He pulled his arm back and nailed her with an *are-you-fucking-kid-ding-me* glare. "What the fuck do you think I'm doing with the money now?"

"Then why do you find your ability so distasteful? You're helping people." Her confusion increased.

"Because it's not the same. I'm not saving people's lives. Not like Kait and Wolf," he snapped.

"But you *are* saving people. Every time you give someone money, you're helping them. You're probably helping a lot more people than Kait or Wolf have."

"It's not the same thing," he insisted tightly, a blindly stubborn look in his eyes.

She studied him. There was an odd expression on his face. Stubborn, yet lost. It was like he didn't know why he was so dissatisfied with his gift. Or at least he hadn't been able to come up with a valid reason. She didn't want to argue with him. He was entitled to his feelings, even though they made no sense to her. But her intuition screamed that his frustration with his ability was crucial to understanding him.

"Why is the way Wolf and Kait help people so much better than the way you do? All three of you are helping people in need."

For a moment, it looked like he wasn't going to answer. His mouth flattened. So did his gaze. But then his eyes lost focus, as though he were considering the question.

"Their gifts impact people immediately, people they know—friends, family, coworkers. They're hands on. It's a visceral process for them."

Something clicked in her head. Was there too much of a distance between the people he was helping and himself? Was there an emotional and physical detachment there? "How do you disperse the money to people in need? Are you in contact with them?"

He looked horrified. "Christ, no. I don't want them feeling indebted to me. The thought of accolades or thank yous—" He broke off to shudder. "I fund a foundation that people run for me—good people. They handle the requests and disbursements. I just dump more money in when the foundation runs low."

So, he had no personal relationship with the people he was helping. He never saw how his generosity affected them. Kait and Wolf, on the other hand, instantly witnessed their gifts' effects.

Aiden probably knew on a subconscious level that his gift helped people, but he didn't see its affect, so he didn't feel it on a visceral level, an emotional level, so for him, the gift had little value.

"Have you ever helped someone with your gift that you knew or were close to? A friend or family member who was desperately in need of financial aid, where you saw the immediate effects of your gift?"

His jaw tensed, and caution flickered through his eyes. Obviously, the answer was yes, but why was he so uneasy with her question? She thought back over the nine years she'd known him, trying to identify the benefactor of his gift. Of course, the event could have happened prior to his stepping into her life.

"Was it Kait?" she asked absently. Kait never seemed short of cash. The condo in Coronado had to have cost her close to a million dollars. Or at least that's what hers had cost Donnie, according to the real estate agent who'd brokered the deal.

Something about that niggled at her, buzzing for attention.

"Kait never needed financial attention. Our dad had the same gift as mine, although he used it sparingly to avoid attention. Because I'd already developed my ability by the time he died, dad left his estate to Kait. She's set for life."

Aiden's explanation came from a distance. Memories were flooding her mind. While they'd had insurance, Donnie's catastrophic injury, along with the surgeries and days in the ER, had left her mired in debt. Their savings hadn't come close to covering the hospital costs. Donnie had been the breadwinner in the family, while she'd been content manning her coffee cart. The only jobs she could find after Donnie's death had been waitressing ones, which had barely covered food, utilities, and rent.

And then a miracle happened—two miracles, actually. An unbelievably huge life insurance policy had unexpectedly paid out, one she hadn't even known Donnie had acquired. She'd even questioned how he could afford the premium without her knowledge. The two-million dollar policy payout had covered all the hospital bills, with enough money left over to set her up for life.

The second miracle had been her condo, the one Donnie had supposedly bought from an inheritance left to him by an estranged uncle. He'd known how much she loved Kait's condo, so the gift itself made sense. But Donnie had never spoken of this uncle. And since Donnie didn't have any family left, there had been no one to question. According to the real estate agent, Donnie had planned to surprise her with the condo on their next anniversary.

The insurance policy and the gift of her new home had been such a blessing she hadn't investigated the circumstances surrounding them. Instead, she'd thanked the universe for providing for her. Only it hadn't been luck, or the bounty of the universe that had stepped in to smooth her world.

It had been Aiden.

"It was me, wasn't it? I was the benefactor of your gift?" Demi whispered. "You were the insurance payout. You bought my condo."

As a man who guarded his secrets behind closed lips and a flat face, she expected Aiden to deny his involvement. He grimaced instead, his gaze dropping to the floor, like he was dreading her reaction. "I knew you'd put everything together once you found out about my stupid fucking ability."

Demi digested that, and another piece fell into place. "Is that the reason you didn't tell me what you can do? You didn't want me to know what you'd done for me."

He grunted and shrugged, his gaze finally lifting to her face. He studied her with guarded eyes. "Maybe."

She frowned over that. "Why?"

He scowled so hard his eyes squinted. "I didn't—hell don't—want you to feel like you owe me." His voice was ferocious.

Like he didn't want a thank you from the people he helped through his foundation? Her chest went mushy. He was a good man, a giant teddy bear of a man.

She got why he hadn't told her. But why hadn't Kait? "Kait knows what you can do, right? Does she know what you did for me?"

"Yeah, she knows about my *ability*." There was less disgust coating the word this time. Not much less, but some. He shrugged. "I never told her I was behind the insurance payout or your condo, but she suspects. She asked about it a couple of times, but I sidestepped."

Kait must have felt the news was Aiden's to share, not hers, even though they'd been friends for years by that point.

"Are you mad about this?" Aiden finally asked, the cautious look back in his eyes.

Demi refocused on him. It wasn't just trepidation on his face, there was uneasiness, too. Like he was worried this news changed everything between them. "You saved my ass back then, Aiden. I could never be mad about that. I'm stunned and grateful, not angry."

He recoiled, his eyebrows slamming down over his flinty gaze. Every sinew in his body tensed. "I don't want your gratitude. I didn't do it for you. I did it for me."

Her eyebrows flew up. She cocked her head quizzically. "You did it for yourself? How's that work?"

His shoulders drew back. His face hardened. Even his stance squared.

This must be how he looks when he's headed into battle.

"Yeah. I did it for me. I hated how stressed out you were because of the hospital bills. I hated how exhausted you were after waitressing at that cafe. I hated the way guys were constantly hitting on you while you were working. I was spinning up for a deployment and I needed to know you'd be safe before I left. I needed to know that you had the money to take care of your bills and still live comfortably. I knew I wouldn't be able to focus on the mission if I was worried about you. So, I took care of things. End of story."

Her lips twitched. Wow, he'd sure spun his kindness into selfishness.

"What about the condo?" she asked, curious how he was going to spin that extravagant generosity into an act of self-interest.

"I wanted you somewhere safe. Bonus points if you were close to Kait, so she could look after you while you were grieving. I knew you loved Kait's condo, so I hired a realtor to find me a unit in Kait's building." Pure stubbornness sat on his face, like he knew she was amused by his explanations.

"I see." She was tempted to thank him again to see his reaction, but bit her tongue against the impulse. He was just so damn determined to portray himself as the selfish asshole, when in reality he was a mushy ol' sweetheart.

Eventually, his face softened and his battle-ready stance relaxed. "You're not pissed?"

"Good lord, no. I'm surprised," she admitted. "We didn't even know each other well back then."

His gaze dropped to her face, lingering on her lips. "I wasn't lying the other night when I told you I fell in love with you years ago. Long before our friends with benefits arrangement. I fell in love with you the moment Kait introduced us, while you were still married to Donnie. I wrestled that love back, locked it down, because you were married and committed to him. But that didn't make me love you any less."

"Really?" It was hard to be skeptical after finding out what he'd done for her.

"Really." His gaze warming, he stepped forward and cupped her cheeks. "The instant I saw you, I knew you were the only woman for me. It sucked that you weren't free and didn't feel the same way about me. Hell—you never even noticed me, but that didn't lessen my feelings or my certainty."

I knew you were the only woman for me.

His confession was very close to calling her his soulmate, and almost identical to what Livvy had said about Samuel.

Maybe there was something to this soulmate cliché, after all.

Chapter Forty-Eight

Day 23
Denali, Alaska

Her mouth was so close he could smell the strawberry balm glossing her lips and the scent of roses drifting up from her hair.

Roses.

The scent had saturated every erotic dream he'd had for years—long before he'd finally hooked up with her. From the day he'd met her, way back when she'd been married and off-limits, the smell of roses had haunted him. His cock had locked onto that sweet scent like Pavlov's dog on the bell. It had taken him years to figure out why roses had become an aphrodisiac. Nine years, to be exact, which was how long it had been between their first meeting and their first lovemaking. That was when he'd realized Demi smelled like roses. Hell, every product she used, from shampoo to body lotion, was rose-scented.

His gut clenched beneath the sensual punch of roses and strawberries. Memories strobed through his mind like a string of flash grenades. *The arch of her body beneath his thrusts...smooth, strong legs cinched around his waist...her fingernails digging into his back...the quake of her muscles and tremble of her skin beneath his mouth...and the scent of roses cocooning them.*

Christ, he wanted to close the distance between their mouths and sip that strawberry sweetness from her lips, steep himself in the heady fragrance of roses.

But one taste would unravel him. He was balanced on the edge of need and hope, his control hanging by a thread. The feel of her lips, the taste of her mouth would set fire to that thread. If she wasn't looking to get back together, kissing her would make it a thousand times harder to walk away.

He forced himself to pull back, even though every fiber in his body wanted to drag her into his arms, and from there to his bed. But he couldn't. Not yet.

While he was almost certain now she'd come to his quarters to resume their relationship, she hadn't brought that possibility up. And considering the serious complications she'd outlined earlier when she'd called it quits on them, problems that hadn't been resolved, it was best not to make assumptions. Nor did he want to sexually manipulate her into a situation she hadn't intended.

"Before things go further, I need to know whether you've changed your mind about us." Aiden studied her face. His cock twitched, recognizing the flush to her cheeks and the haze in her eyes. Signs of arousal. Beneath her shirt and bra, her nipples would be peaked and pebbled, begging for his mouth. "Is this visit about rekindling things between us?"

Fuck. Please say yes.

The haze cleared from her eyes. A frown pleated her forehead.

Ah, hell.

He swallowed a groan as she drew back. She didn't go far though, less than a foot, which was a consolation.

"I did a lot of thinking while I sat by your bed, waiting for you to wake up." Her eyes darkened to mahogany. "And I realized something." She searched his face, her gaze narrow and intense. "I don't want to give up on what we have, on what we could have. There's a connection between us, one I've never felt with anyone before, not even Donnie. I want to find a way to make this relationship work—but on a level that accommodates both of us."

Aiden released a shaky breath. "I want that too."

Relief touched her face, but instantly vanished. "The thing is—" she drew a deep breath. "Are you going back to the SEALs, Aiden? Those long, constant deployments—" She broke off with a dismayed shake of her head.

"No." The answer came easily. Apparently, his subconscious had already reached a decision.

"You're sure?" She looked conflicted; half hopeful, half worried. "I don't want you making that choice because of me. That would just lead to resentment, which would eventually tear us apart."

"I'm sure." And he was. The decision sat comfortably inside him. Sure, there was some sadness, a tinge of loss and grief. But deployments wouldn't be the same without Squirrel and the rest of his teammates beside him. He'd be assigned to a new team, but it wouldn't be the same. Maybe if he'd lost his brothers through less suspicious circumstances, he'd feel differently.

But there were so many questions about what had happened in Karaveht, like who was behind the testing on his team. Truth was, he didn't trust the boots on the WARCOM ladder. Someone had set them up. Somebody had betrayed them. And that someone could be in SEAL command. If you didn't trust those who were supposed to have your back, it was time to get out.

"My contract is almost up, and I'm not going back. I don't know what's going to happen, whether they'll release me from my contract a couple of weeks early, or if I'll be AWOL. Hell, I might already be AWOL. But we don't know who was behind what happened in Karaveht, and I'm not ruling out WARCOM. Either way, with a bounty on my helmet, I'd be a danger to any new crew, anyway."

He was at peace with the choice. It felt right.

"Are you joining Shadow Mountain, then?"

He glanced up, hearing the relief in her voice. It softened the lines of her face and blunted the stubborn edge to her chin. He wished he could give her reassurance on this subject, too, but he'd never lied to her, and he wasn't about to start now.

"I haven't decided what I'm going to do after we lock down this new weapon and track down the bastard behind it." From the lack of surprise on her face, and the slight bob of her head, she'd expected that response. He paused, giving her a chance to protest or question him. When neither was forthcoming, he continued. "This battle hasn't even started, Demi." He hesitated; she'd been honest about her difficulty with the dangers inherent in his job. The possibility of his death wouldn't lessen anytime soon. Not with the creator of this doomsday device in the wind. He softened his voice, hoping his next words wouldn't detonate the possibilities stretching between them. "I'm neck-deep in this situation, babe. When we get a name and a location, I'll be the first man on the chopper. I can step away from the SEALs program, but I can't step away from this mission. This new weapon is too dangerous. It needs to be locked down. The bastard who created it needs to be secured. I owe Squirrel and Lurch and the rest of my crew that much."

She sighed but held his eyes. A smile trembled on her lips. "I know."

"Is that a deal breaker?" He reached out to tuck a strand of aqua hair behind her ear.

"No." She drew the word out on a long, wobbly breath.

The quiver in her voice drew a frown from him. "You don't sound sure."

"I'm sure." Her breathing steadied. "I'm not saying I won't be worried from the moment you leave until you come back, but I'll figure out how to deal with that. I'll have Kait and Olivia and the rest of the book club brigade to help me process the anxiety." Her shoulders squared. "If they're able to deal with their men being in danger—" Her chin rose. "So can I."

"So, where does that leave us?" He forced his hands to remain at his sides.

"Back together?" Her voice lifted into a question. "If you're up for that."

A slow, teasing grin painted her lips. From the fire gleaming in her eyes, that last question had been deliberate. Warmth flooded his chest, swept down his arms and legs, and exploded in his crotch. His cock hardened.

"Fuck, am I ever up for it," he rasped. One step closed the distance between them. He caught her hand and drug it down to his achingly hard cock. "As you can see."

"But I can't see." Her lips formed an exaggerated pout as her fingers closed around the tented material of his tactical pants. Her fingers slid up to the zipper and tugged the tab down until there was a large enough gap to slip her hand inside. She wound her free arm around his neck and tugged it downward until she could nibble at his bottom lip. Cool fingers slipped beneath his boxers and curled around his achingly hard shaft. "But I can feel, and it feels...very...upright."

He leaned down and slid his tongue between her strawberry-sweet lips. "Christ, you taste good."

She huffed out a laugh. "It's the lip balm. It's guaranteed to please my man—at least that's what the packaging says."

"Fuck, no. It's your lips...your mouth...your tongue," he growled against her lips. "They never disappoint."

"Well," her voice became a sultry tease. "Don't you think we should test the accuracy of the claim on the packaging?"

He grunted in disappointment as she pulled back, only to catch his breath as she slid down his torso and onto her knees. She dragged his pants and boxers down, leaving them pooled around his legs. And then her hot, wet tongue started licking up and down his cock, from base to head, where it paused to swirl around the sensitive slit and the even more sensitive ridge beneath the head. When his cock started twitching, her mouth replaced her tongue, closing around his aching shaft. A deep, guttural groan broke from him as she sucked and slid. She knew exactly what he liked, how much pressure to use, the perfect pace to extend his pleasure. Each time she slid her mouth up to the sensitive head, she gently sucked and swiped her tongue around the slit or that sensitive ridge beneath. And the whole time, the fingers of her free hand fondled his balls—caressing, gently squeezing until they were tighter than hell and pulled up against his body.

Christ, behind his closed eyelids, his eyes crossed. He groaned again, leaning his head back, basking in the feel of her hot, creative mouth, and even hotter and more creative tongue.

After a couple of minutes of bliss, the base of his spine started tingling.

His eyes snapped open. He reached down and hauled her to her feet.

"Hey." There was indignant laughter in the protest. "I wasn't done."

He tossed her over his shoulder, holding her in place with one arm. With his free hand, he yanked his jeans up, anchored them against his hip and headed for the bedroom. The tingling was dispersing. Thank Christ. At least he'd have some self-control during the next five—maybe ten minutes. Fifteen if he was lucky. "Much more of that and I'd be done for the night."

"I don't see a problem with that." Her voice was breathless. Maybe from trying to hold the laughter in. Maybe from his shoulder pressing into her diaphragm.

"I do. A big one. I want to come inside you. Not in your mouth."

"My mouth is inside me."

Her voice was even more breathless, but he could hear the laughter. Even feel it. It bubbled out of her and sank into him—an effervescent joy he hadn't felt in what seemed like forever.

"That's not the inside I'm talking about," he growled, practically running to the bedroom. He was that desperate to reclaim her tight, hot pussy.

Anchoring his jeans in place with his elbow, he flipped the bedroom light on as he passed the switch.

When he reached the bed, he swung her down from his shoulder and dropped her onto the middle of the mattress. Even as she bounced, he tore his shirt over his head. As much as he wanted to get totally naked, skin to skin with her, it would take too long. He'd have to unlace and remove his boots first. Instead, he let go of his jeans and shoved them back down, where they pooled around his knees again.

"Really?" Laughter erupted from her. "You can't even wait to take off your boots?"

"You're lucky I have the patience to take off my shirt," he growled as he yanked her sneakers off and tossed them over his shoulder. "But I know how much you love digging those talons of yours into my chest and back."

"You do have a superb chest," she agreed, her laughter turning into a purr. Her hands skimmed from his shoulders down to his abs, and from there to his crotch. Cool fingers wrapped around his throbbing cock. "But other parts are even more...superb."

He unbuttoned her jeans, ripped the zipper down, and tugged them off. "You could at least make an effort to get your clothes off," he complained as he shoved her blouse up and slid his fingers beneath her silky bra to tweak her nipples.

"Sorry!" she offered the apology in a sing-song voice. "But my hands have more important things to do." She reached lower and tickled his sack. "Much more important things."

He groaned, his hands stilling, before grabbing each side of her blouse and jerking it apart. Buttons popped and flew everywhere. Impatience gripping him, he slid his hands beneath her upper back and grappled with the delicate clasp of her bra. The clasp didn't survive the assault. He whisked her lacy bra aside, freeing her tits for his mouth and hands.

Fuck—what a perfect sight—the high, firm globes beckoned to him, the rosy nipples peaked and waiting for his mouth.

She stretched languorously beneath him, her eyes twinkling. "I don't know, baby. Are you sure you're up for this? It's barely been an hour since you were released from the hospital."

He thrust his cock into her caressing hand. "Absolutely. I've never felt better."

Which was true. He felt fantastic. Strong. Steady. Healthy. Something about that niggled at him, but he was too focused on the feel and sight of her to track the thought down.

Her hair was fanned out across his blanket—a brilliant burst of blue-green. A new memory in the making, as her hair had been pink during his last trip stateside. But the rest of her...fuck...she looked and felt even better than he remembered, her skin glowing, her eyes burning. He traced an unsteady line up her ribcage, her skin like silk against his fingertips, and circled her nipple. Her breath caught, and her muscles twitched with each caress. Mesmerized, he eased down and took the pebbled nub between his lips.

She tasted like roses; floral, sweet, perfect.

When her legs opened in welcome, his fingers slid down to trace circles around the inside of her thigh. Her breath huffed with each stroke.

"Wait!" she stuttered. "There's something I want to try."

His hand froze. Her voice vibrated, but it wasn't with arousal. Or at least not only arousal. There was laughter there, too. Joy. That's what it was like with Demi. That was the difference with her. It's what he'd craved over the past weeks of deployment. It's what he'd mourned when he lost her.

The joy. The laughter. The love. He hadn't understood the difference between fucking and lovemaking until her, how sex could be more than physical, that there could be a mental and emotional component too.

"I want to try an experiment," she announced, her voice breathless with suppressed laughter and arousal.

This could not be good. His forehead beetled. "If you think we're going to postpone this until you don your *fuck-me-now* ensemble—"

"Of course not." Her righteous tone dissolved into giggles. "I never had time to pack—remember? My *fuck-me-now* clothes are down in Coronado. I've got another experiment in mind."

"No shit?" His hand started moving again, circling closer and closer to her soaked core.

"See, I watched this documentary that hypothesized that men can smell the scent of female arousal, and that the smell makes men more possessive and aroused themselves." Her breathless explanation tightened as he slipped a finger into her wet heat. "I want too...want to...test—" she gasped as his finger scraped against the inside of her pussy. "—that hypothesis."

He chuckled. "Hate to break it to you, babe, but you signal your arousal with more than scent. It's in your eyes, which turn the color of cinnamon. And your nipples, which pebble and turn rosy." He reached up and tweaked her nipple, then returned his hand to between her shaking legs and his finger to her dripping core. "And then there's this—" He pumped his finger in and out of her pussy. It tightened around his finger. "Look how wet you get for me." He chuckled again. "I know when you're aroused."

"Well, of course, *you do.*" She squirmed beneath the thrust of his finger. "We'd have to test the hypothesis on other men, like at the cafeteria, and see if they can smell my arousal."

Aiden froze. *What the fuck?* His head shot up.

A peal of laughter broke from her. "Oh, my God, you should see your face."

"Fuck that." Aiden reared back and grabbed her calves, lifting them over his shoulders.

He was ninety-nine-point nine percent certain she was joking, but no sense in taking chances. Time to pull out the big gun and distract her. With one hard thrust, he buried his cock inside her. She shifted to align them better and wrapped her legs around his waist. Her arms wound around his sides, all the better to dig her talons into his back as she approached her climax.

He couldn't wait.

After giving her a few seconds to adjust to him, he started a slow, steady thrusting. She hummed and shivered beneath him. He sucked back a groan and kept pumping, his tempo increasing until he was hammering into her like his life depended on it.

In no time, the tingle at the base of his spine started back up. Her body tightened beneath him. Her pussy convulsed and she flew. He followed, chasing her toward the sunrise, and the unicorn, and the pot of gold at the end of the rainbow.

He was home again, Demi in his arms, her magic back in his life.

Chapter Forty-Nine

Day 24
Denali, Alaska

Wolf stepped into the darkness of his quarters without turning on the lights. He let the door swing shut behind him, welcoming the shroud of silence and obscurity. For several long seconds he just stood there, his shoulders slumping, staring into an infinity of emptiness while a flash grenade of memories exploded in his mind.

Flash. Crack. Boom! Samuel and Kuznetsov swallowed by a ball of orange and white fire. Samuel's body lifted and thrown, limp as a ragdoll. The crackle and spit of flames. High pitched screaming, shouting. The acrid smell of smoke, burning metal, spent accelerant, and roasted flesh.

The images vanished, but his flight or fight response continued. His heart slammed against his ribs. His pulse pounded in his ears. His harsh, loud breathing filled the room. His mouth had gone bone dry, his throat tight. His muscles were so tense they ached. No doubt his pupils were dilated too. All symptoms of an adrenaline burst, even though the danger had long since passed.

A low, frustrated grunt broke from him, fracturing the silence. Without hitting the light switch, he stumbled toward his bedroom. He was tired. So damn tired. The exhaustion was so heavy, it carried weight and heft. Each step was a battle. While lack of sleep, along with constant meetings over the past four rotations played a part in his exhaustion, most of the fatigue came from internal rather than external sources.

He'd lost warriors before. Jude, for one. His *anisbecco's* death had left a bloody crater within him, one that hadn't quite healed, even now, three cycles later. In one exceptionally painful case, he'd lost an entire helicopter of warriors. So many lost lives, so much vanished potential.

It was frustrating that his gift forewarned of some deaths, yet not others. He'd seen Aiden's death multiple times, and early enough to prevent it each time. He'd prevented Kait's death with it, too. Samuel's as well. Yet he hadn't seen Jude's. He hadn't seen the chopper crash that led to the end of all those warriors' lives.

He hadn't seen Daniel's murder.

His gift was a fickle beast, serving only a chosen few.

Benioko said the warning pulse could not prevent all deaths, only those brought about through the meddling of the younger gods. The Shadow Warrior's and Blue Moon Mother's shadow children were a petty and jealous lot, envious of the love their parents showered on their earthborn offspring. Sometimes, the lower gods acted behind their parents' backs, orchestrating events to bring about the demise of the favorites among their parents' earthborn children.

Such deaths were not woven into the web of time by the elder gods; thus, they could be circumvented. Shadow Warrior created the warning pulse to prevent such unsanctioned fatalities. But other deaths, those that had been woven into the tangle of time, could not be prevented, thus his gift never warned of their passing.

Still, even knowing this, some fatalities were difficult to accept. Daniel, for instance. His murder should have been preventable. Maybe not through Wolf's gift, but through his knowledge, training, and instincts. Daniel had died because of Wolf's failure, because of his lack of foresight.

The sucking guilt of this was constant. It kept his eyes open deep into the night while he weighed what he'd done against what he *should* have done, where he picked apart every single decision. Every single command. Every single action.

If he'd left Kuznetsov's mistress behind in Petropavlovsk, if he'd refused to let her off the Thunderbird to use the bathroom, if he'd assigned a more experienced guard to accompany her to the shed, if he'd gone with her rather than Daniel. Any of those decisions could have changed the outcome, saved the young warrior's life.

Instead, Muriel was grieving the loss of her first borne child, and Samuel— Wolf flinched. Samuel didn't even know his *jnaaee*, the youngling more like a son than nephew to him, had journeyed to the web of his ancestors.

Samuel's condition was easier to accept. Not his maimed and broken body. That would never be easy to see. But Wolf's *what ifs* over the past five rotations had proven that nothing he could have done would have offered a better outcome.

If he and Samuel had switched places, his *Caetanee* would have been directly in the RPG's path. The grenade would have hit him before it reached anyone else. The only reason Wolf and O'Neill had escaped death was because of Wolf's gift, which gave enough warning for him to tackle O'Neill and drive them both to the ground, so the grenade had gone over their heads.

But O'Neill had been within tackle range.

Even if he'd received a warning flash aimed at Samuel, he would have been too far away to reach him. His *Caetanee* would have taken the blast full force. Even if Wolf had screamed at him to drop, between the wind and the engine noise from the Thunderbird, his second might not have heard him. Reaching him through the *Neealaho* would have been an option, but

Samuel would have had to react instantly. The RPG had hit within seconds of the vision.

No matter how he adjusted the situation in his mind, Samuel would not have lived through a direct blast. His *Caetanee* would survive his injuries. It would not be easy. He faced a slow and painful recovery. But he would survive.

Daniel's murder was more difficult to accept, as his crossing was on Wolf's shoulders. If he hadn't misjudged Kuznetsov's mistress, Daniel would not have died. He'd let the woman's tears and apparent openness blind him to her nature. She'd fooled him completely. Because of this massive failure of insight, Daniel was dead, and she was gone.

Their only link to who'd created the nanobot weapon was gone.

With a low, pained grunt, he sat on his bed. Without bothering to turn on the bedside lamp, he bent, untying the laces of his boots by touch. He retrieved his phone from the pocket of his tactical pants and set it on the table beside his bed. Once he was naked, he laid down and pulled the top sheet over his aching body. His eyes closed, he settled deeper into the pillow, willing sleep to take him. Instead, Daniel's blank eyes and rigid face stared back.

The face he saw behind his closed eyes was identical to the one he'd found in the shed. The empty gaze. The frozen expression. The young warrior had likely already died, when the sound of an engine had roared to life inside the shop. They'd burst into the building to find the roll-up door open, Kuznetsov's mistress gone, and Daniel journeying to the web of his ancestors. Their healers—already weakened from their efforts to heal Samuel—could not revive the young warrior. But then, not even the strongest healer could circumvent death and return a spirit to its mortal shell.

Wolf had found snowmobile tracks outside, and a syringe embedded in a lipstick tube lying on the shop floor. If he'd confiscated that crimson tube back at the house in Petropavlovsk-Kamchatsky, Daniel would be alive.

With a deep, shuddering breath, he banished Daniel's frozen face and empty eyes from his mind. But both followed him into sleep.

A deep, rattling vibration and musical ringtone pulled him from dreams of death and severed limbs. Groggy, with the nightmares still seething through his mind, he reached for his phone.

According to the name lighting up the diminutive screen, the call was from his mother. He sat up, tension flaring. It was not like her to call so late.

"*Anistaa*—" He coughed the thickness from his throat. "What is wrong?"

"*Ho'cee!*" Her voice rattled down the line, choppier than normal, without its normal smooth cadence.

His heart started pounding. The edge to her voice tightened his chest and pierced his gut. His mother wouldn't call with a personal problem. Certainly not so late. She was too independent and unwilling to ask for help. She hadn't even told him about her cancer scare until her second screening had proved negative.

This call must be about Jillian.

Jillian had lived with one foot in the Shadow Realm for three cycles. None of his attempts to drag her back to life had worked. She seemed to slide further across the veil every year. Had she finally given in to her ghosts and stepped fully onto the path to her ancestors? An ache spread across his chest.

"Is it Jillian?" He braced himself.

The breath his mother drew sounded like a hiss. "Yes—"

"She's dead." He flinched, his heart dulling.

It was a statement, not a question. He'd been expecting this call. Still, even expected, the news hit like an arrow to his chest. The breath left his lungs. Hope fled his heart.

"No, no." His *anistaa* sucked in a deep, raw breath. "She lives. It's...just...she's been chosen."

"Chosen?" Wolf shook his head in confusion. "By the shadow people?"

They beckoned to her; her lost children, her dead brother. But if her shadow family had finally enticed her to step across the veil, she would be dead.

"No, not by the shadows. She's been chosen by the woodland spirits—by an animal clan."

Wolf froze, then glanced around his dark bedroom. Was he still dreaming? The woodland clans did not choose Anglos. Never in the history of the Kalikoia had a *woohanna* been chosen by a woodland clan spirit.

He stared down at the bright white screen of the phone warming his palm. The heat of the metal against his skin assured him he was not dreaming. Indeed, he was wide awake now. Yet this news made no sense.

Few among the Kalikoia were chosen by the animal clans. And most of those who bore the mark and carried the totem were men—warriors who had been gifted an animal's essence to keep the tribe safe. The few women who had been chosen through the cycles, like Kait, were gifted by the Blue Moon Mother in ways that kept the tribe nurtured and healthy. Or like Samuel's Olivia, who had been given the ability to recognize heartmates, thus keeping the tribal ties intact.

But for an animal clan to claim a *woohanna*—one with no tribal blood? Such a thing was not possible. His mother must be mistaken.

"*Ho'cee!* Did you hear me? Our Jillian has been chosen by the woodland spirits."

Wolf frowned. His mother sounded so certain.

"Such a thing is not possible. She is Anglo. She has no tribal blood." His words didn't lessen her worth. Wolf had chosen her as his own, even though she never reciprocated. But why would the spirit clans choose her? It made no sense. "You must be mistaken." His voice was flat. Unbending.

"I am not mistaken." His mother's voice chilled. "I know a claiming when I see one. She was visited by her spirit animal. I saw it. She bears the claiming bite. She was gifted a totem." The chill in his mother's voice gave way to dryness. "The spirit animals know better than you or I who is worthy of claiming. They chose Jillian."

"You saw this claiming?" Could she have been dreaming? "Which clan claimed her?"

"Yes. I saw it. I heard it." She hesitated, then rushed the rest out. "I heard the scream of the *heschrmal* first. It woke me from my sleep. It was close. So close. I followed the lion's screams until they stopped. Jillian was sitting in the rocker on the porch. The *heschrmal* was curled in her lap. Purring."

"A lion?" His voice rose beneath a combination of shock and protest.

No one within the Kalikoia had been chosen by the lion clan in centuries. Besides, according to tribal mythos, the lion spirit was a warrior totem, as was the wolf spirit. These two woodland clans only claimed males—the mightiest among the warriors.

Why would one claim a woman? A white woman at that.

This news made no sense.

Chapter Fifty

Day 24
Denali, Alaska

A sound—a grunt or a groan—woke Demi from a partial doze. She lazily stretched, listening for anything out of the ordinary. Beneath the blanket and sheet, she was cocooned in warmth. Her own personal furnace burned against her back, while a band of muscle and heat wrapped around her waist. Even as he slept, Aiden clung to her. She liked to think it was because he was afraid to let her go, afraid he'd lose her again.

Probably wishful thinking.

Still—she'd missed this, the heat of her man in bed beside her, the lethargic, well used ache of her muscles, the way his hard frame fit the contours of her body, as though they'd been individually crafted to complement each other. As though they were meant for each other.

The concept of soulmates was increasingly plausible.

He'd turned off the bedroom light after disposing of that last condom. They'd forgotten about protection during the frenzy of that first joining. She'd done the math though, and they should be alright.

She stretched again. Somehow, the lack of light enhanced her contentment. It allowed her to focus solely on her satiated body, full heart, and the prospect of her own happily ever after, something she'd always believed was a mythical beast at best.

It horrified her to think of how close she'd come to tossing this contentment away, to tossing Aiden aside and severing the connection between them because of fear. What a short-sighted response that would have been.

Thank God she'd opened her eyes and heart in time.

A raspy groan came from behind her, and the arm around her waist tightened with bruising force.

Her lazy stretch stilled. The sound was familiar. Aiden's voice, but not his normal, smooth baritone. No, this voice was gritty, almost guttural. It was the voice he used at night while dreaming.

The dreams, although she suspected they were more nightmares than dreams, had occurred often enough over the past three years. She'd asked him about them. He'd brushed her questions aside or distracted her with sex. Awesome sex, true. But sex, as a means of distraction, was ultimately unsatisfying, at least in the aftermath. She'd laid there beside him, panting and spent, yet emotionally empty.

She tugged on his arm until it loosened and fell away. He stirred against her back as she leaned across the mattress, reaching for the lamp on the nightstand. Bright light temporarily blinded her, but her eyes had already adjusted by the time she twisted around to face him.

He'd pushed the sheet and blanket to his waist, giving her eyes plenty to appreciate. Hell's bells, the man was gorgeous. His chest and shoulders were bronzed and muscled—a living classical sculpture. His thick black hair stood upright, mussed and spikey. A layer of stubble darkened his lower cheeks and jawline. Dark, sleepy eyes caught her gaze. But they were vague...distant...like he was still trapped in whatever dream he'd awakened from. Even as she watched, the fog dissipated from his eyes.

His gaze focused on her face, sharpened. A small frown pleated his forehead. "What's wrong?"

"That's my line." She reached up and smoothed the furrows from his brow. "You were having a bad dream."

"Yeah?" That inward, distant expression touched his eyes again. After a moment, he sighed, caught her hand and drew it down to his lips. He feathered a kiss across her knuckles. "I woke you? I'm sorry."

She shrugged, studying his face. He wasn't pulling away. In the past, the mere mention of his dreams brought a reaction. He'd either roll out of bed to use the *head*, or lean in for a kiss, which always led to another bout of sex. This time, the light kiss he'd dropped on her hand felt more like an apology.

He'd opened up the night before, shared some of his secrets. Was he ready to share this one too?

"You know you can tell me about your nightmares, right?" she offered cautiously. "Sometimes dragging them into the open lessens their power."

"This wasn't a nightmare. At least, not like my normal ones." That distant look fogged his eyes again. He shook his head. The frown was back, but it looked more puzzled than stressed.

This was the first time he'd even admitted to having nightmares.

"You've never wanted to talk about your nightmares. What about these dreams? Do you want to talk about them?"

He cocked his head, his gaze sharpening on her face. "It's not that I didn't want to tell you about the nightmares...it's..." He broke off and scooted up until his back was against the headboard. "I didn't want to infect you with the ugliness inside my head."

She sat up and scooted back, too, mirroring his position. "Ugliness?"

"Yeah, ugliness. Ugly images. Ugly memories." He shifted to face her. "I replay all the fucked-up missions in my nightmares. Chopper crashes. Ambushes. Insertions gone wrong. Executions." He lifted his hands and stared at them. "Blood." He shook his head. "So much damn blood."

His face looked hollow, even haunted. She knew soldiers often returned from deployments with PTSD. But other than the nightmares, Aiden had exhibited none of the common symptoms. No flashbacks. No halluci-nations. No reactions to loud noises. No trouble sleeping. No difficulty distinguishing dreams from reality.

Still, he'd obviously been affected by his time in the field.

"I never told you about my nightmares for the same reason I never told you about my deployments." He grimaced, then pressed her hand against his cheek. "You're everything pure, Demi. Pure light and joy and innocence. You sparkle like sunlight against the snow. I hate the thought of my experiences, my darkness, extinguishing your shine." His face hardened in resolve. "I'll never share my nightmares or missions with you. I need to keep you separate, unaware of the ugliness I've seen, the ugly things I've done."

Demi thought about that. If he needed her light to balance his darkness, she could do that for him.

"Okay." She smiled slightly as his face relaxed. She scooted over and leaned against his side until they were pressed together—shoulder to shoulder, hip to hip. "But what of this new dream? You said it was different from the nightmares?"

"Yeah." His voice was slow, absent. He stared straight ahead, his gaze narrow and thoughtful. "It wasn't about a mission, or any of the brothers I've lost. It was..." he shook his head. "...odd."

"How so?" She kept the question soft, non-intrusive. She could almost feel the puzzlement radiating off him.

"It's just...strange. Full of mist and shadows and weird, stretchy people that don't talk but give plenty of attitude."

Demi's eyebrows rose. "Stretchy people?"

Aiden grimaced. "Yeah, stretchy. Elongated. Completely white, like plaster. Vaguely human limbs and torsos. But their faces—" he broke off, his frown digging deeper into his forehead. "They remind me of that Ghostface mask in the Scream movies, the one with the stretched-out mouth and eyes. All warped and creepy."

His description was interesting. "Have you watched any of the Scream movies recently?"

He huffed out a laugh. "Fuck, no, not since I was a kid."

She laid her cheek on his bare shoulder and snuggled into his hot torso, her personal furnace to repel the cold. "Well, dreams can be weird. You probably saw or heard something that didn't register consciously, but your subconscious latched onto it and stuffed it into your dreams."

"That's the thing." His voice was quiet, reflective. "It didn't feel like a dream." He shook his head. "It felt like I knew that shadowy place, and those weird stretchy people. It felt real, I guess."

He glanced over at her and frowned, then bent to grab the sheet and blanket. Drawing them up, he tucked them around her shoulders.

"Is this the first time you've had this dream?" The chill was already giving way to warmth and lethargy.

"No." His gaze narrowed. "I've had them as long as I can remember. But intermittently. Maybe once or twice a year. They started hitting more often six months ago. Since Karaveht, they've escalated to every night." After a brief hesitation, he continued. "I spent the entire time I was unconscious in the ER in that shadowy, twisted world."

Something about his description niggled at her, but she couldn't put her finger on it. "Do any of the people seem familiar to you? Do they talk to you?"

"They don't say a damn word. And I only get fleeting glimpses of them. They're wrapped in shadows and fog." His voice held a baffled note. "But in the dream, I know they want something from me. They're waiting for something, and their impatience is...palpable."

That's when it clicked. Demi straightened. Perhaps his subconscious had picked up on the Kalikoia motifs of shadows, realms, and gods. Weird, twisty people in a misty underworld could be his subconscious's representation of the Kalikoia shadow gods. That would explain these dreams he was having—or at least the escalation of them.

Although it didn't explain why he'd had them before arriving at Shadow Mountain.

"Have you talked to Wolf about these dreams?"

He snorted. "Hell, no. They have nothing to do with him."

She suspected his resistance to the idea had more to do with perceived weaknesses. Wolf, after all, had final say on who joined, or didn't join their missions. Aiden wanted to be first on the chopper when the Shadow Mountain forces went after the people responsible for killing his teammates. Maybe he was afraid that Wolf would see the dreams as a weakness and bump him from the team.

"You should talk to Benioko. Isn't he supposed to be an expert on dreams?" Wasn't deciphering dreams part of shamanism?

While Aiden looked exceptionally dubious, he didn't outright nix the idea.

"You mentioned there were shadows in your dreams," she continued, her voice thoughtful. "I wonder if your subconscious picked up some of the Kalikoia tribal mythos—like the Shadow Warrior and all the Shadow Realm stuff. For God's sake, the base is even called Shadow Mountain, and it's full of people who are committed to the Kalikoia mythology. The theme of shadows and gods is everywhere. You could have subconsciously eavesdropped on a conversation between two believers and integrated it into your dreams." When he didn't immediately shoot that idea down, she continued quietly. "You really should talk to Benioko. These dreams are obviously bugging you. Maybe he can help you figure out why."

It surprised her that his demeanor seemed more thoughtful than dismissive, like he was considering her suggestion, which was a giant leap from their former couple's dynamic—where he'd hop out of bed or distract her with sex to avoid sharing his secrets.

The change made her feel invincible, like they really could work through their problems and share a life together.

Day 24
Denali, Alaska

"I do not know why the *heschrmal* has chosen your *le'ven'a* after centuries of absence. But she has been chosen. This I have seen with my own eyes."

Wolf frowned. Perhaps not centuries of silence. According to the *Taounaha*, O'Neill was lion chosen as well. O'Neill's claiming was difficult enough to believe, and he was male with a splash of Kalikoia blood.

Jillian was *woohanna* and far past puberty.

"You said a lion's scream woke you from—"

"I did not dream this, *Ho'cee!* It happened. Jillian carries the spirit lion's bite and totem. She is lion clan now."

Squinting into the darkness, Wolf grunted thoughtfully. His *anistaa* would not mistake a spirit animal bite or the totem cementing the claim. Such things were impossible to mistake. If she saw what she said, then Jillian had been chosen by the *heschrmal*. Which, if the Old One spoke true, made her clanswoman to O'Neill. Wolf grimaced.

And of the cat clans. Ice pierced his gut.

Cat and bird clans often clashed. While there were no lion clan members on base—with the possible exception of O'Neill—there were lynx and bobcat. He was often required to smooth ruffled feathers and fur after clashes among his men.

The thought of Jillian's reaction to him, through the lens of her spirit animal, sent the ice in his gut churning.

"Why would the woodland spirits gift Jillian with a warrior's animal?" Even to his own ears, his voice sounded numb.

"This I do not know." His *anistaa*'s voice softened with sympathy. She well-knew the rift between the bird and cat clans. "Perhaps the *Taounaha* knows?"

Wolf frowned. As the earthside voice and eyes of the Shadow Warrior, Benioko knew many of the Shadow Realm's secrets. But the Shadow Warrior was the essence of the male life force—the provider, the protector, the hunter, the warrior. He did not meddle in the Blue Moon Mother's sphere of influence, which was the female life force—the harvester, the healer, the supplier, the nurturer.

As a female, Jillian fell under the Blue Moon Mother's web of influence. But there was no way to ask the great mother why she had gifted Jillian with a warrior's animal. The Blue Moon Mother had not chosen an earthside mouthpiece since Silver Spruce had crossed to the web of her ancestors nearly two hundred cycles ago.

Would Benioko know why Jillian had been chosen? Or what gift she had been given? Each animal gifted something different. Both he, Aiden, and Kait had been chosen by the *thae-hrata*. Yet he and his *javaanee* had received the gift of future sight, while Kait had received the ability to heal.

"To be chosen by such a powerful animal, our moon mother must want something from Jillian." Wolf's voice tightened.

He was expected to save the lives of those shown in his warning flash. Kait was expected to heal when her ability flared. The expectations for

Aiden's claiming gift were unknown, as his *javaanee* had refused to seek the counsel of the *Taounaha*.

"Jillian must have been gifted an ability by the *heschrmal*. What is it? What will be expected of her?"

"We are not equipped to answer these questions," his mother responded.

She was right. But who was equipped to answer them?

The obvious place to start was with the *Taounaha*. If the Old One could not answer Wolf's question, at least he could reach out to the Shadow Warrior and report back on what the Shadow Realm was up to.

After a few seconds of idle chatter, he hung up, his mind buzzing with what he'd learned. It was too early to visit Benioko. He would have to wait for his answers.

By 8:00 a.m., Wolf was more exhausted than ever, but oddly wired. He grabbed a cart from the charging hub and headed for the cafeteria.

The thought of food rolled his stomach, but he piled a plate with scrambled eggs, bacon, sausage and hash browns. Benioko, indeed most of his warriors, approved of the *woohanta* breakfast. At least he could provide the *Taounaha* with a hot meal upon arrival at his door. He snapped plastic lids onto the plate, and the two cups of piping hot coffee—no cream, no sugar—and boxed his haul up. Normally he would have walked to the old section where the Old One lived, but the food and coffee would cool during the walk, so he carried the box out to his cart and climbed onboard.

Benioko's door was propped open with an old boot when he arrived. This was not a surprise. The shaman often knew of Wolf's visit before Wolf did himself.

He pushed the door open and stepped inside, letting it swing shut behind him. The *Taounaha* was not on hand to greet him. Unusual. The propped-open door proved Benioko was expecting him. He deposited the covered plate and both coffee cups on the small Formica table with its chipped and stained surface and took a seat on the sagging couch.

You wouldn't know from the thrift store relics that Benioko, as the earthside mouthpiece, was the most important member of the Kalikoia tribe. The shaman chose a thrifty life, one without creature comforts or ostentatious symbols of status. The *Taounaha's* life was spent in dreams and visions and service to his people.

"*Ho'cee,*" Benioko said, surprise in his thin, crackly voice as he shuffled into the living room. "You are here. Why?"

Judging by the question, along with the surprise in Benioko's voice, Wolf was not the visitor the Old One had expected, which was odd. Few people visited the shaman. Those with spirit trouble went to Wolf first, and Wolf reached out to Benioko. As base commander and the *Taounaha's Betanee,* Wolf facilitated spiritual ceremonies and Shadow Realm connections.

"Who are you expecting?"

"Your *javaanee.*" Benioko shuffled into the kitchen, stopping at the drawer next to the sink.

Wolf heard the clink of metal. When he returned to the table, Benioko held a fork. With a deep, tired sigh, he pulled out a chair, sat down, and popped off the lid to the plate and coffee.

"You're expecting Aiden?" Wolf concealed his surprise.

What business did his *javaanee* have with the *Taounaha*? Aiden still wasn't interested in learning the Kalikoia ways. Indeed, he actively avoided Benioko. It was strange that his brother would seek out the shaman now.

Although curious, he locked the questions behind his teeth. Benioko would speak to him of Aiden's visit if it was meant for his ears. Instead, he sat in the chair across from the shaman, pulled the capped cup of coffee toward him, and waited.

Respect called for the *Taounaha* to begin the conversation.

This didn't happen until Benioko had plowed through the food on his plate and finished his coffee. Once the last morsel of eggs had been caught and transferred to his mouth, the Old One carefully set the fork down and leaned back in his chair. Milky, yet shrewd, eyes snared Wolf's gaze.

"Why have you come, *Ho'cee*?"

Wolf chose his words with care. "My *anistaa* called last night. She spoke of Jillian. Of a claiming by a spirit animal."

A slow frown wrinkled Benioko's lined forehead. "Your shadow-locked *le'ven'a* was claimed by the forest spirits?"

Wolf flinched at the description, although it was accurate. Jillian was locked between the living and the dead.

"Yes. By the *heschrmal.*"

Benioko straightened at that news. Shock widened his eyes. Had the Blue Moon Mother withheld this claiming from her mate? Or had the Shadow Warrior withheld the information from his mouthpiece?

"A *heschrmal?*" The *Taounaha* straightened even further. His eyes flared, some of the milkiness burning away. "Is your *anistaa* certain of this?"

"She saw it. She heard the *heschrmal's* scream," Wolf said quietly. "She says Jillian bears the claiming bite and carries the totem." He steadied his voice. "What does this mean?"

Several moments of silence were followed by the slow shake of Benioko's head. "This I do not know. I will seek answers."

Unsettled, Wolf slumped into his chair. The Shadow Warrior's *Taounaha* was unaware of Jillian's claiming? This was not normal. The shaman was rarely left hanging like this. Not when it came to the elder gods or the dynamics between their earthborn children and the Shadow Realm.

Uneasiness crawled through him. Why had the elder gods turned away from Benioko?

What was going on in the Shadow Realm?

Chapter Fifty-One

Day 24
Denali, Alaska

The strangeness of the day started before Aiden rolled out of bed.

The cell phone he'd pulled from his tactical pants and dropped on the nightstand woke him from a fragmented sleep. That weird shadow world, with its terrifying residents, had taken over his dreams again. The certainty that they wanted something from him...demanded something from him...followed him into wakefulness. The tension from the dream still pressed against his chest as he reached for the lit-up and vibrating phone.

The message icon showed someone had texted him, but he didn't recognize the number the message had come from. After reading the text, he blinked and read it again. He closed his eyes, counted to ten, and read it a third time. The message hadn't changed. And the damn thing still made no sense.

> I am informed that you have need to speak with me.

1301. In the old section. Come now.

--Benioko

What? Who the hell told the shaman I needed to talk to him? He scowled, his fingers tightening around the phone. *Is this summons about the damn dreams?*

It couldn't be. The only one who knew about them was Demi, and she'd been with him all night. Besides, she wouldn't contact Benioko behind his back. Maybe Wolf was behind the summons. Because that's what it was. A summons.

But that didn't track either. While Wolf had brought up Aiden's lack of knowledge regarding their shared Kalikoia heritage, he'd never pushed—at least not hard—for Aiden to learn their tribal history. And he'd sure as hell never suggested that Aiden meet with the base shaman.

So, who the hell had gone blabbing to the Old One?

The shadowy dreams with their stretchy inhabitants flashed through his mind. Demi had made a connection between the shadows in the dreams and the Shadow Realm. But according to Wolf and everyone else in this damn place, Benioko was the only mouthpiece of the Shadow Warrior, which meant he was the only one who interacted with the elder gods and knew what they looked like.

Was it possible?

Of course not!

He grunted in annoyance and glared at his phone. Those damn dreams were fucking with his mind. The note said 'come now,' but no way in hell was he leaving Demi to wake up alone. They'd just patched things up. He wasn't letting anything come between them. Certainly not this unexpected and unwelcome summons.

He switched on the lamp next to the bed and rolled over. Demi was lying on her side, her back to him. His roll had taken him so close, her ass cradled his cock, which had warped awake and was ready for action. You'd think the damn thing would be fully satiated after the marathon of sex they'd enjoyed the night before. But no, it was all revved up and raring to go. No surprise. His cock had been hyper-focused on her since their first meeting all those years ago.

He wrapped his right arm around her waist, his hand sliding up to cup her breast. Squeezing gently, he buried his face in the curve of her neck and suckled the silky skin. She stirred against him, the movement languid and sleepy.

"I see someone's having a good morning," she said in a sleep-thick voice, as she cuddled her ass against his crotch.

"Any morning I awake with you is a good morning," he mumbled against her neck. Christ, she felt good—soft and warm and silky. But she tasted even better; a little salty, a little sweet, with a hint of flowers.

He barely got a couple of nibbles in before his phone rumbled against the nightstand again. He pulled back with a scowl. Worst. Timing. Ever.

"Ignore it." She twisted until she faced him, her arms twining around his neck.

Good idea.

Her face rosy with sleep and growing desire, she leaned in closer. Cupping her cheeks, he bent to take her lips just as the phone rumbled again. And damned if it didn't remind him of a summons, which reminded him of Benioko's text.

Fuck.

He froze, releasing Demi's cheeks.

"What's wrong?" Worry replaced the desire in her eyes.

Double fuck!

"I need to take this." With a frustrated growl, he rolled back over and grabbed his phone. Two more texts, same number as earlier.

And then...

Now.

Neither text had a signature, but Aiden knew who'd sent them. What was so damn urgent Benioko needed to see him immediately, in person? Why couldn't he wait a damn hour?

"Aiden?" Demi's voice rose. Worry darkened her eyes. "What's wrong?"

He flopped onto his back, thumping his head against the pillow. "I've been summoned by Benioko."

"Really?" Surprise nudged aside the worry. "Why?"

"Hell if I know." Scowling, Aiden turned to face her. "He says he's been *informed* that I need to speak with him."

Her brows drew together. "By who?"

He shrugged, trying to squelch the irritation. "No clue. Guess I'll find out when I meet with him."

A frown pulled at the corners of her eyes. "Which is when?"

"Apparently now."

"Oh." Disappointment echoed through the word.

"Yeah." After another annoyed growl and a head thump, he rolled out of bed. Damn, she looked so adorable lying there, the covers pulled up to her chin, her face flushed and mildly disappointed, her hair an aqua blaze against the white pillow. Every fiber in his body and synapse in his mind urged him to say fuck Benioko and rejoin her beneath the blanket.

But duty called. In the Shadow Mountain hierarchy, Benioko was the top dog. Wolf was his war commander, but the old man oversaw everything, which made him Aiden's current CO. Hell, maybe this summons was about the nanobot weapon. If so, he couldn't afford to miss it.

"I'd invite you to join me in the shower, but then I'd never make it to this damn meeting." His good mood had soured amazingly fast.

He showered in record time and returned to the bedroom. Demi had already rolled back onto her side and fallen asleep. His chest warmed as he stared down at her. She looked so relaxed and comfortable. But even more importantly, she was back in his bed.

His. All his. Forever.

Because he wasn't fucking things up this time.

He dressed as quietly as possible, then stopped at the desk in the living area long enough to write her a quick note and backtracked to the bedroom to drop it on the pillow beside her.

> Don't go. When I get back, I'll make you my special French toast for
> you. PB bananas—the works.
> Love you.
> A

Love you was increasingly easy to say. A relief, as he intended to say it often.

He grabbed a utility vehicle and headed for the ramp and the main level. The old section of the base was easy to differentiate from the new. The tunnel was darker, the lights dimmer, the walls grimy and formed from stone, rather than that weird spongy shit. Numbers ran along the tops of the buildings in red-glowing paint. 1000...1100...1200. He slowed when he reached the 1300 block. He pulled in next to another vehicle.

The cold was more intense out here amid the stone and grime. Why the hell did Benioko live all the way out here? As the top dog on base, he could have any quarters he chose. One of the newer, brighter—hell, warmer—apartments was his for the asking. Yet he was buried out here in the bowels of Shadow Mountain.

He stopped in front of the first unit to the right. According to the 1301 stenciled above the door in red—faded to pink—paint, he'd arrived at Benioko's quarters. The old man was obviously expecting him, as the door was propped open by a worn leather boot. A flash of irritation brought a scowl. Apparently, the old shaman was so certain Aiden would jump at his summons, he'd left the goddamn door open.

He almost turned around. But maybe the shaman had bot-related news to impart. Shoving the door all the way open, he stalked through, his patience for autocratic personalities at an all-time low. He stopped dead at the sight of Wolf.

"What the hell are you doing here?" Aiden's tone skated awfully close to an accusation. Had Wolf been behind the texts?

A look of irritation flashed across Wolf's face before it smoothed again. "I had business with the *Taounaha*." He paused, his thick eyebrows quirking. "What of you?"

"I was summoned," Aiden drawled.

Wolf cocked his head. "Summoned? Why?"

"Hell if I know." Aiden mirrored his brother's stance—shoulders back, feet spread, hands clasped behind his back. He strove for the same expression of bland indifference. "Ask your pet shaman."

Everything about Wolf—his face, his body, his eyes—hardened at Aiden's flippant response. "You would do well to mind your tone."

"Enough." A screeching-scraping sound came from around the corner to Aiden's left. The shuffle of footsteps followed. Benioko's fragile frame rounded the corner. The Old One split his disapproving gaze between Wolf and Aiden. "We have no time for squabbling."

A flush heated Aiden's face. Okay, yeah. He might be letting his annoyance with his recently fucked up morning sour his mood. With a grunt, he scrubbed his palms down his face and worked on an attitude readjustment. Time to get this meeting over with so he could get back to pampering his woman. He dropped his hands and raised his eyebrows at the shaman.

"I got your message." Had he ever. He frowned when he remembered the wording of the first text. "Who told you I needed to speak to you?"

"Come. Sit. This concerns you, too, *Ho'cee.*" Benioko turned and shuffled back around the corner.

Wolf and Aiden followed. The kitchen the old shaman retreated into was even smaller than the one in Aiden's quarters. It contained one short counter, which housed a surprisingly fancy coffee pot—which currently sat full and steaming, a well-scrubbed stainless-steel sink, a stove with two burners, and a tiny, dorm style fridge.

That earlier screeching came again. He turned as Benioko sat and scooted his mint green chair beneath a red Formica table. A pair of empty Styrofoam cups sat on the table. It looked like Wolf had been with the shaman long enough to finish a cup of coffee.

An off-putting smell suffused the room—a combination of dust, burned coffee and old cooking, with the acrid undertone of incense, or maybe weed?

"Sit." Benioko gestured to the empty chair across from him.

Aiden hesitated, then took the chair the old shaman indicated.

"*Ho'cee,* coffee."

Wolf took a ceramic cup down from the open cupboard above the counter, grabbed the coffeepot and returned to the table. He filled all three cups and took a seat. With a distant expression in his eyes, Benioko gazed into the steaming Styrofoam cup Wolf placed in front of him. Aiden glanced at his big bro, who shook his head.

The seconds ticked past. Aiden fidgeted, frowned, and glared at his wristwatch. He could be in bed with Demi right now instead— The Old

One suddenly lifted his head, pinning Aiden with surprisingly sharp eyes, considering the film clouding them. "Your *le'ven'a* will wait for you."

What the hell was a *le'ven'a?* Although he suspected the word had something to do with Demi. He shifted uncomfortably beneath the shaman's scrutiny.

"The Shadow Warrior grows impatient," Benioko said, his gaze still locked on Aiden's wary face.

Okay, and this concerned him how? "With what?"

"With you," Benioko snapped.

"Me?" Scowling, Aiden pulled back.

"It is time for you to step past this stubborn selfishness and accept your role among the Kalikoia. The Shadow Warrior is done waiting," Benioko announced, his gaze hard on Aiden's face, his voice flat, yet somehow cutting.

Selfishness?

Aiden stiffened. "I have no role in *your* tribe."

He didn't soften the rejection. This was his life, his choice, not Benioko's, and not the fucking Shadow Warrior's. Aiden turned to Wolf, who stared back with his usual impassiveness.

A long, weighty silence fell. Benioko finally turned rheumy eyes toward Wolf. "How much of the old times have you told him?"

Wolf stirred. For the first time in Aiden's memory, his brother looked defensive. "I have not forced our history on him. Allegiance and belief are not forged through force." He paused. "This you taught me."

The shaman nodded, but almost immediately shook his head. A weary expression settled across his face. The deep crevices bracketing his nose and mouth deepened even further. "There are exceptions. Your *javaanee* is such."

Aiden had heard the word Benioko used enough to know it meant brother. In this context, Wolf's brother. Which meant the old man was talking about him. Yeah—fuck this bullshit. Aiden shoved back his chair and rose.

"Sit." Benioko said without raising his voice.

But there was power in the order. Immense power. It reached out and snared him, slamming him back down in his chair where he sat frozen, unable to move, his body under someone else's—or something else's—control.

Chapter Fifty-Two

Day 24
Denali, Alaska

His muscles bunched and straining, Aiden fought to move something, anything: his arm, his hand, even a finger. But Benioko's unseen power wrapped around him, throughout him, locking his muscles in place and his body in stasis. The only thing he could move were his eyes.

Jesus, am I still dreaming? This can't be happening. Hell, I can't even open my mouth.

"*Taounaha.*" It was Wolf's voice. The title sounded like a protest—guttural and shocked.

"This I like even less than you, *Betanee.* But time has fled. He is needed. He must listen and learn." The shaman's voice was thin and strained, but his gaze caught Aiden's and held it like a snare. "The Kalikoia spirit gifts were bestowed upon the *Hee'woo'nee* to repel the elder gods' jealous shadow children. They were gifted to defend us against the younger gods' envy and spite."

Whatever invisible power Benioko wielded came with effort. And that effort was already showing in the crevices carving up his face and the crackle in his voice.

How long could the old man maintain this invisible fist around him?

"Some among the Kalikoia, those necessary to keep the tribe strong, are double-gifted. I am one." Benioko continued, his voice cracking. "This, the swaddling, is the first talent the elder gods bestowed on me. The second, the ability to see and hear the Shadow Warrior and cross the veil, while living, and enter the Shadow Realm, came later. That talent, the *Taounaha* gift, did not manifest until the mouthpiece before me began his journey to the web of his ancestors."

What the hell did any of this have to do with him?

Aiden concentrated on his little finger, willing it to move. He was rewarded with the faintest of shimmies. He wanted to look at Wolf, see if any of what Benioko was saying was news to him. But his neck wouldn't turn.

"You, too, are double-gifted," Benioko continued.

Double-gifted? Bullshit. His one talent was trouble enough. He didn't need a second one fucking up his life. He went back to concentrating on his finger, urging it to move. It responded with another shimmy, a stronger one this time.

"Even the youngest of the Kalikoia know the purpose of their gifting and how their talents are meant to be used."

Bully for them!

His finger wiggled freely now. He turned his focus to his hand.

"Your first gift, that of foresight as a means to riches, is meant to profit the *Hee'woo'nee.*"

Foresight as a means to riches?

Shock dragged Aiden's attention back to the Old One's words. That sure described his Midas touch. How did the old man know about that? Someone must have tattled. But who? Only two people knew of his talent for acquiring money. Kait and Demi. Neither would blab to Benioko. Had Wolf guessed what Aiden could do and told the shaman? While that seemed the most likely scenario, it didn't feel right.

"The gift of succor, the one you squander so recklessly, is prized among the Kalikoia."

"No shit?" To Aiden's surprise, he managed to push the snarky question out of his paralyzed mouth.

With a disapproving grunt, the Old One opened his arms and gestured widely around him. "How do you think such things are possible?"

Such things? The old man couldn't be talking about his quarters. The shaman lived an austere lifestyle. His table was from the sixties. His couch was even older than that.

His disbelief must have showed on his face, because Benioko elaborated.

"The base. The scientists. The labs. The equipment." He shot Wolf a dry look. "All the flying toys."

Aiden frowned. He'd wondered who funded Shadow Mountain. The costs associated with running this place must be astronomical.

"No way," This time the protest came easily. He glanced down. He could move his hand now and his feet. Whatever *talent* Benioko had used against him was dissipating. "There's no way this base is run off lottery winnings, stock increases, or horse races. Not without attracting attention."

His father had insisted on using their gifts sparingly, lest their sudden influx of wealth lead to unwanted attention. Acquiring the kind of money to keep Shadow Mountain operational was certain to catch someone's eye.

Benioko shrugged, as though the answer was obvious. "Those with the gift of succor knew to buy Microsoft, Amazon and other stocks when each share sold for pennies. These shares are worth billions now and carefully harvested. Those with the succor talent have always shared their visions with the *Hee'woo'nee*. The riches foreseen are harvested and turned over to the *Hee'woo'nee* council, where the money is dispersed." The shaman's voice turned grim. "This is the way it has always been. Until your father and now you. The elder gods are not pleased with your usage of their gift."

Well, fuck them. Maybe they should have tagged their gifts with instructions.

"I use the gift for the greater good." Well, mostly. A burning sensation spread through his chest, almost like shame.

"This is known. It is not enough." Benioko's voice flattened. "Your talent is meant to provide for the *Hee'woo'nee* in our battle against the younger gods. You use it for other purposes. Therefore, your gift brings you no ease."

Aiden's jaw set. To hell with that. If the money he foresaw only went to the Kalikoia, what would happen to his foundation? To the people it helped? "The money I get from my gift goes to charity. It helps people."

Benioko inclined his head with a regal nod. "This is known. There are enough riches for both purposes. But future foresights must also be gifted to the *Hee'woo'nee*."

Talk about ironic. He was being scolded by entities he didn't believe in.

"Fine." He expelled a relieved breath when his legs agreed to push his chair back from the table. "Even though I don't believe in your elder gods."

The Old One cackled. "They do not care."

Aiden glanced at Wolf, who had the strangest look on his face. Half stunned, half horrified. What the hell was going on with his big bro? The realization he could turn his head distracted him. He lifted his arm, then stood up. His body was under his control again. Time to get the hell away from this not-so-toothless shaman.

Wolf slowly rose to his feet as Aiden skirted the table. That strange expression was still on his face, but it had gravitated more toward horrified than stunned.

"You said he was double-gifted." Wolf shot Aiden a quick, searching look. He seemed to push the next question out, but in such a tense tone, he obviously didn't want to know the answer. "What was he gifted secondly?"

Benioko broke contact with Wolf's gaze and stared at the surface of the table for several seconds. When he looked up, he looked drained, and regretful. "You know this, *Ho'cee.*"

"No!" Wolf's voice was so tight it vibrated in his throat. "He has not accepted our ways. He does not *know* our ways. He is not prepared. You cannot ask this of him."

"*I* do not ask this of him. Just as Old Joseph did not ask it of me. We do not choose our gifts." Benioko shook his head, fatigue darkening his filmy eyes. "Nor can we refuse them. You know this, *Ho'cee.* So it has always been."

Aiden stopped at the kitchen door and turned to stare at the two men behind him. Benioko still sat at the table. But Wolf stood frozen beside the chair he'd vacated. Aiden couldn't see his face, but his brother's muscles were tense, his feet braced, his shoulders rigid and pulled back.

Something was wrong.

And Aiden suspected it had everything to do with him.

"This cannot happen. Another must be chosen." Wolf's voice hardened.

Aiden's eyebrows rose. He'd never heard his brother speak so harshly to the shaman.

"It has already happened. He transitions now," Benioko retorted.

Benioko turned his head toward Aiden. Pity folded the old man's face. Even beneath the film in those ancient eyes, Aiden could see sympathy.

The shaman felt sorry for him?

What the hell?

His mind flashed to those weird-ass dreams—the foggy terrain with its otherworldly, twisted landscape, the strange beings with their elongated limbs and death mask faces. Ice crashed over Aiden's head and pierced his gut.

The conversation suddenly felt ominous.

"What are you two yapping about?" Aiden asked, trying to ignore the overwhelming certainty that his life was about to go off the rails.

He thought about their earlier conversation. There had been something about him having a second gift, one Wolf was horrified by. Something about him not being prepared. Something about him transitioning.

Transitioning? Into what?

Those damn dreams shot into his mind again. He suddenly remembered something else the old man had said. How his second gift—the gift of the *Taounaha*—had not manifested until the mouthpiece prior to him had died.

The ice migrated from his gut to his chest, chilling his entire body.

Fuck, no. Benioko is not dead. That can't be what they're talking about.

Although, the Old One didn't look well. His skin was close to gray, his body thin...his eyes vague...

Stretchy limbs...white faces...gaping mouths.

"What do your elder gods look like?" Aiden asked, his voice hoarse. The ice encased his entire body now and froze him from the inside out.

A sound broke from the old man; a cracked, dry husk of a sound. Resignation rode his eyes. "You know this. They have called to you for many cycles."

Wolf grabbed the back of a chair, as if he needed stability, as if he'd suddenly gone weak. "Cycles? He's seen them for *many* cycles?"

"*What?*" Aiden asked, the question breathless, like he'd taken a double tap to the chest. "*When?*"

Although he knew...*elongated limbs, white, screaming faces.*

"Your dreams." The old shaman confirmed Aiden's suspicion.

Fuck that.

His body one big charley horse, Aiden squared off against the old man. "How the hell do you know about my dreams?"

The knowledge of his dreams hadn't come because of Kalikoia gods, or the Shadow Realm. It couldn't have. There had to be a simpler answer to how Benioko knew.

He'd told no one but Demi about the damn things. And she wouldn't have told anyone. Then it hit him. His quarters must be bugged. That would explain how Benioko knew about the damn dreams.

The old man drew himself up until he sat tall and stiff in his chair. "I am the *Taounaha*, the earthside eyes and ears of the Shadow Warrior. I have seen him summon you while you sleep. Soon he will summon you during your waking." He suddenly cocked his head, his eyes losing focus. Stillness claimed his frail form. His face went taut. "It begins."

Aiden hadn't yet processed Benioko's first statement when the old man uttered the ominous warning.

"What begins?" Christ, when had *what* become his favorite question?

"The beginning to the end."

Wolf's phone rang.

The timing of the call felt menacing, like an exclamation point to the shaman's dire warning.

"Go," Benioko said, before Wolf even accepted the call.

His brother glanced at Aiden as he lifted the phone to his ear. Whatever news came down the line was bad enough it shifted Wolf's expression from shell-shocked to grim.

"On my way," Wolf said after a few seconds of listening.

"What's going on?" Aiden asked before Wolf even lowered the phone. Not that he wanted to know. He'd barely recovered from Benioko's first proclamation, not that he believed it. Not that he believed any of it.

There was no fucking way he was the next *Taounaha*.

Wolf shook himself. Pivoting, he strode toward the kitchen entrance, where Aiden waited. With each step, his face hardened. "That was the lab—Faith. She says the nanobots we retrieved from Kuznetsov are vibrating."

Chapter Fifty-Three

Day 24
Denali, Alaska

Wolf avoided Aiden's eyes as he brushed past him and headed for the front door with long, urgent strides. Aiden followed. The nanobot update had certainly put a damper on Benioko's summons.

He waited until the door closed behind him before asking the obvious question. "Vibrating? What the hell does that mean?"

There he went, asking *what* again. Wolf, he noticed, was pretending he didn't exist. No glances in his direction, no adjustments in his strides to accommodate Aiden's pace, no response to his question. He'd never seen his big bro so passive aggressively determined to avoid something that obviously bugged the shit out of him. Benioko's *Taounaha* nonsense had sure shoved a bug up his brother's ass.

"Come on, bro." Aiden raised his voice and increased his speed to keep up. "You can't actually believe all that bullshit back there. I'm not the mouthpiece of your gods."

"Not yet," Wolf agreed, except he sounded grimmer than ever.

"Not ever."

Wolf slowed and flicked an intent glance at Aiden's face. "Yet you dream of them."

White screaming faces...

Aiden banished the image. He was not letting those assholes haunt him during the day. "I don't know what my dreams represent, but they sure as hell aren't about your shadow gods."

Wolf's grunt was full of disbelief. So was the look he turned on Aiden.

"Jesus, man." Aiden's voice rose. So did his blood pressure. He was not the mouthpiece of the Shadow Warrior! No fucking way! "I admit the dreams are whacked. But, if I'm the fucking mouthpiece to your Shadow Warrior, why the fuck doesn't he give me anything to say? Nobody says a damn word in those dreams."

His brother stopped so abruptly, Aiden cruised past him and had to wheel back around.

"Perhaps..." Wolf's voice was so tight, Aiden had to strain to hear the words. "You refuse to listen."

What the hell was that supposed to mean?

Yeah—this was getting them nowhere fast. Time to focus on what was important, which wasn't trivial superstition.

"Look, let's shelve this discussion and move on." He waited for Wolf to walk again. "You said the nanobots are vibrating. What's going on there?"

The last he'd heard, the bots Wolf had retrieved from Kuznetsov were still sitting in their containment tank in one of the labs.

His brother shrugged but accepted the change of subject. "The case the bots are in started vibrating. This is all I know."

"Is the vibration coming from the bots?" Aiden asked as they reached the two utility carts. Wolf climbed into the driver's seat of the vehicle that was there when Aiden arrived.

"It appears so. The case has no cause to vibrate. Faith says the bots are huddled together. The vibrations appear to be coming from them."

Aiden hopped into the passenger seat.

Before the phone call from the lab, Benioko had announced the beginning of the end of times—or something to that effect. He'd issued the warning prior to Faith's report about the nanobot vibrations. The two warnings had to be connected.

"We should turn back and talk to Benioko, find out what he knows about these vibrations. He knew something was up before Faith called."

Wolf frowned at the suggestion, his finger hovering over the cart's start button. His phone rang again. Wolf plucked it from the cargo pocket of his tactical pants and lifted it to his ear. Even from the passenger seat, Aiden could hear the shrill voice coming over the cell phone. Not the words—but the tone, the sharp pitch and urgent cadence to it.

His scalp tightened beneath a sudden surge of foreboding.

What the hell was wrong now?

His brother's face paled, going from flat to stunned, and then horrified. Even more horrified than it had been earlier during that fucked up conversation with Benioko.

"This is not possible," Wolf huffed out. He listened more. "Lock them in. Vent the oxygen from the room. They must not escape. We are on our way."

Aiden's gut twisted. Memories slashed through his mind.

Squirrel's snarling face and twitching fingers. Muddy, enraged eyes. Rifles rising. The crack of gunfire.

"The bots got out?" Christ, what a catastrophe.

Had they already infected the lab techs? How were they going to contain a microscopic entity that could slip through the smallest of cracks? According to Kuznetsov, when Samuel had interrogated him, the bots had a built-in kill switch, which had been activated after the testing on his team. Which was why no one from the Shadow Mountain team had been infected. How the hell were they going to turn this new batch off?

"It is not just the nanobots in the lab." Wolf punched the start button with a stiff index finger, slammed the cart into reverse, and rapidly backed the utility vehicle out onto the main thoroughfare. He glanced at Aiden, disbelief heavy in his eyes. "Your teammates just sat up. All of them. At once."

"What?" Aiden reeled back in the passenger seat. "That's not possible. They're dead! They've been dead for weeks."

"Nevertheless..." Wolf's voice, hoarse with shock, trailed off.

There had to be some mistake. The dead didn't sit up.

The trip to the new section of base was silent, tense. Wolf pulled into a parking slot in front of the ER. The isolation unit had no dedicated morgue, so one of the sealed chambers had been filled with gurneys and flooded with cold. His teammates' sheeted bodies were stored there. A short dude with thinning red hair and a full-body tic met them as soon as they stepped out of the cart.

"They sat up. At the same time. Like fucking zombies!" The redhead sounded winded, as if the sight had knocked the breath from him and he hadn't gotten it back yet.

"Zombies..." Wolf repeated beneath his breath. A startled look flashed across his face. "Have they spoken? Moved beyond the sitting?"

"No." The isolation tech's green scrubs fluttered around him. There was no breeze, so the dude's wired energy had to be creating the movement. "But they're sitting upright."

Aiden still didn't believe it. Outside of Hollywood and the Bible, dead men didn't suddenly arise.

The isolation wing was next door to the ER. The glass doors sprung open allowing them entrance. The hallway Aiden found himself in was icy. The air was stagnant, the walls a chilling white. The corridor seemed to go on forever, twisting left, and then right. Doors periodically popped up with metal, eye-level labels. *IT1. IT2. Supplies.* They rounded another curve, which deposited them into a large, rectangular room with glass-enclosed chambers along the right and left. The air was even colder here, which was odd. Aiden didn't remember freezing during his stint in the isolation chamber.

The redheaded tech led them across the room to the last glass-enclosed chamber on the right. Aiden froze, staring in morbid fascination at the five gurneys. Or more like stared at the five tattered, man-shaped *things* sitting with sheets pooled over their crotches and their legs draped over the edges of the stainless steel exam tables.

Not. Fucking. Possible.

"I told you to vent it."

Wolf's voice was a distant, gritty rumble as Aiden's eyes drifted from one shimmering table to the next.

"We did," said a high, nervous voice. "It had no effect. They're still sitting up."

Movement on the first gurney caught Aiden's attention. His eyes tracked the motion. The *thing* on the table tilted its head. The motion was jerky, almost birdlike.

High on the creature's neck, just below its ear, a tattoo flashed beneath the overhead lights—the bronze and gold scales of a coiled snake.

Squirrel's tattoo.

Squirrel's dead body.

His moving, dead body.

A tangled combination of horror and hope climbed his throat.

Flashes of memories reeled through his mind. Brashness and a firm hand-shake as Squirrel introduced himself during those first days of BUD/S. His dress whites and grim face, the brashness gone, at their first pounding of the Trident after Booker had taken a round to spare their lives. His steady aim and unrelenting focus during assault after assault. His squinty-eyed laugh and squinty-eyed frown.

Twitching fingers and twitching eyes. A snarling face. His rifle rising.

Christ. Aiden massaged his burning eyes.

When he dropped his hands, the Squirrel *thing* was wobbling toward the window. His face was a mangled mess—empty eye sockets, missing nose, chunks of forehead, cheeks, and chin gone.

But he was standing.

He was walking.

New, fragile tissue was forming over the missing parts of his face. The abdominal stitching running the length of his torso after the autopsy looked like a healing wound rather than a stitched cut.

Dead flesh did not heal. Yet...it was healing.

The Squirrel *thing* took another wobbly, shambling step forward. The movement was uncoordinated and reeked of effort. Yet its dead legs were holding it up. Its dead legs were walking.

The thing that used to be his best friend stumbled up to the window and stopped. Its empty eyes sockets, with their delicate webbing of new tissue, stared directly into Aiden's face. It cocked its head in that oddly birdlike movement.

Then, it opened its mouth.

To be continued in Shadow Boxed.

https://www.amazon.com/Shadow-Boxed-Warriors-Book-ebook/dp/B0 D7Z32GL5

More From Trish McCallan

Dear Reader

If you want to read how Aiden and Demi hooked up, and their whole friends with benefits arrangement, click HERE.

If you're curious about what happened between Zane, Cosky, Rawls, Mac and the NRO, you can find that story arc in the Red-Hot SEALs series.

If you're interested in reading more about Tag and Tram, you can find their storylines HERE.

If you're interested in book progress updates, new release information, or discounted and free book offers, sign up for my newsletter HERE!

Find Me

Facebook

Join Trish's Readers Group

Trish's Website

Kalikoia Glossary

A cycle—One year

aggress —attack or assault

anestoo—Father

anisbecco—Uncle- mother's brother

anistaa—Mother

anistino—Wife

anvaa—Child

anvaat—Children

Betanee—First in command—Wolf

betanei—Leader or commander or boss

breen—Equals a mile

brenahecee —The reservations—Refers to all three

Brenahiilo—Reservation—Wolf's specific reservation

Caetanee—Second in command—Samuel

cee'syca—Gym

enesolo—Training

eseneee—The ignorance of a child

hee—Blood

Hee-Hee-Thae—Spirit Healing

hee-javaanee—Blood brother

Heemitia—Sister Moon

Hee-nes-ce—The elder God's breath or grace

Hee-nes—The elder gods

Hee'woo'nee—The chosen people

heschrmal—Mountain lion

hetazenee—Main or first

Ho'cee—Wolf—Wolf's tribal name

Hokalita—Sister Earth

holini—Cafeteria

jaee—The sick

javaacee—One's sister

javaanee—One's brother

jeetce—Sickness/ plague

jenaaee—Nephew- sisters side

jie'van—Outcast

le'ven'a—Woman of the heart

Neealaho—Mental web/ neural net—Mind link between warriors

rotations—days

Tabenetha—realm of the elder gods

Taounaha—Earthside Mouthpiece—Benioko

thae-hrata—Spirit Eagle

umbretan—Thunderstorm

Wanatesa—The apocalypse/ end of everything

woohanna—Anglo women

woohanta—Anglo men

About the Author

 Trish McCallan was born in Eugene, Oregon, and grew up in Washington State, where she began crafting stories at an early age. Her first books were illustrated in crayon, bound with red yarn, and sold for a nickel at her lemonade stand.

Trish grew up to earn a bachelor's degree in English literature with a concentration in creative writing from Western Washington University, taking jobs as a bookkeeper and human- resource specialist before finally quitting her day job to write full time.

Forged in Fire came about after a marathon reading session, and a bottle of Nyquil that sparked a vivid dream.

She lives today in eastern Washington.

An avid animal lover, she currently shares her home with four golden retrievers, and a cat.

Made in the USA
Monee, IL
20 October 2024

68350264R00281